D1051997

The Olive Grove Mysteries

ONE FOOT IN THE GROVE
COLD PRESSED MURDER

COLD PRESSED MURDER

AN OLIVE GROVE MYSTERY

KELLY LANE

BERKLEY PRIME CRIME
New York

BERKLEY PRIME CRIME
Published by Berkley
An imprint of Penguin Random House LLC
375 Hudson Street, New York, New York 10014

Copyright © 2017 by Claire Talbot Eddins
Penguin Random House supports copyright. Copyright fuels creativity, encourages
diverse voices, promotes free speech, and creates a vibrant culture. Thank you for buying
an authorized edition of this book and for complying with copyright laws by not
reproducing, scanning, or distributing any part of it in any form without permission.
You are supporting writers and allowing Penguin Random House to continue to
publish books for every reader.

BERKLEY is a registered trademark and BERKLEY PRIME CRIME and the B colophon
are trademarks of Penguin Random House LLC.

ISBN 9780425277232

First Edition: March 2017

Printed in the United States of America
1   3   5   7   9   10   8   6   4   2

Cover illustration by Anne Wertheim
Cover design by Sarah Oberrender
Book design by Laura K. Corless

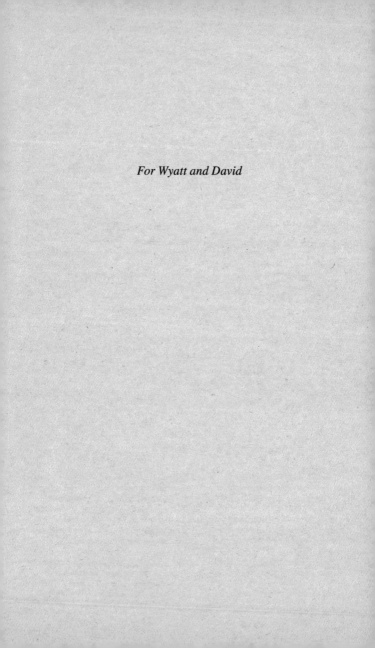

For Wyatt and David

ACKNOWLEDGMENTS

Thank you, literary agent John Talbot, for your vision, confidence, and championing regarding the Olive Grove Mystery series. You've ignited a passion for writing fiction that I never knew existed.

To my editor, Bethany Blair, sincere thanks for your kind patience, insight, and spot-on recommendations. You've helped me to increase my vision and get better at my craft.

Senior editor Michelle Vega, I'm so very grateful that you took on the Olive Grove Mystery series. Also, to the entire team at Berkley Prime Crime—especially Sarah Oberrender, cover designer; Anne Wertheim, cover illustrator; Laura K. Corliss, interior text designer; Eileen Chetti, copy editor; Daniel Walsh, assistant director, production editorial; and Danielle Dill in publicity—thank you all for sharing your talents and hard work on my behalf.

Bibiana Heymann, I cannot tell you how much your steady support and endless enthusiasm mean to me. Your infectious zest and zeal always inspire!

Thank you, readers, for taking the time to purchase and read my books. I am most appreciative. And special thanks to all those folks who have taken additional time to write reviews and/or contact me. I do seriously consider and appreciate your thoughts.

And to the two men in my life, Wyatt Morin and David Eddins, my heartfelt thanks for your never-ending love, patience, and support. Especially when I'm eyeball-deep into a story—oblivious to real life—as I plot, write, rewrite, and edit . . . rewrite and edit . . . rewrite and edit . . . rewrite and edit . . .

CHAPTER 1

Ambrosia Curry looked like a cross between a campy pinup and a burlesque queen. Posing behind waves of intense heat wafting from the Big John M-15B charcoal grill, the raven-haired beauty wore a black lace bodysuit with a pink heart-shaped apron tied around her teeny waist. She gave us a kittenish smile before plunging her perfectly manicured finger into a cauldron of melting chocolate and my family's olive oil.

High in a magnolia tree, a loudspeaker crackled.

"Oooh!" she tittered into the microphone clipped to her décolletage. "This warm chocolate and olive oil feels as good as . . . making whoopee!"

I slammed a hand against my forehead, and the crowd around me roared.

Known as Chow Network's "Orgasmic Chef," the thirty-something forties-styled siren was one of three celebrity chefs preparing food with our olive oils on that sultry summer Georgia afternoon. Twirling her finger in the chocolaty sauce, the sexpot gave a flirty wink to a thousand sweltering fans on the plantation lawn as they watched, squinting against the brilliant sun behind my family's antebellum farmhouse.

"Sooo sumptuously silky . . . I could bathe in it!" she squealed.

Ambrosia Curry pulled her finger from the sauce, wiping it on her retro-style apron before blowing a kiss to the mob. Standing about halfway back in the crowd, a weatherworn farmer next to me jumped up and down excitedly.

"Now, that's entertainment!" he bellowed.

Shifting a mammoth wicker basket in my arms, I nodded and smiled politely to the farmer as I pressed my way through the shoulder-to-shoulder crowd. The glaring sun was killer that Saturday and I'd been on my feet since dawn. I was hot. I was sunburned. I was tired. Just a few minutes more, I thought, and the giveaways in my basket would be gone. Then I could finally retreat to the sanctum of my cottage across the lawn.

"Ow!"

I slapped at a bug buzzing under my ponytail, and my sister's oversized Jackie O sunglasses slid down my nose. I shoved the vintage glasses back up with my finger just as an Elvis impersonator on stilts, wearing dark glasses and a white bell-bottomed jumpsuit, bumped my basket, offering a giant bowl of kale chips grilled in olive oil, coated with garlic and Parmesan cheese.

"No, thanks!" I said quickly.

Dress it up any way you like, I thought. *I'm not eating kale*—even though the Orgasmic Chef had announced to the crowd earlier that the collard was a new superfood, whatever that is. Of course, I knew foods cooked in olive oil could help improve health and lower the risk of heart disease. Still, I also knew darn well that raw kale tasted like lawn clippings, and whether you coated it, seasoned it, dipped it, or grilled it—disguise it any way you like—even drenched it in a vat of healthy extra virgin olive oil, I just couldn't eat it.

I waved off Elvis.

A young woman in a sundress and her four little kids,

dressed in matching outfits, reached into his bowl, grabbing handfuls of the savory, crispy kale chips.

"These healthy snacks are so good for y'all!" the mother cheered, grabbing an extra handful. I smiled and nodded to the little family, making my way past them with my big basket.

The loudspeaker in the magnolia tree screeched and crackled.

"You know," Ambrosia Curry purred, "olive oil is not just for cooking, ladies and gentlemen. Why, just imagine what you can do with it . . . in the boudoir!"

"Yee-haa!" cried a man, tossing his baseball cap into the air. The crowd cheered.

Our community fund-raiser was a hit.

It was the first-ever Knox Plantation Olive Oil Chefs' Challenge for Charity, part of the annual Abundance Farm Family Fare weekend, when farms and restaurants all over Abundance County sponsored food-related events to raise money for local families in need. Our ticket-only cook-off was the brainchild of my eldest sister, Daphne Knox Bouvier, forty-something Southern socialite and local eventrix extraordinaire. Just a year or so earlier, using money from her divorce, Daphne had turned our family's run-down farmhouse into a posh country inn for agritourists. In addition to helping a good cause, we hoped the weekend charity event would put Knox Plantation on the map, garnering positive publicity and guests for the inn, as well as buyers for olive oils made from my dad's olive trees.

After an eighteen-year stint in New England, I'd returned home earlier that summer, and I was in charge of plantation PR and guest relations. I'd spent the sizzling-hot day out on the lawn, first setting up cooking stations in the wee hours of the morning. Then I'd been meeting and greeting folks, offering free bottle spouts from a ginormous wicker berry basket that Daphne had found online.

A hand reached into my basket.

"Y'all sure know how to put on a killer bah-be-cue!"

A young woman in a halter dress and flip-flops grinned

as she grabbed a handful of freebie bottle pourers. Just a
few more left. She shoved the spouts into a colorful Vera
Bradley bag before she sipped something that looked like
tea, but smelled more like whiskey, from a red plastic cup.

"Thanks," I said. "You know, the spouts fit perfectly onto
our bottles of olive oil. Have you tried some? We've got
samples and a bunch for sale under the red tent over there."

I pointed to a gathering of tents on the far side of the
lawn, where our olive oils were for sale and student chefs
from the college in the next county worked to replicate
dishes prepared by the celebrity chefs to ensure there'd be
enough food for everyone—both for sampling and for selling. In another tent, checkered-cloth-covered picnic tables
were lined with balloon-festooned baskets of bread and
shallow bowls of olive oil for dipping, along with the
student-prepared celebrity dishes, iced sweet tea, and lemonade. There was a tent where student chefs churned out
freshly made ice cream from a commercial ice-cream maker
that Daphne had rented. Another tent was for kids and
offered face painting, a napping area, a magician, and a
clown twisting balloons into animal shapes.

"We're donating today's proceeds to Farm Family Fare,
so you'll be helping a wonderful cause," I added.

"Thanks!" gushed the woman. "Ya know, my pops lost
our farm during the recession. We mighta made it if Farm
Family Fare had been around back then. I'll buy some of
y'all's olive oil when I go for more ice." She grinned. "Gotta
make a quick stop back at the car first." She lifted her red
cup. "Brought my own Jimmy Beam 'cause I knew this place
would be drier than happy hour at the Betty Ford Center."

Snatching another pourer out of my basket, she chugged
her bourbon and tottered off.

A blanket of smoke from the grills rolled through the
crowd, mingling with pungent body odors, coconut-scented
sunscreens, cheap perfumes, drugstore aftershaves, and
spirit-laden scents of bootlegged bourbons and beers. I
fanned the smothering fumes from my face as I squeezed
my big basket between more high-spirited sunbaked guests.

"Ooooooh!" squealed Ambrosia Curry over the loud-speaker. "Remember, ladies and gentlemen, taste all our dishes and vote for your favorites! Samples are being passed around and you can find more under the tents. The chef whose dish receives the most votes will be awarded a key to the village!" She squealed again. "Isn't that exciting?"

Everyone cheered and clapped. The symbolic key was a small reward, I thought. But then, it was all for charity, and the visiting chefs were on board with that. Plus, there was the publicity . . .

"Of course, we all know who's got the best dish!" Ambrosia Curry threw her arms up into the air and spun around, twirling a pink dish towel over her head like a striptease artist.

The crowd went nuts, stamping, hooting, and cheering. You had to laugh.

The only female chef at our fund-raiser, Orgasmic Chef Ambrosia Curry oozed nonstop Hollywood sex appeal while preparing one mouthwatering dish after another. First it'd been olive oil kale chips. Then she'd made two olive oil frozen treats: a "boozy" peach bourbon ice cream and a gelato with chocolaty drizzles—perfect for a sweltering-hot Georgia afternoon. After that, she'd cooked olive oil cup-cakes on the grill. Next up, strawberries dipped in olive oil chocolate sauce and fresh Georgia pecans.

With a dirty smile, Ambrosia Curry glanced over her shoulder and tossed the dish towel into the crowd. People fought good-naturedly to snag the coveted pink cloth.

"I got it!" cried a woman happily.

"Chef Ambrosia, I love you!" shouted a deeply suntanned farmer. No doubt he had quit work early that day—something no hardworking Abundance farmer ever did unless there was a family death.

Or an equipment failure.

Or the sky was falling.

What I mean is, chances of having a famous celebrity visit my backwater little hometown of Abundance, Georgia, was akin to having a meteor strike the place—it just didn't happen. No one famous ever came to Abundance.

Heaven knows how my sister Daphne had convinced the superstar chefs to come.

In fact, since the time the railroad stopped coming to Abundance more than half a century ago, unless you farmed, or worked at the chemical plant, or had a job at the prison on the far side of town, there wasn't much reason to be in our little corner of Southern Georgia wire grass country. Hunting was the exception, of course. For Abundance, with its open fields and rolling hills; longleaf pine forests teaming with quail, pheasant, and deer; streams and ponds with trout and other game fish—as well as some of Georgia's biggest and nastiest swamps—hunting and fishing for sport were the biggest game around. Yes, Abundance's picturesque Victorian downtown was quaint and lovely. Still, no one was about to drive two or three hours from anywhere else just for that.

"Ahh!" sighed the Orgasmic Chef. Slowly, she slid her hands down her curvy figure. "Melted chocolate and olive oil send me into orgasmic raptures!" She bent over and posed, burlesque style, peeping into her big pot on the grill.

"Omigosh!" I slapped my forehead.

Someone bumped my elbow.

"No wonder the woman sells millions of cookbooks, eh?"

A tiny, just-past-middle-aged lady with a Northern accent and a big beak for a nose, dressed in black with oversized black glasses, and short, tousled, henna-colored hair, trundled through the crowd carrying a stack of pink heart-shaped potholders. I recognized Miriam Tidwell, the celebrity handler from the Chow Network. She'd arrived the day before with Ambrosia Curry.

Without waiting for me to answer, Miriam added, cackling, "People can't take their eyes off the hussy. Men want to have her. Women want to be her. My network producers love Ambrosia Curry. She's a spot-on recipe for success." Miriam chortled before mumbling under her breath, "Just hope it stays that way."

She made a nasal-sounding noise—I think it was a laugh—as she nodded to herself and waddled into the crowd with her pile of potholders.

The loudspeaker up in the magnolia tree crackled.

"I see we have potholders coming." Ambrosia Curry tittered. "I'll be autographing them after this demonstration. If you haven't purchased a ticket to win one, please do. All proceeds go to charity!"

The audience cheered. Carrying a tray of snacks, a Hulk Hogan impostor wearing a bright yellow wrestling suit, lace-up booties, and a purple sweat rag tied around his head sauntered past the rack of Schwinn cruiser bicycles in the parking area next to the big house, where people queued up, waiting forty minutes or more to take tractor-pulled wagon rides around the plantation.

All day long, my dad and his farmhands toured folks around the pond, on nature trails winding through a three-hundred-year-old longleaf pine forest, and over dirt farm roads that passed by acres of flat, tended fields planted with row after row of my dad's crops—including the commodity that everyone wanted to see, the one-hundred-acre orchard of Arbequina, Arbosana, and Koroneiki olive trees. The trees, just a few years old, made up the Southeast's first commercially successful olive crop. And so far, my dad's olive oils had been an award-winning success. Everyone wanted to see the olive trees.

Pshhhhisssssht.

Heads turned as something sizzled and popped at another grilling station. The magnolia tree loudspeaker let out an earsplitting screech.

Glen Pattershaw, Chow Network's "Crusty Baker," growled an expletive into his microphone. The husky, red-faced fellow wearing a navy blue chef's uniform and tall chef's toque on his head had been "baking" bread loaves on his grill.

"Don't forget to visit our Chow Network tent, where you'll find all sorts of crap you never knew you wanted," he barked. "Some of it's even autographed. There's tee shirts, key chains, refrigerator magnets, canvas bags, potholders, aprons, kitchen utensils, and cookbooks—if they haven't sold out already. Damn, folks, it's hotter 'n hell out here!" He wiped the back of his hand across his forehead.

Along with his gruff personality, the owner of the famous DaBomb Bakery chain and host of the television show that carried his name was famous for barking out enough cuss-words to have earned him more censor bleeps than any other human in the history of television.

"How about toasting some of the bread that we baked on the grill?" he snarled. "Add some of this fresh, buffalo-milk mozzarella, some Southern Virginia ham, and grilled fresh tomatoes drizzled with rosemary-infused olive oil—and holy crap! You've got a perfect snack!"

The baker held his hands on his hips and barked out another expletive as he surveyed the items on the red-and-white tablecloth. There were hand-crafted wooden bowls filled with boules of freshly "grill-baked" olive oil bread; giant platters of sliced meats, vegetables, and fruits; wheels of artisan cheeses; and a dozen dark green long-necked bottles beribboned in purple and filled with Knox olive oils.

"Oh, there it is, rosemary," he mumbled. "Damn!"

He grabbed a green bottle, popped the cork, and drizzled Knox Liquid Gold Rosemary Olive Oil over sliced fresh tomatoes sizzling over the piping-hot charcoal. Smoke exploded upward as the oil and tomato juices sputtered over fired-up flames. Wiping his sweaty brow with his sleeve, he gathered up toasted tomato slices with a spatula while mumbling something obscene.

A thin, harsh-looking woman in the crowd with a toddler at her side spun around to give me a dirty look. She kept her arms crossed over her shapeless denim jumper, pressing to her chest what looked to be a brand-new book.

"Eva Knox!" scolded the preacher's wife, Emmylou Twitty. Her toddler son, Kyle, spit. "You and your two highfalutin sisters haven't changed a bit since high school!" She leaned in to me and whispered hoarsely, "Y'all have no sense of decency. This is supposed to be a family event to help raise funds for the needy." She pointed toward the Crusty Baker. "That man has a potty mouth!"

The herbal-scented fumes from the baker's grill smelled delicious.

"I'm sorry he offends you, Emmylou. I admit it's pretty bad. Still, apparently, that's what folks have come here to see this afternoon. And it's all for a good cause." I smiled. "We're grateful for your support today. Did you get one of our bottle pourers?" I held one out in my hand. "They're free."

Emmylou's mouth twitched as she snatched the pourer, handing it to her son. The crowd cheered at some obscenity the baker barked out. Emmylou's son bit the pourer, then spit before tossing the pourer into the bucket of his toy John Deere tractor. Two cowlicks made the boy's hair stick straight up, like little devil horns.

"Mmm, heavenly scents of herbs and spices," moaned Chef Ambrosia, melodramatically heaving her chest. "Almost as divine as my chocolate and olive oil drizzled over fruit and rolled in nuts. I love licking chocolate off nuts and fruit."

Emmylou clucked her tongue and glared at Ambrosia Curry as she dragged her son deeper into the crowd. The loudspeaker crackled.

"I remember how you like licking nuts, sweetheart," boomed a man's voice over the speaker.

From behind the third grill, Master Chef Slick Simmer waved a long-handled fork. For hours, the world-renowned TV star, restaurateur, and bestselling author had been wowing folks with his mouthwatering dishes, devastating good looks, and sharp-witted commentary. Looking tan and dapper, with a tall, slender frame and neatly trimmed salt-and-pepper hair, Slick Simmer wore a madras plaid shirt and khakis that were pressed and spotless. He smirked at Ambrosia Curry across the lawn.

"Our Orgasmic Chef just can't keep herself from stirring everybody's pot." He sniggered.

"Well, at least I haven't got a finger *in* everybody's pot," retorted Ambrosia Curry.

"Get a room, you two," growled the baker. He dropped a tomato slice on the ground. "Crap."

Slick Simmer, glancing down at his five-foot-long grill, poked the long-handled fork into a chicken leg, turning it over.

Alongside dozens of sizzling chicken parts on the grill, there were several sauce-filled copper pots and pans. He grabbed one of the copper saucepots and slid it closer to him before stabbing a small piece of chicken with the fork. He dipped the chicken in some sauce, then waved it in the air a moment to cool. Popping the morsel into his mouth, he smiled.

"Mmm. Folks, my Sweet and Slightly Spicy Barbecue Sauce is *killer*! Rhubarb is the key . . ."

"Don't y'all love his *Slick Eats America* show?" cried a little biddy in a floral sundress. Standing just behind me, she carried a black umbrella over her head. "In every episode, he drops into a restaurant and finds something wrong with every dish, every server, and every chef!"

"He samples every hostess, waitress, and female kitchen worker, too," said a blue-haired lady next to me wearing dark green wraparound sunglasses. She stamped her cane on the ground.

"Why does he do that?" asked an elderly lady in a big, floppy straw hat.

"'Cause he's on a crusade to rid the United States of crummy restaurants," answered Blue Hair. "And he's a horny bastard." She grinned.

"He's just the tomcat's kitten," sighed Umbrella Biddy.

"Slick! You make me melt, sugah-pie!" shouted a fan from up front.

Slick Simmer pointed his long-handled fork toward his fan.

"I'll see you, darling, privately, after the demonstration! My motor home is parked over there. We'll make some of our own heat and melt together."

As the crowd laughed, the chef motioned toward the far side of the plantation, where his motor home was parked out of sight, many acres away, in our warehouse lot. Unlike Ambrosia Curry, Glen Pattershaw, and Miriam Tidwell—who were our weekend guests in the Knox Plantation big house—the epicurean Hugh Hefner preferred to spend his nights in his legendary bachelor pad on wheels. And rumor had it, he was rarely alone.

Raising his eyebrows, he teased, "You can show me some of that Southern hospitality I keep hearing about, if you know what I mean." He shot a sharp, blue-eyed wink at his fan.

The crowd cheered and laughed.

I wrinkled my nose with a grimace.

"Chef, you'd better be careful what you wish for," shouted the fan, "'cause I might be aimin' to take you up on your offer, you sweet-talkin' thang!" The crowd cheered. Then she called out, "C'mon! Give mama some sugah, baby!"

"Hey, girl, he's mine!" shouted another young woman up front. "Tell her, Slick! Tell her! You're mine!" She had a long blonde braid and wore an official SLICK EATS AMERICA yellow tee shirt. The shirt featured an illustration of Slick taking a bite out of the United States.

"Savannah, it looks like you'll have to take a number tonight," said the chef.

People jeered. Slick Simmer fans standing up front clanged pots, pans, and kitchen implements.

"Unless," said Slick Simmer, outstretching his arms in a welcoming manner, "you two ladies would like to make it a threesome?"

Wow.

"Gad night a livin'! What a pig. I bet plenty of women wanna wring his neck," exclaimed a woman wearing a frowzy housedress.

Blue Hair giggled. "Sure wish I were thirty or forty years younger!"

Charm bracelets jangled from somewhere in the crowd. "*Pahrw-dun* me."

Making her way through the audience, my tall and lithe sister, Daphne, looked perfect and as fresh as a daisy, even in the sweltering heat and standing-room-only crowd. She wore a baby blue silk georgette dress with a fitted waist and swirly skirt, and her fine strawberry-blonde hair was put up in a loose French twist. Little tendrils of hair framed her watery blue eyes.

"I see, Eva, darlin,' *y'all* decided not to take my advice about wearin' a pretty little sundress this afternoon."

Though she was still smiling, her eyes shot me a look of disappointment, an expression with which I was all too familiar. Daphne's tasteful, expensive French perfume—like crystalline flowers with a hint of citrus, woods, and spices— wafted around us as she contorted herself around my big basket to air-kiss my cheeks.

I sighed.

She was doing that "y'all" thing again, intentionally over-using the Southern colloquialism. Like most of the uppity women in Abundance, and some men as well, Daphne directed the normally plural or associative address to a single person every time she felt compelled to show her disdain— which was most of the time. She also used it to soften her demands—which came often. Sometimes, to make things really confusing, she'd use it when she felt particularly close or friendly with someone. And almost always, Daphne said it for social effect around Northerners who didn't know any better. As far as I could tell, using the phrase that way had started as kind of a subtle one-upper in our little town. Growing up with it, I'd never really noticed or thought about it until I'd moved away and then returned. Regardless, in Abundance, as well as in a handful of rural pockets in the South, using "y'all" to address just one person was creeping into the Southern vernacular, becoming more and more common—although most Southerners denied it. And many likened it to the painful screech of nails dragging down a chalkboard.

"Sorry," I said.

I wasn't really sorry. My shirt—it read GEORGIA VIRGIN with OLIVE OIL in little print below—had been specially made to promote the family business. What better time to wear it?

"Please don't tell me you're wearing a skort," Daphne whispered, clearly chagrined.

And, yes. It was a skort. It was black and made from some sort of stretchy material—I'd bought it at Dick's Sporting Goods and I often wore it when I went running. It was perfect for a stinking-hot summer afternoon on the back lawn.

"At least you're wearin' the sunglasses I gave you," said Daphne. "Keep them. They suit you."

Daphne'd insisted that I borrow her vintage Jackie O–style specs after my own sunglasses sank to the bottom of the pond during an . . . altercation . . . with my longtime nemesis, Debi Dicer.

Okay, truthfully, it'd been a big brawl with Debi.

Long story.

Anyway, I was destitute since I'd lost my PR business and practically everything else I'd owned when I ran away from a bad relationship in Boston a couple of months earlier. When Daddy offered me a job and a place to live back home, it'd been a lifesaver. I was just trying to earn enough money to buy food. And on my dime-store budget, decent sunglasses weren't in the picture.

"Thanks, Daph. I appreciate the gift. I'll make it up to you. Promise."

"Well, you can start by not wearing a skort." Daphne sniffed indignantly. She paused as the crowd roared at something Ambrosia Curry said. "I see that our glamorous chef Ambrosia has all the men hot and bothered."

Daphne's "hot and bothered" sounded like "hah-wot un barhw-thud." Her Southern drawl was far more pronounced than most. At some point, she'd taken to the notion that a true Southern belle had to speak with an accent as thick as molasses.

"When you think about it, Daph, marrying sex and cookery is kind of a no-brainer." I chuckled.

"Make fun, Eva. However, folks notice when a woman makes an effort to look her best. One doesn't just wake up in the morning looking ravishing. We work at it! Why, Miss Ambrosia Curry herself arrived last night with enough luggage to stay on here for a month or more. Daddy's farmhands had to hoist her big wardrobe trunk upstairs. That woman is prepared, and it shows. Look around. Men can't take their eyes off her."

"Wardrobe trunk? Are you kidding? Who travels like that these days? Not even you, Daph."

"It's all vintage Louis Vuitton. And she must be doin' something right—it's worth a small fortune. I'd roll over and die to have it!"

Daphne reached out and smoothed my hair with her hand like a mother fussing with a child. Something snagged.

"Ouch! What is that?"

"Hold still, Eva. It's my elephant charm—the one Big Boomer gave me during our honeymoon in Thailand. Oh! Fiddle-dee-dee. It's caught." Daphne let out an exasperated sigh as she tried working the charm loose from my hair. "Oh dear! I can't seem to get his little trunk free. Hold still. Tip your head down."

"Yes, ma'am." I made a face. Daphne fiddled with my hair. "Ouch!"

"There. All better." Daphne pulled her freed wrist away from my hair. "Eva, please stop scowling. I know you've been down in the dumps lately, but it's time to pick yourself up and get a man. After all, you're a Knox woman."

"I'm not scowling. And, Knox woman or not, I don't need a man."

"No woman in her thirties should be single. It positively smacks of 'old maid.' Even your sister Pepper-Leigh managed to wrangle herself a husband." Daphne was the only person in the universe who called our middle sister, Pep, by her given name, Pepper-Leigh. Except maybe our mother, and we'd not seen her in more than thirty years.

The Hulk Hogan impostor in his yellow wrestling suit juggled his way through the crowd, tossing peaches. Daphne tried smiling, but she ended up wrinkling her nose instead, looking like she'd just bitten into something bitter. Eventually, she averted her eyes from the spectacle.

"Don't worry, Eva. I'll find you a husband. It's what I do best."

"Yeah, right!" I laughed. "This coming from a woman who ran back home to Daddy with five kids after going through the biggest, ugliest divorce in the history of Atlanta. Maybe even the entire state of Georgia. I'll pass on your matchmaking services."

Daphne sniffed indignantly. "Big Boomer paid hand-somely for his indiscretions, now, didn't he?"

I shrugged.

"I'm very good at what I do," she insisted. "In fact, Pickles Kibler told me this fund-raiser is the most newsworthy event in Abundance since you tripped over that poor dead man a few weeks ago. And the crowd just adores Slick!" she said dreamily. "I knew they would. He has that certain je ne sais quoi about him, doesn't he?"

She smiled and her eyes softened when she spoke about the playboy chef. I stopped laughing to stare at her a moment. I couldn't remember when I'd seen such an expression on her face.

"I'm so glad I thought to ask him to come this weekend," she continued, dreamy eyed. "Speaking of which, I've got to check on our celebrities." Leaning around my big basket, Daphne managed to smile and whisper in my ear at the same time, "Please, stay out of trouble. Your scandalous behavior these past few weeks has nearly torpedoed my good reputation. And, really, Eva, it isn't helping you one bit in the man department."

She turned and glided into the crowd.

Scandalous behavior?

Hey, just because I'd run off from my wedding in Boston at the last minute didn't mean it was my fault, despite what the media reported. And it wasn't my fault that I'd tripped over a dead guy a few weeks after I'd returned home, either. It could've happened to anyone. I mean, it's not like I killed the guy. Although Sheriff Buck Tanner—another man I'd ditched at the altar, eighteen years earlier—had ruefully called me a "magnet for disaster."

Come to think of it, where'd Buck been during these last few weeks, anyway? I thought we'd reconciled our differences during the murder investigation. Still, I'd not seen Buck since then.

Huh!

Guess he was too smitten with his new squeeze, Debi Dicer—of all people—to give me another thought after the

murder was solved. Tsk. Looks like the sheriff's friendliness
toward me had been nothing more than a calculated ruse to
wheedle information while working a case. Once the mystery was solved, Buck moved on.

Fine.

Like I said, I wasn't interested in men.

Especially Buck.

Besides, I'd declared a man moratorium after my Boston
wedding blew apart . . .

I jumped as a deep voice whispered in my ear.

"Care for a nibble of Chef Ambrosia's mini olive oil
cupcakes with fresh blueberries and mascarpone? Positively
deee-lish!"

A man dressed like a frownie-faced circus clown offered
a tray of mini cupcakes smothered in soft cheese and blue-
berry topping. The treats looked yummy. However, the the-
atrical makeup on his face was greasy from perspiration.
He looked like he'd just stepped from a scary horror flick
rather than an afternoon charity event.

"No, thanks," I said. "I'll pass."

I tried moving away, except with my stupid basket and
the mob closing in around me, there was nowhere to go. The
clown grinned. Then I nearly jumped out of my skin again
when he held up a clown horn and blasted the noisy thing
right in my face.

"Well, thank you, Billy Sunday!" cried Blue Hair. "That
was rude."

It was a wonder the horn hadn't given the little biddy a heart
attack. It'd almost given me one. The clown sneered and
honked his horn again before shuffling away. I shook my head.

No doubt when planning the charity event, Daphne had
envisioned a highbrow Southern-style lawn party with so-
cialites charming one another on the lawn behind our newly
renovated neo-Gothic and Victorian–style plantation house.
The guests would've gossiped in hushed tones, nibbling on
toothpicked delicacies, admiring the pristinely landscaped
lawn and gardens, while listening to stuffy musicians playing chamber music.

However, Daphne had erred . . . big-time . . . when she'd delegated. She'd charged our middle sister, Pep, with securing the afternoon's help. And true to form, Pep had put her own twist on things.

For servers, Pep had amassed a bizarre collection of circus and freak-show entertainers, including half a dozen rainbow-haired clowns with painted faces, bulbous red noses, and oversized shoes. In addition to squeezing obnoxious, blood-curdling bulb horns, the clowns squirted guests with water from fake flowers on their lapels. Given that it was well over one hundred degrees that afternoon, the squirting flowers had their place. Kids loved them. No doubt many of the adults did as well.

Still, looking around, I thought the event was more of a tawdry carnival than the posh society event Daphne'd envisioned. However, don't let Daphne know I said that. A stickler for Southern niceties, my social-maven big sis would go into fits of hysteria if she heard she'd organized something construed as even remotely carnivalesque. And even though a look around proved that "carnival" was as plain as the little nose on Daphne's flawless, porcelain face, she'd never admit it.

Oh no.

Not in a million years.

CHAPTER 2

"I swear, Eva, it's busier out here than a funeral-parlor fan in summer!"

A pair of arms wrapped around me from behind, squeezing me in a bear hug.

"Pep! I was just thinking about you."

My sister smelled of velvety old garden roses—the dark kind that are half dead and well past their peak—mixed with jammy blackberries, soft violets, a dash of pepper, and a smoldering, plushy hint of musk. Cutting through the smoke from the grills, her close-to-the-skin scent was warm, confident, and darkly robust with a slight animal note. Sensual and sinfully rich.

Very much Pep.

"Nice basket!" she teased, taking her arms away and laughing at my monster-sized wicker carryall. "You planning on carrying off a table or two of snacks?" She burst out in little piglet snorts of laughter.

Petite and curvier than I am, my sister ran her fingers though her spiky, boyishly cut platinum hair. Yanking up her tight black corset top, she spun around to watch the band playing in a far corner of the lawn. The group broke into a punk-rock, razor-edged version of "Polish Wedding March."

"Nice music," I said, laughing. "You planning some sort of punk beerfest?"

Staged under a gnarled live oak tree, half a dozen musicians dressed in studded and spiked black leather lederhosen— with piercings, tattoos, and neon-colored Mohawk hair—had been belting out the afternoon's "background music" for hours, oompah-pahing punky, brittle, electrified versions of the "Beer Barrel Polka" and other traditional tunes.

Hardly a Southern lawn party.

"Don't laugh!" cried Pep. "The Polkapunks are nearly impossible to book. Lucky for us, they had a cancellation. And their lead singer is an Ambrosia Curry fan."

"Who isn't?" snapped Chow Network celebrity handler Miriam Tidwell, bumping Pep's arm as she trundled by. She made that nasally chortle again.

"Howdy, Miz Tidwell!" Pep laughed.

Tapping the toe of her black leather boot, Pep followed the beat of the jaunty Polkapunks tune. Her boots stopped just short of her black leather miniskirt, folding over curvy thighs to disclose dark purple fishnet stockings. The afternoon was so oppressively hot that I couldn't imagine how Pep could stand to wear all that leather. Any leather. Let alone the crazy stockings.

"I'm not even going to ask where you found a punk-rock polka band in Southern Georgia," I said. "And what is it with all the clowns and weird carnival people?"

"Eva." She snorted. "This event is part of Farm Family Fare, correct? So I figured, why not go all out and give folks a real carnival?"

"Um, Pep, it's Farm Family Fare, F-A-R-E, not F-A-I-R. You know that, right?"

Pep snorted big-time. "Of course. I just thought the play on words would be fun. Besides, it's not all carney stuff. The servers are dressed like famous folks from Georgia—didn't you notice? Except the clowns and the Elvis, of course. You gotta have an Elvis."

"You're kidding."

"Dyin' if I'm lyin'. Besides, it's worth it, just to see the traumatized look on Daph's face. I love that expression she makes—like she smells something dead but doesn't want anyone to know it." Pep giggled little snorts and batted a wink. "Hey! Did ya see Jimmy and Rosalynn Carter? They're so cute, selling bagged peanuts. And there's a teeny, tiny Paula Deen around, somewhere."

"I'll never understand why you and Daph take such pleasure in distressing each other," I said, chuckling.

"Coming through! Clear the way, folks!"

Balancing two wooden crates of peaches labeled CLATTERBUCK AWARD-WINNING PEACHES over his immense head, crimson-faced local farmer "Big Bubba" Clatterbuck—looking like he weighed well over three hundred pounds, with giant sweat stains under the arms of his blue chambray shirt—puffed and wheezed through the throng of people as he trudged toward Slick Simmer's cooking station. Like everyone else, Pep and I quickly parted to let the hulking farmer squeeze by. Covered in grimy sweat, he reeked of body odor.

Pep grimaced.

Lumbering in his wake, Big Bubba's two linebacker-sized, high school–aged daughters, Peaches and Sissy, wearing their own sweaty chambray shirts and jeans, huffed and puffed as each lugged a wooden carton filled with freshly harvested peaches. The peaches—the very last in an unusually late season—smelled divinely fresh and sweet.

"Hey!" said Pep, after the Clatterbucks lumbered past. "That reminds me. Is Chef Ambrosia's peach ice cream ready yet? I never knew we could make ice cream with olive oil. And with the bourbon, I bet it's to die for!"

"I don't know. It was all hauled off to freeze in the Clatterbucks' truck more than an hour ago."

Big Bubba's peaches were keeping cool in his refrigerated truck parked over at our warehouse. While the fresh peaches took up space in the refrigerated section of the truck, a separate freezer section chilled Ambrosia Curry's freshly made ice cream and gelato. Given the huge crowd on hand that day, the Clatterbucks' fancy truck had been a lifesaver. We had only one refrigerator and one freezer in the big house, and Daddy's old reefer truck was on the road. Without the Clatterbucks' truck, we'd never have been able to keep enough frozen treats chilled to accommodate all the people at the plantation that day.

"Care for some crostini with fresh tomatoes and garlic-infused olive oil?"

A Scarlett O'Hara bearded lady emerged from the crowd holding out a tray, her hooped skirt knocking everyone aside.

"Ooooh, looks yummy. Thanks." Pep grabbed a crostini from the tray and popped the entire slice of grilled bread in her mouth. "Ummmmm," she mumbled as she grabbed another.

"Pep, you didn't!" I whispered. "A bearded Scarlett?"

Blue Hair poked her cane into Scarlett O'Hara's hoop skirt and giggled.

"What?" With her mouth full, Pep's eyes twinkled as she swallowed the crostini. "We all know Daph loves Scarlett O'Hara. Heck, she thinks she is Scarlett O'Hara. I'm just honoring her fantasy." She popped another crostini into her mouth. "There's a Rhett Butler and a Prissy around here, somewhere."

"No, thanks," I said, waving the woman, er, man, off. Up front, Ambrosia Curry moaned again.

"Don't y'all just love the way Ambrosia Curry does that?" Pep said, speaking to no one in particular, grabbing another crostini. "I should try it with Billy. Not that he'd notice."

Billy Sweet was Pep's husband. Together they lived in a small ranch on the other side of the plantation.

Pep frowned before she shoved the third crostini into her mouth. "Okay. Eva, baby, I gotta go," she mumbled with her mouth full. "My shift at the Roadhouse starts soon."

Pep tended bar at the local watering hole when she wasn't helping Daddy at the farm. A heavy-equipment junkie and mechanical genius, Pep had always been Daddy's right-hand farm gal, and she still was, when she wasn't tending bar.

"Tootles!" she cried, slipping into the crowd.

I shifted the big basket in my arms and watched an egret

fly up from the pond and over my one-room cottage on the other side of the lawn—reminding me that I'd left my little black dog, Dolly, in the cottage so she wouldn't be underfoot. I needed to get back home and check on Dolly. Besides, my pourers were gone. And I was worn-out and crashing fast.

A woman's voice rang out from the edge of the crowd. "Master Chef Simmer!" It was Pat Butts, a local reporter. "Sources say you're about to call in a big loan on Chef Pattershaw's DaBomb Bakery chain. Care to comment?"

"I don't know what you're talking about," snapped Slick Simmer.

"What the hell, Slicko!" shouted Crusty Baker Glen Pattershaw.

"Chef Pattershaw, do you have anything to say?" asked reporter Pat Butts.

"Sure. Thanks for the heads-up," barked the baker. "Now I know who my friends are . . . er . . . aren't." The loudspeaker screeched as he called Slick Simmer some bad words.

"Little reporter lady, why don't you butt out of my beeswax?" snapped Slick Simmer. "When I want the world to know my business, I'll let them know. Meanwhile, take a flying leap!" Then he added, "Unless, of course, you aim to meet me in my motor home later?"

The audience laughed. "Will it get me the story?" asked the reporter.

"No. But I guarantee you'll have plenty to write about afterward."

"Eva Knox!"

Scowling preacher's wife Emmylou Twitty poked my arm.

"I could've gone to any of the other plantations on the charity tour today. But no, I just had to come here to see Slick Simmer." She blushed, squeezing his new book to her breast. "He's my idol. I've wanted to meet him for years. Except when I got here, I couldn't find a place to park! Then the ticket line was so long that I waited almost an hour to get in. Then I had to take Kyle to the portable potty—that

line took forever and I missed the entire autograph session!"
She put a hand on her hip and glowered at me, like it had
all been my fault. "Now I've got to wait until all *this* nonsense is over to ask Chef Simmer to autograph my new
book—I've even got some of his old books in the car for
him to sign." She groaned. "I'm tired of waiting and I don't
want my child to hear this vulgar talk!"

Emmylou seemed strangely blind to the fact that her idol,
Slick Simmer, was the mouth behind much of the smutty talk.

"Hot. Hot. Hot!"

A juggler made up to look like musician Little Richard,
dressed in a sequined turtleneck and white pinstriped suit
with big, bouffant hair and a pencil-thin mustache, pressed
his way through the crowd, tossing mini loaves of the Crusty
Baker's just-baked bread. Emmylou continued lecturing me
about how miserable she was as her son picked his nose. The
loudspeaker crackled and Ambrosia Curry moaned into her
microphone, swirling her finger in the chocolate sauce again.

"You always were a moaner, Ambrosia," Slick Simmer
teased with an evil grin.

The crowd roared. Emmylou's devil son, Kyle, spit—just
missing my sneaker. Then he smashed his green tractor into
his mother's thigh. It left a big dirt spot. Regardless, Emmylou rambled on. I caught a whiff of something cooking
on the baker's grill. He was using our rosemary olive oil. It
smelled sweet and woodsy, with spicy, peppered aromas.

Delish.

". . . not to mention all the stuff Tammy Fae Tanner's
been sayin' about y'all at the beauty shop . . ." Emmylou
yammered.

It was a no-brainer that anything Tammy Fae Tanner had
to say about my sisters and me was bad news. Tammy Fae
despised all of us, especially me. She'd been out to take
me down since the time I'd left her only son, Buck Tanner,
at the altar.

Emmylou flapped one of her hands around for emphasis.
She raised her voice and prattled on about more unflattering
things folks were saying about me. I heard "man eater,"

"runaway bride," "shameless Jezebel," and worst of all, "Yankee."

Nothing new.

Then, probably due to the fact that I'd tripped over a dead man a few weeks back, there was "klutz," "stumblebum," "bad juju," and even "man killer."

I'd heard it all before.

Out of the corner of my eye, I saw my little black dog, Dolly, tail curled over her back, sniffing under people's feet. Already that week, Dolly'd plowed through my cottage screen door and a window screen. I hadn't closed the main door to my cottage since I'd arrived back home—without air-conditioning, the cottage was too hot in the summer to keep it closed up. Dolly must've busted through another screen.

I groaned.

Emmylou didn't notice.

Still listening to Emmylou's list of everything that was wrong, I tried to follow my notorious chowhound with my eyes as Dolly scuttled between people's legs, nose to the ground, scarfing up tidbits of dropped food. Finally, Emmylou paused to breathe.

"We appreciate your coming today," I said quickly, touching her arm. Keeping my eye on Dolly, I started to move away. *Aw, shoot!* I lost sight of Dolly. "You're helping a wonderful cause."

Emmylou snatched at my sleeve and prattled on. "Abundance used to be such a nice place. It's just not safe anymore . . ."

The crowd cheered. There was a metallic *pop* as someone opened a beverage can from somewhere behind me. Probably a beer. No one was supposed to be drinking alcohol, but it was intensely hot . . . and, well, that's what folks did on hot summer afternoons in Abundance. Kyle wailed as he twirled on the end of his mother's arm. Then the brat spat out a giant gob of spit, hitting my ankle. His mother kept rambling. Chef Pattershaw barked something profane into his microphone. That's when Emmylou finally yanked Kyle from the ground, scowling and wagging her finger at me.

"Maybe if you had a child of your own, you'd understand!" she screeched. "It's all about the children. Don't you know that?"

She spun on her heel and began shoving her way through the crowd, dragging Kyle, who turned to me and spat one last time before they disappeared.

A hand fell on my shoulder.

"Don't feel bad, Eva. It's not your fault."

Daphne's best friend growing up, forty-something, brown-haired, Palatable Pecan restaurant owner Lark Harden, smiled at me. Next to Lark stood her daughter, pretty, twenty-something Robin, who worked as the hostess at her mother's restaurant. They'd lent a pile of pro-sized copper pots and pans for Slick Simmer to use that afternoon—the master chef refused to cook with anything other than copper, even on an outdoor grill. Lark's longtime friendship with Daphne, and the fact that Lark was the person who'd started the Farm Family Fare a decade earlier, made the copper loan a no-brainer.

"Emmylou Twitty got dumped by her hubby last week," Lark explained. Tall and elegant, she looked chic in a tailored black suit over a pale green chiffon blouse. "She's still in shock."

"And mad as a wet hen," I added with a chortle. Then, all at once, I put it together. "Wait! You mean, Emmylou's husband . . ."

Daughter Robin stepped in with a giggle. "Yes, ma'am. Emmylou's husband, Preacher Twitty, ran off with the church organist!"

Tan and lean, Robin wore a pistachio green and white blouse over a trim black skirt. Her thick, wavy brown hair was tied in a ponytail with a pale green ribbon. When she smiled, her deep aqua eyes sparkled like her diamond earrings.

"Shame on Preacher!" hissed Floppy Hat from behind us. "I'd like to take that ol' scalawag across my knee."

"And his little organ stroker, too!" Blue Hair sniffed.

"Eula had wonderful fingers." Umbrella Biddy sighed.

"And Preacher knew it," said Blue Hair with a huff. Then she chortled.

The biddies sniggered.

"Eva, I've got to run," said Lark with a smile. "Please tell your father that we'd like to put in a standing order for his extra virgin olive oil at the restaurant. It's fabulous. We're even changing the menu to offer seasoned dipping sauces for our homemade breads."

"Daddy will be thrilled! And thanks for loaning Slick Simmer the copper pots and pans today."

"No problem. Ten years ago when I started the Farm Family Fare, I'd no idea it would grow to become such a big event. Getting these famous chefs to come here is quite a feather in Daphne's cap. I can't imagine how she pulled it off! It'll be our honor to treat y'all to dinner."

"Thanks! We never go out—except Daddy; with all the marketing and growing of his olive oil business, he's never home. We'd love to come. And since Daddy's heading out of town Sunday evening, is it alright if we bring Precious Darling in his place? She's family to us."

"Of course!" Lark smiled, then turned to her daughter. "Robin, I'm checking with Daphne to make sure she doesn't need anything else. Will you meet me at the car?"

"Sure, Mum."

"Nice seeing you, Eva." Lark gave me an air-kiss.

Robin giggled. "I have to tell you that I was so excited to get a close-up peek at Master Chef Simmer's copper collection when I brought him our big copper pots and pans. Did you know he's got several pieces with significant provenance, from royal estates in Europe?"

"Really? I'd no idea."

Robin nodded. "In Europe, his copper is more renowned than he is. I used to read all about his famous collection when Mum and I lived in Belgium. It's beautiful stuff."

When she'd been in high school, Lark and her family had moved away from Abundance and gone to Europe for Lark's father's work. Years later, Lark married some sort of duke or count, or something like that, and they'd had Robin. After the older duke died, Lark had returned to Abundance with her daughter.

"I've got to get Mum back to the restaurant before the dinner rush," she said. "Please don't forget to come by the restaurant tomorrow. It's our treat."

"Thanks!"

The magnolia tree loudspeaker crackled.

"I've been meaning to ask you," grumbled the Crusty Baker, "Slick—how'd you manage to afford all that fancy copper cookware?"

Ensconced in billows of smoke, Glen Pattershaw wiped his white goatee with the rumpled sleeve of his blue chef's jacket, rubbing flour on his cheek.

"Mmmmm," purred Chef Ambrosia. "Yes. Do tell, Master Chef Simmer."

Facing the crowd, just like a burlesque queen taking a final bow, Ambrosia Curry bent over from her waist and peeked into the big pot on her grill.

"Careful, honeybun," blasted Slick Simmer. "You don't want to get grill marks on those precious titties." The caddish chef wagged his fork and smiled devilishly. Then he turned to face the Crusty Baker. "And the pricey copper collection? Maybe it's because I'm actually masterly at what I do, and people pay me for my talent. Not like you, doughboy."

A bearded man wearing dirty overalls and a cap with a chicken logo grumbled something about talking disrespectfully to Ambrosia Curry as he worked his way toward the front of the crowd. Something wet hit my arm—a clown was squirting water from his giant lapel flower. I shook my arm and turned on my heel to find Dolly. Except, with my gigantic basket I couldn't see where I was going and I tripped over the clown's big shoe.

"Oh, excuse me!" I crashed into Blue Hair, who steadied us both with her cane.

"Watch your step, honey," she said.

I righted myself and looked up to see Ambrosia Curry blowing a kiss to the crowd.

"Chef Ambrosia is offering more lip service, I see," Slick Simmer joked. "You've always had loose lips, Ambrosia."

Clanging kitchen implements, fans up front hooted and howled.

"You just clang those pots and pans to your hearts' content, folks," cooed Chef Ambrosia. "I can take anything your favorite horndog can dish out. And I can dish it right back."

"Even with all those fancy copper pots and pans, Slick needs all the support he can get," grumbled the Crusty Baker. "Ha!"

Chef Ambrosia smiled. "Yes. He'll pay dearly for his indiscretions. And if he didn't know it before, he knows it now." She looked over at Slick and gave him a long stare. "Payback's a bitch, sweetheart," she said brightly.

I was sure I'd missed something . . .

"Clear the way! Move it, folks!"

With their empty cartons, Big Bubba Clatterbuck and his linebacker daughters plowed through the crowd.

"Did you hear how that Slick guy talks to women?" asked Peaches Clatterbuck, swaggering past me.

"He's a sexist, chauvinist pig who's wasting our peaches," answered Sissy. "Wish he were dead."

Big Bubba growled over his beefy shoulder, "Y'all quit gabbin', girls, and hurry up! We ain't got all day." The crowd scuffled and closed in after the Clatterbucks slogged by.

"Have y'all seen Miss Daphne?"

Daphne's employees, twins Charlene and Darlene Greene, both petite and pretty with freckled heart-shaped faces and dark wavy hair, emerged from the crowd. Each wore a Knox Plantation "uniform"—a short black skirt with poufy crinoline underneath, covered by a frilly, floral half apron, and topped with a white off-the-shoulder blouse with ruffles. It was Daphne's "Southern belle" design, cute to look at, but hardly practical. Really, the uniforms reminded me of French maid outfits.

"She was here a few moments ago," I said to the twenty-somethings. "You must have passed her."

"Okay!" Before I could say more, the twins giggled and wriggled themselves back into the mob.

Who knows what the twins are up to, I thought. At least they'd shown up for the day. Although they were supposed to be full-time employees, as far as I knew, they'd only ever managed to work a part-time schedule.

A lanky teenaged boy wearing Western boots, tattered jeans, a plaid shirt, and a cowboy hat stepped in front of me. I peeked around him to see Chef Ambrosia holding her chocolate-covered finger in the air.

"Ummm. I bet this tastes good," moaned the sexpot chef.

"I love a woman with good taste . . ." joked Slick Simmer. He gave Ambrosia Curry a lewd grin. "And a woman who tastes good. Reminds me of the old days, babe."

I couldn't help but make a face. Even teasing, it seemed the chef might've gone too far . . .

"Ambrosia, you're such a tart," he taunted. "Why keep teasing everyone? Just lick it."

Suddenly, the bearded farmer with the chicken cap surged from the front of the audience and ran behind Slick Simmer's grilling station, growling and hurtling his fists at the chef. From Slick Simmer's microphone, we could hear the angry farmer.

"Don't ya be talkin' about Miss Ambrosia like that! She's a lady. It ain't nice. Ya hear me? I'll kill ya if ya talk like that again!"

Quickly, Daddy's burly plantation manager, Burl Lee, hustled up and strong-armed the farmer before dragging him away.

The shocked crowd mumbled.

"No worries, folks," boomed Slick Simmer's voice over the loudspeaker. "Just another poor fool taken in by Chef Ambrosia's smoke and mirrors. Believe me, she ain't what she pretends to be." Slick smirked, straightening his shirt.

Ambrosia Curry glowered at Slick Simmer.

If looks could kill.

Clearing his throat, the Crusty Baker snatched absently at his signature diamond earring before he sputtered, "Damn!" Then he grabbed a block of cheese. "Let's get back to cooking. Now, you folks could substitute Emmenthal, fontina, or cheddar cheese for the mozzarella . . ."

"Glen," interrupted Slick Simmer, "you're an idiot. Surely you know that if you use cheddar, it will totally change the flavor and texture of the dish. It's a hard cheese that doesn't take well to melting. Use it, and you'll have a gritty mess."

The Crusty Baker looked annoyed and embarrassed as his face flushed.

"Remember, ladies and gents, Glen here is only a baker. And a half-baked one at that." Slick Simmer laughed. "His cupcakes taste like crap, by the way. Like the buttinsky reporter lady said earlier, his DaBomb Bakery chain—perfect name for it—is ready to go under, isn't it, Glen?"

"Simmer, you're gonna pay!" The baker huffed.

"At least I can cook. Unlike you, Glen. You can't even make a simple cupcake taste good!" He made "cupcake" sound like a dirty word. "Even hers are better than yours," he said, jabbing a thumb toward Ambrosia Curry, who was blowing kisses to the crowd. "Aside from the fact that you've never run a successful business in your life, you're no chef. Stick to making bread, doughboy!"

The crowd started laughing.

Someone shrieked.

"Hey! Gimme that, you damned mutt!"

The Crusty Baker grunted something profane into his microphone as he threw down his spatula and lunged toward his table of plated food. Whatever he'd lunged for, he must've missed it, because he landed chest first into the table. The table and everything on top of it crashed to the ground.

A stream of expletives coursed through the loudspeaker.

I stood on my tippy-toes, peering around the tall cowboy teen, trying to see what was happening. The crowd up front closed in, jabbering and wee-wobbling this way and that.

There was another loud crash followed by more profanity from the baker.

"Runaway pooch!" someone shouted. "Catch it!" someone else yelled.

More bad words.

Miriam Tidwell grabbed a microphone. The loudspeaker in the tree screeched. "Ladies and gentlemen," she chirped, "please remain calm!" No one listened. "Ladies and gent—" It sounded like someone crashed into the bitty woman.

"Can you see what's happening?" I asked the cowboy teen.

Laughing with a high-pitched donkey squeal, the skinny teen tipped up his hat and turned to look over his shoulder. "A kid just knocked over the mean-looking lady with the purple hair. She's okay. Looks real mad, though."

"She always looks that way! What happened before that?"

"A dog jumped up on a table and stole a stack of cheese. When the baker dude tried to grab the dog, he fell into the table." The cowboy kid broke out laughing, hee-hawing hysterically. "Now the dog is running through the audience, coming this way, I think . . . No . . . Nope, the dog is still somewhere up front. People are trying to grab it."

Hee-haw. Hee-haw.

"Black? Wavy hair? Floppy ears?"

"I can't see . . . There's a clown in the way . . ."

"Tail curled up over her back?"

"Near 'bout as I can tell, the dog is short, black, and . . . yup! Tail curls up over her back!" The teen took off his straw hat and wiped his forehead on his sleeve. "Oh man, I wish I had my camera!"

Hee-haw. Hee-haw.

Oh crappy, I thought. It had to be Dolly. But, then, of course it was. Daphne was going to kill me . . . Using my basket as a sort of battering ram, I shoved my way through the crazed crowd. There was another loud crash and more shrieking. Clowns honked their horns. I blasted past a very tiny person carrying a huge pitcher of lemonade, nearly knocking her over. Wearing an apron and sporting a big bouffant hairdo, the little person was a dead ringer for celebrity Paula Deen, except for her diminutive size.

"Sorry!" I called out.

"The dog just jumped up on Chef Simmer's table and snagged a chicken," the lanky teen shouted after me. "Looks like there's olive oil spilled everywhere!"

"Lord 'a' mercy!" someone cried.

As the crowd parted for a moment, I caught a glimpse of Dolly, panting and drooling on Slick Simmer's table. At least the table was still standing, I thought. As someone tried to grab her, I saw Dolly snatch a barbecued chicken leg from the table. There was a flash of red-and-white-checked cloth in her mouth as well. Then, as someone else lunged, arms outstretched, Dolly flew to the ground . . . dragging the checkered tablecloth and all that was on top of it with her. Bubba Clatterbuck's precious peaches, spice jars, platters, cooking utensils, and a dozen bottles of olive oil all crashed onto the lawn.

"Noooo!" someone cried.

There was a terrible clanging noise.

More shrieking. More laughter. Bedlam. People were slip-sliding everywhere.

"Dolly! Dolly!"

I tried to run forward, wedging my basket between people who were crowded together, yelling, doubled over laughing, or craning their necks to see.

"Crappy!"

I saw the twins Charlene and Darlene, scrambling through the crowd in their Southern belle outfits. Bending over as they picked up debris, with their black skirts and white crinolines tousled and puffed up over their backs, they looked like a pair of tom turkeys skittering along. Daddy's farmhands scrambled, helping people who'd been knocked down, righting tables, and collecting spilled goods.

"Dolly!"

"There she is!" someone shouted. "Grab that mutt!"

"Dang-nabbit!"

I tripped over a giant clown shoe and fell forward, bumping

into someone else's elbow and purse—which went flying—before I lost my wicker basket and hit the grass, face-first.

"Ouch!"

The crowd closed in. I tried to stand, but the legs and torsos around me were moving chaotically, one way and another, as people shouted out sightings of Dolly. An eight-foot-tall Walt Frazier wearing a New York Knickerbockers uniform and carrying a basketball and an armload of olive oil bottles slipped and took a tumble in front of me.

"I know how you feel, guy," I muttered.

"There she is," I mumbled to myself, "over by Chef Ambrosia's table." I shuffled on my knees as fast as I could, weaving through the busy legs as the Polkapunks rocked out a frenzied version of the "Fruit Salad Polka."

I heard reporter Pat Butts shout, "Make way, folks! Media here!"

"Eeeek!" shouted a woman.

Kids laughed. Something bounced on my head. A chicken leg hit my arm, dropping onto the grass.

"Mutt on the run!" someone shouted. "Over here, quick, y'all! Grab that pooch!"

"Critter ran by me like a scalded haint . . ."

"Anyone have a leash?"

"That aggravatin' dawg's faster than a bell clapper on a goose's butt!"

A string of bad words blasted out over the loudspeaker. The Crusty Baker's microphone must've still been on. People howled with laughter.

I crawled over a sandaled foot with painted toenails. "Oh. I'm so sorry . . ." I bumped into a metal walker. "Excuse me." I power-crawled past more legs . . . jeans, skirts, pressed slacks, overalls, a pair of circus stilts . . . "Pardon."

The grass was slick with olive oil. Someone stepped on my hand. Yanking my fingers from under a crushing, muddy work boot, finally, I saw Dolly just seven or eight feet away, licking a slice of cheese.

"Dol-ly!" I growled.

Crouching, I shoved my way through two pairs of skirted

legs and past a cane and another leg in a plaster cast. I lunged toward Dolly, my arms outstretched, diving into the air. I was just fingertips away from my dog when a pair of expensive, pressed moleskin slacks stepped right in between me and my mutt.

"Umph!"

Hitting firm, muscled legs under the pricey slacks, I crashed. Again.

Chapter 3

"Will ye care for a lift, now?"

The brogue was unmistakable.

Scottish.

"Will" sounded like "well." Soft vowels. Hard consonants. There'd be shallow double "T's" and discreetly rolled "R's."

Ian Collier, my mysterious neighbor from Greatwoods Plantation next door, held back a chuckle.

The handsome, tall, broad-shouldered, forty-something hunk reached out as I sat at his feet covered in food and olive oil, scratched and grass stained on Daddy's trashed lawn. Could I be any more embarrassed?

I don't think so.

My cheeks flushed hot. A circle of onlookers tittered. An Alan Jackson under a ginormous ten-gallon hat winked at me as he sauntered past with Umbrella Biddy on his arm. A Nancy Grace put her hands on her hips and shook her head disapprovingly as a Burt Reynolds unicycled past with an armload of trash bags. I heard a click as someone took a picture. Ian's head quickly turned, scanning the crowd as if he were trying to see who took the shot. It was a little girl—no more than

seven or eight years old—with a smartphone. Harmless. Ian
turned back, still holding out his hand to me.

My hands were slick with olive oil. "I got this," I said,
embarrassed, waving him off.

This wasn't the first, or even the second, time Ian Collier
had been my knight in shining armor. In fact, it seemed that
every time he ran across me, I was muddied, bloodied,
bruised, or just plain in a heap of trouble.

Sitting next to me, Dolly yipped and wagged her tail.
Delighted.

Dragging myself to my knees, I glared at Dolly as she
sat unapologetically at the heel of Ian's pricey leather moc-
casin. She gobbled up a torn slice of provolone cheese.

"Drop that," I hissed, slapping the cheese from Dolly's
mouth.

Behind Dolly, I noticed an enormous pair of red-soled
yellow Louboutin pumps cradling monstrous feet that led
to a pair of toffee-colored tree-trunk legs under a designer
yellow silk shift that encircled an Amazonian woman.

"Hey there, Sunshine," said my friend Precious Darling.
"What happened this time?"

Standing as tall as Ian, Precious blinked her dark,
almond-shaped eyes before wiping a paper party napkin on
her coppery face around her close-cropped hairline. Her
brown hair glistened in the bright sun. Looking into the
glaring late-afternoon sky made my eyes hurt.

Uh-oh.

I'd lost Daphne's Jackie Os.

"Hang on," I said.

I was back on my hands and knees, surveying the slippery grass. Daphne would kill me if I lost her sunglasses.
Still, given the overall circumstances, I was pretty sure that
if Daphne had anything to do with it, my life was pretty
much over anyway.

I found my gigantic wicker basket and dragged it behind
me as I searched for the Jackie Os.

"Woo-wee! Y'all could pull a baked potato right out of
the ground, it's so damn hot out here today," said Precious.

She fanned herself with the paper party napkin. "Aw, shoot. Lookee there. I got my heel stuck."

"I don't know how you can wear those things," I croaked, crawling around my friend's feet. "They make my feet hurt looking at 'em."

Precious slapped a big hand on my head. "I'm afraid that I'm aerating your pa's precious lawn." Leaning on my head, pushing me into the ground, she pulled her spiky heel out of the sod. Then she wiped the heel with her paper napkin before gingerly lowering her foot, trying not to put weight on it. She dropped the soiled napkin into my basket.

"Gee, thanks," I said with a smirk.

"No prob, Sunshine."

For several weeks, Precious, who managed Ian's magnificent Gatsbyesque estate next door, had been helping out in the Knox Plantation kitchen while Daphne looked to hire a permanent chef—ours had left unexpectedly. Another long story. Anyway, Precious described straddling the two jobs as the perfect mix, saying that although she adored Ian Collier, she was happy for the change of scenery at our place.

Besides, she'd said, "Y'all need my help like a flea needs a dog."

It didn't seem as if Daphne was in any hurry to find a permanent chef. And Ian seemed content to share his estate manager with us indefinitely.

"Eva? Do ye hear me?" Ian was staring down at me. Lost in thought, I'd no idea what he'd said.

"Sunshine, you're a sight for sore eyes. The green on your knees really brings out that pink hair of yours," Precious razzed.

"Don't it, now?" Ian laughed.

"It's not pink," I huffed. I looked at my knees. Sure enough, they were green. I found the Jackie O sunglasses, snatched them up, and shoved them over my face. I wiped my oily hands on my skort.

"Nice glasses," teased Ian.

Precious burst out laughing. "Ya look like a little ladybug in those big specs. Careful, or somebody might step on you!"

"They already did."

Ian reached down and wrapped his hands around my waist. I felt like a feather as he lifted me to my feet. I expected his hand on my back to drop. It didn't. Instead, his palm stayed pressed to the little dent in the small of my back as we stood side by side. My stomach fluttered.

"You feelin' okay, Sunshine?" asked Precious. "You're lookin' kinda flushed."

"Aye, yer cheeks are quite pink, Eva." Ian chuckled. His eyes twinkled when he looked at me.

"I . . . I'm just hot," I said.

"That ye are, lass." Ian chortled.

"More like a hot mess, I'd say," Precious chirped, shaking her head.

I could smell the starch in Ian's creamy cotton shirt. It draped beautifully over his wide shoulders, fitting neatly around a slender waist. Ian had a rugged elegance and a way of wearing the most exquisite clothes and making them look . . . comfortable. Plus, the touch of his skin, the way he smelled, fresh starch mixed with his sexy, woodsy cologne . . . I stepped away. The spot where his hand had lain felt oddly cool. I reached down and picked up my basket.

"It's alright, folks. Ye can go about yer business now. The rogue pup has been neutralized," Ian announced to the people around us.

Ian bent down to scoop up Dolly, who was holding another damned piece of cheese in her jowls. Immediately, she dropped the cheese and started wagging her tail and licking Ian's face.

"Dolly! No!" I was mortified.

"It's alright." He beamed at my wretched dog as she soiled his immaculately pressed, smooth-as-silk shirt.

"Make way!" Big Bubba was headed in our direction.

Ian plopped Dolly into my basket, and I almost dropped it. Dolly felt ten pounds heavier than she looked.

Time to cut back on doggie treats.

Standing amid total chaos at his station, the Crusty Baker mumbled something profane. The crowd laughed. Fortunately, all three burning charcoal grills had survived Dolly's rampage without turning over, starting a fire, or burning anyone. Daddy's farmhands and a bunch of Chow Network fans in their SLICK EATS AMERICA tee shirts scurried madly, reconstructing the cooking stations. Miriam Tidwell arranged items on the Crusty Baker's righted table as a smiling Daphne worked alongside her, smoothing out a fresh tablecloth. Daphne picked up a microphone.

"While we work quickly to get everything under control, why don't y'all give Big Bubba Clatterbuck a round of applause for bringing his wonderful, award-winning home-grown peaches!"

The crowd cheered. Fans clanked cooking utensils, and Ambrosia Curry squealed and blew a dramatic two-handed kiss from behind her grill.

"Press coming through!" someone shouted from the far side of the crowd.

"Now, you asked about my shoes," continued Precious.

"I did?"

"Sunshine, when I was little, I didn't have nothin' to wear on my feet. I swore I was gonna make me a pile of money, and when I did, I was gonna get me the fanciest shoes money could buy. There ain't a day that goes by when I can see not wearin' my Louboutins. They go where I go. Squishy lawn or not."

"Coming through!" I heard a camera click. I looked to say something to Ian, but he'd disappeared.

The crowd clapped in response to something Ambrosia said.

"Anyway, this has been fun. But I can only stay out here a few minutes," continued Precious.

I spun around, still looking for Ian. The crowd focused on the chefs as they talked more smack. I heard Chef Simmer's taunting laugh. The Crusty Baker's voice grumbled something unrepeatable. Chef Ambrosia tittered. I saw reporter Pat Butts alongside her partner in crime, photographer Tam See, looking my way just as Tam lowered her camera, grinning. Then the duo quickly turned away, heading toward the celebrities. I was sure Tam had snapped a photo of me. I looked down at myself. *What a mess.* Torn, bloodied, oily, and grass stained. Dolly stood up in the basket and licked my face.

"Dolly, stop it!"

"I gotta start preppin' dinner for Miss Daphne's guests tonight," continued Precious. "Mister Collier brought me over here on account of the tires bein' rotated on my car, and Mister Lurch has to be at his ballroom dance class."

Mister Lurch was a manservant, of sorts, who worked for Ian Collier. I'd seen him a few times, yet almost never heard him speak. Silent and shadowy, the guy looked remarkably like the tall, shambly character of the same name on the old *Addams Family* television show.

Precious and I mashed ourselves out of the way as Big Bubba's girls lumbered by, each hauling a fresh load of peaches. Precious grabbed a perfectly ripened peach from Sissy's box and bit into the purloined fruit. Sissy whirled around, narrowing her eyes. Then she mouthed the words "I'll kill you" to Precious before trundling behind her sister.

"Oh, scary." Precious laughed.

"It kind of was," I said. "Who does that?"

"Those linebacker girls are grumpy on account o' them not bein' able to take this kinda heat. Why, it's hot enough to peel house paint out here! Someone's gonna have a heart attack luggin' those boxes through this multitude of people. I'm just glad it ain't me." She bit into the peach, wiping juice from the corners of her mouth.

"Precious?"

"Yes, Sunshine?"

"Where's Ian?"

Before Precious could answer, the loudspeaker crackled.

"Where were we?" asked Ambrosia Curry. "Oh, I remember! I was rolling my strawberry in nuts."

She looked skyward and dangled a huge chocolate-and-nut-covered strawberry over her lips before biting into the berry. She swallowed hard, moaning and rolling her eyes.

"Now, that's a mouthful," she purred.

The crowd broke into applause. Precious laughed out loud. I just shook my head.

"Comin' through!" Big Bubba pressed his way through the throng with another box of peaches.

"That Ambrosia chick has it goin' on," said Precious. "I love the way she does that with the fruit. And don't y'all just love her lacy kitty-cat suit? I gotta get me one of those."

Thinking of mammoth Precious in a lacy, formfitting "kitty-cat suit," I slammed my hand on my forehead as the crowd shuffled to let Big Bubba pass.

"Ladies," said Ambrosia Curry, "rub olive oil on your lips before bed; they'll be smooth and supple by morning. Olive oil, kept bedside, is extremely useful—extra virgin, of course!"

"You'd know all about bedside oils, wouldn't you?" Slick Simmer snapped. "Not the extra virgin part, of course."

Chef Ambrosia shot him a dirty look.

"Gotta get through here!" Big Bubba wheezed as he lumbered closer.

"Make way, Sunshine," said Precious, looking over her shoulder as Big Bubba closed in on us.

"Comin' throoooough . . . !"

Just as the crowd opened up, out of the corner of my eye I thought I saw Ian. I turned to look.

"Arggghhhh!"

An unbearable weight crashed into me from behind, throwing me forward. Dolly and the big basket flew from my arms before I found myself pinned to the ground, desperately struggling to breathe.

"Daddy!" Sissy and Peaches shrieked in unison.

CHAPTER 4

In the big house kitchen the next morning, my sisters and I were so busy comparing notes about Big Bubba's collapse that we didn't pay much attention to the guests in the dining room. I'd just assumed that they were all there—except Ambrosia Curry, who'd insisted on breakfast in her suite upstairs. Everyone else was supposed to be chowing down on Precious's scrumptious meal in the dining room before heading off for a late-morning farm tour with Daddy. They'd all been eager to visit the olive grove.

"Anyone hear any more about Big Bubba?" I asked.

"Other than the man's deader than a doorknob?" Pep replied. "Nope." She wore a black midriff top with a glittery skull and crossbones printed on the front with a lacy mini-skirt and black combat boots.

"Sissy and Peaches were fit to be tied last night. All that caterwauling . . ." Precious sighed.

"It's a shame," Daphne said. With her pressed peach linen shift tailored perfectly to fit her sylphlike figure, Daphne looked remarkably rested, perfectly coiffed and made-up. Surprising, given all the events of the day before. Her gold charm bracelet jangled as she pulled open the refrigerator door. "Meg, please see to it that your brother finishes his waffle."

"Yes, ma'am," answered Meg.

Twelve-year-old Meg was the oldest of Daphne's five kids. The neat strawberry blonde had happily assumed the role of caretaker to her siblings, much like the way Daphne had done after our mother abandoned us when Pep and I were little.

Daphne narrowed her eyes, glancing at her six-year-old daughter, Amy, seated next to me at the table. Amy'd returned from summer vacation at her father's in Atlanta with her waist-length fair hair dyed inky black, giving the freckled, fair-skinned child a mini-Vampira look that only Pep seemed to appreciate.

"Eat your egg, Amy," ordered Daphne. "Precious scrambled it with chopped pickled olives, just the way you like it."

I couldn't help but make a face.

"Big Bubba doted on his two daughters," Pep said. "And Sissy and Peaches worshipped him. Heaven knows what they're goin' to do without him now."

"Still, I hardly think that the girls' threatening to kill whoever did this to Big Bubba was an appropriate response." Daphne sniffed, crossing the room. "Clearly it was the poor fellow's health that caused his demise."

"Obviously, not enough olive oil in his diet," said Pep, rolling her eyes.

"Gracious! Pepper-Leigh, have some good taste."

"I think I will, thank you." Pep grabbed a balsamic, berry, and peach olive oil scone and bit into it. "Mm, tastes good," she mumbled. Her big gray eyes twinkled.

Daphne shook her head. "Violetta Merganthal called and told me this mornin' that Big Mama might have to sell the farm. She's got two girls to put through college."

"I told y'all it was too hot for them big folks to be luggin' heavy cartons back and forth across the lawn all day." Precious shut off the faucet. "Hang on . . . I gotta check on folks in the dining room. Be right back."

Carrying a porcelain water pitcher across the kitchen, Precious leaned into the door, swinging it open to the formal dining room.

"How y'all doin' out here? You folks need anything?"

The door swung shut.

Daphne, Pep, and I chatted as Daphne's youngest kids scarfed up their breakfasts. Meg bustled about the old kitchen, serving and cleaning up after everyone.

Daphne's two-year-old son, Little Boomer, squealed delightedly as he squished homemade waffles drenched in melted butter and warmed maple syrup between his fingers. Freckled ten-year-old Jo, her strawberry-blonde hair pulled back in a ponytail, bounced a tennis ball the entire time she sat at the table. The constant *thunk-thunk-thunking* of the ball hitting the floor nearly drove me insane. I was surprised that our manners maven, Daphne, didn't object. But then, I was learning that rules and politesse are often overlooked when it comes to one's own kids.

Bookish eight-year-old Beth never said a word. She just kicked her chair rhythmically, humming "99 Bottles of Beer on the Wall" while keeping her nose buried in *The Mystery at Lilac Inn*, a Nancy Drew mystery. Absently, she shoveled mounds of waffles, fresh fruit, and whipped cream into her mouth, slathering more food on her face and the book than into her mouth.

And, yes, Daphne had named her girls after the characters in her favorite book, *Little Women*. Her other favorite book was *Gone with the Wind*, and we all knew that from the time she was little, Daphne saw herself as a contemporary Scarlett O'Hara.

"Folks are finishing up," announced Precious, stepping back into the kitchen. "They're headin' out to the front porch, where your pop is waitin' to take 'em to the olive grove. And I'm almost done here with Chef Ambrosia's room-service breakfast. Just gotta finish these last waffles."

Daphne clapped her hands. "Children, y'all have fifteen minutes to get ready for the church canoe trip today. Meg, help your brother, please."

"Yes, ma'am," replied Meg, picking up her brother.

In a flurry, the kids tossed napkins and sent utensils clattering as they jettisoned themselves from their chairs and raced from the kitchen into the adjacent laundry room, where they clamored up the back stairs, past the second-floor guest rooms, and to the family bedrooms on the third floor.

Daphne smiled. "Aren't they just priceless!" It was a statement, not a question.

"Sure. As long as they're not mine," Pep said, chortling.

"Oh, Pepper-Leigh. You'll see. Wait till you have your own someday. You'll do everything for them." She sighed wistfully.

Pep made a face.

"Anyone seen Chef Slick Simmer this mornin'?" asked Precious.

"No . . ." answered Daphne cautiously. Pep and I shrugged.

"I saw Miriam Tidwell and the Crusty Baker guy. I didn't see Slick Simmer in the dining room," said Precious.

"Maybe he's busy boffing someone in his motor home," said Pep with a silly smile. "I mean, that's what he does, right?" She raised her eyebrows and looked at Daphne.

Daphne gave Pep a stern look before focusing on me. "Eva, dear, after everything that happened yesterday, did you sleep alright last night?" I had the sense that Daphne's inquiry was more about wanting to change the subject than about any concern for me.

"I'm still having nightmares about the dead man I tripped over in the olive grove a few weeks ago," I said. "Now this. Honestly, I barely slept at all."

Crawling out from under dead Big Bubba had been no small feat. As sorry as I was for him and his family, I knew that I'd have nightmares for weeks. Still, chronically suffering from insomnia, I'd had weird dreams for years, often awakening startled, in a panic. During most nights, I'd clear my mind by going outside to run. Sometimes it worked. However, so far that summer, it hadn't worked much.

"Perhaps, Eva, you should seek out some counseling. Sadie

Truewater says there's a new doctor in town. And he's single."
Daphne smiled.

Daphne was totally into counseling. It always made her feel good to talk about herself. And, clearly, she figured that finding me a man would be a cure-all. Combining a beau and counseling would be a slam dunk. Except it was the last thing I wanted.

No counseling.

No drama.

No man.

"No, thanks. It's not like I've ever slept much anyway," I said.

"No official word on how Big Bubba bit the big one?" Pep asked.

"Pepper-Leigh!" Daphne looked aghast.

Precious said, "My friend Coretta Crum—she works at the bank, y'all remember? She called this mornin' and said that her brother Bigger, who works at the morgue, told her that Doc Payne said it was probably a heart attack and that Big Bubba passed instantly."

"A shame," mumbled Daphne.

"Say, did anyone check Big Bubba's refrigerated truck? Is it still over at the warehouse?" I asked.

"Oh yeah . . . the ice cream!" cried Pep. "I never got any. Peach bourbon, right?"

Daphne chirped, "The truck was still there last night. I saw it comin' back from . . .".

Pep raised an eyebrow.

Daphne stopped herself and said nothing.

Pep pressed on. "Slick Simmer's motor home?"

Precious and I looked at each other. Daphne's eyes flashed at Pep.

"You were there last night, weren't you, Daph?" Pep grabbed another scone and took an oversized bite. "And you seem to have an extra bit of spring in your step today," she said with a mouthful. "I haven't seen you look like this since way back when you were with . . ."

"Stop!" hissed Daphne.

"Daph, I saw you," Pep said. "When I was coming home from the Roadhouse."

Daphne narrowed her eyes at Pep before looking down. Slowly she took a ladylike sip from her tea. She reached over to a doily-lined platter and picked up a scone, breaking it into small pieces, placing each piece carefully on her plate. Ignoring Pep. Ignoring all of us.

We waited for Daphne to respond.

She didn't.

"More fresh-squeezed orange juice?" Precious asked, finally breaking the silence.

"Not for me, thanks," I said.

"No, thanks. I'm still waiting for an answer," Pep said. "No one else drives a big-ass Buick around these parts, Daphne, especially comin' from over at the warehouse. It was you."

"Yes. Alright! I was visiting with Slick last evening," Daphne finally said. "We're old friends. It's no big deal."

"You're friends?" I asked. "Why didn't I know that? Is that how you got the famous chefs to come here?"

"I heard no woman ever gets into the chef's motor home without paying for it with favors," pushed Pep. She raised her fingers, bracketing the word "favors" in air quotes.

"Really, Pepper-Leigh." Daphne sounded completely disgusted.

"I also heard he's got a water bed in there."

"Really?" asked Precious and I at the same time.

"Uh-huh. And I read in the *Celebrity Stargazer* that he has some sort of bizarre disorder," Pep said.

"Pep, I can't believe you read that rag. I'm crushed," I said. And really, I was . . . The tabloid had devoted an inordinate amount of ink to scandalous gossip about me.

"The article said he can't fall asleep unless he's with a woman," continued Pep. "So, Daph, were you the woman to help our playboy go beddy-bye last night?"

"Well, if he was with a woman, then he was hardly sleepin', now, was he?" Precious laughed hard.

"Actually, now that I think about it, maybe that's what

you need to help you sleep, Eva—a sleeping buddy!" Pep grinned.

Sitting at the table, stony faced, Daphne said nothing.

She'd never admit it, but just from looking at Daphne, we all knew she'd had some sort of intimate liaison with Slick Simmer. With her eyes bright and sparkling, her mood was better than it had been in weeks—despite our razzing and dealing with her five rambunctious kids, not to mention dead Bubba Clatterbuck, the busy charity cook-off, and all the Dolly hullabaloo the day before.

Finally Daphne said, "That's just Chow Network publicity bunk. Made-up stories as part of Slick's image. People just love a bad boy. He's really not like that at all."

"I'll bet." Pep let out a snort.

"Methinks the lady of the house has stars in her eyes," said Precious with a laugh.

Daphne left the table, crossed to the counter, and peeped into a steeping floral-patterned teapot.

"How come I never knew about this?" I asked.

"Some things are better left unsaid," joked Precious.

"Who'da thunk it? Scarlett O'Hara makin' whoopee in a motor home," Pep teased.

Daphne picked up a coffeepot next to the teapot and floated over to the big oak table, pouring a second cup of coffee into Pep's dead-roses mug, and then into my favorite blue-and-cream glazed hand-thrown mug. She offered coffee to Precious, who shook her head no. Setting the coffeepot back down on the counter, Daphne focused on the breakfast tray that Precious was prepping for Chef Ambrosia.

"Gracious!" exclaimed Daphne. "For such a fit woman, Chef Ambrosia is no skimpy eater."

With her charm bracelet jangling, Daphne grabbed the floral-patterned teapot and poured herself more hot tea in her flowery china cup before she pulled out one of the pressed Larkin oak chairs and joined us at the table.

No doubt about it, the discussion about Daphne and Slick Simmer was over.

"Lord knows," said Precious, dropping a dirty bowl into the farm sink, "Ambrosia Curry asked for a breakfast big enough to feed a family of four."

"I feel like that's what I just ate myself," I joked. "Those strawberry Belgian waffles were killer."

"I'm imagining one paired with the peach bourbon ice cream I never got yesterday," said Pep.

"We really should go over and check on the Clatterbucks' truck," I said. "You think the freezer is still running?"

"Oh, sure," said Pep. "I saw the truck last month when Big Bubba brought it over to show Daddy, right after he bought it. It's a hybrid with a movable wall between the refrigerator and freezer compartments and a big battery, like the kind in the Prius cars. It's really cool. Any food inside—even ice cream—should be fine. In fact, he may have plugged in the battery to charge at the warehouse. Hmmm, now that you mention it, Eva, someone really needs to rescue all that peach bourbon ice cream!" Pep smiled evilly.

"Yes. There's at least a dozen tubs of ice cream and gelato in the truck. Why don't y'all check on it when we're finished here?" said Daphne. "Eva, take Daddy's Kubota all-terrain vehicle. Although, goodness knows, I don't know what we'll do with all that frozen deliciousness—or where we'll keep it!"

"I can bring it to the Roadhouse, where we've got a walk-in freezer," said Pep. "It'll be easy to store those big tubs while we figure out what to do with it all."

"Thank you. That sounds like a fine idea, Pepper-Leigh," said Daphne. "After we get the tubs out, I'll ask some of Daddy's men to clean the truck and return it to the Clatterbuck family."

Precious opened the waffle iron and picked out the last waffle, dropping it on a small serving platter.

"Waffles are ready. And famous celebrity or not, I ain't climbin' no stairs to serve Miss Ambrosia Curry. I gotta hustle and clean up the dining room before I race back to Greatwoods. Mister Collier said he needs me today."

"I'll help clean the buffet, Miss Precious," Daphne said.

"I'll take Ambrosia's breakfast up," I said.

Precious had prepared a huge silver tray with waffles, warm grits, cinnamon toast, fresh fruit, yogurt, scrambled eggs, an assortment of flavored butters, syrup, jams, hot tea, and a carafe of orange juice. I had to marvel at how Ambrosia Curry could eat such a big breakfast and still maintain her figure.

"Eva, I'm thankful for your help takin' up the breakfast, but please don't let anyone see you," said Daphne. "Don't y'all have anything to wear besides tee shirts and sneakers? Even yesterday's skort would be better than those ratty cutoffs."

Pep looked at me from across the table and stuck her finger in her mouth.

"The twins look so adorable in their Knox Plantation uniforms," continued Daphne. "I can have Earlene Azalea make one up for you, lickety-split."

Earlene Azalea Greene was Daphne's current best friend and mother of Daphne's employees, Charlene and Darlene. Daphne's friendship with Earlene Azalea explains how we ended up with the twins as "full-time" employees and why Daphne overlooked the fact that the two were missing in action half the time they should've been working.

I bristled. "If the twins had actually shown up for work this morning, they could be wearing their own 'adorable' uniforms. However, since they're not here—again—you're stuck with me and my ratty cutoffs."

Pep chortled as she grabbed her dead-roses coffee mug. She added half a mugful of cream to her steaming fresh coffee.

"Eva, Charlene and Darlene worked so hard, for such a long time, cleaning up the lawn after your mutt destroyed it yesterday, I told them to come in late today," Daphne said pointedly.

Pep dumped half a dozen teaspoonfuls of organic sugar into her mug. "Touché."

Watching Pep dump her sugar, I said, "Who needs teeth?"

Pep smiled. Her eyes looked full of mischief. "I can take the tray upstairs," she offered.

"Dressed like that?" Daphne cried. "Goodness gracious, no! Pepper-Leigh, I'm sure there's something in the book of good manners about not wearing skulls to Sunday breakfast."

"Oh dear." I laughed, standing from the table. "Pep, we've both failed the fashion test this morning."

"So what else is new?" Pep slapped the table and snorted like a piglet.

Precious handed me a monster-sized silver tray with a heavy domed silver cover. "Here, Sunshine. Take this up to Chef Ambrosia. Maybe she's feedin' a midget who came in that big fancy trunk of hers. If she is, there's plenty of food for 'em both."

"Aw, shoot," I said, balancing the oversized salver. "This tray is so big, it won't fit into the dumbwaiter, will it?"

There was an old dumbwaiter next to the back stair in the laundry room. We used to play in it as kids. After shoring it up, Daphne had been using it to move laundry, cleaning supplies, sundries, and occasionally meals to and from the second- and third-floor bedrooms.

"Nope." Pep laughed. "It'll stand up sideways in the dumbwaiter, but it won't fit flat with things on it. Ya gotta go around and carry it up the big front stair."

Daphne sighed. "Eva, unload the food into the dumbwaiter and send it up while you carry the empty tray up the back stair. Then reload the tray on the second floor before serving Chef Curry."

"Too much trouble." I kicked the door open into the dining room.

"Eva, *puh-leese*, don't kick the door!" scolded Daphne in a loud whisper.

The dining room was empty.

"Everyone left with Daddy," I told Daphne. "I'll go up the front stairs, the way Pep said."

"Sunshine, when ya come back down, we'll go check on the ice cream before I leave for Greatwoods," Precious called after me.

"Oh nooo!" Daphne wailed. "My little elephant charm . . . it's gone!"

CHAPTER 5

Balancing the loaded silver tray, I lumbered past the mahogany buffet and dining table centered under my great-grandmother's crystal chandelier. Tossed linen napkins, dirty silverware, and food-spattered china patterned with little pink roses, along with a dozen empty china serving bowls and platters, made up the remains of Precious's magnificent breakfast in the dining room.

I wondered how Precious had missed seeing Slick Simmer as she'd gone back and forth all morning. Surely the man had been at breakfast. Then, thinking of him with Daphne, I grimaced and shook my head. It was hard to imagine Daphne—anyone, really—being intimate with a man who seemed to treat women so irreverently.

I used my hip to scoot a dining chair out of the way and trundled into the front parlor, where the grandfather clock ticktocked. Shelves flanking the fireplace were stuffed with cherished family books to share with guests. I remembered the times I'd curled up in the squishy rolled-arm couch by the window overlooking the wraparound porch. I'd dip warm, homemade Toll House cookies in milk, reading a good mystery, waiting for Buck to stop by after he finished his farm chores . . .

Stop that!

Enough about Buck, I thought.

Reaching the big curved stair, I pressed the heavy tray into my hips and wobbled carefully up the steps, struggling to balance the tray and its contents. Feeling like a wimp, I decided a new workout routine was in order. Heck, maybe it'd help me to sleep, I thought. I remembered hearing about a new gym in town called Ringo's.

I'd ask Daphne about it.

Nearly to the top of the stairs, I heard light footsteps scurrying down the second-floor hallway. Still, when I reached the top stair, I didn't see anyone. I made my way down the hallway and knocked on the door to Ambrosia Curry's suite. I heard a voice inside. *Must be on the phone,* I thought. I knocked lightly again.

"Miss Curry?"

No response. Just a quick flurry of footsteps. I waited another ten seconds or so.

"Miss Cur—"

Suddenly, the door opened a crack. Ambrosia Curry peeked out. Wrapped in a fluffy white bathrobe and without the dramatic penciled eyebrows, false eyelashes, black eyeliner, and crimson red lipstick, the pale-skinned woman could have been any average woman. Except she was tall and slender, like a dancer. I even noticed a few freckles . . . easily camouflaged by makeup. And her shoulder-length black hair was not coiffed into her trademark forties-style waves. Instead, her curls were wild and unkempt. The only hints of her glamorous pinup persona were the beauty mark and gorgeously manicured crimson-polished nails at the tips of her slender fingers.

"Set the tray outside, please," she snapped. "I'll get it in a minute." She started closing the door.

"Wait! Miss Curry!" I braced the mammoth tray against the hall wall. "I'm happy to set this up for you in your suite. I'd hate for you to be disappointed if the waffles, tea . . .

well, everything, gets cold. And the tray is heavy . . ." Her request for me to leave the tray outside on the hall floor surprised me.

"No need. I can get it in a minute," she said hastily. She started to close the door.

"Okay. But . . . when you're finished, just let us know. Our housekeeping staff will come up and take it all away."

If the twins decide to show up for work, that is.

"No!" She stopped the door and poked her head out. "I mean, no, thanks. I'll just set it all on the hall floor when I'm done. And I don't need housekeeping today. I'm working on my recipes and don't want to be disturbed."

She smiled. Then she closed the door.

I knocked.

"Miss Curry? I'm sorry to bother you again. It's just that, there's a dumbwaiter at the end of the hall. Perhaps you could leave the dirty dishes in the dumbwaiter instead of out here on the floor? Just set the tray against the wall when you're finished loading the dumbwaiter so we don't risk a fire."

And Daphne wouldn't go apoplectic at the sight of dirty dishes littering the floor.

"Fine," she called out from the suite.

I lowered the tray to the floor. Still, something about leaving food on the hall floor seemed wrong. I stared at the tray for a moment before finally turning and heading for the stairs. When I heard Ambrosia Curry's door squeak open, I looked over my shoulder to see her reach out and slide the big tray into her suite. A little giggle came from inside the room just as the door clicked shut.

Hands on my hips, I stopped for a moment and stared at the closed door down the hall.

That was weird.

CHAPTER 6

Precious, Dolly, and I stood in the gravel drive next to the big house between the bike rack and Daddy's orange all-terrain Kubota—something akin to a cross between a jeep and a golf cart with a dump bed in the rear.

"Wouldya look at that!" Precious exclaimed, eyeing the dozen or so bikes in the rack. "That one there looks like a big tricycle!"

I laughed. "There are two. See?"

I pointed to another Schwinn trike cruiser on the end of the line. It had three wheels, fenders, a three-speed shifter, and a big basket in the back.

"Pep insisted Daphne buy the two trikes when she purchased the regular bikes. Turns out the three-wheelers are guest favorites. Families love them."

Precious huffed. "Ha! No one's catching me riding around on an oversized tricycle. Nuh-uh!"

"Somehow, Precious, I don't see you riding around on a two-wheeler, either. You just don't strike me as a biker type."

Precious burst out laughing. "Ain't it the truth, Sunshine!"

I slid behind the wheel of the Kubota and turned the key.

As the engine growled and rattled, Dolly jumped in, standing with her front paws on my bare leg, sniffing the summery air. Precious plopped onto the seat on the passenger
side before I shifted and backed away from the house. We
were off to check the Clatterbucks' truck before Precious
returned to Greatwoods for a few hours.

Suddenly Daphne appeared on the porch, waving her
arms.

"Yoo-hoo! Eva! Wait!"

She rushed down the stair, through the flower garden,
and over to the Kubota in the drive. I shut off the noisy
engine.

"Y'all, I can't find my little elephant charm anywhere!
And I've got to take the kids over to the river. Since y'all
are already goin' to the warehouse, can you peep around
Slick's motor home and see if I lost my little elephant there?
I'd never ask if it weren't one of my most precious things . . ."

Precious raised her eyebrows. "The chef is supposed to
be on the plantation tour with the other guests and your
daddy. So are you meanin' for us to go inside and rifle
through his motor home . . . while he's not there?"

"No. No. Of course not," answered Daphne, sounding
flustered. "I just thought maybe y'all could look around outside. Since y'all will be right there and all." She blushed.

"Seems to me, if you were makin' monkey business between the sheets in the motor home last night, that's the
place you should be lookin' for a lost charm," Precious
said bluntly. "Hey, by the way, I forgot to ask—is it really a
water bed?"

I chuckled. Daphne frowned. I could see she wasn't going
to answer that one. Was a water bed in a motor home even
possible?

I wondered.

"Truth be told"—Daphne looked contrite—"we were
making out on the bench next to the woods when Slick
picked me up and carried me into his motor home. He's such
a romantic!" Daphne flushed.

Precious and I looked at each other. I rolled my eyes. I'd

never heard Daphne use the phrase "making out" before, especially referring to herself. It made me oddly uncomfortable. Precious looked down and shook her head in mock disgust.

"I might've caught my charm on the motor home steps, or the doorway . . . or maybe at the bench when he first caressed my hair. I got kind of tangled—"

"I get it," I said, raising a hand in protest. "Too much information, Daph. We'll look. Come on, Precious."

"Thank y'all so much! I'd look myself except the children—"

"Yeah, yeah. We get it," I said, waving her off. "Bye, now. We'll see ya later."

I turned the key and quickly backed away.

Dolly licked my arm as we motored along, passing sweetly scented hedges of roses and dogwood and magnolia trees near the big house. I ran my hand over Dolly's wavy black fur as we crossed the sunny lawn. A couple of Daddy's farmhands raised their caps and waved as they worked around the yard. I waved back.

"How y'all doin' today?" called Precious, waving like a beauty queen to the men. "Now, there's a bunch of brawny beasts," she mumbled to herself with a smirk.

"Nice day!" she said to no one in particular. Dolly yipped excitedly.

"Precious, do you think that Slick Simmer could be with Ambrosia Curry this morning?"

"You mean, in the big house?"

"Yes."

"Why do ya ask? I thought he had the hots for your big sis."

"I didn't want to say anything to Daphne, but, like you said before, no one saw him at breakfast—and that was a ton of food you made for Ambrosia Curry. Certainly, it was enough for more than one person."

"Yeah, so . . ."

"Well, when I went up with the tray, she was acting kind of . . . squirrelly."

"Squirrelly?"

"Uh-huh. She didn't want me to come into the suite. She even had me leave the tray on the floor in the hall."

"All my good food . . . on the floor? Why, that's just plumb gross! Not to mention totally disrespectful."

"When I told her someone would be up later to remove the dirty dishes, she went ballistic. Said no one was to come into her suite. And I could swear she was talking with someone in there."

"You don't say!" Precious looked thoughtful for a moment. She shrugged. "I dunno!"

With her dangly gold earrings jangling in the wind, Precious raised her sparkly cell phone to her face, flashed a toothy smile, and snapped a selfie.

We whizzed under the shade of giant live oak trees. Overhead, gnarled branches were laden with foamy green moss. We picked up a narrow trail and headed out into bright sunshine again, then followed the dirt road over a couple of gently rolling knolls.

"Woo-wee! It's hot as Hades today!" Precious said. "This little breeze we're makin' feels *fab-u-lous*!"

She grabbed the handle on the roll bar under the Kubota's black roof and fanned herself with her free hand. Dolly wagged her tail. The hills flattened and the land stretched out in front of us. We followed a rough dirt lane between smooth, level crop fields until we hit a gravel drive at the end of a field and turned ninety degrees around the bottom of the field and down the gravel drive. Straight ahead, we could see Daddy's red warehouse with the corrugated metal roof. The Clatterbucks' white box truck was parked alongside the building. Slick Simmer's flashy silver motor home hulked on the far side of the parking area, close to a stand of hardwood trees on the edge of the woods.

"What's that?" asked Precious, pointing.

Parked behind and not too far from Slick's motor home was a junky-looking old yellow Volkswagen van.

"Daphne said the van belongs to a woman named Savannah Deats," I said. "She's kind of a groupie who follows Slick everywhere." I chuckled as Precious raised her eyebrows.

"And Daphne's actually charging the woman money to park here and use the warehouse bathroom. Like a campsite."

"Well, I'll be. Your big sis sure is a businesswoman, now, ain't she?"

"Our superfan is supposed to leave tomorrow when Slick leaves. She'll just follow him out like she followed him in."

Just as the words were out of my mouth, a young woman with a long blonde braid stepped out from behind Slick's motor home. I remembered Slick insulting her in front of the crowd during the cooking demonstration. I'm sure she saw us—we were no more than a quarter of a mile away and the Kubota made a ton of noise. Still, she didn't stop or wave. Instead, she stomped across the gravel and yanked open the door to her van before climbing inside. The door slammed shut just about the time we hit the gravel around the warehouse.

"Well, that's a fine how-de-do," said Precious, chuckling. "Ya think she's been in the motor home this mornin' gettin' a little nookie with your big sister's boyfriend?" Precious laughed.

"Omigosh, Precious!" I grimaced. "Don't say a word to Daph. Slick is supposed to be on the tour with Daddy and the others. I hope he's not with Ambrosia Curry *or* Savannah Deats!"

"Or both." Precious laughed. "Remember what he said to this Savannah girl yesterday, during the cooking demonstration? About the threesome? Surely your big sis knows he's a total cad. I mean, it's not like the guy hasn't been with just about every woman he comes across. That's just . . . what he does. Right?"

"Far as I know." I navigated down the gravel drive, closing in on the warehouse. "Maybe, like Daph said, it's all an act. After all, the media says all sorts of stuff about me, and none of it's true." I shrugged. "Really, now that you mention it, I can't imagine Daphne wanting to be with a man who's been with everyone. Of course, I can't imagine her sharing a man, either."

"Me, neither, Sunshine."

We stopped next to the warehouse.

"This is the fanciest warehouse parking lot I've ever seen!" Precious said. "Why, it looks like a national park out here."

"Ha!" I laughed. "That's because last week Daphne decreed that no Knox Plantation guest is going to feel like he—or she—is staying at a 'truck stop.'" I flagged my fingers like quote marks when I said "truck stop." I continued. "Obviously, she knew Slick Simmer was traveling in his motor home. I didn't get it at the time; however, now I understand why she had Daddy's crew plant all these shrubs and rosebushes that you see all around the warehouse. She even had them set up benches and picnic tables over by the woods. I'm surprised she didn't set out a barbecue."

"Probably not enough time." Precious laughed, then looked around and whistled. "Mm-hm. It looks pretty nice out here, awright."

I shut off the Kubota engine. Dolly scrambled ill-manneredly across Precious's lap, then leapt out of the Kubota, landing in a belly flop on the gravel. Nose to the ground, she sniffed and scooted toward the woods, tail wagging over her back, following the scent of some squirrel, no doubt.

"Don't go far, Dolly!" I stepped out of the Kubota as Dolly shot off into the woods on the scent of something.

The cab of the Toyota box truck featured a big rounded windshield and windows nearly as big in each of the doors. Standing at the driver's side of the truck, I heard a mechanical hum from the front of the box compartment behind the truck cab.

"The compressor's running. Everything should still be cold inside." I reached to the side door on the refrigerator box behind the cab. I tried the latch. Locked. I headed to the rear of the box.

"Toyota Dyna," mused Precious, looking over the truck. "Looks like a little bug towing a bread box."

The high-set black bumper was well above my waist. Reaching up the left edge of the box, I grabbed ahold of the silver handle on the bifold-style back door.

"I like this little truck," prattled Precious, following me to the vehicle's rear end. "'Cept, lawdee! You're gonna have to hand me the ice cream one container at a time, Sunshine. I ain't haulin' myself up there to get it. The bumper is clear up to my boobies!"

"Correction. My chest. Your waist, Precious. And if you'd worn more practical shoes, you could climb inside as well."

I reached up and yanked the bifold door open and folded it to the right. A cool blast of air shot from the refrigerated compartment.

"Oooh, that feels nice as ice!" Precious bent forward, pulling the neckline of her blouse away from her skin, fanning cool air toward her chest.

"There's still a few cartons of peaches left. Here. Give me a lift, will you, please? We can take them back in the Kubota."

"Sure, Sunshine."

Precious let go of her neckline and plaited her fingers together. She held her gargantuan hands down at my knee, like a stirrup. I placed one sneakered foot into her hands, grabbed on to the frame of the truck, and hoisted myself up as Precious lifted her hands to help raise me into the chilled container.

"Hey, Precious, can you bake something with these peaches?" I stepped into the compartment.

"Sure can, Sunshine."

Looking around, I saw three wooden cartons of peaches set along the right sidewall. I headed toward them.

"Omigosh, these peaches smell great! Maybe we can bring something made with the peaches to the Clatterbuck family."

"How many peaches you got up there?" asked Precious. Shielding the bright sun from her eyes with her hands, she peered into the darkened truck box. "Mmm, it does smell good and peachy! Maybe I can make one of my famous Cold Pressed Peach Cakes."

"Famous?"

The overhead compressor clicked off as I grabbed a peach from one of the cartons.

"Sure, Sunshine! It'll be famous once I make it!" Precious laughed.

"Think you can make a couple? There are enough peaches up here for at least a dozen cakes."

I tossed the peach to Precious, who caught it with a smile. About two-thirds up inside the container, a dividing partition that slid on rails was mounted to the compartment sidewalls. In the partition was a door to the freezer section in front. It was closed. I headed toward the freezer door.

"Sunshine, if y'all will eat 'em, I'll make two dozen famous Cold Pressed Peach Cakes!"

I grabbed ahold of the latch to the freezer compartment.

"Yummy! I can't wait. We'll put a sign over the kitchen door: Precious Darling's Cold Pressed Peach Cake Factory. I'll be your taste tester!"

I looked back over my shoulder at Precious and grinned. She gave me a thumbs-up as she bit into the peach I'd tossed to her. Yanking open the freezer door, I stepped into the compartment. A blast of frozen air hit me hard.

Then I fell forward, stumbling over something on the freezer floor.

"Oh my gosh! Precious . . ." I dropped to my knees. "I need your help . . . Dial 911! Hurry!"

"Wha?" she mumbled, holding the peach in her teeth. "I got a cheach in gny gnouth . . ."

"It's Slick! He . . . he . . . he's *ice-cold*!"

CHAPTER 7

Sheriff Buck Tanner was right. Like he'd said once, I was a magnet for disaster. I'd been back home just a couple of months and already I'd tripped over, fallen under, and stumbled into not one, not two, but three dead men.

The first man—the one I'd tripped over in Daddy's olive grove weeks earlier—had been murdered. The second—Big Bubba Clatterbuck, who'd fallen on top of me—died from natural causes. However, the third man—Master Chef Slick Simmer, whom I'd stumbled over just hours earlier—had died . . . *oddly*.

His cause of death remained officially "undetermined," pending an investigation.

Remembering the way he'd looked—lying lifeless in the truck freezer, eerily off-color, with a cold, frozen, blue-eyed stare—gave me the chills. Next to Slick, there'd been an ice-cream scoop and an open tub of peach bourbon olive oil ice cream with little gouges in it. I shuddered. Then I pulled the Jackie Os down over my face as I tried sinking deeper into the tight, black-leather bucket seat of the late-model red Corvette Stingray.

"Yup," said Precious, pressing the accelerator pedal with her spiky cherry red pump, "one person bumpin' into two dead bodies in the same weekend must be some kinda record."

Her man-sized hands tightened around the leather-wrapped steering wheel. Keeping her head slightly bent to the side, ostensibly to keep it from hitting the roof of her racy little car, she pressed harder on the pedal as we sped under a green canopy of moss-draped oaks along the country road.

"That makes three dead guys you've bumped into since you've been home," she said brightly.

"Yeah. I'll have to check in with the Guinness book of records," I said sarcastically.

All joking aside, I was bummed. It'd been an insane Sunday. After Precious and I had discovered Slick Simmer's body, two officers—Deputy Price and Deputy Pierce—had arrived quickly. They'd been very kind and understanding as they interviewed us, several times, and secured the area. Still, it'd been chaos as emergency workers, law enforcement, and media people arrived one after another, crawling all over the plantation. Not to mention the hoards of Slick fans and gawkers who'd swarmed our place after hearing the devastating news about their beloved chef. Finally, after discovering a videographer hiding under the big house porch, and another reporter sitting up in one of the live oak trees, spying on us, Daphne'd hired a couple off-duty deputies to round up all the trespassers and kick them off the property.

A few hours later, the kids were safe with Daphne's bestie, Earlene Azalea. The guests had all gone out for Sunday dinner—everyone, that is, except Ambrosia Curry, who remained holed up in her suite with dinner delivered from Saucy's Pizzeria. And Precious and I were headed to Main Street in the village, where we'd meet Pep and Daphne for our gratis meal at the Palatable Pecan.

The little car hurtled along the twisty country road, whizzing past antique farmhouses and dilapidated barns alongside flat, sandy fields used to grow cotton, onions, soybeans, peanuts, pecans, and fruit. We left each farm behind in a noisy blur. Precious chuckled.

"Your sister Pep said folks down at the Roadhouse are calling your place 'Knox-'em Dead Plantation'! Great, huh?"

"Yeah. Great." I sighed. I didn't think it was funny.

Precious gave me a look. "C'mon, Sunshine. Quit poochin' your lips out like that. Life ain't that bad. We gotta be happy for what we have. Not what—or who—we lost."

"Two more deaths," I said stubbornly. "Who'd ever believe such a thing? And I'm sorry for Daphne. I really do think she cared for Slick. This is gonna go down hard."

Tightening her grip on the wheel with one hand, Precious downshifted the stick shift in the center console with her other hand as she rammed her foot down on the accelerator pedal. Like a bullet, the car roared, shooting smoothly across the pavement through a shaded green tunnel of moss-covered oak trees.

It was the first time I'd ridden as a passenger with Precious. In fact, I'd become completely dependent on riding with others or borrowing their vehicles for errands or trips to town. As of a few weeks earlier, I no longer had a car of my own. In fact, for what it's worth, it helps to pay your auto insurance when it's due. That way, when your car gets totaled in an accident, you can at least buy another car, even if it's a crappy one. *Sigh.* It'd be a year or more before I could save enough money to purchase anything.

Live and learn.

Flying into the left lane, we passed a crawling John Deere tractor, yellow flashers warning us that it was a slow-moving vehicle. Precious jerked the wheel, and we slid over onto the right side again.

Singer Tina Turner's voice, crooning, "You're simply the best . . . ," blared suddenly from Precious's sparkly cell phone.

"Hello?" answered Precious. "Oh, hiya, Coretta. Whatchya know, hon?" She slammed the sports car around a corner.

As Precious listened to Coretta, I watched as swaths of flat, sandy farmland stretching out next to old rambling farmhouses and barns flashed by. There were more farms, then blurs of longleaf pine forests. Every now and again, there'd be a gate in front of a dirt drive that disappeared into the wilderness. *Hunting lodge.* Then, before I could blink, it'd be gone.

"Uh-huh. Ya don't say!" A variety of scandalized expressions crossed Precious's face as her friend chatted on the other end of the line.

We blew by Carter's Country Corner Store, the local hangout for hunters and codgers.

"Really? Uh-huh." Her eyes bugged out. "Well, I'll be a monkey in a barrel!"

I closed my eyelids and felt the car jerk right, then left, as we careened down the twisty road. When I opened my eyes again, we were just a few miles from the village, passing one Georgian- or Federal-style mansion after another, each set well back from the road. There were white fences, big wrought-iron gates, cobblestone drives, and well-tended lawns and gardens with flowering magnolias and roses. The antique estates had been built by wealthy railroad and lumber magnates during an earlier century.

"Ya don't say! Ain't that something," said Precious into her phone. She nodded emphatically.

Blowing past more wilderness, we drove by a few stately Victorians. Then about a mile outside the village, we passed a white farmhouse with painted gnomes on a scraggly lawn with rosebushes. Mister Moody's place. The old codger's rocking chair on the big porch was empty. Probably inside for dinner, I thought. Normally, Mister Moody would be out on his porch, waving to every passerby. Even though he wasn't there, I waved anyway. It was habit. I'd been doing it since I was little.

"Okay. Thanks. Talk with ya soon! Bye, hon." Precious took her foot off the accelerator. The engine quieted as the car slowed. "Well, it's official," announced Precious.

She punched the brake pedal as we closed in on the village. The wide, tree-lined boulevard ahead of us was bathed in the rosy, warm light of approaching dusk. We cruised past freshly painted, picture-perfect Victorians with gingerbread trim.

"Coretta says that Bigger says that Doc Payne says Slick Simmer was murdered. Looks like someone choked the life outta the poor bastard before lockin' him in the freezer last night."

Chapter 8

Slick Simmer, murdered?

"Oh. No."

I slid my Jackie Os on top of my head and rubbed my face in my hands.

Another murder.

I remembered Daphne and her missing elephant charm. When, exactly, I wondered, had she been with Slick? And when had she left him? And why had Slick gone to the Clatterbucks' truck in the middle of the night? Had he gone to the truck alone or had someone followed him there and surprised him . . . ?

"At least he lived life to the fullest," said Precious cheerily, downshifting the Corvette. "Had his way with more babes than you can shake a stick at. And ya know he ate well. What more could a guy want outta life? Great food. Great sex. Right up to the end." She shook her head. "What a way to go."

"This is bad, Precious. Really bad news. I'm worried about Daphne. And our business. Who's going to stay at a place where everyone dies? Who's going to want to buy Daddy's olive oil?"

Precious downshifted again. The car slowed.

"Uh-oh," she said. "Speakin' of bad news, looks like everyone in town is waitin' to get into the restaurant. It's a plum-pickin' mob scene!"

Even from a block away, there was no mistaking that the huge crowd on the sidewalk ahead was waiting to get into the Palatable Pecan.

"I guess with the Farm Family Fare weekend, everyone decided to dine out tonight."

"Uh-huh."

"Look! Someone's leaving," I cried out, pointing to a white midsized Chevy leaving a parking space. "Hurry! It's right in front of the restaurant."

"I'm on it, Sunshine!"

Precious shifted and stomped on the accelerator pedal. I shot back in my seat as the car launched forward and we sped down the boulevard. Precious suddenly downshifted and slammed on the brakes, throwing me forward. The car skidded to a stop right in front of the pistachio green Victorian with ornate white gingerbread trim. A wrought-iron sign read PALATABLE PECAN. On the sidewalk, people turned their heads to stare. Already, I could smell the burned rubber from the tires.

"Precious, you just laid rubber. Right in front of all these people."

Precious grinned. With fast, jerky transitions she maneuvered the growling car into the parking spot and shut off the engine. Quickly, she checked her makeup in the rearview mirror, then opened her door, throwing out one tree-trunk leg and then the other, before hoisting her big self out of the tiny bucket seat. Wearing lots of gold jewelry over a poppy red sleeveless silk top, matching Louboutins, and a black skirt, like a celebrity, Precious flashed a big, red-lipsticked smile and waved to the staring crowd of nearly one hundred people as she lumbered around the front of the Corvette.

Well, that was an entrance, all right.

Slowly I opened my door and slid out of the low bucket seat onto the sidewalk, trying to be as inconspicuous as possible. Keeping my Jackie Os down over my face, I stood slowly, smoothing out my black jeans before quietly clicking the car door shut. I wore my low-heeled black Cole Haan sandals, a black silk top with cutaway sleeves, and a pair of dangly Navajo turquoise-and-silver earrings—some of the staples from my very limited wardrobe after I'd walked away from most everything I'd owned back in Boston, including my clothes.

We pressed our way through the clamoring crowd, passing the few people lucky enough to have snagged seats at half a dozen marble-topped sidewalk tables, where they sipped on drinks and munched on appetizers as we headed toward the stained oak door flanked by giant cement urns potted with roses and perennials. Food aromas wafting from the restaurant smelled delicious.

"There y'all are! Look who I found!"

I looked past dozens of faces until I spotted Daphne. And him.

As always, Daphne was the ultimate Southern belle, oozing charm, sophistication, and graciousness, meeting, greeting, and air-kissing folks, even as she unabashedly crashed through the crowd towing a somewhat sheepish-looking Ian Collier.

"Isn't it positively lovely to find Mister Collier here tonight?" Daphne gushed as she reached us.

I saw Ian exchange an odd glance with Precious.

Daphne's charm bracelet jingled as she reached up to adjust a big straw hat that drooped in front of her face, which was already obscured by a pair of dark Dior cat-eye sunglasses. Given that it was almost sunset, I guessed my big sis wore the hat and glasses in order to deliberately hide—kind of like I was with the Jackie Os. Still, even in her "disguise," I could see she'd been crying—her lipstick had worn off and her neck was red and blotchy. And, really, she was way too cheery to be believed. Fake cheer was always a dead giveaway with Daphne.

She really had cared for the dead chef, I thought. I felt bad for her.

Still, regardless of how she really felt, Daphne seemed determined to put on a good show. And she had her sights on Ian, at least for the night. No doubt our mysterious neighbor was a welcome distraction from Daphne's grief.

"I caught our handsome neighbor crossing the boulevard!" she exclaimed breathlessly. "We never see him around town!" Daphne was like a cat with a prize mouse.

And she was right about Ian's never being seen. In fact, except for his brief appearance at the charity cook-off, the man seemed to spend all his time alone in his Greatwoods mansion—well, except for Precious and Mister Lurch, of course. Still, I hadn't yet figured out what Ian did all the time. And even though we were best buds, Precious was uncharacteristically mum when it came to her boss. She never said a word about him or what he did, holed up day after day in his palatial digs. Several times, I'd tried picking her brain about the mystery man.

To no avail.

Ian mumbled sheepishly, "Missus Bouvier, ye must call me Ian."

"Oh, goodness gracious, Ian, please, call me Daphne," gushed Daphne, flapping her wrist. The bracelet jingled again. "Especially now that I'm a divorcée." She flashed her smile and fawned all over Ian, keeping her frail arm bent around his forearm, leaning into his side. She couldn't have pronounced "divorcée" with any more fervor if she'd tried.

I rolled my eyes.

Why not wear a sandwich sign that reads I'M SINGLE?

I watched as Ian took in Daphne's perfectly tailored navy silk shift. Multiple strands of creamy-colored pearls adorned her neck. And there was a matching pair of cluster pearl earrings. Gifts from her ex. I was sure the gems had cost a fortune.

"Yer looking like a bluebell in summer, Miss Daphne," he quipped.

My mouth dropped open. Ian wasn't falling for Daphne's ridiculous Southern belle act, was he? Men fell all over themselves for Daphne. I didn't know why, but I'd imagined

Ian was different from the rest of them. This was a disappointment.

Precious shook her head.

"How terribly kind of y'all to notice, good sir!" Daphne purred.

"Good sir?" I asked aloud. I lifted the Jackie Os, placing them on top of my head. "Are you kidding?"

Daphne gave me a sharp look.

I wanted to puke. Even for Daphne, she was laying it on pretty thick.

The good news was that Sister Code dictated that if Daphne had even the slightest pretentions about Ian, I needed to be sure not to interfere. If I'd been tempted at all to retract my self-imposed man moratorium, Daphne's open interest in Ian—whether for just a night of "grief relief" or a lifetime—gave me all the reason I needed to stick to my guns. No tangling with any man in whom either of my sisters took interest. That was the rule. Daphne'd laid it out when we were kids, and we'd always stuck to it. All three of us. Fortunately, it wasn't hard to do. We'd never been interested in the same guy.

So, it was settled. No Ian for me. Even if he did smell like heaven.

I shot him a glance.

Ian was staring right at me with his devilish, sexy smile. He winked. My insides fluttered. I dropped my Jackie Os back down on my face. Daphne was so busy pressing her flat breasts into Ian's side, she didn't seem to notice Ian noticing me.

"Eva," he said.

Bending down, he brushed my cheek with the side of his face. His day-old beard tickled. My stomach flipped as I took in his woodsy scent. And, as always, there was that fresh, starchy smell of his custom-made cotton shirt. This time it was pink and it set off his evergreen eyes. My chest pounded as ancient tribal tunes—bagpipes, drums, and fiddles—pulsated in my head. I staggered backward, bumping into Precious, who groaned.

That's when I caught Daphne's glare.

Okay, so Daphne'd noticed Ian noticing me.

"Eva, dear, close your mouth, dahhwr-lin', and stop staring at Mister Collier." She squeezed Ian's arm and looked up at him, batting her eyes. "It's not polite."

"What?" My sister was treating me like a grade-schooler.

"Y'all know that Eva has absolutely no sense when it comes to men," Daphne quipped, still smiling at Ian. "After her heartbreak in Boston, I'm finding her a nice Southern man to settle down with—I know what she needs."

Of course, "Southern" was the key word here. No sexy Scottish neighbor for me.

"Do ye now?" Ian looked at Daphne, amused.

"Why, yes." Daphne smiled. "Did y'all know that I practically raised Eva?"

There she went . . . inferring, of course, that I was too young for Ian. My cheeks flushed. Even when I knew she was being ridiculous, Daphne had this way of making me feel childish.

"Ooh! Eva, look over there," cooed Daphne. "It's Maddox Keeper!" she cried cheerily. "The new warden over at the prison. I hear he's a bachelor. And just your age!"

With a too-big, too-fake smile, Daphne cranked her head around, lifting her chin, indicating where I should look. I'd caught Ian's eye and it'd made her mad. Now she was going to show me Big Sister was still boss.

"I'm sure you could get used to his height." Daphne smiled.

"His height?"

Okay, so I took the bait.

"Why, yes, he's only about five feet tall. Although, just last week, Bubbles Bolender said during our jujitsu class that he's really only about four foot nine. Anyway, I know you prefer shorter men, Eva."

"Jujitsu?" I asked, purposely ignoring Daphne's suggestion about the shrimpy prison warden. She was acting idiotic. I was chalking it up to shock and unresolved grief over Slick Simmer. Where she came up with the "shorter men" line, I'll never know. Most likely she'd said it because Ian was anything but short.

No matter. I was changing the subject to jujitsu.

"Oh yes!" She flapped her hand. "Alice Spencer told me about jujitsu class when I was over at her farm picking up eggs last winter. Why, just everyone in town goes . . . Bubbles, Alice, Earlene Azalea, Asta . . . you know, all the club ladies. It keeps us limber."

Daphne smiled and looked up at Ian. He blinked as her big hat bumped him on the chin. Like he needed to know she was "limber." *Barf.* At least she'd let go of the prison-warden bunk.

"Anyhoo, y'all can learn about it yourself, Eva. I told the ladies you couldn't wait to join us in class on Monday! That's five o'clock, sharp, tomorrow. We're expectin' you in the village at Ringo's Gym. And don't forget y'all are leading the olive oil tasting party for the ladies club on Tuesday night. Everyone who is *anyone* in town will be there!"

I nodded. I'd come up with an excuse later to bug out of Monday's jujitsu class. Still, I couldn't get out of the ladies club gig—that was work. Given that most of the ladies club members were colossal gossips, and certainly many had been behind all the nasty rumors about me—especially club president Tammy Fae Tanner and her cohort, real estate agent Debi Dicer—I'd been dreading the Abundance Ladies Club meeting for weeks. Still, the tasting was all part of promoting the family business. So in two days, I'd put on my big-girl panties, face all the tattlers, and make the best of it.

"Of course I remember," I said, smiling. "I've got everything planned."

I lied.

"Now, back to warden Maddox Keeper. Since y'all claim not to be interested in men anyway, as long as he brings home the bacon, what do y'all care that he's a bit height challenged? Just wear your silly sneakers. Y'all wear them all the time anyway. Oh! Since he's the prison warden, maybe he's got some handcuffs y'all could use in the bedroom! Wouldn't that be fun?"

Peeking over the top of Daphne's big hat as she clung to his arm, Ian grimaced. Precious burst out laughing.

"Y'all would never notice his height," Daphne continued, completely unaware of Ian's expression. "Now that I think about it, this could be a match made in heaven!" Daphne dropped Ian's arm and clapped her hands together, bracelet jingling as she spun herself around, surveying the crowd. "He's here somewhere . . . Fiddle-dee-dee. It's so difficult to find a small man in a big crowd. Y'all just give me a moment . . ."

Y'all, y'all, y'all . . . every other word was "y'all." I wanted to slap Daphne. Shake her out of it. Anything!

"Too bad about Big Bubba," said someone, tapping Daphne on the arm.

It was Floppy Hat from the cook-off. The little biddy stood next to Blue Hair, who peered at us through thick red-rimmed glasses. Daphne turned and started to say something, except Blue Hair beat her to the punch.

"I just heard that Slick Simmer's been bumped off! That can't be true. Why, we just saw him at your place yesterday. He looked happier than a dog with two peters!"

Daphne opened her mouth to say something when Blue Hair turned and tapped my foot with her cane.

"Aren't you Robert Knox's youngest daughter . . . the runaway bride? The one who dumped Tammy Fae's boy and ran up north a few years back?" She tipped her chin down and peeked over her red eyeglasses, looking me up and down. "I thought it was you yesterday," she said. "I read all about you in my *Celebrity Sneek Peek* paper!"

"Why, if that don't beat the band. It is you!" cried Floppy Hat, looking me over and smiling. She chortled. She turned to her friend. "You were right!"

Before I could respond, arms flung around me from behind as someone gave me a big kiss on the cheek.

"Hi, y'all!" cried Pep. Releasing me, Pep bear-hugged Precious next.

Already, Blue Hair and Floppy Hat were prattling away with another biddy behind me.

"Ahh, I see y'all are sleeveless today, Pepper-Leigh," Daphne said, frowning.

"Another fashion faux pas." I shook my head. "Pep," I said, "seriously. I have to side with Daph this time. How can you wear those tall boots? It's well over ninety degrees. Aren't you hot?"

"Not really." Pep made a face, batting long eyelashes over her smoky eyes. She had a fresh coat of grape lip color and wore a torn black midriff tee with the sleeves ripped off that had ROADHOUSE printed across her chest. She gave Daphne a hug, then slapped Ian on the shoulder, sniggering like a piglet. "Hey, Ian! Ian! How ya doin,' sweetheart?"

Daphne looked horrified. Ian greeted Pep with a warm handhold. "How ye doin' yerself? Yer lookin' quite gallus today, Missus Sweet."

"Honeybun," said Pep, "I don't know what that means, but I'm takin' it as a compliment." She grinned.

"Aye, as it's intended."

"Pepper-Leigh, you look like Puss in Boots," said Daphne with a sniff.

"Daph, I'd rather look like Puss in Boots than act like Scarlett O'Hara," Pep shot back, chuckling in little piglet snorts.

Ian was looking most amused as he took us all in. He whispered something to Precious. She nodded. Someone brushed my arm.

Looking flushed and overworked, restaurant owner Lark Harden smiled. "Hello, folks! I'm so glad y'all made it today. We're a bit overwhelmed with diners this evening . . . We've never had such a crowd!"

Dressed in a chic black suit, Lark pushed a stray strand of hair away from her face with the back of her hand.

"Lark, dahhwr-lin'!" Daphne cried.

Daphne and Lark air-kissed.

"Really, if y'all are too busy, we can come another time," said Daphne. She leaned close to Lark and whispered, "It's been a wild weekend. You must be exhausted."

"No, no. Not at all. Robin said you'd be coming tonight.

I've got a lovely table for you in the back where it's quieter. It's the least we can do after all the money you folks raised for charity yesterday—more than twenty thousand dollars!"

Precious whistled.

"It's our pleasure," said Daphne.

"That reminds me, Missus Harden," said Ian, reaching into his breast pocket. "I promised I'd come up with a contribution for yer charity. As long as ye keep it anonymous, as we agreed."

Ian handed Lark a check.

"Oh my!" Lark was clearly dumbstruck. "This is as much money as we brought in during the entire weekend, from all the venues combined!"

"I'd hoped to match what ye managed to raise."

"You've done that and more! I don't know how to thank you."

"Just keep the donor's name anonymous and put it to good use; that's all," Ian said. "Make sure local folks get the help they need."

"Thank you. Thank you. I will."

Daphne looked all mushy as she batted her eyes at Ian.

"Well, there's a happy ending to the weekend after all," said Precious.

"Yes. And we feel dreadful about Big Bubba and . . . and . . . Master Chef Simmer," said Lark. "I just can't believe it. Two terrible, terrible accidents. I don't know how you folks can cope with all this. It's . . . overwhelming."

Lark and Daphne hugged.

"Let's do lunch next week, shall we?" asked Daphne. "We could both use a little girl time."

"Sounds wonderful," Lark said. "And you're right. Despite the tragedy, it feels good to help those in need. Slick and Bubba would both be pleased. The money y'all helped raise will change people's lives. Folks are still climbing out of the recession. Especially our farmers."

"Tell me about it," Pep said. "Daddy almost lost the plantation a few years back. If he hadn't taken a gamble on the olive oil market, I doubt we'd be here today."

"Well, I hope y'all can rest a bit and enjoy your evening out tonight," said Lark. "We're clearing a table now. There are four of you?"

"Five," Daphne answered, reaching for Ian.

Except Ian was no longer standing with us. In fact, he was nowhere in sight.

Slipped away.

Daphne frowned as she looked quickly around. Precious smiled and shrugged, as if she had no idea what'd happened to her boss. I doubted it. I was pretty sure that Precious always knew what Ian was up to. And she never said a word to any of us.

"Oopsie, my mistake. There are just four of us." Daphne smiled politely as her eyes darted around, scanning for Ian. "Excuse me," she said suddenly, "while I powder my nose."

"Table for four it is!" said Lark with a smile.

Daphne and Lark headed into the building. Pep raised her eyebrows.

"Slick," I said. "She's putting on a good front. Still, she must ache for him."

Pep nodded. "I know that. Still, boohooing about him isn't gonna bring him back."

"Oooh, that's cold," said Precious.

"Sweet tea?" A waitress offered a tray filled with tall glasses of sweet iced tea with mint sprigs.

"Sorry. I remain corrupted by the North," I said. "I'll wait until we're inside to order a plain, unsweetened tea."

"I'll have one. Extra sweet!" Pep laughed. "Thanks, hon."

"Me, too. Thanks." Precious reached for a cool, sweaty glass. Then she looked over my shoulder. "Uh-oh." She frowned. "Miss Eva, you might wanna go inside and get that Yankee tea now."

I started to turn—

"Oops," said Precious with a grimace. "Too late."

CHAPTER 9

Precious shot me a warning look and the corners of Pep's mouth curled up mischievously. Turning in the crowd in front of the restaurant, I stopped short.

Too late, indeed.

Tall, tan, and toned, with a blonde inverted-bob hairstyle—shoulder length in front, nape skimming in back—the flawlessly made-up woman I'd nearly bumped into wore a neon pink and green Lilly Pulitzer shift over Tory Burch thongs with oversized gold ornaments that showed off her perfectly painted and pedicured toes.

"Eva Knox. Aren't you a sight! I see for once y'all are not wearing that little tee shirt, advertising yourself as a virgin!" Debi Dicer cackled with a wicked smile. "I've always said y'all have a mah-velous sense of humor. Of course, everyone knows you're not a virgin." She laughed at her own joke.

She'd invoked the infamous "y'all" in the singular. Game on.

"Debi," I answered coolly. "I'm surprised to see you here. Alone tonight?"

Debi raised her long, tanned arm and flicked a lock of bleached hair. "Of course not. I just finished work. I'm meeting someone."

"I hear you do your best work at night."

"Of course," Debi prattled, completely unfazed, "I'd be here tonight even if I didn't have a date. You of all people, Eva, know how it is bein' the sheriff's fiancée—one must see and be seen!" Debi smiled a sickly-sweet smile. "Oh, wait!" A smudge of hot pink lipstick ruined an otherwise perfect set of pearly whites. "He wasn't sheriff when y'all ran off and dumped him, was he? Come to think of it, he was still just a boy then. Bucky's come such a long way without you."

"Bucky?" I laughed. "Did you say 'Bucky'?"

Pep snorted loudly before she mumbled, "Talk about how to emasculate a guy. Just call him 'Bucky.' Sheesh." She snorted again.

"Got that right." Precious tittered.

"And here you are, Miss Pep." Debi whirled around to give Pep the once-over. "Looking like . . . like you always do. My, aren't those tall boots swanky!"

"Aren't you sweet. Thanks, hon."

Quickly, Debi shifted her gaze to check out Precious. She smirked. The smirk might've actually been intended as a smile. Still, it came out as a smirk.

"Hello," she said, looking up at Precious. "Do I know you?" Debi was quite tall. Still, she had to look up to meet Amazonian Precious eye to eye.

"Hello," said Precious coolly. No smile. Hands on hips. "No. I don't believe you do."

And that was that.

"So, Miss Eva," said Debi, spinning around back to me, "I'm thinking that we should start calling you Venus."

"Venus?"

I knew that I'd regret asking.

"Why, yes. I hear men are still dropping like flies around you!" Debi let out a wicked cackle, clearly pleased with her cleverness. "It's a joke, sweetie." She touched my arm, still laughing. "Get it? Venus? As in flytrap?" She laughed again.

I smiled just as sweetly as I could manage. "Say, Debi, where's your big engagement ring?"

Just a few weeks earlier, Debi'd wasted no time bragging to me how she and Buck were engaged to be married, gloating that all she had to do was pick out her big, fancy diamond ring and they'd soon be hitched. Still, I didn't see a ring on her left hand.

"Don't y'all worry your pretty little panties over my diamond ring. It's in the works. And once I've got it on my finger, y'all will be able to see it from clear across the county!"

There she went again, y'all-ing away. Debi glanced over my shoulder and twisted her head around, as if she was looking for someone.

"Lose your man again, Debi?"

I was not so subtly referring to the time a few weeks earlier when Buck had ducked out on an important date with Debi. In fact, I'd gathered it was the night she thought he'd be proposing marriage to her. And when Debi'd discovered that Buck had been with me instead, she'd blown a gasket, accusing me of having an affair with "her" man. Of course, his being with me hadn't been personal—Buck had been working a case. Still, I'd never refuted Debi's accusation. It'd been fun to let her think the worst.

And that's just what she'd done.

Folding her arms over her chest, Debi looked me in the eye and smiled. It was totally bogus.

"I'll give you credit, hon. You're a real go-getter," she said, gritting her teeth.

"Thank you." I smiled back and crossed my arms. Two can play that game. I opened my mouth to say something more, when a heavy hand landed on my shoulder. Precious bent her head close to my ear.

"Sunshine, never kick a fresh turd on a hot day," she whispered. "Besides, our table's ready."

CHAPTER 10

Inside the restaurant, white latticework trim, potted palms, and hanging white birdcages with live orange and yellow canaries decorated the leafy green lobby and dining room. Chamber music tinkled from loudspeakers in the ceiling. Underneath whirling white ceiling fans, bare marble-topped dining tables and reclaimed ice-cream parlor chairs with itty-bitty cushions lent a bistro vibe to the garden-like dining space during the day. However, it was evening and the overhead lights were dimmed and the marble tables were draped with evergreen velvet tablecloths topped with pressed white linens and candles in hurricane lamps, lending a plusher feel to the place.

Precious, Pep, and I made our way through the crowded lobby and into the room of seated, chattering diners at their velvet-topped tables. We headed over to Daphne, who was seating herself at a table in the back corner.

A friendly young waitress with a name tag that read WENDEE came to the table. Dressed in black with a pistachio green three-pocket waist apron, she handed out menus and took our drink orders. Minutes later, she returned with our drinks, first serving Precious a "grande"-sized piña colada sporting a humongous skewer of tropical fruit. Daphne got a white wine spritzer garnished with a lime slice. Although she'd said she craved a beer, instead Pep ordered an iced sweet tea with lemon because she'd be working the late shift at the Roadhouse after dinner. And finally, Wendee handed me an unsweetened tea, no lemon, which came with a pretty mint sprig. In hindsight, the tea was probably a big mistake—the caffeine would make it impossible for me to sleep.

Next, Wendee took our dinner orders, then brought an assortment of artisanal breads, along with little bowls for each of us filled with herb-infused Knox Liquid Gold oil with minced fresh herbs for dipping.

"Y'all enjoy!" she said with a big smile.

We chatted for twenty minutes or more, munching on bread dipped in the flavored olive oil—it was delicious. For Daphne's sake, we all avoided discussing the elephant in the room—Slick Simmer's murder—which I found ironic, really, because after all, Precious and I had been the ones who'd discovered the dead chef. Also, we were careful not to bring up Daphne's missing elephant charm, because after we'd found Slick, we'd completely forgotten to look for the charm over by Slick's motor home. For all we knew, it was gone forever.

"Mmmm, this stuff is great," purred Pep, dipping a big chunk of bread into the herb-flavored olive oil. She popped it into her mouth and reached for another.

"Mmm-mmm." Precious nodded, gnawing on a chunk of oil-soaked bread.

"The herbs are from the Pickenpackers' herbary," I said absently. I watched as Lark seated Debi Dicer at a nearby table. Lark set down a second menu across the table from Debi.

Pep reached for another piece of bread.

"Pepper-Leigh, don't spoil your dinner," scolded Daphne. "Ah, here it is now!"

Wendee set each of our dinner plates down on the table. "Is there anything else I can do for y'all?" she asked.

"No, thank you. We're doin' just fine," answered Daphne.

Daphne was still wearing her straw hat and cat-eye sunglasses, despite the dim lighting. Normally, I would've teased her about it. However, I figured it wasn't the night. I'd set my Jackie Os on top of my head.

"Now, y'all enjoy your dinner," Daphne said to us with a smile. She was actually beginning to relax. "This has been lovely so far. We'll continue not talkin' about any sad or bad things for the rest of the evening."

We all nodded. The queen had spoken.

With my fork I stabbed bits of my Palatable Pecan Signature Apple, Peach, and Pecan Green Salad with Sirloin Strips, then took a big bite. "Mmmm."

"I love this place, but I just hate these chairs," complained Precious as she squirmed on the teeny round seat of her wrought-iron chair. "My butt always hangs off the edges." She skewered a chunk of Palatable Pecan Perfectly Grilled Salmon with Olive Oil and Herbs.

"Well, I think the ice-cream parlor chairs are positively dahhwr-lin'."

"I agree with Precious. They make my ass hurt," said Pep, gnawing off a huge bite of her Palatable Pecan Bleu Cheese Buffalo Burger. "But then, the dinky bentwood chairs at the Roadhouse aren't any better," she added with a mouthful. "Mmm! This is a damn good burger."

"I think y'all are way too critical." Daphne sighed. "It's just lovely here." She used her fork continental style as she picked at her Palatable Pecan Salade Niçoise. "Pepper-Leigh, I can't believe you ordered a hamburger. Why not the filet mignon? It's divine."

"And it's on the house, so it's free!" added Precious with a wink.

"Where is Robin, by the way? I haven't seen her tonight," I said.

"It's a buffalo burger, not a hamburger," said Pep to Daphne. "I like buffalo. Besides, I've only got forty-five minutes before I need to be back at work. I've got to hurry and eat." Pep stuffed a big bite into her mouth. "There's no pretension about a burger. I can cram it down and run," she said with a mouthful. A chunk of bleu cheese fell from her mouth.

"Gracious, Pepper-Leigh, where are your manners?" hissed Daphne. "That dreadful Roadhouse is ruinin' you." Then she looked at me.

"What?" I said. "Why are you staring at me?"

"I'm surprised. And, er, overwhelmed, Eva. By your appearance."

"What's wrong with my appearance? I dressed up tonight! I even put my hair up in a chignon! For you!"

My outfit may have been simple, yes. But hardly criticizable. Besides, Daphne often wore her hair in a chignon . . . I thought she'd be pleased that I'd made the effort.

But no.

"I've brought it up before. And I'm tryin' to hold my tongue," Daphne continued. "Eva, you haven't looked this savaged since that time you fell out of the tree when you were sneaking around with that snake in the grass Buck Tanner. Of course, your little silk top is lovely; it's just that it's black. Everything is black. I'm afraid you're followin' Pepper-Leigh's example, wearin' all that ghastly black! And it's just deadly with your fair skin. With those big circles under your eyes you need a bit of color. Some makeup wouldn't hurt. And I don't know why you insist on wearin' jeans all the time—you should wear a little skirt to show off your lovely legs. They're really your best asset—"

"Hey!" I said. "Hang on, here. Daph, how . . . how do you know about the tree? Who ever said I was sneaking around with Buck?"

"Why, dear, just about everyone—"

"Never mind," I mumbled, holding my hand up in protest. "It was a lifetime ago," I explained to Precious. "I don't want to hear it. It'll just make me mad. And I'm too upset about all this other stuff to be mad. I mean, we've got another murderer on the loose!"

Oops. I'd said it, something sad *and* bad, breaking Daphne's dinner rule.

"We are not havin' this conversation!" hissed Daphne. "Remember? I said, nothing sad or bad. It'll upset me terribly. Besides, there'll be plenty of time for it startin' tomorrow, I'm sure. I can't *wait* for another visit from our favorite detective, Eli Gibbit," she snapped.

No doubt she was being sarcastic.

Daphne'd been a thorn in Eli Gibbit's side since they'd been in grade school. And now that he was county detective, he was more interested in moving his career along than he was in actually solving crime. If there was a quick way to make some charges stick, right or wrong, he'd be sure to make it happen, just as long as the public thought he was doing a better job than his boss, Buck Tanner, who, according to some folks in town, had somehow "stolen" the sheriff's job for which Eli had been campaigning for years. Eli Gibbit would be all too happy to press unfounded murder charges against my sister.

"Precious, I remember when Eva fell out of the tree," said Pep, ignoring the fact that I'd just said I didn't want to hear it. She wiped her mouth with the back of her hand. "She was in high school." Pep snorted a laugh. "Said she fell out her window while trying to reach a cat hollerin' on the roof. That was lame, Eva. We didn't have a cat back then. Even Daddy didn't buy it."

"That's rich," said Precious, chuckling as she impaled another forkful of salmon.

"And I recall Daddy had words with Buck Tanner," said Daphne.

"He did? Buck never told me Daddy spoke to him . . ."

"Hmm, yes. I imagine there's a lot Buck hasn't said." Pep smiled at Daphne. She threw her head back and laughed.

"Shhh! Pepper-Leigh, lower your voice," whispered Daphne.

A woman at the next table tipped her head toward us, obviously listening. Her companion sat with a frozen grin. Debi smirked at me from her table. I looked down and took a deep breath. *Stay calm, Eva.* I was grateful for the violin music wailing from the speaker above us. Hopefully, Debi couldn't hear any of our conversation.

Pep let loose a series of little snorts and chortles. "Eva, I always figured y'all were more scratched up from messing around with Buck in the prickers than you were from the tree fall!"

"Prickers?" asked Precious.

"Eva and Buck made out everywhere," explained Pep. "Especially that first summer, when Eva came home from college in Massachusetts. They made use of every nook and cranny on the farm, didn't you, sis? They found places that even I never knew about. Come to think of it, I should've thanked y'all, Eva, for showing me around. I made good use of those spots for years!" She chomped a homemade pickle wedge.

"Pep, what are you talking about? And how would you know, anyway?"

"Maybe once in a while we followed you—you know, just to make sure y'all were alright." Pep winked as she reached for a couple of sugar packets in a glass container.

"You followed me? When . . . when I was with Buck?" My voice went up, and I felt my chest and jaw tighten. My face flushed hot.

"Who's kicking me?" Pep looked up and smiled brightly.

Daphne glared at Pep from across the table. Precious laughed. Pep tore open the packets and dumped more sugar into her already sweet tea.

"Shhh!" warned Daphne.

Pep shrugged and kept talking. "It was easy." Pep turned to me. "You and Buck were so wrapped up in yourselves that y'all never noticed me." She twirled her spoon in her tea, clinking the ice cubes against the sweaty glass.

"I can't believe you followed us!" I put my fork down. Suddenly, I wasn't hungry. "Why?"

"I was a regular Nancy Drew. Remember the time you two spent most of the night in the bat cave? Oh yeah, and the canoe? The corncrib? The blackberry patch? The tree house . . ." Pep took a swig of tea. Then she ripped off another bite of buffalo burger.

"Pep! I can't believe I'm hearing this. I've been totally betrayed, by my own sister!"

"Sisters. Make that plural, hon. I'm not taking the rap by myself," Pep mumbled with a mouthful. "Daph was the mastermind."

My face felt hot. My ears burned. My chest tightened. Twenty years later, it felt as if it had just happened. My sisters had spied on me when I'd snuck out of the house at night to be with Buck.

"Both of you? How awful!"

Precious chuckled.

"Ha!" Pep laughed. "If y'all only knew." She smirked at Daphne.

"What does that mean?" I demanded.

The women at the nearby table glanced our way and whispered. I needed to lower my voice. I reached on top of my head, pulled down the Jackie O sunglasses, and jabbed them over my face. As if that would fix everything. No doubt I looked ridiculous. Just like Daphne, in her Dior glasses and floppy hat.

I didn't care.

"Oh, Eva, don't pout," said Daphne. "Put it into perspective. Buck Tanner was older. He had a reputation for being an animal. Your virtue was of utmost importance."

"My virtue? My relationship with Buck was private. It wasn't your place to know or to weigh in about what we did. Ever. Either of you! Besides, Buck always treated me right."

"Yes, yes. That's what you always said . . ." Daphne chided, dismissing me with a flip of her hand. "Of course, then you ran away from him . . ."

"I said that Buck treated me right because it's true!"

". . . and you never said a word to anyone about why you took off so suddenly. Naturally, everyone always assumed the worst." Daphne looked smug.

"Well, everyone was wrong," I said, disgusted. "My reasons

for leaving were private. I didn't need to explain anything to anybody. I still don't. This makes me sick. You spied on us!"

"Pepper-Leigh did most of the groundwork," said Daphne coolly. "And I was right about those sunglasses, Eva. They suit you."

"Don't try to change the subject."

"Thanks for throwing me under the bus, sis," said Pep to Daphne. "You might want to tread lightly. And stop kicking me under the table!"

"Well, you did do most of the fieldwork," said Daphne with a shrug.

"At your behest!" cried Pep.

"And I thought y'all were prim-and-proper ladies," teased Precious. "I never reckoned the folks in the beauty shop might actually be onto something."

I turned and glared at Precious. "You went to Tammy Fae Tanner's salon?"

"What? I got to get a pedicure *somewhere*." Precious stabbed another bite of salmon. "Shear Southern Beauty is the only place in town. Tammy Fae told me all about you and Sheriff Sweet Cheeks, by the way. Said you were tryin' to steal her son back from the lovely Debi. And she couldn't let that happen on account of you already dumpin' him and bein' the town tart and all. Course, I know better. In fact, I think you and the sheriff are cute together. But I didn't let on."

"Oh puh-leese, Eva, tell me you're not fraternizin' with Buck Tanner!" Daphne dropped her fork and dramatically hit her forehead under her hat.

"Oh gosh!" cried Pep with a big grin, dropping a fry. "You've been doin' it again with Buck! That's why Debi Dicer is so fit to be tied!"

Pep looked over to Debi's table and wriggled her fingers in a wave.

Debi pursed her lips and glared.

"Shhhhh!" hissed wide-eyed Daphne. "Folks will hear you!" She slapped Pep's hand down onto the table. "Stop that, Pepper-Leigh!"

"Oh, c'mon! A night or two in the sack might do her some good, Daph," said Pep to Daphne, as if I weren't sitting right there. "Maybe she'd finally stop stressin' about the wedding mess up in Boston and all these dead people she keeps fallin' over. Time to move on . . ."

"Stop it. I'm not with, nor do I want, Buck Tanner," I said. "Besides, he's engaged. Remember? To the lovely Debi?"

I waved my fork in the direction of Debi's table.

Debi smirked. Clearly, we had her attention.

Pep continued. "I told you that a little spank would do you some good, Eva. And I should've guessed you and Buck wouldn't be able to resist each other. Especially after all these years. Still, I hardly expected you to get back at it this quick. Good goin'!" She raised her hand for a high five.

Someone at the next table tittered.

"Oh my God!" I said, ignoring Pep's raised hand. "I've not been—"

"Daphne, please, stop kicking me under the table," interrupted Pep.

Daphne looked daggers at Pep. Then she turned to me. "Eva Knox, if y'all have taken up with the likes of Buck Tanner again, then I will surely roll over and die. *Just die!*" Daphne's "die" sounded like "die-yuh."

"What's the matter, Daph? Jealous?" Pep teased.

Precious slammed the table with her big hand and let out a belly laugh. "You Knox girls slay me. This scene is better than a soap opera." She grabbed the table. "Oh, whoops! Nearly fell off my itty-bitty chair!"

"Stop it, both of you. All three of you!" I cried.

"Lower your voices. People are staring," warned Daphne in a hushed tone.

"They'd be staring anyway," said Pep matter-of-factly. "They always do." She popped another fry into her mouth. "Besides, the two of you look goofy, sitting at the table wearing sunglasses at night. Who wouldn't stare? And, Daphne, you're not fooling anyone with that silly hat. You still look miserable underneath all that makeup."

"If you don't want folks starin', perhaps then y'all shouldn't dress like Puss in Boots meets the walking dead," Daphne hissed through clenched teeth.

Pep rolled her eyes.

I picked up my fork, then put it down. I'd completely lost my appetite. There were too many thoughts swimming in my head. I needed to sort it all out. I was tripping over dead people again, and my own sisters had spied during my romantic trysts with Buck.

Pep leaned forward and winked at Precious. "After Eva ran off, Buck had every woman in town and then some."

"Pepper-Leigh . . ." warned Daphne.

"Seriously, Eva. I think it's great that you two are gettin' back together," Pep gushed. "And if y'all ask me, since he came back last year from wherever it was he disappeared to for all those years after you left, Buck's way hotter now than he was eighteen years ago." She winked. "Lost all his baby fat."

"And replaced it with some fine muscle, I see." Precious chortled.

Daphne grabbed her chest melodramatically. "Please, don't! The thought of that man!" The word "man" sounded like "my-ahnn."

"Oh, Daphne," said Pep, "you're just a sore loser. Everyone knows—"

"Stop!" I whipped off the Jackie Os, tossing them on the table, and pressed both my hands into my forehead as I took a deep breath.

"Go on, Daph. Tell her," Pep said to Daphne.

"Pepper-Leigh, do not go there," whispered Daphne dramatically.

"Oooh, this is gettin' good," said Precious. She plopped her napkin on the table, leaned back in her little chair, and smiled.

"I don't want to hear any more about me and Buck!" I cried.

The words came out louder than I'd expected. People at the tables near us stopped talking and stared. I didn't care.

"Let me be clear, one more time," I said, louder than I

should have. "I don't want to be with Buck. Not now, not ever. He can have Debi!"

A utensil clattered to the floor nearby. I could feel the heat rise in my neck and cheeks. I was pretty sure half the people in the restaurant had heard me. I didn't dare look over to Debi's table.

"You're blushing," said Pep quietly.

"I am not blushing."

"You are blushing. Big-time!" Pep gave a little piglet chortle. "It's cute. You and Buck are made for each other."

"Methinks Miss Eva doth protest too much about Sheriff Sexy Pants." Precious giggled.

"Yup," said Pep. "Hard to get Buck outta your blood."

"I don't want to hear that man's name anymore tonight," Daphne hissed. "Or ever again."

"I bet you don't," grumbled Pep. "Tell her. Or I will."

"Pepper-Leigh, *puh-leese*!"

"Tell me what?"

"Nothing," snapped Daphne.

We all sat motionless at the table, staring silently at one another. It reminded me of a game my sisters and I used to play as kids. We'd sit around the kitchen table and stare, daring one another to be the first to blink. This time, no one blinked. Or said anything.

Until Pep burped.

"Oh dear. Excuse me," she said with a giggle before taking another swig of sweet tea.

Daphne gasped. Even under her hat and from behind her glasses, Daphne looked like she would die. Precious burst out laughing. People around us chuckled. Then, finally, all the tables around us started humming as people began talking among themselves again. I leaned forward and looked hard at each of my sisters.

"For the record, I'm angry at both of you for spying on me. Really angry. And disappointed. What you did all those years ago was a horrible betrayal," I said quietly.

"We were not 'spying' on y'all," said Daphne. "We were simply looking after our baby sister. It was not a betrayal."

"Right," said Pep. "Spying was not a betrayal. However, sleeping with Buck was a betrayal."

"What?"

She raised her voice. "I said sleeping with Buck was a betrayal."

"Oh, Pepper-Leigh." Daphne sighed.

"What are you talking about?"

The room seemed eerily quiet again. Or maybe it was just in my head.

"I've been trying to tell you," said Pep. "After you left town, everyone in town slept with Buck."

"Yes. You've said that. Many times. What does that have to do with me?"

Pep looked at Daphne. Daphne looked away.

"What . . . ?" I was at a loss for words.

"Look," said Pep, "the guy was a total wreck after you left him at the altar. It was like something snapped. No one saw him for days. Weeks. Daphne went over to check on him. Tell her, Daph."

"Tell me what?"

"I slept with him," whispered Daphne.

CHAPTER 11

"I slept with that lousy womanizing scoundrel Buck Tanner," whispered Daphne, still looking down at her plate in the dining room of the Palatable Pecan restaurant. Then she looked up and turned to Pep. "But, then, I wasn't the only one. Was I, Pepper-Leigh?"

"What . . . what are you saying?"

Already, I knew.

"I've wanted to tell you for years," said Pep. "Of course, I ran into Buck long after Daphne's affair with him . . ."

"I did not have an affair with him. He . . . he . . . he took advantage of me." Daphne sniffed.

"Yeah. Right," scoffed Pep. "Anyway, by the time I came along, there'd been plenty of others. And you were long gone, Eva, sweetie. No one imagined you'd ever be back. So, I figured as long as the cat was out of the bag, so to speak, no harm, no foul. Really, it was all harmless fun. It meant nothing—to me or Buck. In fact, he left town the very next day."

I heard Daphne click her tongue in disgust.

"And that's supposed to make me feel better?" I managed to say. I couldn't see. The world was a whirling blur.

"Eva," said Daphne again. "It was a long time ago. I thought he needed comforting . . ."

"More like you wanted a little nookie. Not to mention, to pick his brain about why Eva really left," interrupted Pep.

"That was part of it . . ." admitted Daphne. "The picking his brain part." Daphne scowled at Pep. "Not the nookie." Then she faced me. "After all, Eva, dear, you never said a word to any of us about why you ran away. I wanted to understand. I waited weeks after you'd left to go see him. And, well . . . the man's an animal. He gave me some wine—y'all know I can't drink—and he took advantage of me. It was only one time. And it was a mistake. A terrible, terrible mistake." She wiped a tear from her cheek with her napkin.

"Oh, give me a break." Pep snorted, rolling her eyes. "Don't be such a drama queen, Daph. Buck gave you some wine because you brought it to him. And you brought it to him because you wanted to loosen him up to pick his brain about why Eva left. You and I both know that you have the remarkable ability to drink just about any man in Abundance County under the table. Except Buck Tanner. Turns out, after two bottles of wine, you couldn't resist him yourself. You were all over the guy. I saw you the morning after you'd been with him. Remember? You were dancing on air. Bragging to me about how you'd slept with Southern Georgia's hottest bachelor. You couldn't have been happier."

"That's not true!" cried Daphne.

Pep laughed. "Buck never took advantage of you or anyone else. After Eva left, every babe in this town was falling all over herself to get it on with him. You were the first, Daph. And he never came back to you for more. It made you crazy."

"Don't be silly, Pepper-Leigh."

"You couldn't take the fact that in your lifetime, just one man, Buck Tanner, turned you down. You still can't take it!"

"How dare you, Pepper-Leigh!" scolded Daphne.

I was shaking. Without a word, without looking at Precious or my two damned sisters, I dropped my napkin and stood from the table. "So much for Sister Code," I heard myself say.

Both my sisters had been intimate with Buck Tanner. The love of my young life. And I'd never known. I had visions of each of them, Daphne, then Pep, with Buck. In a flash, I saw them together in all the places Buck and I had made out around the farm . . . my happiest days, ever. I barely heard Daphne and Pep speaking to me from the table as I fumbled my way around the backs of their chairs, focusing on the front of the restaurant.

"Let her go," I heard Precious say.

As I glided like a dazed zombie under whirling fans, around suspended birdcages, and between dining room tables and chairs full of chatty diners, the world I knew faded away. I stumbled toward the lobby, trying to wrap my head around what they'd said, but it still wouldn't stick . . .

"Eva?"

The restaurant was a blur as I staggered forward. My two sisters were jumbled and crowded in my memories of a time when I'd been head over heels in love. I bumped into an empty chair. I'd almost reached the lobby. The front door was in sight . . .

Then I saw him.

Just inside the front door, those damned cute dimples smiled at me from clear across the room. Dressed in a white-collared shirt—tailored to fit his tanned, muscled body—with perfectly fitted, pressed black jeans, big-shouldered, handsomely buff Sheriff Buck Tanner was making small talk in the doorway with Blue Hair and Floppy Hat. The biddies looked tickled pink to be chatting it up with their favorite officer. Laughing easily, Buck ran his brawny hand through his close-cropped brown hair before shaking hands with the biddies. Threading his way through the lobby crowd, his infectious smile lit up the room as people around him smiled, patted him on the back, and waved him greetings. No doubt Buck was headed for Debi's table.

It was the first time I'd seen Buck since the whole dead-man-in-the-olive-grove scandal a couple of weeks earlier. I'd thought we'd kind of gotten closer then, leaving our past behind us. He'd insisted on putting his cell phone number in my phone, claiming that even his squeeze, Debi, didn't have the number.

Right.

Then I never heard from him again.

Of course.

It'd just been bad-boy Buck working another case. And it'd been loneliness, guilt, and nostalgia working on my part. I should've known.

And now this.

As I crossed behind the last table in the dining room, Buck caught my eye and grinned at me. As I thought of him with Daphne, and then with Pep—my two sisters, of all the people in the world—my heart wrenched. And then Debi. My biggest foe. I felt sick with humiliation and grief. At that moment, arrogant, self-serving, womanizing, grinning Buck Tanner infuriated me.

Striding up to Buck, I looked right into his velvety chocolate eyes. And before he had time to say a word, before I could stop myself—in front of everyone in the restaurant—I raised my hand and slapped the sheriff of Abundance County right across the jaw. Then I turned, punched the door open, and marched outside into the steamy night, headed down the sidewalk to who knows where.

CHAPTER 12

Okay, so sometimes I let my emotions get the best of me. *Eye roll.* As I flounced down the boulevard, headed out of the village toward home, it occurred to me that I'd just assaulted an officer of the law. I'd probably be going to jail. I mean, it's not like I could deny it—everyone in the Palatable Pecan restaurant had watched me smack the sheriff.

What had I been thinking?

Clearly, I hadn't been thinking. And it's not like I'm a violent person. If I'd actually thought about it, I never would've physically hit or hurt Buck . . . or anyone, for that matter. It'd just been terrible timing. I'd been in such a state of . . . shock.

Maybe it was what they call "temporary insanity."

Of course, making matters worse, I'd self-righteously stormed out of the place, like a movie heroine riding off into the sunset. Except the reality was that sunset had taken place about thirty minutes before I'd stomped out of the restaurant. It was getting dark fast. I had no ride—into the sunset or anywhere else. The walk home could easily take me several hours.

Down a dark, twisty backcountry road.

Good one, Eva.

Still, I was too upset—and too proud—to turn back. And really, I was too foolish. So, foolishly determined to walk home, I picked up my pace and stomped past precious Victorian shop after precious Victorian shop, slowly making my way out of town. When I reached the edge of the village, I started jogging, my mind still awhirl.

My sisters had broken Sister Code. Thinking of Daphne with Buck was almost like thinking of my mother with my boyfriend. I mean, Daphne raised me after our mother abandoned us. *Gross.* How dare she tell me—tell anyone—how to behave! What a hypocrite. Same thing for Pep. She'd broken code and then hidden the secret for years.

I had nothing against Precious, of course, even though she'd admitted going to Tammy Fae Tanner's place for a pedicure and everyone in town knew that Tammy Fae wanted to take me down for abandoning Buck all those years ago. Since my return home, Precious had quickly become my best friend. And that wasn't about to change. I just didn't want to talk to Precious that night. Or anyone, really.

A hot tear rolled down my cheek as my sandals slapped the sidewalk. My sisters had spied. And slept with my boyfriend—my fiancé! Well, my former fiancé. That was the same thing, wasn't it? And they'd kept it all a secret for years. That was the worst part. All three of them knew. Daphne. Pep. Buck. And not one of them had told me. Over time, the rest of it was probably forgivable. But the secret? All these years? Unforgivable.

I kept running.

Then I heard it before I saw it. The growly motor of Precious's red Corvette. Quickly, I jumped over a little white picket fence and ducked behind a bush in the yard of a purple Victorian.

Fourth-grade Eva.

There were several gazing balls and whirligigs in the yard, and a sign out front read PALM READING. Before I knew it, the little red Corvette whizzed by on the other side of the road. I waited for the car to get a ways down the boulevard before I headed out to the sidewalk again.

Thirty minutes later, it was pitch-dark and I was thinking how stupid it was to have hidden from Precious, who would've picked me up in a heartbeat and happily driven me home to Dolly. Outside the village, the sidewalk had stopped and the boulevard had merged into a two-lane rural highway. Already, I'd crossed to the other side of the road, where there was a narrow dirt walkway. The path was ending. It was just me, the winding backcountry highway, and very little shoulder next to the pavement.

And I didn't even have my phone.

Still, as far as I could tell, none of the sheriff's deputies had driven by looking to arrest me for hitting Buck. Maybe they'd show up at the plantation in the morning. They were probably all at the Palatable Pecan. Or at the Roadhouse, enjoying a few beers with Pep behind the bar. I jogged on. The road dipped down into a valley, where it was cooler. An eerie mist rose around my legs. Quickly, I jumped onto the shoulder as a car whizzed past, leaving a wide berth around me. Then another car followed, again pulling out into the middle of the road, leaving me plenty of room. As they left me behind, purring engines and red taillights faded slowly into the distance before me.

This is stupid, Eva.

I was starting to come to my senses.

Too late.

Off in the woods, an owl hoot-hooted. I tried to think of things to distract myself. Of course, the first thing to come to mind was Slick Simmer. I remembered his cold, lifeless body in the truck with the little ice-cream scoop at his side. Could the woman in the yellow van, the groupie, have been with him? What was her name? Savannah. That was it. Savannah Deats. Maybe she'd caught Slick with Daphne and killed him out of jealousy, I thought. Sounded plausible. She could've lured him to the truck for ice cream after Daphne left, then *whammo*!

Then, right on cue, Big Bubba came to mind. I could still

smell his sweaty stench on my skin—I remembered dragging myself out from under him, while Precious tried CPR
and his daughters shrieked hysterically. Why did this kind
of thing keep happening to me? It'd started with the dead
man from the olive grove from a few weeks earlier. How
rubbery his foot had been when I tripped over it . . .

I was running. Faster and faster again. I ran for I don't
know how long, my Cole Haan thongs spanking the pavement. As I ran, I tried to erase my thoughts. Finally I had
to stop. Had to breathe. Huffing and puffing, I stepped off
the road. A car whizzed past, high beams illuminating the
mist and dark pavement.

Taillights faded into blackness.

There were no houses, barns, or buildings of any kind
that I could see. Not even any lights. Just the noises of bugs
and tree frogs screeching in the darkness. I started running
again. This time, I tried to think of nothing. Just one foot
first, then the other. One, then the other. A few minutes later,
there was no shoulder alongside the road. Just a big ditch.
It was five or six feet deep. If I remembered the road cor-
rectly, it'd be that way for at least a couple of miles. Quickly
I picked up my pace, sprinting ahead.

The backcountry road was as dark as sin. I was still a
mile or two away from where the shoulder beside the road
would begin again. And still, there'd be no houses. Next to
me, the six-foot-deep ravine looked as if it stretched down
to the center of the earth—a foul and final resting place for
lost items, discarded trash, and roadkill. In the distance
behind me I heard an engine approaching. Straightaway,
headlights illuminated the black-tarred roadway. The vehicle sounded like it was moving slowly. With nowhere to go,
I eased to a walk, hugging the edge of the road, turning my
head to keep an eye on the approaching auto.

The driver of the vehicle snapped on the high-beam headlamps. *Good,* I thought. *This person sees me.* I inched over
to the narrow strip of dirt and debris along the pavement
perimeter, mindful that the edge of ground fell sharply into
the trench beside the road. Behind me, the auto accelerated

quickly, heading straight in my direction. I turned and stood for a moment, staring, as if somehow looking at the headlights would make the driver more aware of my presence. The vehicle kept coming. I waved. There was no change in the oncoming auto's speed or direction. I turned and started running, hoping to get past the ravine and reach a flat piece of ground beside the road . . . anyplace where I could step off the pavement and not end up in the ditch. Nothing. Nothing. Nothing. More ditch. *No!* I heard the vehicle's engine rev up as it continued accelerating.

It was headed right for me. No question . . . I was running for my life. The engine roared as the driver steered along the very edge of the road, barreling toward me, headlights blinding me when I turned to see. Closing in. Fast. I sprinted as quickly as I could. There was nowhere for me to go! The car kept coming . . . coming . . . coming . . .

I threw myself into the ditch five or six feet below the road. And none too soon. Another second more, and the auto would've mowed me down.

The dark vehicle flew past.

I scrambled up the bank to see it swerve away from the roadside, back into the center of the lane, before careening around a curve, out of sight. Had it been an SUV? It'd been too dark and the lights had been too blinding to tell for sure.

I bent down for a moment and tried to catch my breath. Instead, tears came.

Then, a minute later, there was another set of headlights headed in my direction. *Oh my gosh,* I thought, *not again!* I was completely paranoid. This time, I didn't wait.

I jumped right back into the ditch.

Chapter 13

I huddled in the ravine as the vehicle slowed. Then I heard it pull to the side of the road, its blinking red emergency flashers lighting the sky above me. I heard the door slam. Then footsteps. I pressed myself into the damp ground and lay still, holding my breath, hoping whoever it was on the road wouldn't see me hiding in the ditch. I was going to die. I just knew it.

Then came the voice.

"Eva? Are ye okay? What are ye doin' out here?"

Ian Collier. My knight in shining armor.

"Eva?"

"Yes. Yes, I'm fine," I said as I gathered myself up. I was covered in dirt and roadside sludge. At least I hadn't landed in any broken glass. Or roadkill. Standing tall above me, Ian shielded his eyes as he tried to get a better look at me in the ravine below him.

"What are ye doin' in the ditch, girl? Let me give ye a hand."

"Umm. I . . . I . . . think someone just tried to run me down."

I'd started to scramble up the side of the ravine when Ian reached down and pulled me up to the road. His hands felt strong and reassuring. And, as always, he smelled divine.

"Run ye down? Are ye serious?" He gripped my shoulders, turning me to face him.

Nodding, I wiped a tear and brushed myself off. It was a useless effort, of course. I was sure that I looked like crap. I sure as hell felt like it. Grazing my face with his fingers, Ian gave me a look of concern and disbelief. I resisted the urge to burst out crying and to throw myself into his arms.

"Yer head's not minced?"

I shook my head no.

"And yer okay? Let me look at ye."

I nodded again as Ian gave me a once-over, then shook his head, pulling me toward him into a hug. I could've stayed safe in his warm, muscled arms forever. He felt so safe. Smelled *so* good.

I took a deep, shaky breath.

"Alright, now. Let's get ye off the road." He pulled away and led me to his navy blue Hummer. He opened the passenger door. "Coorie up; get inside."

I climbed in.

"Fasten the seat belt," he ordered, closing the door behind me.

Quickly Ian strode around the front of the Hummer, past the light beams highlighting his tall, athletic frame. He opened the driver's-side door, slid behind the wheel, and then quietly closed the door. Clicking my seat belt around me, I leaned back in the black leather seat and heaved a sigh. Ian shut off the blinking emergency lights and pulled easily out into the road. Soon after, we cruised around a dark curve. I shuddered. Looking out into the blackness, I thought about walking the road alone. What had I been thinking?

"Eva, did yer car break down somewhere? Did I pass it?"

I shook my head.

"No?"

I shook my head again.

"Yer just out there walking? Alone? In a night that's black as coal?" He said it kiddingly, I was sure.

I nodded. Ian grimaced. "Aye, right!" His face looked like he didn't believe me.

I shrugged.

"Are ye bladdered?"

"Blattered?"

"Ye know—blootered?"

I shrugged my shoulders, not understanding.

"Mad wi' it? Wrecked? Hammered? Smashed . . ."

Oh. I got it.

"Do you mean, am I drunk?"

Ian raised an eyebrow and waited.

"No. I'm stone-cold sober. Although at this point in the evening, a good stiff drink or two couldn't hurt." I tried to laugh.

"Have ye gone totally doo-lally, Eva? What the hell are ye doin' out on the road at night? Ye could've been killed. And if you'd ended up in the ditch, no one would've found ye!"

"Something happened at the Palatable Pecan. I . . . I just got upset and decided to walk home. It's no big deal." Even I knew that I was talking out of both sides of my mouth.

"Walk home? From the village? Home? Ye walked all that way . . . alone? Surely yer playin' with me. It'd take ye all night to walk to Knox Plantation. If ye didn't get killed first. What the hell are ye thinking? What happened to ye?"

"Someone—two people, actually; no, make that three people—betrayed me. Unforgivably. And I just found out about it tonight during dinner."

"Betrayed ye? Yer bum's out the window! What could drive ye out into the night, to walk along a dangerous road alone? Are ye nuts?"

"Probably." I thought for a minute. "Besides, when I first started walking I kinda half thought that I'd get arrested before I got too far out of town."

"Arrested? What for?"

"I hit Buck Tanner."

"What?"

"Slapped him, actually. Right across the jaw. Hard as I could. In front of everyone."

"Eva, I realize yer a bit of a hammerhead, but have ye lost yer friggin' mind?"

"Probably. Anyway, he deserved it." I folded my arms.

Hammerhead? Huh! Good to know that's what Ian thought of me.

Ian shook his head and gave me a look that I couldn't quite read before he turned his attention back to the road. We rode silently for a bit, passing darkened fields, farms, and forests. My mind raced back and forth over everything that had happened during the last day or so. I couldn't seem to make sense of anything. I felt completely worn-out and it was all a giant jumble—Big Bubba, Slick Simmer, my sisters, and . . . Buck.

Damn him.

Then, all of a sudden, I felt tired. Really, really, really tired . . . I remember looking outside as we passed a white farmhouse and then laying my head on the Hummer window. The air-conditioned glass felt cool against my skin.

Next thing I knew, Ian's warm hand was brushing against my cheek.

"Eva, yer home now."

I sat up and rubbed my eyes. We were parked in the gravel drive next to the big house, between the bicycles and the Kubota.

"Oh. Ah . . . thanks. Did I drift off? Sorry."

Still half asleep, I grabbed the handle, yanked the door open, and tumbled down from the Hummer into the gravel. It was farther down than I'd expected and I stumbled. Ian started to open his door to get out and I raised my hand in protest.

"No. No. Stay there. I'm fine. Thanks for the ride." I slammed my door shut and turned to head across the lawn to my cottage.

"Ye got no more to say?" Ian asked as the Hummer window rolled down.

"Nothing you'd want to hear," I shouted as I waved. I never turned to look at him again. Already, I was halfway past Daphne's flower garden. "Thanks again. I really appreciate the ride."

"Get some rest, Eva," I heard Ian call out. "Please."

I ambled across the lawn to my cottage. A minute or two later, I heard Dolly woofing excitedly—she'd heard me coming. I couldn't wait to give her a hug. Before I opened the non-screen door, Dolly blasted outside, all licks, wags, and whimpers in the yard. Then she followed me inside the cottage. As I started to close the door behind me, I saw that Ian had watched and waited until I'd reached home before pulling away from the big house across the lawn.

"I should've treated him better," I said to Dolly, lightly touching the spot on my cheek where his fingers had brushed me awake. "But I just couldn't." I bent down to give Dolly a big hug. "It wasn't him. It was me. I'll apologize next time I see him. Promise." I stood up and went over to the nightstand, opened the drawer, pulled out a doggie biscuit, and tossed it to Dolly.

"You're a loyal little pup, Dolly girl."

CHAPTER 14

Of course, after falling asleep and then waking up in the Hummer, it was a sure bet that I'd never get to sleep again. And the caffeine in the iced tea that I'd had during dinner didn't help one bit. Still, I tried my best to get into a bedtime routine.

I poured myself a glass of water from the sink in the kitchenette. I let Dolly out, sipping my water while I watched from the stoop as Dolly sniffed around the yard. Then I brought her back inside. I drew a bath and took a long soak in the slipper tub with some lavender-scented olive oil Daphne'd given me. After the soak, I brushed my teeth, changed into my oversized BOSTON POPS tee shirt, and turned up the speed on the overhead fan—it was sticky hot that night, but of course, the fan did no good. It never did. I kissed Dolly good night as she lay on her fluffy cushion beside my four-poster bed. I turned down the matelassé bedspread, climbed up onto the mattress, and settled in, flipping lazily through a book about olive oil before finally turning out the light on my nightstand and punching my pillow just the way I liked it.

Then I tossed and turned for three hours.

I actually longed for the comforting city noises of night-time Boston: the constant amalgam of motorized vibrations and humming traffic noise from city streets and the Southeast Expressway, which wrapped around the city. I missed the rumbling and soft hissing and squeaking of brakes from the MBTA trains, the jet engines flying overhead from Logan Airport, and the vehicle honks and muffled chatter of human voices on the streets below.

Sleeping in my country cottage that night was not going to happen. Ask any of the tree frogs yammering outside my window. Or the incessant trilling crickets jingling in the yard. Along with the deep-throated moos of the bullfrogs as they slopped around the pond at the bottom of the knoll. Every single time I started to drift off to sleep, all the crap about Big Bubba, Slick Simmer, and my turncoat sisters came floating to the surface of my mind. Of course, that was the real problem, wasn't it? The whole Buck-and-my-sisters snafu. Thinking about it pulled my mind and emotions into complicated places. And then there'd been the car chasing me on the road. Surely it'd just been a careless driver . . .

"Argh!"

Then I thought about Ian, with his ruggedly handsome face and tousled dark hair. The way his custom-made clothes hung perfectly against his ripped physique. His taut muscles and long-legged stride. The way his deep green eyes twinkled when he watched me. And his long fingers against my skin as he softly caressed my cheek . . .

Savage Celtic music pulsated wildly in my head.

"Omigosh!"

I threw off the sheet and clambered out of bed.

"Come on, Dolly. I'll never sleep tonight. We're going for a ride."

I had to do something to distract myself. Call me crazy—I decided to look for Daphne's stupid elephant charm over at Slick's motor home. I wasn't doing it for Daphne, mind you. I was doing it for myself. A puzzle to distract my distraught

emotions and occupy my overactive mind would be better
than tossing and turning all night. And maybe if I could find
Daphne's charm, it'd help me figure out who'd actually murdered Slick Simmer. After all, I'd figured out the last murder
on the plantation . . .

I yanked off my BOSTON POPS tee and put on a strappy
black yoga top. More black. Daphne wouldn't approve. Ha!
I laughed. I slid on a pair of cutoff jeans, then slipped into
a pair of cheap sneakers that'd replaced my favorite running
shoes after they'd melted a few weeks earlier.

Long story.

"Okay, come on, Dolly. Kubota ride!"

Dolly jumped up on my leg and yipped before she spun
around and galloped through the torn screen door.

"Great." I sighed.

With Dolly, you only had to say "Kubota" once. She was
sure never to miss a ride.

Outside, with the moon hiding behind the clouds, everything was inky black. A little breeze swished leaves on the
dogwood tree. I followed Dolly as she skittered across several acres of lawn, headed toward the Kubota parked at the
big house. A single light was on in one of the guest bedrooms upstairs.

A minute or two later, passing some empty boxes near
the bushes at the porch, probably left from the charity
cleanup, I walked behind a couple of cars in the drive. *Rentals.* I remembered Glen Pattershaw had arrived in one, Miriam Tidwell and Ambrosia Curry in the other. Still, I was
so focused on the cars and the upstairs light that I didn't pay
attention to the bicycles on the other side of the Kubota as
I slid behind the wheel.

"Come on, Dolly, hop in!"

Dolly jumped up and parked her butt on the bench seat
next to me. I turned the key and the Kubota engine growled,
making a terrible noise as the vehicle shook and rattled.
Hoping I hadn't awakened everyone in the big house, I
quickly worked the gearshift into reverse and backed away.

I toggled on the headlamps and shifted again. The engine smoothed out as Dolly and I rolled forward over the grass.

Moonlight played hide-and-seek with the clouds, alternately lighting and darkening the plantation grounds as we motored across the lawn. Soon we rolled into darkness, under giant live oaks and hardwood trees, as the headlamps illuminated the way. Then the landscape opened up again and we sailed over grassy knolls before driving past one flat crop field after another. Several minutes later, Dolly and I rounded the bend at the last field, hitting the gravel drive. Ahead in the darkness, I made out the massive rectangular shape of the warehouse, about a quarter of a mile away.

"That's odd," I said to Dolly. "The dusk-to-dawn light is off at the warehouse."

Dolly stood up, front paws on my arm, and licked my face.

Mounted to one end of the building, a big vapor light usually came on at night and ran until dawn, illuminating the entire parking area as well as the warehouse entrance. Without the light, like everything else that night, the area was dark. Except when the moon peeked from behind the clouds.

"Aw, shoot, Dolly."

I hadn't brought a flashlight . . . I'd assumed the dusk-to-dawn light would be working.

Dolly whimpered and wiggled excitedly on the seat as I slowed, nearing the warehouse.

Wrapped in yellow police tape, the Clatterbucks' truck was still parked alongside the warehouse. Over on one side of the parking area, Savannah Deats's yellow van was parked behind Slick's fancy motor coach, which sat undisturbed next to the woods.

I didn't want to wake Savannah, so I rolled to a stop on the far side of the parking area, near the warehouse entrance. Before I could shut off the engine, Dolly flew from the Kubota and raced ahead of me across the parking area, headed toward the woods behind Slick's motor home. I shut off the headlamps and turned the key. The Kubota shuddered and fell silent.

I stepped from the Kubota as the eerie, high-pitched whinny of a screech owl warned of my arrival. Picking my way through the darkness, I crunched in the gravel, slowly making my way past the Clatterbucks' freezer truck. I stopped for a moment. It'd been only hours since I'd discovered Slick Simmer dead inside. I shuddered as the screech owl wailed again.

Continuing across the gravel, I headed toward the motor home. Then, moments later, I jumped as a night heron's noisy barking squawks screamed out from the woods behind Slick's motor home. Visitors to the plantation unfamiliar with night herons were always "sure" the hoarse, spine-chilling screams came from a bobcat, fox, or coyote. Of course, night heron or not, I knew there really were bobcats, foxes, and coyotes in the woods . . .

Shuffling through the darkness, I made my way around the front of Slick's fancy motor home, passing the front tire and driver's-side door. Moonlight popped from behind a cloud and quickly I surveyed the hidden side of the motor home next to the woods, scanning the ground for Daphne's charm. I saw a couple of candy wrappers and an empty cardboard box beneath a limp strip of yellow police tape hanging from one side of the motor home door. The moon disappeared again. Behind me, a light breeze ruffled leaves in the forest trees. The night heron screamed again. I jumped, clutching my chest.

Dang!

"Dolly, are you still here?" I called out quietly.

I heard shuffling in the detritus under the trees, about twenty or thirty feet away, not far from Daphne's new bench on the edge of the woods. As I was about to turn my attention toward the trees to look for Dolly, there was another puff of wind and the police tape at the motor home door fluttered. The moon peeked from behind the clouds and something caught my eye.

The door to Slick Simmer's luxury coach was open a crack.

"What the . . . ?"

I moved closer to the motor home. Grabbing the handle on the side of the big coach, I stepped up to the open door. The last thing I remember was a terrible clattering noise and Dolly's shrill barking from somewhere behind me as the coach door burst open.

CHAPTER 15

I heard Dolly growling. Then voices. When I opened my eyes, I saw blue lights flashing from the other side of the motor home. A white light blinded me.

"Over here! Quick! She's getting away!" shouted a woman.

"Hands up and over your head! Now!" growled a man.

"What's going on?" The back of my head ached. My brains felt jangled. Dolly was barking like mad.

"Someone shut that mutt up!" ordered the man.

"Dolly, quiet!" I scolded, finding my voice. It sounded far away. My head ached terribly.

Dolly kept right on barking. In fact, Dolly was so excited that she'd found what I'd come to call her "hound voice," letting out a nonstop series of ear-piercing *yeee-ooooowww, yeee-oooowww* howls. It was awful.

"Quick, quick! Arrest her. Before she gets away!" cried the woman.

I could see now. It was the yellow van owner, Savannah Deats, hopping up and down behind Slick's motor home, her long braid flipping in the air as she bounced excitedly, pointing a flashlight at my face.

I was lying flat on my back on the gravel drive, next to the motor home near the woods.

"It's you!" Savannah shrieked. "I shoulda known! Murderer! Officer, Officer, I recognize her! It's one of the Knox sisters! The one in all the newspapers! Hurry, arrest her!" She moved closer to me, blinding me with her light, hissing between gritted teeth, "All those stories I read about you are true!"

"Oh my gosh . . ." I struggled to stand up. Dolly kept screaming and barking from somewhere behind me. What was happening? "What are you talking about?" I started brushing myself off. "Dolly, stop!"

Already, I felt a big, hot lump on the back of my head.

"Ma'am, put your hands over your head."

A no-neck deputy wearing a uniform with a wide-brimmed hat, shoulder patches, a badge, and a service belt strode toward me, clanging and jangling as he made his way around the back of the motor home. He flipped on his flashlight, and it was even brighter than Savannah's. He pointed his light right into my eyes, blinding me as I finally stood up.

"Arrest her!" Savannah demanded. Then to me she shouted, "I heard you out here, sneaking around tonight. You've been in Slick's motor home. You murdered him!"

"Me? Arrest me?"

"Raise your hands where I can see 'em. Now!" The deputy's voice was sharp. Still with his flashlight in one hand, the officer fiddled with his other hand at his service belt.

"Me?"

Okay. Wait. I get it.

I'd hit the man's boss, Abundance County sheriff Buck Tanner, just hours earlier. The deputy must've come to arrest me. Static squawked over a radio in his vehicle on the other side of the motor home—tiny backwater Abundance County couldn't afford uniform radios or cameras for their deputies.

"Turn around; face the other direction! Put your hands above your head where I can see 'em!"

The big deputy stepped over and grabbed one of my wrists with a massive, hot, sweaty hand. Pulling my arm, he spun me around, yanking my arm up behind my back.

"Hey!" I cried. He was rough.

Suddenly, Dolly threw herself at the deputy's leg. She didn't bite him; she just growled and jumped up on his leg and barked. And squealed. And barked. And squealed.

"Git off me, ya damn mutt!" The deputy shook his leg. Letting go of my wrist, he seemed to be fumbling around for his gun. "Y'all better shut that varmint up, or I will!"

"No!" I cried out, spinning around to face him, "Dolly, stop!" The spin made me dizzy.

"Arrest her!" shouted Savannah, jumping up and down excitely. Her big flashlight jiggled and the light bounced with her.

"Please!" I cried.

"Don't move!" the deputy yelled. "And git your damn mutt off me before I shoot it!" This time he was genuinely reaching into his holster. Grabbing and holding my wrist tightly with one hand, he whipped out his handgun with his other hand and pointed it toward my little dog.

"No! Stop! Dolly, get down . . . please!" How was I supposed to be still and manage Dolly at the same time?

I scrambled to get ahold of Dolly, while the deputy kept his sweaty hand clamped onto my wrist. As I reached for Dolly, somehow I slipped free from the deputy's grasp, landing on my knees in the gravel as he kicked at Dolly. She yelped and jumped away, tearing around the back corner of the motor home, whimpering.

Somehow in all the chaos, I thought I heard a vehicle rolling over the gravel on the other side of the motor home. Were there more lights?

The deputy's hot, fat hand yanked me up again by my wrist. I tried to read the nameplate pinned to the right side of his chest, but he jerked me close and got in my face so bad that I turned away, trying to avoid being nose to nose.

He seemed like the archetypal dirty-dealing Southern

backcountry law officer that we've all read about in books and seen in movies. And he was every bit as sinister.

"Don't listen to her!" insisted Savannah. "Arrest her! She killed Slick!"

"I did not!"

"Shut up," the deputy snapped. He spit a gob of tobacco on the ground and then pulled me right up to his face. He wheezed when he breathed. The big man had sunburned skin, jowly cheeks, and a shaved head under his flat hat, and his dark eyes glinted in the glare of Savannah's flashlight.

"Well, ain't you a pretty little thang," he purred under his stinky tobacco breath. A little bead of sweat rolled down the side of his face. "Why, I believe it's little Miss Eva Knox herself. Shame on you, darlin'." He shook his head. "Hittin' the sheriff earlier tonight was nahw-tee! And now here you are, causin' more trouble for yourself."

"Please. You're hurting me."

"Did I say you could speak? Someone needs a little lesson about respect." He grinned, and his uneven rows of tobacco-stained teeth looked like kernels of colored corn. "You an' me, we're goin' fer a ride, little lady!"

I heard Dolly yipping excitedly from behind the motor home as suddenly the deputy spun me around hard, twisting my arm up behind my back.

"Ow!"

"Hold still!" ordered the deputy. I thought he was fiddling with handcuffs. "I'm orderin' you!"

"Stop! Please, there's no need for this!"

"Yes! Arrest the murderer!" cheered Savannah.

"Aren't you supposed to read me my rights? What have I done?"

"Shut up."

The deputy clamped tighter, jerking my arm hard, pulling me backward. I almost fell to the ground. Arresting me was one thing. Manhandling me and threatening me was something else completely. I remembered how during the last murder investigation, Buck had warned me about some of the county deputies. He'd told me to steer clear of the group who aligned themselves with his political nemesis, Detective Eli Gibbit. Probably this guy was one of them.

"You're pissing me off, little lady," he whispered, spittle hitting my ear. "Looks like I have to teach a spoiled, naughty little Knox girl a lesson in the cruiser on the way to town. And believe me, I'm gonna enjoy it . . ."

I was frightened out of my wits. Still, I'd be damned if I was going to let him know that. If I was going down at the hands of a dirty deputy, I was going down with a fight.

"Like hell!" I declared. I tried to wriggle free. "Savannah, don't let him do this! You're a witness!" I called out.

"You asked for it . . ." He clamped harder and started dragging me backward.

CHAPTER 16

"That's enough, Deputy," drawled a silky smooth masculine voice.

"Sir!" cried the no-neck deputy. His hand clamped harder, crushing my wrist.

"Holster your weapon." The voice was calm. Authoritative. "That's an order."

"But, Sheriff . . ."

"I'll handle it from here, Deputy Riddley." Buck strode around to face us. "Put your weapon away. Now." His poker face was stern and he sounded very calm. He showed no hint of emotion.

"There's been a complaint, sir! A 459 in progress . . ." One hand still clamped on my wrist, the deputy holstered his gun. Then he pointed to Savannah. "This woman over here. She called in and—"

"I said, I'll handle it, Deputy." Buck's voice remained unemotional but commanding.

"Sir? This one committed a 240 downtown in the—"

"I know who she is. And I know what happened, Chigger.

I was there. Remember? Release Miss Knox, please. I won't ask again."

"Sir? I don't get it—"

"You're officially off duty, as of now. Go home, Detective Riddley."

There could be only one Chigger Riddley. He'd been in Daphne and Eli Gibbit's class in school. And he'd always been meaner than a junkyard dog. His glinty eyes narrowed as he stared at his boss in disbelief.

"Yes, sir. You're the boss." I thought I heard him mumble "For now" under his breath.

Buck crossed his arms and never batted an eye.

Finally, Deputy Riddley threw my wrist down before spitting another gob of tobacco on the ground and huffing back toward his cruiser on the other side of the motor home.

Feeling my wrist—it hurt like crazy—I looked away from Buck, trying to hold back tears for the second time that night. Whether the tears were from fear, humiliation, relief, or all three, I wasn't sure.

"You're gonna arrest her, right?" asked Savannah. "She killed my Slick."

Buck began, "Eva, do you need—"

"I killed him?" I whirled around to face Savannah, wiping my eyes. "You mean, you killed him!"

"Ladies—"

"Sheriff, aren't you gonna arrest her?" demanded Savannah.

I heard a vehicle door slam from the other side of the motor home. Buck's head turned to listen as Deputy Riddley's cruiser spun out over the gravel, racing away. Buck turned back, looking me over, and his mouth tightened.

"Quiet, please, both of you. Eva, do you need medical attention?" he asked me.

I shook my head no.

"Can you answer me with words?"

"No. I mean yes. I can answer. No, I do not need medical attention."

Buck pointed to Daphne's bench on the edge of the woods. "Sit, please."

"But—"

"Sit!" he ordered. Then he looked at Savannah. "And you are . . . ?"

"Savannah Deats. I'm the one who called your office to report this crazy woman breaking into Slick Simmer's motor home."

"And this yellow van back here is yours, correct?"

Savannah nodded. "I kinda live in it."

Buck stared at the van a moment, then took in the scene around us. "Yes. I remember your statement, Miss Deats, regarding the chef's death. I hear you were close to him. I'm sorry for your loss."

"Thank you."

That was pretty magnanimous, I thought. Considering Savannah was surely a prime suspect for the murder.

"Let's start at the beginning. Miss Deats, what time did you call?"

"About thirty minutes ago."

I jumped up from the bench. The leap made me feel queasy. "Thirty minutes ago? I wasn't even out here thirty minutes ago!" I felt hot tears on my cheeks. I wiped them away with my good arm.

"Eva, please! Sit down and be quiet. You'll get your turn."

"Well, I wasn't. I was in the cot—"

"Eva! Enough. Do you want me to arrest you?"

"Well, you're going to anyway, aren't you?" I plopped down on the bench.

"She was there, in Slick's motor home!" Savannah blurted, pointing to the fancy motor home. "I saw her inside, sneaking around with a flashlight."

Again I jumped up. "I'm not the one with a flashlight. You are, Savannah! Look . . . where's my flashlight?" I raised my arms and spun around. The spin made me dizzy. My head pounded. My wrist throbbed harder. I stopped short, trying to keep from toppling over. "You don't see one because I don't have one," I managed to say. I was still confused as to what had happened that had left me blacked out on the ground . . . I flopped back down on the bench.

"What were you doing in the motor home, Eva?" Buck asked.

"I wasn't *in* the motor home. I was *outside* the motor home when someone must've come out of it and knocked me down. And I don't have a flashlight. Search me if you want. Have a look around. There's no flashlight. Or smartphone with a flashlight app, if you want to get technical. If anyone was in the motor home, it was Savannah. From what I hear, she practically lives there anyway." I put my head in my hands. I wasn't feeling at all well.

"Why would I call the sheriff's department if I was in the motor home?" Savannah shrieked. "To turn in myself? That's the stupidest thing I've ever heard! Sheriff, she did it, I tell you. She murdered my Slick and she came back to steal all his stuff!"

Buck raised an eyebrow. "Please, Miss Deats, try to remain calm. We'll get to the bottom of this. Why don't you take a seat?" He motioned for her to sit next to me on the bench. She stood still. Then to me, Buck said, "Not carrying your smartphone again, Eva? That's not safe. Do you ever learn?"

I just sat with my head in my hands.

"Eva?"

I looked up. "Well, if I had been carrying my phone," I said quietly, "then it'd be difficult to prove that I wasn't in the motor home with a flashlight or a flashlight app on the phone, like Savannah mistakenly says I was. I'm not carrying any light—as you can plainly see—because I didn't think I needed one. I didn't know that the dusk-to-dawn light isn't working. So if you can even believe what the woman says about there being someone in the motor home earlier, it couldn't possibly have been me."

"Liar!" screeched Savannah.

"Ladies—"

"Okay, Savannah." I pulled myself upright. "Has it occurred to you that the reason I was out cold, stretched flat on my back on the gravel, when you and the deputy arrived is because someone knocked me there? It's the only explanation. Of course, it was probably you—"

Buck quickly asked, "Eva, again, do you need medical attention?"

I ignored Buck. "Savannah, if I'd wanted to sneak around surreptitiously inside the motor home, why on earth would I have brought my busybody, howling dog and not brought a flashlight?"

I was pretty sure that I saw Buck raise an eyebrow.

"In fact," I continued, "I never saw you, Savannah, before I opened my eyes on the ground. You certainly could've been the person inside the motor home who opened the door, knocking me down. Just maybe, I surprised you and then you called the sheriff's department to cover for yourself. Makes sense to me."

"She has a point," said Buck to Savannah. "Except, Eva, by your own words, the timing is off."

"She's a liar!" screeched Savannah. "I love Slick. I've always been loyal to him. I wouldn't hurt him. Or sneak around his stuff! I'd do anything for him!"

"I don't know, Savannah. Out here, all alone, with no one watching . . . It must've been pretty tempting to check out Slick's stuff," I said. "Maybe you thought you could help yourself to his things, now that he's dead. After all, who'd notice anything missing? Precious and I saw you out here earlier today, just before we found Slick in the freezer. What were you doing then?"

"Eva, I'll handle this—" Buck said.

"I don't need to check out his stuff, as you say. Slick and I are together all the time . . . or at least we were . . ." Savannah started heaving. "I don't want his things. I want Slick!"

Then came the waterworks as Savannah began sobbing. Then wailing.

"I hadn't seen him. I just knocked on his door this morning; he didn't answer . . . but that's because you'd already killed him and left him frozen in the freezer! Oh. My. God!" she shouted, lifting her arms up high and looking at the night sky. "Frozen! He's frozen! My Slick is gone!"

Either she was totally gaga over the dead chef or she was the best actress I'd ever seen.

I'd been about to suggest that Savannah'd been jealous of all Slick's flings with women and that she'd killed him after catching him with Daphne. However, I checked myself. As angry as I was at Daphne for lying to me about her dalliance with Buck all those years ago, I didn't want to implicate her in a murder. This was Abundance, Georgia, after all, and shady Detective Gibbit and his deputies would do anything for a quick conviction. Anyone would do. And I didn't know whether I could count on Buck to make it right. So I said nothing, figuring that in the end, what the cops didn't know about Daphne and her relationship with the murdered chef wouldn't matter. After all, she might have lied to me about Buck, but I knew darn well that my sister hadn't killed the chef.

So for several minutes, Savannah blubbered away. I ranted about my innocence. Buck threatened to take us both downtown as he listened to our disparate stories and tried to piece together what had happened. Then, out of nowhere, Dolly appeared. She was carrying something in her mouth.

"Oh, gross. What the hell has that mutt got?" asked Savannah, pointing and wiping tears from her face. "A deer leg? Ugh. That dog is disgusting."

Dolly trotted over to Buck. He bent down and patted Dolly on the head. She dropped something at his feet. Buck picked up a wooden-handled copper ladle, about twenty inches long.

"Hey! I know that!" said Savannah, wiping her nose on her shirtsleeve. "It's one of Slick's antique ladles. It came from some French castle. He uses it all the time."

"You say this belonged to Chef Simmer?" asked Buck as he stopped turning the ladle over in his hand. "Damn," I heard him mutter. I noticed that he didn't reposition his hands on the ladle. We'd all realized, too late, that it was probably evidence.

"Yes." Savannah motioned toward the motor home door. "He keeps it hanging over the cooktop, on the rack with all his copper pots and pans."

"Alright. Sit tight. Both of you."

Like a cat, quick and sure, Buck moved to the motor

home door. Taking one hand off the ladle, without touching the flung-open door of the motor home, Buck leaned his head into the big coach and swept his flashlight around the ritzy interior.

"You mean the stainless cooktop, over on the left?" he shouted to Savannah.

"Yes," she answered. "With all the pots and pans hanging above it." She pulled up her tee shirt and blew her nose into it.

I made a face as Savannah wiped her tears with her shirt. Dolly jumped up on my leg. Then she spun excitedly in a tight circle and sat down with a bark.

"Shhh. Stop, Dolly," I whispered.

"Are you sure?" Buck asked, still looking inside the motor home.

"Of course I'm sure!" Savannah called back to Buck. Then she glared at me.

"That's interesting," answered Buck, pulling his head out of the motor home and turning to face us. "There are no pots and pans hanging over the cooktop. Or anywhere else inside, that I can see."

CHAPTER 17

Buck knew the copper pots and pans had been in the motor home when it'd been checked during Slick's murder investigation. Someone had removed them since then. He called in a second team of deputies. I listened while he spoke with the dispatcher, specifically requesting each deputy by name, Deputy Pierce and Deputy Price—the same men who'd been on the scene after Precious and I had found Slick Simmer dead in the truck. Also, I heard Buck tell the dispatcher to contact Detective Gibbit about the burglary.

"Let him know there's no rush. The deputies will secure the scene, do preliminary interviews, and wait here for him."

Buck came back holding out a lead for me to use with Dolly. "I don't want her messing up my crime scene any more than we've done already."

"You carry a leash?"

"For people like you," hissed Savannah.

I started to shake my head, but it hurt too much. I put the lead on Dolly and she lay down at my feet while I waited on the bench. My throbbing head and wrist worsened. Savannah just stood, pointing her flashlight at stuff, whining and complaining about my not being arrested while Buck looked around.

The night heron barked in the woods. Dolly barked back.

"Shhh!" I whispered.

Savannah picked at her nails and glared at us.

Minutes later, two cruisers rolled in and Buck's deputies marched over to speak with him. Deputy Pierce, a young, lanky fellow with intense hazel eyes and dark brown hair, checked out the motor home and the surrounding area. Deputy Price, a middle-aged, brawny, blue-eyed Viking type, with a soft voice and a quick smile, interviewed Savannah. Then Deputy Price told Savannah to stay inside her vehicle for the remainder of the night while the deputies looked around. Professional and courteous, he came over and I stood as he asked me questions for several minutes. Sometimes he asked the same question a different way. My answers were the same, regardless. When we finished, I asked if I could go home.

"Sheriff, we're through here. Miss Knox asked if she could go home now."

From the other side of the motor home Buck answered, "No. Tell her to wait."

"Have yourself a seat, Miss Knox." The deputy gestured to the bench. I sat down and waited ten minutes or more, holding Dolly on the lead. She lay down and started snoring.

"Alright, Eva, let's go," Buck finally said, after ending a conversation on his phone.

Dolly jumped up.

"Let's go?"

"I'm giving you a ride."

Dolly whimpered and wagged her tail.

"A ride?"

Of course, I thought. It was time for the assault charge for slapping Buck earlier in the restaurant. I was headed to jail.

"Bring Dolly," Buck said to me as he waited. "This way."

He gestured over to his SUV. "Night, Deputy. Call me if you find anything significant. And don't let Eli screw this up. Everything by the book."

"Yes, sir. Got it. Night, sir."

Buck held open the back door for me. "Get in, please, Eva."

CHAPTER 18

I slid onto the backseat and Dolly jumped up and into my lap. Buck slammed the door closed. Well, I thought, at least I wasn't handcuffed as I went to jail. Did they still use handcuffs in Abundance? Or did they use those plastic zip-tie thingies I'd seen on TV? I fiddled for the seat belt, working to fit it between Dolly and me. I snapped it closed.

"Can we stop so I can leave Dolly at home? I don't want her to go to the animal shelter," I said as Buck slid behind the wheel.

Buck turned and gave me a funny look as he clicked his seat belt shut. Without a word he turned on the ignition and we roared out of the parking area. Suddenly very tired, I tried resting my head back on the seat, but the lump on the back of my head was way too sore. I was thirsty. I sat erect as we passed the left turn for the fields and the big house— the way I'd come on the Kubota. Instead, we were headed down the narrow gravel drive through young, overcut woods toward the plantation's unmarked working entrance off the main road. The same way Buck and the deputies had arrived.

About half way down the gravel drive, lights from another vehicle hit the windshield. Buck pulled off the drive as far as he could, into the bushes and briars, as a big black sedan headed in the other direction sped past us, spewing gravel and dust. As the other vehicle flew by, Buck raised his hand in a wave. I recognized jug-eared, grim-faced Detective Eli Gibbit behind the wheel of the sedan. He didn't wave back.

Buck pulled back onto the worn grooves of the old farm drive. Dolly settled in on the seat next to me as I reached back with my hand and checked the bump on my head. It was hot and sensitive to the touch. And it was a good-sized lump—nearly the size of a billiard ball. Touching the lump, I winced.

"Are you hurt, Eva?" asked Buck. He'd been watching me in the rearview mirror.

"No."

"You should have it checked out."

"No need."

We drove along for a few more moments.

"Alright, Babydoll. Let's cut to the chase, then," he said. "What were you doing at Slick Simmer's motor home in the middle of the night?"

"I already told you. And Deputy Price. I couldn't sleep. So Dolly and I went for a ride. You know I have insomnia."

"Right. And when you can't sleep, you go for a walk. Or a run. Except you didn't do that tonight. You took the Kubota and parked it beside a murder scene. Then you went poking around the dead man's motor home. What were you doing in the motor home?"

"I told you—I never went inside."

"We'd better not find your prints inside that motor home."

"You won't. Someone knocked me down— Hey! Where are you going?"

Abruptly, Buck made a hard left turn off the farm road, onto a barely visible trail in the woods that led through saplings and brambles. If you didn't already know it was there, you'd never find it. It was an old logging trail, made during a time when the hardwoods had been clear-cut for timber. Buck must've remembered the trail from when we were teenagers. Although I don't know how. I certainly wouldn't have ever remembered it, let alone found it again.

With my left hand braced against the door to steady myself, I grabbed Dolly with my free hand to keep her from falling off the seat as the SUV slammed and bounced down the rough trail, bumping over stumps and whacking through bushes and sapling branches as tangles of briars screeched like nails on a chalkboard against the outside of the vehicle.

"Ouch!" The vehicle bounced. I banged my sore wrist on Dolly.

All at once, when we were nowhere in particular, Buck braked hard and stopped. He shut off the engine and turned off the headlights. Without a word, he opened his door, stepped out of the SUV, then opened the back door. Frogs and night creatures chirped and screeched in the dark woods around the vehicle.

"Move over," he ordered, unsnapping my seat belt. Dolly and I scooted over as Buck slid onto the seat next to me and slammed the door shut. Dolly yipped excitedly and jumped over me and into Buck's lap.

Traitor.

"What's going on? Why are we here? Aren't you taking me downtown?"

Moonlight popped out from behind the clouds, filtering through the trees and into the SUV window, highlighting Buck's poker face. I couldn't read him at all. Should I be worried? His honeyed skin smelled soft and powdery, with whiffs of oriental spices, sandalwood, and patchouli. I could feel the heat from his shoulder as his shirt brushed against my skin. He was wearing the same clothes he'd worn at the restaurant. Then something grabbed Buck's attention. His expression darkened. He picked up my right hand, gently holding my arm up.

"What are you doing?"

"What's that?" Buck studied my wrist.

"What's what?"

"It's swollen. And there's bruising. Did this just happen?"

I shrugged. Buck's expression clouded.

"Eva, answer me! How did this happen? Did you do this when you fell?" Buck turned my hand over, examining my wrist.

Dolly jumped to the floor of the vehicle, all over Buck's feet, sniffing.

"I don't know. Maybe it happened when I fell." I snatched my hand back.

"Or maybe not." Buck looked angry. "Chigger did this, didn't he?"

I shrugged. Buck cursed. He clenched a fist, and I thought he might hit the side of the vehicle door. But he didn't. The young, impetuous Buck to whom I'd been engaged eighteen years ago would have smacked the door. And he might've jumped back in the driver's seat, raced off, found Chigger, and beat him to a pulp. Instead, Buck took a deep breath and slowly exhaled. Dolly jumped up on the seat next to me, tail wagging.

"You need to tell me truthfully, Eva. Did Riddley do this? And are you going to press charges?"

I shook my head no. Buck tightened his lips and shook his head, obviously not believing me.

"I promise there will be a fair and thorough investigation. Still, I need to know what happened, this minute. Moving forward, we do this by the book."

"Am I to take it, then, that you're not doing whatever it is you're doing now 'by the book'?" I still couldn't figure out why we were parked in the bushes.

Buck stared hard at me. His jaw was tight. His eyes were like stormy pools of darkness. He looked again at my wrist. I saw him curl his fingers into a ball. Then he finally answered.

"No, Eva. This is not by the book. I'm officially off duty."

"It doesn't matter. I am not going to press charges against Deputy Riddley," I said.

Aside from not wanting to risk my personal health and

reputation, I didn't want to put the plantation and my family at risk by crossing the scary deputy and his cronies. It wasn't worth it. Not to mention all the additional bad publicity it'd cause for my family.

"You know, I know that you're lying." Buck closed his eyes and sighed.

"No. I'm not."

"Yes. You are."

"I'm not pressing any charges," I said flatly.

"You're a terrible liar, Eva." Buck shook his head. "Alright, then. If that's the way you want it, I won't be asking you about this again. Understand?"

I nodded.

"Chigger will be dealt with. I promise you. This will never happen again." Buck's jaw was tight as he ran his hand through his hair.

"Just forget it, okay? Can we go now?" I still didn't know why we were sitting in the middle of Daddy's woods.

"In a minute," he said after a moment, looking straight into my eyes. "I want to talk to you."

"Is that why we're here in the briars? So we can talk?"

"I didn't want us to be disturbed."

"You didn't want anyone to see us, more likely. Is your lovely fiancée, Debi, following you again?"

"Probably." Buck almost chuckled. His low, sotto voce tone and familiar scent made me feel safe, secure. Almost comfortable. He reached down and ever so lightly touched his fingertips to my thigh. My heart did a little flip. He drew his hand back. "Forget about Debi."

"Gladly."

"I'm not . . . We're not . . ." He sighed and narrowed his eyes. "Just forget it. Alright?"

I shrugged. "Whatever. It's fine. It has nothing to do with me."

"Listen, Pep told me what happened between you girls at the restaurant tonight."

I wasn't expecting this. I looked up and my mouth popped open.

"I didn't realize that you didn't know that I'd . . . been with your sisters," he continued. "Pep said that you were in shock when you . . ." He paused. "When you left the restaurant."

I squirmed in my seat and leaned farther away.

What about the part where I'd slapped him?

"It was a long time ago. I barely remember any of it. With either of them. After you left Abundance, I was upset. Not myself. Out of my mind, really. And it wasn't—isn't—important now. Understand?" He touched my leg again.

I was processing.

He went on, "I had no idea that your sisters never told you. I just assumed you'd known all along. You three were always so tight."

Buck had caught me off guard. Welling up from somewhere deep inside me, my gut twisted as I felt strange pangs of heartbreak and despair thinking of him being intimate with each of my sisters. There was a kind of sorrow that cried out, like a hungry child who hadn't been fed. I worked hard to hold back tears. And I didn't even know why. We were over each other, Buck and I. He was with Debi. I was with . . . well, no one. And that was the way I wanted it to be.

Needed it to be.

Still, something wrenched inside. I couldn't stop it.

"You all did a terrible thing," I whispered, trying to quietly quell my distress. I needed to stop my mind and heart from going there. Change the subject. Make it all about him. It was his betrayal, not mine. My cheeks flushed hot. "All three of you. I feel totally betrayed by what you did. And humiliated."

"Don't. It's not worth it, Babydoll." He paused for a moment. "I don't mean disrespect to your sisters. Like I said, it was a long, long time ago. I was angry. I was hurt. Maybe, at the time, I wanted you to be angry and hurt, too."

I felt like someone had punched me in the stomach.

Why do I feel this way?

"It's not even so much that you all did what you did," I

blurted. "Believe me, that's bad enough. I mean, really, that must be quite a coup for you, having carnal knowledge of all three Knox sisters." The words tasted bitter in my mouth.

"Stop, Eva. It's not like that." Buck started to say something more, but I shut him down.

"It's more about the fact that not one of you told me that it happened. Not one! After all these years. It's the secret that hurts the most. The fact that I never knew that you'd had—"

He put his hand down on my leg. Hard.

"Had *sex*? Is that what you think?" He looked at me in disbelief.

"Of course!"

He started to chuckle. Then he laughed out loud, putting his head in his hands.

"What are you laughing at? It's not funny!"

"Yes, it is!"

"No, it's not. Stop it!"

With my good hand, I punched him in the shoulder. It was as hard as a rock. Somewhere inside, I heard a little voice: *Just like old times.*

Buck tried to look serious, but he couldn't keep the corners of his mouth from turning up. "Eva, Daphne and I slept together. Literally. Slept. As in, fell asleep. Sure, we drank some wine—too much, if I recall. Your big sister tried to liquor me up. And she did a damn good job of it. Of course, I returned the favor. And we fooled around a little, but that was it."

"What?"

"Then all of a sudden, she fell asleep and started snoring. I couldn't stand it."

"She snores? You're telling me that my sister—Southern belle cum laude Daphne—snores?"

"You didn't know? How could you not know? You grew up together . . ."

I shrugged. "She's ten years older . . . We were never in the same bedroom . . ." I shrugged again.

Buck rubbed his forehead in disbelief. Then he shook his head.

"Honestly, I've never heard her snore. Ever!" I cried.

"She sounds like Darth Vader."

"Darth Vader? Are you kidding? I . . . I can't imagine . . ."

"Neither could I."

"Omigosh."

"And with Pep," Buck continued, "to be frank, we certainly hit a couple of bases. But we were never intimate. Not in the way that I think you mean. Pep's fun. A lot of fun, actually. But, really, she's not at all my type. I've always thought of her as a sister, and I liked keeping it that way. If we'd slept together, well, that would've been the end of it."

I stared at my lap. Stunned. I fidgeted with Dolly's lead while neither of us said a word for a minute or more. Next to me on the seat, Dolly scratched her ears and yawned.

"Okay. So anyway, regardless of the details, I get it," said Buck finally. He sat back and crossed his arms over his chest. "I understand how you feel. That feeling of betrayal and not knowing, at least."

"You do?"

"Sure."

Buck sat quietly for a moment. Then he turned and looked straight at me, his deep chocolaty eyes full of devilry. They drew me in. I couldn't move.

Sliding closer, Buck put his brawny hands on my shoulders and pulled me closer to him. I could feel the heat from his heavily built body as his massive chest and shoulders closed around me. I let myself fall toward him. *What am I doing?* The familiar sweet scent of his skin, mingled with the newer, more unfamiliar faint scent of his powdery oriental cologne and leather from somewhere . . . all together, in Buck's arms, in the back of the SUV, it was warm, sweet, safe . . .

My cheek was right next to Buck's clean-shaven face. I looked up. *Stop!* His eyes were fiery and soft at the same time. He moved nearer, putting one hand on the back of my neck. Slowly Buck pressed himself closer to me. I felt young, passionate, desirable . . . the same way I'd felt more than

twenty years ago when Buck and I had first kissed. All at
once, I was shocked to realize that I'd never felt that way
with anyone else. Ever. And I'd forgotten how right the feeling was . . .

Buck's hand slipped up to the bump on the back of my
head and I flinched. I couldn't help it.

He pulled back.

My head throbbed. Still, my heart pounded and I felt . . .
heartsick for more Buck.

"I get it," he said in a low, husky whisper. Then he leaned
away and cleared his throat.

"You get . . . ?"

"The feeling of loss and betrayal that you were talking
about." His eyes flashed. He paused. "It's kind of like being
left at the altar in front of a town full of people and never
being told why," he said quietly. "It feels like a crushing
breach of trust. A stab in the back. Heartbreaking. Humil-
iating. Humbling. And so infuriatingly confusing, especially
when you feel . . . like this."

Gently, holding my face in his hands, Buck pulled me
close and kissed me. Lightly. He felt soft and somehow, even
with the lightest kiss, intensely passionate. My insides fluttered. I was mush. Despite my brain, and every part of my
body that ached, my heart wanted more.

Then he stopped. He dropped his hands and leaned back.
My cheeks felt hot. My heart raced.

"What . . . ?" I mumbled.

"Sorry," he said hoarsely. "What I was saying was, in a
situation like that, like ours, without answering the 'why,'
without some sort of explanation, you can't work toward
understanding and forgiving what happened. And it takes
forgiving what happened to be able to move on." He ran his
hand through his hair and sighed. "So, I do get it, Babydoll."

He looked back at me. His eyes held mine.

"And so . . . have you been able to . . . move on?" I whispered, almost dreading the answer.

A moment went by. Finally Buck answered.

"Yes. It took a long time. And a life in another kind of world. But . . . yes."

The bottom of my stomach dropped and I suddenly felt queasy. Heat ran up the back of my neck. My cheeks were burning. It was the first time, ever, we'd spoken about the time I'd jilted him at the altar. I blinked and looked down. I'd known that I'd hurt him deeply; still, I'd never imagined— never wanted to know, really—how much he'd hurt. How much he'd loved me. Truly loved me.

And I'd left him.

For all the wrong reasons.

It made me sad.

"So maybe we're even now," he said simply.

Buck slid away and opened his door and stepped out. I looked up at him. Confused, I couldn't find words. What was Buck doing? Was he kissing me to punish me? Or did he want me back? But then, what was the deal with Debi? My mind was a jumble. Still holding the door open, Buck's face softened. Then he leaned in.

"Don't worry about it, Babydoll. I let it all go after I left town. All I ever wanted was for you to be happy, loved, and safe. I always figured you were."

He started to close the door, then stopped himself.

"By the way, I forgive you for slapping me in public to-night. I probably deserve it . . . for all the women I've really slept with, wishing they'd been you."

He slammed the door shut, got back in the driver's seat, snapped on his seat belt, and threw the car in reverse. I fumbled with my seat belt and snapped it shut. We spun around in the brambles, Buck mashed the accelerator pedal, and the SUV shot forward through the bushes and sapling branches. Riding silently as branch after branch slapped the sides of the SUV, finally we hit the gravel farm road. Then we made it to the main road. Within a few minutes we were back home again—not downtown—parked next to the big house.

"Maybe after you've had some rest and see a doctor in the morning, you'll see fit to tell me the truth about what you were doing out at the warehouse tonight. I'll be back looking—officially—for answers."

Buck stepped out of the SUV, opened the door for me, and gestured that Dolly and I should get out.

I hadn't been going to jail after all.

Far from it.

CHAPTER 19

The screen door slammed with a *whack!* There was a heavy footfall. Then another.

"Well, well, well! Ain't y'all the princess and the pea this mornin'! You bein' the princess, your little mutt bein' the pea . . ."

Precious threw the sheet off me. Bright sunlight hit my eyelids. I fought to keep them closed. I was dreaming about being a Scottish princess in a Highland castle. I loved that dream. Only, the prince kept changing . . .

"Go away," I said, grabbing the sheet and rolling over. I'd been so exhausted after Buck dropped me off early that morning that after taking a double dose of ibuprofen, I'd just collapsed into bed, not even bothering to change my clothes.

"Rise and shine, Sunshine. You've got work to do! Your little mutt just let herself out through the torn screen in the door, by the way."

I groaned. I'd forgotten to fix the door. Which reminded me, I needed to go to the hardware store . . .

"What are you doing here? What time is it?"

"I brought back the sunglasses you left at the restaurant." She plopped the Jackie Os on the Sheridan dresser next to the door. "And I'm here to get you outta bed, sleepyhead. It's after nine o'clock. Honestly, I dunno how you can sleep so late. And in your street clothes! Tsk, tsk. You look awful, by the way."

"Maybe that's because I didn't get home until almost four this morning." I groaned again, sitting up. My head throbbed all over. I looked at my wrist. It was fat and blue.

"Well, ya sure made a heap of trouble for me last night. Mister Collier gave me hell for lettin' you leave the restaurant alone. Said he found you wanderin' in a ditch alongside the road in the dark. Said you coulda gotten yourself killed! I ain't seen him this broody and upset in years. Now I'm payin' for it. He said I'm never to let ya outta my sight again."

"That's a bit extreme." I moaned. "I'm sorry, Precious."

"Really, Sunshine, what were you thinkin,' runnin' outta the restaurant like that?"

"I wasn't. I was just so shaken. And then, when I slapped Buck—I just had to get away."

"Well, you sure caused a pile of drama. Although Miss Daphne has it nearly tied up for queen of the drama department. The minute you slapped Sheriff Sweet Cheeks, she nearly fainted on the spot, right at the table."

"What?"

"Oh yeah. She was moanin' an' swoonin' in her little ice-cream chair. If I hadn't caught her, she woulda hit the floor like a log."

I rolled my eyes. "Daphne's always been the family drama queen."

"Let's give credit where credit is due, Sunshine. Last night, you won first prize. You are the queen of drama queens."

"I am not!"

"Ha! Don't make me laugh. At least, from what I could tell, people thought it was kinda funny, you hittin' the sheriff and all. Everyone was figurin' you and Sheriff Sweet

Cheeks have unfinished business from way back when. 'Cept Debi Dicer, of course. That uppity piece of work was fit to be tied. Went on and on, screechin' to everyone in the restaurant about how you should be thrown in jail. I dunno how your boy can stand her."

I groaned. "Pep says it's because Debi's flexible."

"That may be too much information for my liking." Precious patted my shoulder. "Hurry and get dressed, Sunshine. I gotta get back to Greatwoods, and there's a big breakfast tray on the warmer waitin' for you to take upstairs to the other drama queen, Miss Ambrosia Curry."

"Wait, please, while I change. I'll walk over with you. I want to tell you all about last night."

"Sure, Sunshine."

Examining my wrist more carefully, it looked awful. Still, even though it was terribly bruised and swollen, it didn't feel like anything was broken. I could use it . . . as long as I was careful and didn't hit it. My throbbing head, though, was another story. The lump was nearly the size of my hand and tender.

I slid out of bed and tried to ignore the dizziness I felt. Grabbing some clean clothes from my dresser in the front wall, I hightailed it past Precious at the foot of the bed and past my dining table and kitchenette to the back of the room, over to the bathroom. Quickly and carefully—so as not to whack my wrist or the big bump on the back of my head—I pulled off my dirty shirt and unhooked the bra I'd slept in. Only, when my bra fell away, something tumbled out of it and rolled somewhere on the floor.

"Hey . . . ?"

Slowly I got down on my knees and scanned the bathroom floor.

"Found it!"

I picked up a good-sized diamond stud earring. Or at least, it looked like a diamond. It must've fallen down my top when the person knocked me over coming from Slick's motor home. Hooray for cleavage! I would've laughed,

except my head hurt too much. Then I stopped to think . . .
Did Savannah wear earrings?

I couldn't remember.

I pulled on my clothes, shoved the earring in my shorts
pocket, washed my face, ran a toothbrush across my teeth,
took two ibuprofen, and shoved my feet into my cheapo
sneakers. Moments later, Precious and I were out the door,
hustling across the lawn toward the big house.

Although gorgeous, already the day was oppressively hot
and muggy. The heat and bright sun made my head feel
worse. Raising my hand, I shielded my eyes from the sun
as we crossed the lawn. I explained to Precious how I'd gone
to Slick's motor home to look for Daphne's elephant charm
and everything that had happened next. Except the part
when Buck took me down the logging trail. I was still sort-
ing through that. Really, I didn't know what to think. So I
tried to push it all aside. Besides, I had more pressing stuff
to worry about. I was freaking out about giving the tasting
presentation to the ladies club the next day. I still had no
idea what I was going to say or do. And I needed to solve
Slick's murder before the bad publicity got out of hand. If
it hadn't already . . .

"Look what I found just now." We stopped in the garden
and I dug the earring out of my pocket, handing it to Precious.

"An earring? That's nice. Is it a real diamond? I don't get
it." She studied the gem, holding it up to her eye and squinting. "Hmmm, sure looks real, don't it?"

"It fell out of my bra. The one I wore last night."

"Okay . . . I could make a joke about finding a diamond
in the rough, but I'll let it pass," Precious said with a chuckle.
She handed me the earring.

"Say, what happened to your wrist? It's all puffy and
blue! Did ya hurt it when you fell at the motor home?"

"Yeah, I guess so."

Precious gave me a funny look.

"Precious, don't you get it? This earring belongs to whoever knocked me down at the motor home. It must've fallen off that person's ear and somehow landed down my shirt."

"Are you kiddin' me?"

"No! It's the only thing that makes sense. And doesn't it stand to reason that this is the same person who killed Slick? I mean, that's motive, right?"

"I suppose so . . ." Precious seemed to be thinking it all over. "You should take that earring to Mister Jingle at the jewelry store. Find out if it's genuine."

"Mister Jingle?" Was there someone actually named Mister Jingle? I shook my head, then regretted it, as the movement worsened the ache. "Never mind. Look," I said, touching Precious's arm, "we have no idea who killed Slick or why. Right?"

"Right, Sunshine."

"This famous collection of copper pots and pans—Robin Harden told me they were once owned by royalty and some of the world's greatest chefs—is certainly reason enough for murder. And right now, Savannah Deats is at the top of my list. She had motive and opportunity. And she lives out of her van. Her van! It must be thirty years old or more. She could certainly use the money. Besides, she was all too quick and excited to pin it on me last night."

"Did the sheriff find the goods in her van?"

"No. Not that I know of . . ."

"Well, it don't matter. You'll get your chance to question her right quick. She's Miriam Tidwell's guest for breakfast. They're sittin' at the dining room table now, along with that bad-mouthed Crusty Baker fellow. C'mon. And remind me," said Precious at the bottom of the wooden porch stair. "How come *we* have to figure out what happened with all this?"

"You think Detective Gibbit is up to the task?"

Precious made a face. "He's about as useful as a trapdoor on a canoe."

"Exactly. He's a nincompoop. And a dirty one at that. If we don't get at this, and quickly prove that Knox Plantation had nothing to do with a murder, or stolen copper, it could kill our business."

"Literally." Precious chuckled.

We climbed to the back porch, where a painted wicker settee and chairs flanked a low table showcasing a fresh-picked bouquet of wildflowers—black-eyed Susans, Queen Anne's lace, little pink and white wild roses—clustered together in an old pewter pitcher. Behind a pretty crocheted hammock, stacked along the shingled wall of the house, were several large cardboard boxes with KNOX PLANTATION labels looking ready to mail.

I pulled the screen door open and stepped into the kitchen. And stopped short. Precious bumped into me as the screen door slammed into her butt.

"My stars and garters!" she cried.

"Good morning, ladies," whined a man's voice.

With his hand clenching my sister's elbow, Detective Eli Gibbit stood alongside a distraught-looking Daphne. On the kitchen table was a plastic baggie with Daphne's elephant charm inside, glistening in the sunshine that streamed through the curtained window over the sink. There was a tag on the bag; I could just make out the words: EVIDENCE AND CHAIN OF POSSESSION.

"Dang," I heard Precious say under her breath.

"Miss Eva Knox, Miss Precious Darling, how are y'all this fine morning?" the detective asked with a lopsided grin.

"Detective," Precious and I mumbled in unison.

Eli Gibbit smiled. Except it looked more like he was in pain. With jug ears and buckteeth, the skinny-as-a-rail man looked like a Halloween pumpkin on a broomstick. His unremarkable clothes hung awkwardly. He was all adult-sized body parts on a child-sized frame, like he'd never grown into himself.

"What's going on?" I asked, looking at the detective.

"Missus Daphne Knox Bouvier and I are going to town," he answered.

Daphne's eyes snapped up to find mine. "I've called Earlene Azalea and she's comin' over to take care of the children after school. The detective tells me it will be quite a long day."

"It seems Missus Daphne Knox Bouvier had a secret relationship with the deceased, Spaulding Montjoy Simmerton the Third, otherwise known as Master Chef Slick Simmer," said the detective. "I have questions. Just part of the process." He gave us a weasely sneer.

"Eva, I carried Ambrosia Curry's breakfast upstairs earlier. You'll need to retrieve the dirty dishes. Also, you need to mail some olive trees for Daddy. They're on the porch, boxed and ready to go. Use money from the petty cash," said Daphne quietly.

"Okay," I said.

"Let's go." The detective reached up and grabbed Daphne's elbow, leading her toward the door to the dining room.

"Detective," scolded Daphne, "I am not goin' through the dining room. We've got important guests in there and I will not have them disturbed and fascinated by you parading me past them. We'll leave out the back door."

It wasn't a question.

CHAPTER 20

After the detective hauled Daphne to the station, Precious headed back to Greatwoods. She'd return as quickly as she could, she'd promised. Crossing the kitchen, I stopped short at the dining room door. I heard a woman sobbing in the next room.

"It was one of the Knox sisters," wailed Savannah Deats. "She killed him! I was there when the sheriff took her away. Thank God!"

Pushing open the door just a crack, I peeked into the dining room. Three people were seated at the table. Teary-eyed Miriam Tidwell was wiping her nose with a napkin. Baker Glen Pattershaw was shoving a fresh olive oil donut into his mouth. And with a pile of pancakes on her plate, all puffy-eyed and red-faced, Savannah was waving her knife and fork around, crying and talking at the same time.

"I've read all the stories about her," said Savannah, shoving a forkful of pancakes into her mouth. "Secretly, she hates men," she mumbled with a mouthful. "Just toys with them and breaks their hearts." Savannah swallowed. "That's what the *Celebrity Stargazer* says, anyway."

Miriam Tidwell blew her nose.

"Sounds like a perfect match for ol' Slicko, if ya ask me," growled the baker, reaching for another donut. "Damn, these are good."

"Glen," warned Miriam quietly.

"She's nuts! Have you seen all the stuff about her on the Internet?" asked Savannah. She wiped her teary face on her arm and stabbed into the pancake pile on her plate.

"Wait a minute . . ." Miriam interrupted, looking up.

Savannah continued. "I've been googling. Since she ditched that weatherman in Boston, she lost everything when he kicked her out of their place. Can you blame the guy? And she used to have some sort of PR business up there. She lost that, too. I mean, who wants to hire a person to help with public relations when she makes a mess of it in her own life? No one." Savannah gulped down half a glass of orange juice. "And just everyone says she's flat broke now. That's the reason she came back to Georgia. She had to. No one else would have her! Pass the syrup, please. So, I'm thinking she killed my beautiful Slick so she could steal his collection of copper pots and pans. Slick told me those pans are worth a ton of money."

Ironic, I thought. I'd been thinking the same thing about Savannah.

"Wait!" Miriam insisted. "I thought you were talking about the oldest sister. You're talking about the youngest one?"

"Of course! It's sure not the kooky middle sister."

"No. That's not right." Miriam sighed. "You've got it all wrong." She shook her head.

"Of course I'm right. That's why the sheriff took her away last night. I caught her red-handed, sneaking around Slick's motor home!"

"No." Miriam looked thoughtful for a moment. "Aw, hell. I knew we shouldn't come to this godforsaken place." She took a sip from a china coffee cup with little pink roses patterned on it. "I told Slick no good would come of it. But he wouldn't listen. He was too smitten with that woman. Had a thing for her for years. Called her his 'sweet Southern belle.' Said he had to help her raise money for charity. It was the least he could do, he said. Maybe they'd make it work this time, he said. Of course, he was in love with her . . ."

"No! I'm sure you're mistaken. Slick loved me!" cried Savannah.

"He loved the woman. Except I'm talking about the oldest sister. The divorced one. Daphne Bouvier. She was married to Boomer Bouvier, the ballplayer from Atlanta. I saw her in Slick's Atlanta restaurant. Several times."

"No!" cried Savannah. "He loved me!"

Glen Pattershaw snorted. "Slick never loved anybody. He was incapable."

"Yes. Usually. Except this woman is different. Have you seen her? She's beautiful. And she's the reason he dragged us all down here in the first place. We had a big argument about it. More coffee?"

"You're lying." Savannah spat the words out.

"I'll take some coffee," Glen said.

Miriam continued. "It has to be about her. I know they had a secret rendezvous before. Several, in fact. I saw her come through the back door of his restaurant when I was leaving once. Perhaps she was jealous of all his lady fans. She definitely doesn't seem the type to put up with that sort of thing. That's what I told the detective, anyway."

Crap on that!

So, in addition to finding Daphne's charm, the detective had a statement from Miriam implicating Daphne. My sister was in serious trouble.

"He loved me! Only me," cried Savannah.

"Can someone pass me the sugar?" asked Glen.

"Here, Glen," said Miriam. "Slick's feelings for that woman are what made me nervous about coming here in the first place. People love Slick because he's—um, he was—such an irreverent cad. A scoundrel. A playboy."

"He was not a scoundrel!" insisted Savannah.

Miriam stopped to blow her nose. She continued. "Slick . . . was . . . the cad women love to hate. It's TV magic and our producers know it. We all worried at the network that if he should really fall for someone, he'd lose his edge. That special vibe he has . . . er, had. Worse, he'd get married and quit. And we'd all be out of jobs."

"That's cold, Miriam," said the baker. "And I was thinking that you actually cared for the guy. All you care about is your job."

"I did care for him. Like a son. But you wouldn't understand that, Glen, would you? All you've had on your mind since Slick died is money," Miriam huffed.

"You're wrong!" shrieked Savannah. "He loved me. I know he did. And I was his woman. His only woman. Oh sure, he'd been with others—"

The baker laughed out loud. "Ha! That's the understatement of the century!"

"They meant nothing!" cried Savannah. "He told me so. He just did it for the show. He had to, he said. For the ratings. He had to make everyone think he was a playboy. That's what he said. But really, he thought of me when he was with each one of them!"

"Yeah. Right." The baker laughed. "And you fell for it." He shook his head in disgust.

"Get ahold of yourself, Savannah," said Miriam. "You're sounding a little over-the-top obsessive. I'm sure it will all get worked out."

Savannah jumped up from the table and ran from the room, through the parlor, and out the front door. I could hear her wailing as she ran down the porch steps and past the side of the house.

"If I'd known she was such a kook, I never would've asked her to breakfast," said Miriam, sniffing. "I just felt sorry for her. All she's got is that wretched van of hers. She's followed Slick everywhere for years. Cooking for him. Pressing his clothes. Running errands. He took advantage of her."

Glen swore. "He treated everyone like dirt."

Looking out the window, I saw Savannah riding one of the three-wheeler bicycles across the lawn toward the warehouse.

Help yourself, I thought.

"Not the Bouvier woman. He loved her. I worried he was thinking of actually asking her to marry him. And now he's dead . . ." Miriam choked back a sob and slammed the table with her little balled-up fist. "How could this have happened? And we're stuck in this godforsaken place until that miserable detective says we can leave." Miriam groaned. "It's too goddam hot down here! There's nothing to do. You and Ambrosia need to get on the road; you have other scheduled appearances!"

"Well, if you ask me, we could be stuck in lotsa worse places. The digs here are fancy. I got my own fancy marble bathroom. The grub is awesome. And these Southern women ain't bad to look at, either. Choice cuts."

"Try not to be such a pig, Glen."

"Why don't you take up hunting, Miriam? I hear there's no better pace. And it suits you. Go shoot a duck or something. You'll feel better. Hey, I'll make a deal. You go kill something this afternoon and I'll cook it up, real special for ya."

"You're sick." She pushed her black glasses up her nose.

"Face it. Ol' Slicko got what he deserved." The baker chuckled.

"Glen! You don't mean that."

"Like hell I don't. Slick's been a pain in my butt since college. Arrogant SOB. I don't feel bad about it at all. Good riddance."

"You're just sore because he wanted to call in a loan on your bakery chain," Miriam said with a sniff.

"Yeah, I'm plenty pissed about that. Greedy bastard. And to think, he owed me money!"

"I thought you owed him money."

"No. It was the other way around. And I got big bills to pay." The baker threw his napkin on the table and stood up, shaking the table and chandelier. "Now I'll never get the money Slicko owed me." He swore. "That reminds me, I gotta get to town. Take care of some business. I'm takin' my rental car."

"You'll have to pay for your own gas!" Miriam warned.

"Why am I not surprised? They should change the name from 'Chow Network' to 'Cheap Network.'" The baker stomped out of the room.

I took a deep breath and pushed open the door. With her unkempt, purply-red hair, and dressed in a drapey black tunic and leggings, Miriam Tidwell adjusted her glasses and looked up with a scowl.

"Miss Tidwell, my sister did not kill Slick Simmer," I said. "You were wrong to suggest something so heinous."

"Your sister has been toying with my chef for years," Miriam said indignantly.

"Your chef? It seems to me that the man had quite the mind of his own."

"You know what I mean. It was my job to keep him on a leash, on the straight and narrow, so to speak. Every time your flirty sister came around, he'd talk about giving it all up. For love. For her. How stupid is that? I'd have to rein him in every time. Talk sense into him. Keep him away from her."

"Sounds like the chef was a romantic. I'd have never guessed. And besides, if what you're saying is true, then they truly cared about each other. Why on earth would my sister want to harm someone who loved her?"

"I dunno. But it was her idea for him to come here in the first place, and now he's dead."

Miriam honked her nose in the napkin before dropping it on the table and standing up.

"Excuse me, young lady. I need to get some fresh air."

CHAPTER 21

As Daphne'd instructed, I headed to Ambrosia Curry's suite to retrieve the breakfast tray. I started to knock and was surprised when the door fell away from my hand . . .

"Miss Curry?"

No answer.

I tapped lightly on the door. It swung open a bit more. I heard the shower running in the bathroom.

"Hello? Miss Curry?"

"Yeeeee-owwww, wahhhhh-hagnhhhh!"

A voice cried out as something crashed down the hall. Startled, I raced to the dumbwaiter, flinging open the door. Dressed in a pink floral play dress, squatting inside the dumbwaiter closet with a big stuffed bunny, a girl about three years old—with fair skin and black curly hair—wiped a tear with her tiny hand. She was a mini Ambrosia Curry, right down to the pouty mouth that curled up into a flirty smile when I opened the closet door. She had the bluest eyes ever.

"Um . . . hi there, sweetie. What's your name?"

"Clementine."

"Hi, Clementine. My name is Eva. May I pick you up?"

She stuck out her bottom lip and nodded. I wrapped my left arm around the child.

"Let's go find your mother, shall we?"

"Mister Bunny is scared."

"I remember playing in there when I was little. Sometimes it was scary, especially when my sisters locked me inside. But mostly it was just dark. You're okay."

"I don't have sisters. Just Mommy. She said she's going to fix that."

"Clem! Where have you been?"

Suddenly at my side, Ambrosia Curry grabbed her daughter from my arms. The woman was still wet, with her hair wound up in a big towel, her fluffy white bathrobe barely tied around her waist. She scolded her daughter.

"You know you're not supposed to leave our room. Ever!"

"I found her here in the dumbwaiter," I said.

"Oh God! Clem! What were you thinking?"

"Mister Bunny was scared." Her lower lip quivered.

Ambrosia hugged her daughter tight. "It's alright now, honey," she whispered. Then she looked at me and said, "She went with me yesterday to deposit the breakfast tray and dishes. I never let her leave the room. I shouldn't have then. I guess the dumbwaiter looked like the perfect hiding spot."

I nodded. Why was she hiding her child in the first place? I never even knew that she had a child . . .

"Miss Curry," I said, "surely you know that your daughter is more than welcome here—"

"Shhhh!" Ambrosia Curry grabbed my arm and dragged me down the hall and into her suite, quickly slamming the door behind us. Pointing to Clementine, she mouthed the words, "I don't want her to hear this."

"Clem, let's go into the bathroom. I want you to wash your hands and brush your teeth."

"Can I bring Mister Bunny?"

"Of course you can, honey. And remember to sing the happy birthday song once while you wash your hands and four times while you brush your teeth, alright?"

With one finger, Ambrosia motioned me to wait as she reached down and picked up a small wooden stool from among a pile of toys scattered across the oriental carpet. Then she grabbed Clementine's hand and led her into an opulent bathroom with pink and white striped walls. Daphne'd created the fancy en suite bathroom from an old sewing room that'd been accessed off the hall when we were growing up.

Ambrosia squirted toothpaste onto a toddler-sized toothbrush. "Here, stand on the stepstool. That's right, sweetheart." She twisted the water faucet open. "Oh dear, we're out of clean hand towels . . ."

"Look in the basket under the sink," I called out. A fanatic about fresh towels and linens, Daphne had extras stashed in all the suites.

"Thank you," said Ambrosia before handing a fresh hand towel to Clementine. She stepped into the bedroom, closing the bathroom door behind her. "I'll be right out here, Clem, talking to this nice lady."

Ambrosia motioned me toward a small Federal-style settee covered in a rich cranberry-colored velvet. I looked around my old bedroom. When I was growing up, the ordinary room had never looked so lavish; Daphne had replaced my pedestrian hand-me-down furnishings with elegant antiques swathed in ritzy fabrics. Front and center was a king-sized, tall-post, carved plantation bed. A Federal-style mahogany table, covered with the remains of another scrumptious Precious-made breakfast, had been rolled to a mahogany Federal-style settee positioned at the foot of the bed. Under a window adorned with lush new drapes was a brown-patterned Louis Vuitton trunk with the lid open. I could see a little pillow, a pink blanket, and more toys inside the trunk.

"Omigosh!" I said, horrified. "Clementine doesn't *sleep* in there, does she?"

As the words came out of my mouth, I recognized holes in the back wall of the trunk. *I bet that's how Ambrosia snuck the child in here,* I thought, appalled.

"No. No. I need to explain," said Ambrosia. "Sit. That's her playhouse. She loves it."

Maybe, I thought. Still, how else could she sneak her daughter into the room with no one knowing?

"Happy birthday to me, happy birthday to me . . ." Clementine's little voice warbled sweetly from behind the bathroom door.

"Please, just listen," said Ambrosia. "I haven't got much time to explain. It takes Clem about fifteen seconds to sing 'Happy Birthday' and we've only got about five rounds before she comes back."

"I'm listening."

"As I'm sure you've guessed, Clementine is my daughter." Ambrosia spoke in a hurried, hushed tone. "I love her to the moon and back. I'd do anything for her. Anything. However, she's not in my contract."

"Happy birthday to me!" sang Clementine.

"I'm sorry, I don't understand."

"I'm not married. And my getting pregnant with Clementine four years ago was an unexpected surprise. I was thrilled, of course. However, my Chow Network contract expressly forbids me to get married or to have children." She rolled her eyes. "It's all part of the 'Orgasmic Chef' brand."

"Mommy!" Clementine called from the bathroom. "I can't sing and brush my teeth!"

"Just sing in your head, honey. Or listen to Mister Bunny as he sings to you."

"Okay."

"Look," she said to me. "Signing that contract the way it was written was a mistake. I should've hired a lawyer or an agent to look it over. But I was just a dancer. I was nearly broke. I desperately needed a decent job. And I wasn't getting any younger. I'm forty-two, you know."

"You look ten years younger," I said. And I meant it.

"Thanks. I work at it. Anyway, when Miriam Tidwell approached me about becoming the Orgasmic Chef, it sounded like the opportunity of a lifetime. And really, it was. The marriage and kid clauses seemed moot to me; there was no man in my life, and no prospects for one, and at my age, even if I found a man, chances of getting pregnant without extra help were pretty slim."

"I see."

"So now I'm a single parent, my Chow Network career is my main source of income, and I need every penny for Clem. I can't afford to get spanked with a lawsuit."

"What about Clementine's father? Surely he could help."

Ambrosia's eyes flashed. "It was a onetime fling. He's never been in the picture. I just need to keep this out of the media now and protect my contract. For Clem's sake."

"So, let me get this straight. You've been hiding this child, from . . . everyone?"

"Happy birthday to me . . ."

"Yes. I took some time off late in my pregnancy—I told everyone that I needed to work on my *Orgasmic Desserts* cookbook. Then, after Clem was born, I was able to hide her pretty easily. She was a quiet baby. Never cried. Slept for hours at a time."

"In the trunk?"

"Sometimes. Don't look at me like that! It wasn't closed!"

"Still . . ."

"Look, now that Clem's older, it's more difficult to hide and protect her when I have to travel for network appearances. And her future depends on no one knowing she exists. At least until my contract ends. Meanwhile, I can't lose this job! So, please, please, will you promise me that you won't say anything to anyone? If you do, there will surely be a lawsuit, I'll lose my job, and the tabloids will have a field day with this."

"You don't have to tell me about the tabloids," I said, sighing.

CHAPTER 22

About midday, Daddy's farm manager, Burl Lee, knocked on the kitchen door.

"Miss Eva?"

"Hi, Burl. What's up?"

"Miss Daphne said you'd be needin' a ride to town—to mail some of your daddy's olive trees. Is now a good time?"

"Now is a great time! Thanks."

"And she told me that I'm to drive you back to town again later, for a five o'clock jujitsu class at Ringo's Gym . . ."

I'd forgotten all about Daphne's silly jujitsu class. "Don't worry about the class, Burl. I'm not going. One trip to town today is enough."

Burl chuckled.

A big strapping guy in his thirties, Burl had worked for Daddy forever. He was an easygoing fellow with muscled arms the size of telephone poles, a deep, dark tan, and a big smile. We chatted about this and that as he helped me carry the boxes from behind the hammock on the porch and load them into his Chevy pickup.

"Say, Burl, aren't you and LaDonna due to have a baby soon?"

"Actually, she's two weeks past her due date. My wife's gonna have someone's hide if this kid don't come soon!" He laughed good-naturedly.

"Well, I'm happy for you both."

"Thanks."

We jumped into the truck and headed to town. There was no air conditioning in the old Chevy, but the windows were down and the wind whipped my hair around my face. It felt good.

"So, Burl, who's buying Daddy's trees?" I asked.

"Your dad sells a lot of trees to folks who want to grow their own orchards, mostly amateur farmers. Big orders go to commercial growers."

We chugged through a green tunnel of live oaks. On the side of the road, two deer—a doe and her spotted fawn—turned and jumped back into the wire grass, white tails waving.

"I reckon this batch is goin' to folks who just want garden and patio trees. The smaller Arbequina variety works real good for that. And they're super easy to keep in pots."

I watched for more deer as Burl navigated around a curve. The sun was dazzling. Even though they looked stupid on me, I wished that I'd remembered the Jackie Os. I reached up and flipped the windshield visor down. We rode along the country road in silence for a bit, smelling the summer-sweet air, rounding curves, cruising under more tree tunnels, passing fenced fields, red barns, and white farmhouses. As we passed under another shaded tunnel of hanging moss, I remembered something.

"Burl, who was the farmer you dragged away after he hit Slick Simmer during the cook-off on Saturday? Remember? The guy with the beard? After Slick insulted Ambrosia Curry?"

"Yeah. Hard to forget that. Too bad about the chef, huh? Big Bubba, too."

"Yes. It's still hard for me to believe it all happened."

"A real shame. You know, LaDonna's got every one of Chef Simmer's books. She was thrilled when I brought home a signed copy of his latest book. He gave it to me after I helped him haul some of his pots and pans back to his motor home after the demonstrations."

I nodded.

"So anyway," Burl continued, "back to your question. The farmer roughin' up the chef was Frankie Runkle. Frankie's got a chicken farm over on the other side of the county. I reckon he's always been kind of a hothead. In fact, when I went to pick up some late-night takeout for LaDonna at the Roadhouse Saturday, Frankie was sittin' at the bar, still mad as a hatter and goin' on about Ambrosia Curry."

"He was?"

"Yep. Frankie has a 'thing' for her. No one at the Roadhouse could shut him up. He just kept ramblin' about how she was the love of his life." Burl shook his head. "Frankie'd been livin' with Junie Mae Cleaver, from the corner store. We all thought they'd be gettin' married soon. But a few weeks ago even Junie Mae got so sick and tired of hearing about Ambrosia Curry all the time, she kicked Frankie out." Burl laughed. "I think everyone was relieved Saturday night when, after drinkin' too much and arguin' with nearly everyone, Frankie finally got up and stormed outta the bar."

"What time was that?"

"I got there about half an hour or so before closing. That'd prob'ly be about twelve thirty or so."

"Huh." I filed the time in my head. "Thanks."

"You think he had something to do with what happened to Chef Simmer?"

"I don't know. Do you?"

Burl thought for a moment. "Hard to say. I've seen Frankie lose his temper and throw quite a few punches. But kill somebody? I'd hate to think so. Although I suppose if anyone could, it might be Frankie."

"Hmmm. Thanks."

"A terrible thing that was . . ."

"Say, do you remember what time it was when you helped

Chef Simmer move his pots and pans back to his motor home after the cook-off?"

"It was pretty much after the crowd left. I helped Robin Harden load up her restaurant pots and pans; then I went back from her car to help the chef. It was close to supper-time. Maybe five thirty."

Burl drove past scruffy wire grass and pine forests, long driveways leading to hunting lodges, and Carter's Country Corner Store. Midday, the gravel lot outside the store was filled with dusty pickups belonging to farmers and hunters, regulars who visited the junk-food-filled man shack for a snack and a helping of local gossip.

A bit closer to town, I smelled flowers from the manicured yards of rehabbed Georgian- and Federal-style mansions once owned by moneyed railroad and logging magnates. Then the shoulder beside the road disappeared. The land reverted back to wilderness. I recognized the big trench that I'd jumped into the night before. I cringed, thinking about the vehicle that hadn't slowed down. Must've been a drunk driver, I thought. Someone from the Roadhouse.

Someone like Frankie Runkle.

Then I remembered Ian. How he'd stopped to find me. The way he'd smelled, the way he'd felt as he'd held me close. The concerned look in his deep green eyes. The way he'd softly brushed my cheek with his beautiful long fingers . . . And then I remembered how rude I'd been.

When I get back home I'll dig out my phone and apologize, I thought.

Of course, right on cue, my mind blipped. I thought of Buck. My insides fluttered. What had Buck been doing, kissing me like that? What had I been doing, kissing him back? We were over, years ago. We could be friends, I felt pretty sure. But the kisses—they'd been more than friendly.

Much more.

My cheeks flushed as I fiddled with the fringe on my cutoffs. Buck was engaged to Debi, wasn't he? She sure let me know that was the case. On the other hand, Buck didn't seem to give a whit about Debi . . . so, was he using me? Or

Debi? Or both of us? That thought made me feel sick. He certainly had a reputation as a womanizer. The last thing I needed was to be around another lying, two-timing snake in the grass. But then, he'd cleared up the mess about his being with Daphne and Pep . . . I tried to push all thoughts of Buck aside.

Of course, I couldn't.

Burl pulled into the parking lot outside the unremarkable brick post office. We unloaded the boxed trees, hauling them inside the building. Burl's cell phone rang.

It was LaDonna. She was in labor.

"Go, Burl! I'll get these trees mailed and call someone for a ride home."

"But, Miss Eva . . ." I could see the worry and excitement in his eyes. "Miss Daphne told me to make sure—"

"It's fine, Burl. Really. Please go. Even Daphne will understand! This is a once-in-a-lifetime event for you and LaDonna. You should be with her. You'll be sorry if you miss it!"

"Okay, thanks!" cried Burl. "I owe you!"

He waved as he flew out the post office door.

CHAPTER 23

"I'll be with you in a minute," said the postmaster from behind the counter. "Just gotta finish taping these boxes up."

I watched the gray-haired man's knotted hands wrap packing tape around a large box marked FRAGILE. There were other boxes like it, already wrapped, stacked on a table behind the postmaster.

"Phew! Glad that's over with. This is the last of about twenty boxes!" he said with a sigh.

There was something about the boxes behind the counter . . . Where had I seen them? I turned to look at my ten boxes on the floor. They were identical. But then, a box is a box, right?

"Alright," he said, "how can I help you? Oh my! More boxes?"

"Yes, I'm afraid so," I said. "Except mine are ready to go."

The postmaster stepped out around the counter and started carrying the boxes, one by one, behind the counter. He read one of the labels and looked up at me.

"Eva! I didn't recognize you. Should've, with your strawberry-blonde hair and all. Haven't seen you around here since you were a girl. I heard you were back home. You're all grown up and famous now! I've been readin' about you in the *Celebrity Stargazer*. How's your dad?"

"He's fine, thank you. Out of town this week. And I hope you don't believe everything you read about me!"

He smiled. "You got more of your dad's olive trees today?"

"Sure do."

"Alright, then. I'll need you to fill out some forms. Back in a minute."

He grabbed one of the boxes he'd been wrapping and shuffled out back. I stood on my tippy toes and squinted, trying to read the addresses on the boxes. None of the labels faced me.

"Here you are," said the postmaster, stepping up to the counter again. "Just fill out these papers while I move these other boxes out of the way. Seems like today is box day!" he said with a chuckle.

He handed me the forms and a pen, then grabbed another big box before stepping out back with it. This time I was in luck. When he removed a box, he uncovered another box behind the counter. It was turned so that I could read the address label.

I blinked twice.

The recipient was Glen Pattershaw, with an address somewhere I couldn't quite make out, in Pennsylvania. Who would be sending boxes to Glen Pattershaw? Was the Crusty Baker mailing stuff home to himself? Had he been shopping?

Then I remembered seeing the boxes on the ground outside the big house when Dolly and I had headed off to the motor home in the night. And there'd been a light on in a guest room upstairs, hadn't there? And there'd been another box outside the motor home. I tried to remember . . .

CHAPTER 24

A few minutes later, Daddy's olive trees were officially in the mail.

I stepped from the post office into the glaring midday sun. All along Main Street, tourists ambled along pristine brick sidewalks. Potted plants flanked Victorian buildings with awnings, hand-painted signs, and fancy window displays. Songbirds chirped from the live oaks in the median of the boulevard. Squinting into the sun, I headed off toward the hardware store, where I planned to buy a new screen for my cottage door. Then I'd grab lunch while I figured out how to get home.

A woman rushing toward the post office bumped into me. Her package fell.

"I'm sor— Oh! It's you!" snapped Emmylou Twitty with a big frown.

"Hi, Emmylou. Lovely to see you," I said politely. Knowing her estranged preacher husband had dumped her, I took Emmylou's dour attitude in stride.

Wearing a baggy denim jumper and clogs, she stooped to pick up her padded mailing envelope. A book fell out. I recognized Slick Simmer's photo on the back of the book jacket. It was his latest cookbook—probably the very same book I'd seen Emmylou clutching in her arms during the celebrity cook-off two days earlier.

"I see you have Slick Simmer's last book. I hope that you were finally able to get his autograph . . ." I was just chatting, trying to get her to crack a smile.

Emmylou surprised me with a furious look.

"That man was a monster! Yes, I got my autograph," she huffed. "And, already, I've sold the book on eBay for five hundred dollars. And if you ask me, he got what he deserved."

She turned on her heel and marched into the post office.

"Woo-wee! Talk 'bout havin' a hissy fit with a tail on it!"

I recognized Pooty Chitty's voice behind me. Pooty owned the Lacy Goddess Lingerie Boutique in town. I turned as Pooty sauntered up carrying a package. She grabbed my arm and crushed me in a big, gushy hug. She smelled of incense, too-sweet fruit, gummy vanilla, and synthetic musk.

"Eva, hon, didn't y'all hear? Emmylou's preacher husband and his squeeze, Eula, got caught doin' the dirty deed in the church boneyard." Pooty laughed loudly. "Emmylou's been as sour as a salty sucker ever since."

With wild dirty-blonde hair strewn about her shoulders, Pooty was attractive in a distinctive, rode-hard-and-put-away-wet sort of way. Her gauzy peasant blouse was sheer enough to clearly show her lacy purple bra underneath—Pooty was always showing off her wares, so to speak. That was probably why she was far more popular with the men in town than the women.

"Hi, Pooty. Yes, I heard."

"Preacher man havin' a quickie with Eula on a gravestone sure killed his marriage, now, didn't it? Who knew Emmylou would show up that night puttin' flowers on her daddy's grave just half a dozen headstones away!" Pooty punched me in the shoulder, tee-heeing. "Poor Preacher. He should've taken a lesson from you, Eva, sweetie, and never gotten married in the first place. Ha!"

Pooty had a big mouth, literally as well as figuratively. She bumped me with her hip and smiled her crooked smile. Like we were best friends. Then she tossed her tangled hair.

"Woo-wee! It's hotter'n balls in a Speedo out here today, ain't it?" she said. "Rushing to mail this special-order garter belt got me all worked up in a sweat." She fanned herself with her hand. "I gotta go, hon, 'cause time's a-tickin'." She waved her package in her other hand. "I left a sign on the shop door that I'd be back in ten minutes. There's lotsa tourists in town today and I don't wanna lose any customers!"

"Yes, I see . . ."

Pooty tossed a wild clump of hair behind her shoulder. "Stop in later, sweetie, and I'll fix ya up with somethin' real pretty." She looked me up and down. "I bet you could use it. You strike me as a thong girl . . . I've got a real cute one in tiger print. Grrrrr!" She growled. Then she laughed at herself. "Catch up with ya later!"

Pooty winked before sashaying into the post office.

I shook my head and headed up the boulevard.

CHAPTER 25

Passing the florist shop, I jumped back suddenly as two people wearing denim shorty shorts, sleeveless plaid shirts, big Western belts, and dusty work boots with no socks spilled out from the doorway onto the sidewalk. I recognized teen-aged Sissy and Peaches Clatterbuck as they lumbered across the sidewalk. Each girl carried a monstrous urn filled with pink Stargazer lilies, gladiolas, and carnations.

"What in tarnation!" exclaimed one sister from behind her tower of flowers.

"Only pink flowers left! Ugh. I hate pink!" complained the other sister from behind her massive bouquet.

I didn't know how either girl could see where she was headed.

"Mama hates 'em, too," said the first sister as I sprang out of her way.

"She's gonna have a cow," said the second sister, shuffling across the sidewalk.

"Too many dead folks this week," said the first sister, imitating a man's voice—the florist, no doubt.

"I'd like to smack that florist's sorry ass." The second sister spit on the ground as she shuffled toward a shiny black late-model GMC pickup truck parked near a curbside meter.

"And why do folks think just 'cause he died that we'd want to talk about him?"

"Well, I, for one, am glad he's dead. Serves him right."

"He treated all of us like dirt."

"Open the truck door!" ordered the second sister.

"I can't! My arms are full. You open it!"

"I asked you first!"

"Sissy, Peaches! Hi." I had no idea which sister was which; their faces were still hidden behind the humongous arrangements. "It's Eva Knox. You probably don't remember me . . . May I help you here?"

"Of course I remember you!" snapped the first sister.

"You were underneath my dad when he died," said the other. "I'll never forget you."

"Me, neither," said the first sister. "And that's not a good thing."

I couldn't see the girls' hidden faces, so it was like the flowers were talking with me.

"Yeah! Folks say that every man you touch dies. You're, like, a black widow."

"Yes, well, that's not true," I said softly. "I assure you. Still, I'm so terribly sorry about your father. I'm sure it's a shock for you both, and your mother. It is for all of us. It was just so . . . unexpected. He will be deeply missed—by everyone in the community."

The first sister held out her hand and a set of keys jingled. Lights on the curbside GMC truck lit up. The door locks clicked. I pulled open the passenger door. The second sister brushed past me, shoving her giant urn of flowers up onto the front seat, filling the cab. The flower stems bent as the blooms hit the roof. The sister hoisted herself into the cab, pressing herself next to the big bouquet. I could finally see that it was Peaches. She glowered at me. Then Sissy loaded the second arrangement, burying Peaches in the cab, before

slamming the door and marching around to the driver's side
of the truck. She yanked open the door, climbed in, and
quickly slammed her door. Right away, the engine started
up, and the truck roared out onto the boulevard.

They disappeared in a cloud of blue smoke.

CHAPTER 26

Inside Abundance Hardware, owner Merle Tritt helped me purchase a replacement screen for the cottage door. Also, I bought a pen and a little notepad that I found at the sales counter. Back on the street, carrying my hardware store shopping bag, I crossed the boulevard and headed back about a block to the Palatable Pecan restaurant, where people were enjoying the afternoon, dining at marble-topped ice-cream tables on the sidewalk. A sign on a wooden stand read PLEASE SEAT YOURSELF. I found a shaded table in a corner under the awning and sat down.

"Hi there! Eva Knox, right?" A waitress handed me a menu. It was Wendee, the same woman who'd served dinner less than twenty-four hours earlier.

"Hi," I said. After the scene I'd made when I'd slapped Buck, it probably wasn't a good thing that the waitress recognized me. Inevitable, though.

Ah, well.

"Wendee, right?"

Wendee grinned. "Yes, ma'am! Would ya like a few moments to look over the menu?"

"I'll just have a BLT and unsweetened iced tea, please. Thanks."

"No problem. I'll bring the tea right out." She smiled and hustled off.

I flipped open my notepad, grabbed my pen, and wrote *Suspects* at the top of the first page. I thought about who could have killed Slick Simmer before jotting down my list of suspects and their possible motives. After that, I studied my list and scribbled a few more notes as I waited another thirty minutes for my sandwich. It was a long wait for a sandwich.

"Here ya go!" said Wendee as she placed the garnished platter of food in front of me. The BLT looked delicious. "I'm sorry your order took so long. Mondays are always rough; it's delivery day and we're shorthanded. I'll be around if you need anything else."

"No problem," I said. "It's a gorgeous day. I'm happy to sit and watch the world go by. Say, is Robin Harden around? I didn't see her last night and I wanted to thank her for inviting us for dinner. And apologize for the scene that I made."

Wendee smiled. "Actually, Robin's out sick."

"Well, then, is Lark here?"

"No, I'm sorry. Monday is Lark's day off. I'll be happy to pass on the message tomorrow when I see her, if you'd like."

"That'd be great, thanks."

When I'd almost finished my BLT, Wendee returned again.

"Can I get you something else?"

"I'd love a slice of lemon merengue pie. And I have a question, if you don't mind." I looked up from my notes. "Do you know whether or not all the copper pots and pans the restaurant loaned to Slick Simmer were returned Saturday night?"

Burl Lee had told me that before helping pack up Slick's copper, he'd helped Robin pack up the restaurant's copper. That was before five thirty in the evening. Maybe some of

Slick Simmer's missing copper pieces got mixed in with the restaurant's copper and ended up at the restaurant by mistake. Maybe I could account for at least some of Slick's missing copper . . .

"Uh, I don't know. Want me to check in the kitchen?"

"I'd really appreciate it," I said. "And, please, can you ask if any extra cookware was returned?"

"Sure can. Be right back!"

Buck and Savannah had said there'd been copper in the motor home after Slick died. Still, maybe there'd been more somewhere else. None of it made sense. And it probably didn't matter. I was grabbing at straws. Still, the copper was all I had to go on. Somehow it seemed important. It couldn't hurt to account for it all and figure out when it'd been where . . .

Wendee returned. "Our sous chef says all the copper came back and there weren't any extras. Is that what you wanted to hear?"

"Yes. Thank you. Please tell Lark when you see her that we're very grateful for the dinner."

"Will do!"

CHAPTER 27

After I'd scraped up every scrumptious bite of Palatable Pecan lemon merengue pie—really, it was all I could do not to lick the plate—I paid for my meal, thanked Wendee, and headed back to the sidewalk. I hadn't taken any time off since my return to Abundance, so I'd decided to be a tourist and tool around town for a couple of hours. Then, at five o'clock, I'd meet Daphne at Ringo's Gym after all. I was sure she'd have a ride home.

As I passed Creed's Goods—Abundance's version of the five-and-dime and the place where I'd purchased my cheapo sneakers—the door opened and a young family with kids holding balloons and whirligigs stepped out behind me, laughing and giggling. In front of the Kibler Gallery, two young women walking arm in arm and laughing, each carrying several shopping bags, bumped into me hard by mistake, never saying a word to me as they plowed on past.

Tourists.

Stepping around a mob peering into Clayworks Pottery, I passed Solventi's Dry Cleaning before waving to owner

Tommy Burnside inside Hot Pressed Tees, where the front door was propped open.

"Howdy, Miss Eva!" Tommy smiled and waved back. He'd printed up all our GEORGIA VIRGIN OLIVE OIL shirts.

After I passed Buy the Book—they had a really cute cozy mystery display—I slowed as I approached the big bay window with purple shears painted across the glass. Last time I'd passed Shear Southern Beauty, I'd made a total fool of myself.

I had a knack for doing that.

Press on, Eva.

Only it was too late. Buck's mother, beauty shop owner Tammy Fae, was standing in the salon doorway, arms crossed over her purple apron. She raised her eyebrows when she saw me approaching.

"Well, well, well, look who the wind blew into town today!" Her voice oozed insincere exuberance.

Fifty-something Tammy Fae clapped her hands together. Through the doorway behind her, I could see two women covered in purple-flower-patterned smocks, who paid no attention as they sat reading fashion magazines, their heads buried under gigantic domed dryers that filled the salon with noise.

"Why, if it isn't Miss Eva Knox, as I live and breathe," gushed Tammy Fae.

Petite, with deep brown eyes, a pert, turned-up nose, and perfectly set whisky-colored shoulder-length hair, the former Miss Abundance and presiding president of the Abundance Ladies Club had always reminded me of a cocker spaniel— without the endearing cocker spaniel personality, of course.

"I hear y'all knocked the life out of another poor fellow down at your place. That makes two dead men, just this weekend! So, tell me, hon, how many dead men have y'all bumped off—oh, excuse me, bumped into—since you've come back home, hmmm?"

"Lovely to see you, too, Missus Tanner."

Not.

"Oh, puh-leese, hon! We've known each other forever."

She winked as she touched my shoulder. "Do call me Tammy Fae. Y'all are catchin' up in years, you know. Y'all will be a little ol' spinster before you know it!"

I gave her my sweetest smile. "Thanks," I said. "But I wouldn't dare call you by your first name, Missus Tanner. My parents raised me to always be respectful of my elders."

Tammy Fae put on a big supercilious smile. "Well, bless your heart."

Without a word I turned, walking quickly past an alleyway.

Tammy Fae called out, "I see y'all only got half the lessons in respect that you should have. That'd be because only half your parents were around raisin' y'all after your shameless mama ran off!"

That was cruel.

I didn't look back as I hurried past Boone Beasley's closed butcher shop. The Lacy Goddess Lingerie Boutique was next. And, I'm embarrassed to admit, Pooty Chitty always had something going on in the window that intrigued me. Not that rainbow-colored teddies, push-up bras, and tiger-print thongs were my thing, mind you. I just wanted a peek at how the other half lived . . .

I stopped to take a peep.

When I looked in the window, my eyes gravitated past scantily clad mannequins in see-through peignoirs, frilly beribboned negligees, and lacy teddies, panties, and bras. Instead, my attention shot right across the shop to the man in the baggy jeans, punk-style metal belt chains, and biker boots. He was leaning over the counter, laughing with Pooty, who was flinging her hair around.

The man was Billy Sweet, Pep's husband. And this wasn't the first time I'd found him around Pooty. Just weeks earlier, I'd discovered Billy's retro red custom Kawasaki motorcycle behind the building, in a parking area reserved exclusively for village residents who lived in second- and third-story apartments above the shops—as Pooty did. And I'd stumbled upon Billy and Pooty alone together at a couple of social events.

Neither of them saw me gaping outside Pooty's shop window.

Quickly, I turned and shot down the alley to the back of the building. And there was Billy's bike. His red motorcycle helmet with black skulls emblazoned on it hung from the handlebar. Could they really be having an affair? And could Billy be stupid enough to park his bike where it could be so easily discovered?

Yes.

Billy wasn't big in the brains department, and Pep never came downtown. And even if she did come downtown, everyone knew parking behind the buildings was reserved for village residents, so no one except village residents ever went back there. That made Billy's parking spot less obvious than you'd think.

I walked around to the street side again, contemplating walking into the shop just to see what Billy would say to me. Only, when I returned out front, the shop door was shut and there was a handwritten sign that read CLOSED.

"What?"

I leaned up to the picture window, shielded my eyes from the sun, and peered inside. No Pooty. No Billy. I walked around back. Billy's bike was undisturbed. Pooty and Billy just had to be inside. Or could they have left the shop and gone somewhere? No, I'd have seen them. Dollars to donuts, they were upstairs in Pooty's apartment. I wrinkled my nose at the thought.

I stood around a few minutes more to see whether Billy came out. Then I walked next door and hung around the Gifts Galore shop window for several minutes. Still no Billy or Pooty. The thought of them together made me sick for Pep. Still, it had to be . . .

I slid the shopping bag up my good wrist and shoved my hand into my pocket. That's when my fingers rediscovered the stud earring in my pocket. I remembered how Precious had told me to get it checked out. And I was in front of the Baubles jewelry shop. So, with one last look back at Pooty Chitty's closed shop, I pushed open the Baubles door.

Cool air whooshed over me, making little goose bumps on my arms as I stepped onto soft carpet. A buzzer went off as the glass door behind me closed with a quiet *thwump*. Gems and precious metal jewelry sparkled from glass cabinets as strategically placed LED lights pinpointed each sparkly bauble. A crotchety-looking man with a white beard and a rumpled suit shuffled out from behind a curtained room.

"Mister Jingle?"

"How may I help you today?"

I dug out the stud and held it out to the old jeweler. "Please, can you tell me if this diamond is real?"

"I reckon that I can."

He put on a pair of white cotton gloves and took the earring from me. Using his jeweler's loupe, he studied the gem.

"Looks quite genuine to me. If I may, I'd like to take it out back for a minute. To test it."

"That's fine."

"Would you like me to clean the piece for you?"

"No. That's not necessary. Thank you."

The old man shuffled to the back room. A few minutes later the jeweler shuffled out.

"It's a real diamond, alright." He handed me the earring inside a mini plastic bag. "May I do anything else for you today?"

"No. Thank you. How much do I owe you?"

"Not a thing. I'm happy to oblige."

"Thank you!"

I felt bad about not purchasing any merchandise. But, really, jewelry wasn't my thing. And besides, other than Daphne's petty cash, I didn't have a dime to my name.

"I had to clean it," he admitted. "It's a lovely stone. You should take good care of it. It's an excellent-quality D- or E-color stone. I'd say VVS1. And it looks to be two carats, maybe more. Worth quite a bit."

"Really?"

The old man nodded. "I don't see many in here as nice as that. Don't lose it."

"I won't. Thank you."

"Have a nice day."

"Thanks. I will."

I shoved the packet with the expensive diamond earring into my pocket. Pushing open the door, I stepped out into the sunshine. As lovely as downtown was, the midafternoon sun made it too hot outside for me to enjoy. I decided to go to the library for a couple of hours. I could google around the Internet on one of the library computers. Maybe I'd uncover something to help me figure out who had killed Slick Simmer. After that, I'd meet Daphne at Ringo's. I didn't know if she was still with Detective Gibbit or not, or how she was getting home. Regardless, I needed a ride home. And since Daphne had asked Burl to take me to Ringo's Gym at five, I figured she had a ride and a plan. Daphne always did.

CHAPTER 28

Abundance's historic library had been built and gifted to the town during the Gilded Age of the late nineteenth century by wealthy cotton broker Duke Dufour and his wife, railroad tycoon heiress Dina Abbot Dufour—the same couple who'd constructed mega-thousand-acre Greatwoods Plantation, more recently acquired by my neighbor, Ian Collier. Built in the Richardsonian Romanesque style, the brick-and-stone Dufour Public Library reminded me of a scaled-down version of Boston's Trinity Church, one of my favorite New England landmarks.

Inside the cool, hushed library, the rooms were nearly empty of people. Little gray-haired Millicent Page—she'd been the librarian since I was a child—helped me get started in the new computer room.

"I'll be right out front if you need anything, dear," she said, doddering back to the main desk.

"Thanks."

I got to work.

Three hours later, I felt pretty good about my Internet research. Except for the extra hour I'd spent trying to learn something about Ian—there was nothing about him on the Internet. Nothing at all. And tax records showed that Greatwoods was owned by some sort of trust.

It made me more curious about him than ever. I'd try pumping Precious for information again.

On a more positive note, I learned quite a few things about Slick Simmer, Glen Pattershaw, Ambrosia Curry, and even Miriam Tidwell.

Someone tapped me on the shoulder.

"Miss Knox?" whispered librarian Millicent Page. "It's nearly five o'clock and we close at five on Mondays."

"Okay. Thank you," I said, logging off the computer. "I found all that I need for today anyway."

CHAPTER 29

Really, I don't know what I was thinking.

Next to the library, in the parking area behind the Duke's Donut building, I walked past two doors: One, marked PRIVATE KEEP OUT, led to the donut shop kitchen; the second door had a FOR RENT sign with an arrow pointing to the second story, along with Debi Dicer's realty information. Next to that was a stairwell leading down to a propped-open basement door. The sign overhead read RINGO'S GYM.

Reaching the bottom of the basement stair, I stepped through the propped-open door.

Instantly I saw what was happening down there.

And still, I stayed.

A dozen or more of Daphne's cronies giggled and twittered together, standing barefoot in the middle of a large mirrored room with mats covering a polished wooden floor. Each wore a traditional martial arts gi—the white, loose-fitting pants and jacket with a cloth belt. Looking at the group, all chatty and dressed in their whites, I couldn't help but think they looked like a gaggle of geese. Certainly, they sounded like it.

Still, I didn't see Daphne. I worried. After meeting with Detective Gibbit, had she been arrested?

From the far side of the gym, a door labeled OFFICE opened. A short bald man with a peaceful, friendly expression stepped into the gym. He wore a gi.

"Welcome to today's *budoshin* jujitsu class," he said. The women stopped chattering. "The gentle art." He gave a short bow.

"Hi, Ringo!" they all shouted in unison, giving little bows.

Someone bumped me from behind.

"Hey, Eva!" Pep whispered breathlessly. She'd just come down the stair.

Ringo continued. "As always, our goal is to learn the fundamentals of jujitsu, through which you will practice patience and efficiency, self-confidence, physical fitness, and self-defense. Are you ready, ladies?"

"Ready!" The women tittered in unison.

"Why are we here?" whispered Pep in my ear. "Daph texted me to come. Man, it's hotter than Hades down here!"

"I don't know," I whispered back. "But I need a ride home. Have you got a car? Please tell me you have a car."

"I have a car. But where's Daphne? Isn't she supposed to meet us?"

"I'm here, y'all," cried Daphne as she glided into the gym from a door marked LOCKER ROOM.

Like everyone else, Daphne was all gussied up in her gi. And as timely as her cry of arrival was, she hadn't actually been addressing Pep or me. Instead, she flew over to the gaggle of ladies.

Daphne gushed, "I'm so sorry to be late, y'all! We've just been so terribly busy at the plantation!"

The locker room door opened again. Much to my horror, dressed in gis, Debi Dicer and Tammy Fae Tanner strutted into the gym.

"Yes, I imagine there's been quite a cleanup necessary at your place," said Tammy Fae, responding to Daphne's comment. "All those bodies!" She let out a harsh laugh.

Daphne blushed as some of the ladies giggled.

"Well, don't that just piss on your parade," whispered Pep. We watched the piranhas join the gaggle.

"C'mon," I whispered to Pep. "Let's get out of here."

Pep and I turned to leave.

Too late.

"Pepper-Leigh, Eva! I'm so glad you're here!" cried Daphne. Then to the group, Daphne said, "My sisters have both been so eager to learn jujitsu, haven't you, girls?" Daphne fluttered over and put her arms around us.

Pep whispered, "Are y'all nuts?"

The locker room door flew open again. Out popped the Clatterbuck sisters, dressed in brand-new gis—crease marks were still in the fabric.

"Welcome, girls," everyone said at once, bowing.

The sisters stomped into the room, glowering.

Daphne grabbed my hand, and wearing her fake smile she whispered, "I suggested Big Mama send the girls over for class; they needed a distraction. And we all thought they could use some camaraderie."

"Of course. Great idea." I nodded.

I didn't actually mean it.

"So glad to see y'all, Miss Sissy, Miss Peaches," said Daphne brightly. "Jujitsu is the perfect art for young ladies. After all, we women can't be too careful these days . . . That's why my two sisters came today, to learn how to take control of their bodies and to be safe, right, Eva?"

Still holding my hand, Daphne squashed it tight as she turned and stared hard at me, making it clear that I was supposed to say something to back her up.

"Ow!" I whispered. Daphne dropped my hand. "Uh, yes." I cleared my throat, trying to ignore my throbbing hand and wrist. "Um . . . Unfortunately, we've all seen how danger lurks, even here in our cloistered little town of Abundance. Threats to our safety will only worsen as more tourists and out-of-towners come to visit . . ."

Pep snorted. The rest of the women nodded. It was a page out of my old PR playbook, addressing the violence head-on and framing it as a community problem—not a Knox Plantation problem.

"We'd love to stay, y'all, really we would," Pep interrupted, "but we left our costumes—"

I hit Pep with my elbow and whispered, "Gis," through smiling teeth.

"Er, we left our gis at home, so we can't possibly work out today. So silly of us!"

"Yes, so silly," I said.

"It's no problem," said Ringo with a smile. He put a gentle but firm hand on my forearm. "We have people come in street clothes all the time, don't we, ladies?"

There was a loud group mumble yes. Smiles and nods. Debi rolled her eyes as Tammy Fae clapped her hands together in mock excitement.

"Just as long as you are dressed comfortably," he continued.

"Oh, they look mighty comfortable alright!" said Tammy Fae. "Casual, at least." The ladies giggled.

Ringo looked us over. I was in my cheapo sneakers, jean cutoffs, and an old MILK & COOKIES FOREVER tee shirt from Mount Holyoke College. Pep wore a torn black tee shirt with bat-patterned rhinestones and a fat leather belt with giant metal studs over black leggings and studded black leather combat boots.

"Yes, yes!" Ringo said. "This will do. Please, take off your shoes, ladies." He looked at Pep. "And your, er . . . belt, please."

"Really, y'all are bein' so gracious," Pep said. "We'll just come back for the next class on another day in our . . ." She frowned, trying to remember.

"Gis," I said.

"Right," finished Pep.

"Fiddle-dee-dee!" exclaimed Daphne. "Y'all are our guests today, right, ladies? And you'll both come each week from now on! My treat. You, too, Sissy, Peaches. We women must stick together!"

"Right!" shouted the group in unison.

"Oh, fiddlesticks," said Pep under her breath.

I kicked off my sneakers.

"Come, ladies." Ringo motioned us to the center of the gym.

"Eva, you know Bubbles Bolender," added Daphne quickly, yanking me over to a pale woman with blonde hair styled in a Marilyn Monroe bouffant. Bubbles lived in a magnificent Georgian colonial outside town. Her place always won first prize in the spring garden club competition.

"Nice to see y'all." Bubbles flapped a pale, wilted hand. Her voice was airy and soft, reminding me, again, of Marilyn Monroe.

Tammy Fae Tanner marched up to me. "Do feel free to come into the salon for a makeover. I'd love to get my hands on you." She smiled sweetly.

Pep burst out laughing.

Tammy Fae looked at Pep and narrowed her eyes. "You, too, dear," she said. "I love a challenge."

Pep snorted and slapped Tammy Fae on the shoulder. "You're a hoot, Miss Tammy Fae."

Standing next to Tammy Fae, Debi Dicer gave us a contemptuous smile as she kept her arms crossed over her chest.

The locker room door opened again.

"And Emmylou Twitty is here today!" said Daphne brightly.

Without a word, plain, miserable-looking Emmylou stepped onto the gym floor. Emmylou's gi looked two sizes too big for her. I smiled and nodded greetings to half a dozen more women. Palatable Pecan owner Lark Harden smiled warmly as she came over to greet me and Pep.

"So glad y'all are here today," said Lark.

"Hi, Lark," I said. "I had lunch at your place today. I wanted to thank Robin for inviting us for dinner last night. I'm sorry I missed her."

"Robin's off visiting relatives. She's been planning this trip for months!"

"Well, dinner was delicious. Thank you for treating us. We all enjoyed it," said Daphne.

"Come, ladies!" called Ringo, clapping his hands together. "Today we will again focus on the art practiced by samurai warriors. You will concentrate on yielding to your opponent's direction of attack as you attempt to control and use your opponent's own force and energy against her. Let's warm up."

We did a series of stretches, then some yoga-like moves, before moving out across the mats and performing one-knee tumbles across the floor, posing before switching knees with each tumble. I tried to protect my injured wrist and the back of my head. Still, the tumbles made me dizzy. Everything hurt. Regardless, I was determined not to wimp out and be a panty-waist in front of the ladies . . . especially Tammy Fae and Debi.

Pep kept falling over and giggling. I couldn't help but notice how Debi aced the movements. Flexible? You bet.

I bet Buck loves that.

Suddenly, the sensation of Buck's kiss swept over me. I felt my face flush. Then I thought of him with Debi. I lost my balance as I tumbled, falling face-first on the mat.

"Easy there, girl!" cried Pep, chortling in little pig snorts.

I heard Debi cackle. "At least she didn't fall over a dead man this time."

Mad at myself for thinking of Buck and Debi, I got serious about the moves as we dove faster and harder into tumbles, ending in a fight stance. I worked hard to be just a little competent. Debi was catlike. Lark, too. Tammy Fae was assertive. Bubbles tried to do everything like a ballet dancer. Daphne was precise. Emmy Lou was pathetic. And although it was their first time at jujitsu, hulking Sissy and Peaches were very aggressive and athletic, grunting and groaning as they slammed hard onto the mats like a pair of sumo wrestlers. I wouldn't want to meet either sister in a dark alley, I thought.

Or a refrigerated truck.

I'd started contemplating that notion when Ringo raised his hand. "Please, find your partner now. Sister Eva, you will be my partner today," he said, pointing to me.

"Ooooh, darn," I heard Debi say. "I wanted Eva to be my partner."

As instructed, I positioned myself on my hands and knees, being careful of my wrist, as Ringo tumbled over me. Each duo did the same. The gym was filled with the loud *thunk* and *whump* sounds of bodies hitting the mats, sometimes followed by little whimpers and cries—usually from Bubbles. Art gallery owner Pickles Kibler cried out when she broke a fingernail.

Ringo gave precise instructions about each move. Each time, he and I bowed to each other before we demonstrated the move, Ringo prefacing it with a description of the kind of circumstances for which the move might be useful in real life. For example, we demonstrated what to do if an attacker grabbed you by the wrists. Ringo didn't say anything; however, I was sure he noticed my severely bruised wrist. He was careful not to hurt it.

"Now, ladies, your turn," he finally announced to the class. "Remember, no punching, slapping, kicking, biting, eye gouging, pinching, hair grabbing, or finger locking."

From across the room, a wide-eyed Pep caught my eye.

Ringo had to remind people not to do those things in class?

I slammed my hand on my forehead as Pep broke out into amused little snorts. Then we practiced thwarting grabs, blocking arm thrusts, and grabbing and disabling our attackers. Next, we added throws.

"These moves are extremely effective for self-defense," Ringo said. "The armlock would work for a woman with smaller hands against a larger man."

I remembered how helpless I'd felt when big Deputy Riddley had grabbed my wrist.

"Now we demonstrate the neck nerve press that we learned last week." Ringo took my arm and we went to the center of the room. Ringo positioned himself behind me. "This press is an extremely effective way to take out your opponent. However, it can be very dangerous and can cause serious injury, or even death, if not executed properly."

Great.

Ringo placed his arm around my neck. I felt a hand on

top of my head. It was easy to figure out that if I were to move forward, he could easily tighten the pressure around my neck and head. I imagined not being able to breathe. He stepped in close behind me.

"Remember, this is just practice, ladies. Maintain close body contact, keeping your thigh against the back of your opponent's leg or butt to remain in control and to reduce the chance of injuring your partner."

The ladies listened to his descriptions and studied our positions as we demonstrated the technique. Then Ringo walked around the room, giving precise and careful instructions to the pairs, allowing each person to play each role.

"It's very important to remain close," he said again. "Many law enforcement agencies limit using this maneuver to only life-or-death situations. I am showing you again today because you never know—your life could depend on it."

CHAPTER 30

"So, don't keep us in suspense. What happened with Detective Gibbit?" Pep asked Daphne.

Flapping her hand in front of her face, Pep tried to cool herself as the three of us walked up the back stair from Ringo's Gym after jujitsu class.

Suddenly, Daphne threw her hands in the air.

"Oh, fiddle-dee-dee! I've forgotten my purse. It must be in the locker room."

"We'll meet you outside," I said. "C'mon, Pep, keep climbing."

Daphne flew back down the stairs toward the gym. Already, Pep and I'd waited on the bench in the gym nearly thirty minutes after class as Daphne'd primped in the locker room. By the time she'd reappeared, we were the very last of the class to leave the stinking-hot basement gym.

"C'mon, Pep. Hurry up! I need air."

"Pass me." Pep, a step or two ahead of me, moved over on the stair so I could get by.

"Thanks." I raced ahead, taking two steps at a time until

I reached the parking lot. I started looking for Pep's car. A puff of warm wind felt great against my overheated skin.

"Look out!" I heard Pep cry as she pushed me hard with both her hands.

I staggered forward as a large urn fell from above us, shattering onto the pavement exactly where I'd been standing before Pep shoved me out of the way.

"Damn," I said, shocked.

Pep and I looked up to a balcony off the upstairs apartment. There was no one in sight. A door leading to the apartment from the balcony was open. A gauzy curtain fluttered in the wind.

"What the dickens?" said Pep, looking at the cement urn shattered on the ground. "That was one heck of a big pot!"

"And heavy, filled with all that dirt," I thought aloud.

"There sure as heck isn't enough wind to blow it off the balcony." Pep frowned. "Do ya think?"

"You don't imagine someone pushed it off the balcony . . . do you?"

Pep grabbed my arm. "Hurry!"

We dashed to the apartment door with the rental sign on it. Debi's blue Realtor's box with the key inside was snapped around the door handle. Pep tried the handle anyway.

"Locked!" cried Pep. "I know another way—c'mon!"

We tore back down the stairs to Ringo's Gym.

"Outta the way! Outta the way!" cried Pep as she pushed past Daphne, who was climbing the stairs.

"Goodness gracious! What on earth . . . ?" Daphne had no time to finish her sentence before I shoved past her as well.

"Wait for us here!" I called out.

Running past a stupefied Ringo as he stacked mats, I followed Pep into the locker room, racing through to the other side, where she pushed open a door labeled EMER-GENCY EXIT. We galloped into a narrow stairwell and up the stairs, until we reached a small foyer and a street-side door. Pep didn't stop. Bolting past the outside door, she turned, continuing up the stairway until we reached the second floor. We both stopped, side by side on the landing. The moment I touched the handle to the apartment door, it swung open with a creak.

Pep followed me inside, waving her hand in front of her face for air. Like cops in some sort of television police drama, we separated, inspecting the suite of four or five rooms, one by one.

"Clear!" shouted Pep jokingly. She threw herself on the wooden floor.

Except for the drapes, window shades, a folding chair, toilet paper in the bathroom, and an old plastic garbage can in the kitchen, the apartment was completely empty.

"Well, this is a bust," I said, stepping in from the balcony. "Clearly, there's no one here."

I sat down on the floor next to Pep. Early evening sun streamed in through the open balcony door as the sheer drapes fluttered in the breeze.

"Someone was here," said Pep.

"Do you think someone left the balcony door open by mistake during a real estate showing?" I was trying to stay positive.

Pep frowned.

"No. If ya ask me, someone hustled outta here faster than a cat with a turpentined ass."

CHAPTER 31

Thirty minutes later, sitting at the hot pink counter inside
Duke's Donut Shoppe, Pep, Daphne, and I sipped tall iced
teas garnished with fresh lemon wedges as we stuffed ourselves silly with warm, just-made donuts. Pep and I had
deemed the donut splurge to be the only proper recovery
from a forced-upon jujitsu class, a near-miss urn missile,
and a mad dash up and down three flights of stairs. Daphne'd
agreed to partake in the binge because it was the only way
she could get home—Pep had the car.

A few weeks earlier, I'd convinced shop owner Duke to
make some donuts with our Arbequina olive oil, a fairly
mild and sweet variety that's good for baking. He'd agreed
to develop a new donut, using olive oil instead of butter.
Moist and chewy, the olive oil donuts had been an instant
hit with customers. So much so that Duke decided to offer
two types of olive oil donuts: plain—that's what the three
of us had ordered—and the daily special.

As my sisters and I chewed on the moist and delicious
treats, I considered the urn missile. It'd been the second near
miss in less than twenty-four hours. Was it just a coincidence?

I told Daphne and Pep about the car chasing me down the road after I'd left the Palatable Pecan.

"Creepy," said Pep.

"It's a good thing y'all have started comin' to jujitsu class," said Daphne, sitting next to me at the counter. "Y'all never know when a little bit of the gentle art might come in handy."

Pep dumped a pile of sugar into her already sweetened tea.

"That's gross, Pep," I said.

"Yes, Pepper-Leigh, mind what you eat." Daphne looked at both of us. "Y'all won't have your young and girlish figures forever."

"Not if a giant pot falls on our heads and kills us," said Pep. "I say, life's too short. Have another donut, sis."

I rolled my eyes and took another sip of my unsweetened tea. The server behind the counter, a round, dark-skinned woman wearing a pink and orange polyester pantsuit, a crown on her head with a hairnet, and a name tag that read LALA, had made the tea especially for me. No one drank tea without sugar in Abundance.

No one.

After a few bites of delicious donut, I continued recounting my saga, filling in my sisters on what had happened when I'd gone to Slick's motor home in the night, how I'd been knocked to the ground when someone came out of the motor home, how Savannah Deats had called the sheriff's department, how the deputies and Buck had shown up, and all about the missing copper.

Of course, I left out the part about Buck taking me down the logging trail.

"Gracious!" Daphne cried. "You certainly do need jujitsu!"

Daphne's cell phone played some sort of classical tune. She reached into her bag and pulled it out, before listening to a message. She looked distraught.

"That's the third cancellation we've had since Slick died. We've just got to solve his murder before we lose everything! Oh . . . poor Slick."

Daphne looked miserable.

"You could always change the business name," offered Pep. "How about 'Bump-off B and B'? People would flock to the place!" She snorted.

Daphne groaned.

"C'mon, Pep," I said, chiding her.

"What? I'm just trying to lighten the mood here," Pep said.

"Seriously, we can't wait for Eli to bungle this," I said. "Or pin it on you, Daphne."

"Okay. So, Daph, you were at the sheriff's department all day," said Pep. "Did you convince Eli to give up his witch hunt?"

"Having a smart, high-powered lawyer up in Atlanta does have its rewards." Daphne sighed. "I do believe that Beverly Bickers, of Bickers, Balls and Slaughter, put the fear of God into Detective Gibbit when she called. He let me go right after their phone conversation. Of course, he could change his mind tomorrow. And I've been instructed not to leave town."

"That's not good," said Pep.

"I just can't have Big Boomer finding out about all this. He'll use it to assassinate my character and take the children away from me."

"So, who are our suspects?" asked Pep.

"Wait. I made a list." I pulled my notepad from my shopping bag.

"Top of my list is groupie Savannah Deats," I said, "because she was head over heels for Slick, he humiliated her in front of everyone at the cook-off, she was jealous of Daphne, and she probably stole the copper for money. Plus, she's been all too eager to pin it on me."

"Ticks a lot of boxes," said Pep.

"It certainly does," added Daphne. She let out a sad sigh. "I should've charged her more to park at the warehouse. Y'all know, I've been lettin' her use the warehouse bathroom for free."

"Free potty? Daphne, I'm shocked!" Pep made a face and shook her head.

"Then there's suspect number two, Glen Pattershaw," I

said, ignoring Pep. "He grew up and went to college with Slick, has a failing bakery business, needs money, and just found out that Slick is calling in a big loan. Slick totally slammed and humiliated him during the cook-off."

"There's an awful lot of history between the two," said Pep. "And he strikes me as a hardheaded, coldhearted kinda guy."

Daphne nodded.

I sipped my tea. "Then we've got suspect number three, Ambrosia Curry, who also was humiliated by Slick in front of everyone during the cook-off. And it definitely seemed as if they'd been together intimately, at least sometime in the past."

"You mean he boffed her," said Pep.

"Don't be crass, Pepper-Leigh," scolded Daphne.

"Bow-chicka-bow-wow," sang Pep.

"Okay, you two. Enough," I said. "Yes, I think it's safe to say they had some sort of . . . let's call it a 'fling' for now. Alright?"

Pep shook her head and clucked. Daphne looked distraught.

"Sorry, Daph," I said.

Daphne sighed but still nodded in agreement.

I was about to tell my sisters about Clementine and how Ambrosia Curry might have killed Slick to keep her secret, when I remembered how my sisters had spied on me, chased after Buck, and kept it all a secret for years. I owed them a secret or two. This little tidbit could wait . . .

"Next up, we have suspect number four, local boy chicken farmer Frankie Runkle, who completely lost it and attacked Slick during the cook-off because, according to Burl, Frankie is fixated on Ambrosia Curry and didn't like the way Slick talked to her."

"I give Frankie extra suspect points for losing it in front of the entire population of Abundance. He's always been a hothead," said Pep. "I see him shoot off his mouth all the time at the Roadhouse."

"Suspect number five, Emmylou Twitty, was bristling mad today and told me that she hates Slick, even though on

Saturday she was totally smitten with him. Something must've happened when she got him to autograph her book."

Daphne began, "She's always been—"

"A total nutcase," interrupted Pep. "I can totally see her offing someone. Who else?"

"Suspect number six, one or both of the Clatterbuck girls, who said on Saturday that they wished Slick were dead, right in front of me."

"Why?" asked Daphne.

"Because he was a chauvinist pig who wasted their good peaches."

"Oh," Daphne mumbled. "That's hardly enough to murder someone, is it?"

"They're just kids, Eva," said Pep. "Although they are known for being pretty mean . . ."

"Right," I said. "And they've just lost their dad. And did you see them in jujitsu class today?"

Pep nodded. "Sumo wrestlers. And in their grief, they may not be firing on all cylinders, as they say," she added.

"Right," I said. I almost added, "Like Daphne." But I held my tongue.

"They might have come back Saturday night for their family's refrigerated truck and found Slick," said Pep. "After all, the truck does belong to them. Maybe they didn't mean to kill him when they surprised him in the truck and something . . . happened. They're awfully big."

"Hmmm," mused Daphne. "I hadn't considered that."

"And," I said, "I heard them on the street today coming out of the florist shop saying something about being glad 'he was dead' and that 'he deserved it.' At the time I was horrified, thinking the girls were talking about their own dad, Big Bubba. However, remembering what they'd said about Slick on Saturday, maybe they'd been talking about Slick again."

"It all fits," said Pep.

"What about Miriam Tidwell?" Daphne asked.

"Ah, suspect number seven . . ." I began.

"Wait a minute!" Pep interrupted. She hopped off her stool and held up her hand. "I hear something."

She hurried across the black-and-white-checked tile floor to the Duke's picture window, painted with a giant pink-iced donut topped with a crown. Pep peered through the glass just in time to catch the tail end of a red motorcycle as it flashed down the opposite side of the boulevard.

"Is that Billy?"

"Uh-oh," I mumbled.

"It is!" Pep cried. "I'd know that engine sound anywhere. Why is he in the village? He's supposed to be playing a gig at a nursing home outside town."

Daphne and I exchanged glances.

"Excuse me," I said quietly to Lala. "May we please have three of those pink-iced olive oil donuts—today's specials? The ones covered with the obscene amount of dark chocolate bits and rainbow sprinkles."

"Sure thing, sweet cakes," said Lala, grinning. "Comin' right up."

"We're gonna need them," whispered Daphne next to me. "Miss Lala, please throw some extra coconut on them, too. Thank you, ma'am."

"Y'all are quite welcome."

Pep came back to the counter as Lala served us the fresh, sickeningly sweet pink donuts, covered in dark chocolate, rainbow sprinkles, and coconut shavings. I grabbed mine and took a huge bite.

"Oh my gosh, this is disgusting," I said with a mouthful. It was the sweetest, moistest, chewiest, and best donut I'd ever had. "Here, Pep, try one."

Lala chuckled as she headed toward the kitchen.

"Yes," said Daphne. "Enjoy." She broke a piece off her pink donut and took a nibble.

Pep looked us both over. "Daphne is eating another donut? A pink, über-sweet, stomach-turning donut with sugar and vile crap all over it? Now I know something is wrong. What's up, y'all?"

"I'm sorry, Pep. You need to know," I said. "Sit."

Finally I told Pep what I suspected about Billy and Pooty Chitty. And it turned out that Daphne had her own Billy-

and-Pooty stories to tell as well. She'd seen Pooty and Billy cozying up together in the deli section at the grocery store. Another time when she was picking up dry cleaning, she saw Billy coming out of Pooty's shop. Daphne swore he had an "extra spring in his step." Then Daphne said that her friend Asta Bodean reported that her housekeeper had seen Billy and Pooty together during a raunchy party at an abandoned poultry farm outside town late óne night.

"A woman like that . . ." said Daphne about Pooty. She made a face and clucked her tongue as she shook her head in disgust.

"I should've said something sooner," I said. "It's just that after all my own debacles with men, I didn't trust my instincts. I thought that I was being too . . . oversensitive. I'm sorry, Pep."

"It's not all y'all's fault," said Pep. She shoved a man-sized portion of outrageous pink donut into her mouth and chewed. Her cheeks puffed out like a chipmunk's. "Aw, heck. I can't even blame Pooty."

Daphne shot me a look of concern as Pep swigged her extra-sweetened iced tea.

"You'll change your mind when the shock wears off and you come to your senses," said Daphne, patting Pep's arm. "Mark my words."

"Pooty's just naturally horizontal," continued Pep with another mouthful. "She can't help it. Some women are born that way. I blame Billy. After all, he's the one who's married." Pep crammed the other half of the donut into her mouth. I was shocked at how calm she was. "I'm not completely surprised. Still, mostly, I blame myself," she mumbled through the donut.

"No, *dahhwr-ln*', you're not to blame," said Daphne, reaching over and handing Pep a fresh paper napkin. "The man's a cad. It may surprise y'all to know that I've always thought so."

I burst out laughing. Pep choked on her donut. I slapped Pep on the back as she guzzled more tea to clear her throat.

"Hon, your feelings about Billy are no surprise to anyone!" Pep finally said to Daphne. She smiled and shook her head.

Daphne and I waited. "No," Pep finally said after a big swallow. "It's my fault. When we first met, I fell for Billy because he was so sexy, irreverent, and outrageous. What did I expect? That marrying the guy would change him?"

"He's certainly irreverent and outrageous," said Daphne with a sniffy expression.

"I'm sorry, Pep," I said. "I know how it feels when someone you love cheats on you."

"No, Eva, hon. You know how it feels when someone *you think* you love cheats on you. You never really loved that scumbag in Boston. Not the way you loved Buck. I could see it. I still can. Everyone can."

I felt myself blush. Part of me was growing more heartsick for Buck by the moment. Another part of me was dreading seeing him again. I was letting my guilt trick me into believing what I felt was real, I reminded myself. He was with Debi. And I didn't want, or need, a man. I'd moved on.

"Can we not go there, please?" I took a gulp of tea. "I really don't want to hear any more about me and Buck from either of you. I'm still trying to get a handle on the fact that you both chased after him. Yes, it was after I left, so that's on me. And it was a long time ago. I get it. I'll work it out. Still, before that, you spied on us. *Spied!* I haven't come to terms with that. It just seems so disloyal and . . . disturbing."

"Oh, Eva," said Pep with a snort. She went on as if I hadn't said a word. "Best thing that ever happened to you was to find out that the weather guy in Boston was cheating on you. Besides, if you'd gotten married, you would've been divorced within two years. And you wouldn't have come home this summer, and we wouldn't have you here today!" She gave me a hug.

"I'm sorry that I overreacted last night at the restaurant. Buck explained what happened," I said.

"He did? You talked to Buck about what happened at the restaurant?" Pep asked. "When?"

Daphne let out a groan.

I shook my head. "We're not discussing me today. For once." I gave Daphne a look, heading off her sure-to-come disparaging remarks regarding Buck. "We're talking about you, Pep, and Billy."

"Yes," agreed Daphne. "So, Pepper-Leigh, what are you going to do about Pooty?"

"I'm not sure. I've been looking the other way all this time, thinking that my 'not noticing' would save our marriage. That Billy'd get tired of whatever he was doing and just come home. All those nights he disappeared for hours. He'd say later that he was out playin' cards. Or gamblin'. Which was bad enough, but at least there wasn't a woman. And then there are the times he'd get mad and storm out, sayin' he just couldn't take thinkin' about all the men 'lusting' after me while I work behind the bar. And I'd feel guilty."

"Guilt sucks," I said.

"I really do love him," continued Pep. "Or I did. Oh, I don't even know anymore."

"The knave is not worth the dirt he walks on," mumbled Daphne.

"Knave? Daph, did you actually say 'knave'? Is that even a word anymore?" I made a funny face.

"Of course it's a word," scolded Daphne.

"Of course," I said. Then I mumbled, "Knave," rolling my eyes.

Daphne sighed. "Well, I suppose there is some good news today."

"There is?" Pep and I asked in unison.

"Yes. I can think of at least three things. First, after my all-day interrogation, Eli didn't see fit to arrest me. Yet."

We laughed.

"And second?"

"Eva, last night's car and tonight's planter both missed hitting you."

"And the third thing?"

"Pep, you haven't killed Billy . . . yet."

"Oh, y'all know there's still plenty of time for that," Pep said, snorting.

We all laughed again. Then Pep ordered a dozen donuts to take home. Lala gave her thirteen.

"Billy's not going to even know I have these," Pep said with a sly smile.

"And I bet he isn't going to see whatever it is you have coming his way either . . ." I winked.

We tumbled off the swiveling orange stools and made our way to the door.

"Y'all have a nice evening, now," said Lala with a friendly wave.

"Thanks!" we all said in unison.

Still, as we walked around back and headed across the parking lot toward Pep's car, the seriousness of each of our situations wasn't lost on any one of us.

And none of us noticed the folks sitting inside the little black Honda parked behind Pep's car.

CHAPTER 32

"Y'all don't mean we're going home in *that*."

Daphne stopped in front of Pep's car in the parking lot and sighed, taking in the sedan's wood trim and the fifties-style red rims on the wide whitewall tires.

"What?" asked Pep. "This car is one of a kind."

"Right," I said. "That's because Chrysler stopped making them years ago. This is probably the only one left."

"Y'all know nothing about cars," Pep said with a groan as she opened the door to her black 2002 Chrysler PT Cruiser Limited Wagon. "This baby is one of a kind. I just finished customizing her last week. She's got old-timey style and substance!" She tossed her bag of donuts in the backseat.

I rolled my eyes. Pep extended her arm and waved it through the air, showcasing the car like a game-show model displaying a prize.

"Ladies, please, won't y'all take in the nifty fifties red rims and the superwide whitewall tires?" she said. "Cost me a fortune. And the custom hood, grill, bumpers, lights, and mirrors; Borla exhaust; K&N intake system; custom suspension and steering rack. And then there's under the hood!"

The pitch of Pep's normally velvety voice got higher as she became more excited.

"Eight-liter V-10 with five hundred horsepower with the six-speed transmission! Ladies, the power is insane!"

She patted the roof before sliding into the gray leather seat and slamming the door. Daphne and I stood outside, looking at each other.

"It is kinda cute," I said.

Daphne groaned. "Looks like something Great-Grand-daddy Knox would've driven. Didn't we have some broken-down jalopy like this in the old red barn?"

"A family of raccoons lived in the chewed-up seats," I laughed. "Except it didn't have wood trim like this."

"I loved that car!" called out Pep. "That 1935 Plymouth was my inspiration. And it shoulda had wood trim. I was so sad when the barn collapsed on it. Now, c'mon, y'all!" Pep revved the noisy engine. It roared like a race car. "Hop in."

"I'm only doing this because I've got to get home." Daphne opened the front door as I slid into the backseat. "Please, Pepper-Leigh, don't drive like you normally do. Remember, I have young children."

Pep snorted.

"Really, Daphne, it's not that bad. Just a little retro— that's all."

"Oh, fiddle-dee-dee." Daphne moaned. "Pepper-Leigh, must we ride with . . . those?" She fastened her seat belt and pointed to two big fluffy red skulls dangling from the rear-view mirror. "How can you even see out the windshield with those . . . heads?" She wrinkled her nose.

"Oh, don't be such a party pooper," said Pep.

"So, back to our murder suspect list: I did some research at the library today," I said from the backseat. Taking out my notepad as we turned out of the lot onto Main Street, I noticed a black Honda following us out of the parking lot.

"And?" Pep asked.

Referring to my notes, I said, "Slick Simmer and Glen Pattershaw were both blue bloods who grew up in the same wealthy Philadelphia suburb. They were college roommates at Amherst College. Glen's bakery business began as a cupcake cart to help pay for college while he was an undergrad. His moneyed parents wouldn't help with expenses."

"I knew all that," said Daphne.

"Fine," I said. "Now, after more than twenty years, Glen Pattershaw's DaBomb Bakery chain is in trouble because his stuff is made with processed flour and extra-sugary toppings. People want cupcake specialty shops and bakeries using organic wheat- and gluten-free ingredients."

"Yuck," said Pep. She waved to someone crossing the boulevard.

"Plus his designs are dated," I added.

"What about Slick?" asked Pep.

"After Spaulding Montjoy Simmerton the Third, aka Slick Simmer, dropped out of Amherst, he traveled around the world working for some of the greatest chefs. He worked his way up from dishwasher to executive chef."

"I knew that," said Daphne.

I rolled my eyes.

"Slick married twice. The first wife died in a car accident when the chef was in his early twenties and she left Slick a ton of assets."

"She loved him. He loved her," said Daphne, nodding.

"After that, he married right away, then went through a contentious divorce just a year later."

"She was a money-grubbing bitch," said Daphne.

Pep snorted. "Number two is always evil."

"In Europe he worked in kitchens all over the continent. Several years after that, his ex-wife passed away after contracting malaria during a gem expedition in Mozambique."

"Served her right," Pep teased.

"Well, at least we know that an ex-wife didn't kill him," I said. "At some point, he began collecting copper cookware, including antique pieces with provenance. Some experts value his collection at more than one hundred thousand dollars. His fame skyrocketed when he wrote a tell-all book about Europe's finest kitchens, including titillating and sordid details about what kitchen staffers really do behind the scenes, as well as stories about private encounters he'd had with celebrities. Although the book became the first of many bestsellers, our tattletale chef became persona non grata in top kitchens."

"Where discretion is paramount," added Daphne.

"Right. Back in the United States, Slick opened up his own restaurants and continued his book career. His reputation for being a randy womanizer became synonymous with his name."

"What about Ambrosia Curry?" asked Daphne.

"Originally from New Jersey, she was a burlesque dancer at the Crazy Horse cabaret in Paris when someone at the Chow Network 'discovered' her. After she got her own TV series, people criticized her, saying she was a dancer who didn't know how to cook, and that her published recipes couldn't possibly be her own. She's considered a relatively 'private' person."

Of course, I knew why. Clementine.

I sighed.

Might as well spill the beans, I thought. "By the way, did either of you know that Ambrosia smuggled her toddler daughter into the big house?"

"What?" gasped Daphne. "What daughter?"

"Daughter?" asked Pep.

I told my sisters what I knew about Clementine.

"Well, that poor child," said Daphne. "All alone like that! I'll get the kids to make a playdate. I'm shocked you could keep such a huge secret from us, Eva . . ."

"Duly noted. Thank you, Daphne, for sharing your opinion on *secrets*."

Pep smiled, shaking her head, before she accelerated as we headed out of town.

I continued. "Miriam Tidwell used to be a big-shot producer at the Chow Network until she was let go during some kind of shake-up," I said. "No one knows exactly why. Or why she later returned to the network as a lesser-ranked 'promotions guru.' She travels with the chefs and deals with the public. That's about all I've got."

"In other words, you didn't find anything definitive to indicate who might've murdered Slick," said Pep.

"Not really. My money is still on Savannah Deats. Maybe she saw Daphne with Slick and went ballistic with jealousy, then lured him into the freezer truck and killed him there. She's nuts about him."

"Makes sense," said Pep. She tooted her horn at a squirrel on the road. It raced to the side of the road as we cruised by. "Although if she's so nuts about him, could she actually kill him?"

"Pepper-Leigh, mind the speed limit, please," Daphne reminded her as we whizzed past farmhouse after farmhouse. She turned to look at me. "So you think Savannah was in Slick's motor home last night, stealing copper pots and pans?"

Glancing in the rearview mirror, Pep sped up the car again.

"I don't know. She doesn't appear to have any means of her own. That reminds me," I said. "Daph, you were in the motor home, right?"

"Yes."

"Was the copper stuff there when you were there?"

"We were so . . . distracted. I think so . . ."

Pep jerked the car around a corner, glancing in the rearview mirror again.

"Whoa, Pep!" I cried, grabbing the back of Daphne's seat. "Daph, what time did you leave the motor home?"

"Maybe close to eleven. It was later than I'd planned to stay. Still, I was in a hurry to get back to the kids." Daphne bowed her head and sniffed. She looked ready to cry again. "Poor Slick . . ."

"Have a donut, Daph," said Pep. "Eva, hand her the bag of donuts; they're on the seat next to you." I watched Pep check the rearview mirror. She let out a slow whistle.

"Daphne," I said quietly, "did you and Slick have an affair while you were married to Boomer?" I handed her the donuts.

"No! Of course not. Oh, already I miss him so . . ."

"Then why did Miriam Tidwell tell Savannah and Glen that she'd seen you with Slick?"

"I don't know." Daphne hiccupped. "Occasionally, Boomer and I went to Slick's restaurant."

"Slick's Atlanta restaurant?" I asked.

"Yes. Atlanta Simmers, it's called. But we only went a couple times."

"Huh," said Pep, again looking in the rearview mirror.

"What is it?" I asked.

"If I didn't know better, I'd say we were being followed. Know anyone in a black Honda?" She stepped on the accelerator and the PT Cruiser shot forward. I grabbed the armrest on the door.

"Pepper-Leigh! There is a speed limit!" cried Daphne.

I turned to look out the rear window. A couple of car lengths behind us a black Honda followed. I'm not real good at identifying vehicles; I've never known how folks do it. Maybe it was a Civic. Regardless, as our vehicle sped up, the Honda did as well. There was another car—silver— behind the Honda. Both cars kept up with us.

"I saw it follow us out of the parking lot," I said.

"Probably Northerners," Daphne with a sniff. "They all drive too fast."

"Daph, Eli doesn't have any real evidence against you, right?" I asked. "I mean, your elephant charm wasn't even found at the crime scene, was it?"

Pep swerved sharply around a curve.

"No . . . I mean . . . right. Correct!" said Daphne breathlessly as Pep swerved again. "They've found nothing to indicate that I was ever in the Clatterbucks' truck." She turned to look back at the Honda. "Oh, fiddle-dee-dee. They're taking pictures!"

I looked again and saw that someone was holding a huge camera lens out the Honda window, pointed at us. "Reporters." I shrugged. "So, Daph, your elephant charm was . . . where?"

"I don't know where they found it. The detective was asking questions, not giving out answers. Still, it wasn't in the Clatterbucks' truck because I was never in the truck. Hence, they've found nothing to incriminate me."

Pep accelerated again, but the Honda was closing in. Then, suddenly, another car passed the Honda. "Crikey!" cried Pep. "It's another one with a camera . . . looks like a videocam!"

"What?"

I turned to see, and sure enough, a two-door silver something or other was fast approaching. A guy had his head out the window and had his eye to a video camera.

"When are they gonna leave us alone? This is ridiculous."

"Yes. I'm tiring of this game," whined Daphne. "Eva, when we hired you for our plantation PR person, I daresay this runaway-bride-dead-body-finder-tabloid-sensation aspect of your life wasn't what we had in mind . . ."

"Hold tight, ladies," cried Pep. "I'll handle this!"

"Right. So, Daphne," I said, trying to act like everything was normal, "Detective Gibbit questioned you all day simply because he found your charm somewhere in or around Slick's motor home, and Miriam Tidwell told him that you'd had a relationship with Slick before he came here. Is that it?"

"Miriam Tidwell? She told him that I knew Slick?"

"Yes."

"How do you know that?"

"I overheard her talking with Savannah Deats and Glen Pattershaw at breakfast this morning. Then I confronted her about it."

"Oh." Daphne started sniffing, like she was about to cry.

I turned around and saw the black Honda again. It'd passed the silver something or other, which was now following the Honda.

"Pep," I said, "slow down a minute. Maybe we can see who is in the car behind us."

"Sure." Pep slammed on the brakes. We all fell forward.

"Whoa! Not like that—you'll kill us!" I spun around to look out the rear window. The Honda was almost on our rear bumper. I could see the surprised faces of both driver and passenger as they braked hard and their car screeched behind us. "Figures." I turned back around in my seat. "Our favorite rag reporter, Pat Butts, is behind the wheel alongside her sidekick with the camera, Tam See."

Pep groaned as she sped up again. "I'm getting mighty tired of those two," she said.

"You're tired?" I cried. "I'm the one they keep chasing after! I'm the one they keep showing in embarrassing photos on the front page!"

"Maybe, darlin', y'all should settle down a bit. Not be so . . . interesting," scolded Daphne.

"You think that I do stuff on purpose to get attention?" I shook my head. "And who is the interesting Knox sister this week? I'm not the one who had a relationship with a famous murdered chef and got hauled down to the sheriff's department for all-day questioning! Maybe, just maybe, this time it's *you* they're following!"

"Eva, you're the one who ended up with two dead men at her feet. Oh, make that three—"

"So, Daph, are you gonna fess up and tell us the skinny about you and the playboy chef?" interrupted Pep.

"There's nothing to tell. Slick and I met in Atlanta, shortly before Boomer and I were married. It was during a wedding shower that some of my Atlanta girlfriends gave me."

There was a giant curve in the road ahead. I glanced back to see the Honda and the silver something or other still following.

"Hold on!" cried Pep.

Suddenly Pep yanked the wheel hard to the right. The PT Cruiser swerved, then careened off the road, over the grassy shoulder, and up into the air before hurtling down a steep embankment.

"Pepper-Leigh!" screeched Daphne.

We landed on the edge of a huge cornfield.

"It's okay! No worries about the car . . . I told you, I've got a custom suspension!" Pep shouted as she accelerated and we rumbled across the field, spewing dirt everywhere. "Did we lose the Honda?"

"Yes," I moaned, holding my throbbing head in my hands.

Back on the road, the Honda, followed by the silver something or other, whizzed past.

"Okay. Keep talking. This is a shortcut."

"Oh my gosh," I said. "Pep, we're in someone's cornfield!"

Outside the roaring PT Cruiser, a tornado of dirt encircled us as we slammed across the field.

"Where was I?" asked Daphne, trying to regain her composure. The field was bumpy and Daphne's voice warbled when she spoke. "When I met Slick. The girls and I went to this restaurant in Atlanta, and Isis Buckingham was upset because her food wasn't right. The chef—it was Slick—came out and apologized, offered her a new meal, gratis, of course. He caught my eye and, well, I guess I caught his."

"That's nice," said Pep. "Can ya cut to the chase, please?" She honked at a buzzard that flew up from the dirt as we whizzed alongside tall green stalks of corn.

"Husker Pike is gonna have your ass if you wreck his cornfield," I warned Pep.

"No prob. Husker and I are good," said Pep. "I'll make it up to him at the Roadhouse. He's a regular and he likes his bourbon. Besides, I fixed his combine last week."

Daphne looked annoyed as she gripped the dashboard to steady herself. She continued her story. "After the wedding shower dinner, we all went to have cocktails at a jazz club. About an hour after we got there, Slick showed up and sat next to me at the bar. We started talking, and the rest is history." She let go of the dash to bite into a pink donut.

"That was vague," I said, rolling my eyes. "Pep, how can you see through this dirt cloud?"

Pep shrugged.

"What do you want me to say?" cried Daphne with a mouthful of donut. "That Slick and I were passionate and inseparable lovers during the months before my marriage as we professed our undying love to each other?"

"That's a start," said Pep.

"Well, fine," said Daphne, blotting frosting off her dress with a paper napkin. "That's exactly what happened."

"Yikes!" We'd slammed across a giant ditch in the field. "Daph, if you loved Slick, then why on earth did you go ahead and marry Boomer?" I looked back. There was another cloud of dirt behind us. The Honda was following. "Omigosh," I mumbled.

"Because Slick's career was on the upturn," said Daphne. "He wasn't ready to give it up for a marriage commitment. He needed more time. Y'all know that I was too old to be single anymore. I wanted children. Besides, I'd gone too far with Big Boomer to back out."

"Too old to be single . . . ?" I shook my head. Only Daphne.

"You should've taken a lesson from Eva. It's never too late to cut and run!" Pep snorted. "Right, Eva?"

"Hey!"

"Yes, well, at the time I remembered all too well Eva's running away. And all the fallout afterward," said Daphne.

"You're blaming me for your marrying the wrong guy? Pep, the Honda's catching up!"

Pep accelerated. The engine roared louder as we flew in our cloud of dirt past more cornstalks.

"Of course not, Eva, dear," said Daphne, clutching the dashboard to steady herself. She didn't sound too convincing. "Anyway, Slick and I kept in touch over the years, just a phone call here and there. And of course, whenever I could, I visited his restaurant in Atlanta after it opened. Boomer never realized that Slick and I knew each other."

"And you never had an affair with Slick after you were married?"

Pep started the windshield wipers to clear the dirt off the windshield. They only made it worse.

"No. Although I admit, there were times when I wanted to," said Daphne. "When Boomer was on the road, I'd hear stories about him with other women. I tried not to believe it, of course. Then Slick called one day and asked me to meet him at the restaurant. It wasn't unusual. We'd met for lunch a few times before, when he'd meet me at the restaurant kitchen door and we'd share a little meal together between the lunch and dinner rushes. Just catching up on old times—you know. Anyway, that's when he broke the news to me that Boomer had been bringing a young woman to the restaurant and they'd been quite cozy together. Slick told me he was sorry, but he thought I'd want to know. And he promised to let me know the next time they were in the restaurant."

"Ahh," said Pep. "And he did. Right?"

"Yes. They were cozying up in a private room together when I walked in on them."

Behind us, the Honda was falling away.

"And the rest, the divorce, as they say, was history . . ."

"Daphne, the press never mentioned any of that," I said.

"I didn't want anyone to know. For the children's sake. And of course, Boomer didn't want the public to know because he was afraid it would diminish his popularity and cut into his lucrative sponsorships. Of course, I realized that if his income went down, then whatever he'd end up paying me would be less than it could've been. Our marriage was over, and I knew it. Getting Boomer to pay up big-time was much more satisfying than having him crash and burn publicly. In the end, he paid me handsomely to keep what I knew to myself. He still is."

"But then, where does Miriam Tidwell fit into all this, Daphne?"

"I'm not sure. I suppose she might've seen me with Slick during some of our lunches together. But I never had an affair with him while I was married. Or even while I was legally separated. I was a devoted wife to Big Boomer."

"Even so, given Slick's reputation, Miriam Tidwell probably assumed the worst," said Pep.

"Well, in a way," I said, "she was right. Slick was way more attached to Daphne than all the other women he'd been with physically . . . Oh, sorry, Daph."

"It's alright." Daphne sighed. "Difficult as it's been, I've accepted who Slick was. I suppose, after my divorce, it's why I decided to come back home instead of seeking him out. We were star-crossed from the beginning. He understood that."

"Except he sought you out!" cried Pep.

"Yes. Unfortunately, he did," Daphne said with a groan.

"So, Daph, I still don't understand why Detective Gibbit thinks you could've killed Slick," I said. "Why does he think you would've done such a thing?"

"Other than Eli's intense dislike for me since grade school, I really don't know, other than I did make nookie with Slick . . . not long before he passed away." Daphne looked upset, fidgeting with her donut shop napkin. "Maybe I was the last person to see him alive . . ."

"And an obvious suspect," added Pep.

"Want another donut?" I asked.

"No, thank you. I'll be sick as it is," said Daphne.

"Make nookie!" exclaimed Pep, pretending to bang her head on the steering wheel.

I shook my head.

"Well, almost nookie," said Daphne. "We were rushed for time when he saw his watch and said he had to go. Said he'd be back in a few minutes. I was supposed to wait. I told him I'd return in the morning after breakfast instead. That was the last we spoke . . ."

"What was so important that he had to leave the love of his life?"

"I don't know." Daphne's voice got small. "He said it was important. Something about the copper. And, well, when I looked at my own watch and realized how late it was, and I thought about the kids and all, the moment was kind of lost. When I headed home, he was still in the motor home. Maybe if I'd waited . . ."

Pep accelerated and the engine roared again. Looking out the window, I couldn't imagine where she was headed. We'd been in a field that went on for miles. But it was coming to an end.

"We were just star-crossed—" Daphne's voice sounded puny.

"Hold on!" shouted Pep, jamming her foot down on the accelerator pedal.

The PT Cruiser roared like a fire engine, headed straight for a high bank on the edge of the field. Daphne started screaming. I held my hands to my ears as the car sped forward, then tilted upward, and we were suddenly airborne . . .

CHAPTER 33

We catapulted out of the cornfield and hit the main road crosswise. The PT Cruiser slammed onto the pavement in a cloud of dust.

"Now we're talking!" yelled Pep. "Woo-hoo!"

Pep threw the car in reverse and spun around, heading us toward home.

"Oh my Lord," exclaimed Daphne. "I think I'm going to puke!"

"I'll never get into another car as long as I live," I said, gasping.

I turned to watch as the Honda approached the same high bank in the field, following us. In a cloud of dust, the little car shot about halfway up the bank, before it suddenly fell to the left and skidded back down into the field. I watched as the doors flew open and the two reporters scrambled out. Pat Butts kicked the side of the Honda.

We were racing down the road when all of a sudden Pep slammed on the brakes. Then she turned sharply into the gravel lot at Carter's Country Corner Store.

"He's here!" Pep said breathlessly, skidding to a stop.

"What in the world . . . ?" Daphne muttered. She looked as pale as a ghost.

"Frankie Runkle! Suspect number four. He's here! I recognize his truck. It's the black Ford, over there. C'mon, who's goin' inside with me?" asked Pep. She shut off the engine.

Housed in an old general store built shortly after the Civil War, Carter's Country Corner Store was an Abundance institution. Open from six in the morning until eleven at night, seven days each week, with sundries, a deli, and a grill, it was the place where one could find just about any imaginable candy or prepackaged, preserved snack food. Plus, it was the local hangout for hunters, farmers, and geezers who gossiped, played cards, and hid out from their women for hours at a time. It was dark and dirty and smelled rank inside. Men loved the place. A neon sign in the big window next to the door flashed LOTTERY.

"Most assuredly not I," insisted Daphne. "I've never been inside that revolting man cave and I'm not about to start today. It's full of nothing but nastiness and riffraff. Not to mention unhealthy junk food, lite beer, fish bait, tobacco, knives, and ammunition. Why, this is where hunters bring dead animals to be tagged!"

"And buy their toilet paper," I added.

"Y'all go on. I shall not go inside anyplace with license plates tacked to the walls. I would, however, be most grateful for a bottled water." She handed Pep a twenty-dollar bill.

"Okay, c'mon, Eva," said Pep.

Thanking my lucky stars not to have been killed during the ride so far, I was happy to climb out of the souped-up jalopy. I started across the parking lot with Pep. Even in the evening, waves of heat wafted up from the hot gravel as we passed a skinny young guy in a cowboy hat unloading piles of newspapers from a van marked ABUNDANCE COUNTY RECORD. He gave us a smile and waved. I recognized him as the tall teen with the goofy laugh from the cook-off. Pep and I waved back.

"Pep," I whispered, "don't you wonder how Daphne knows about the license plates on the walls if she's never been inside?"

Pep snorted a laugh. We were about ten steps from the store's covered-porch entry.

BANG!

A bearded man dressed in overalls crashed through the picture window. Shards of glass rained around us as the man soared through the air and landed at our feet. His cap, with a chicken logo on it, flew off his head and fwapped into my leg.

Pep and I looked at each other, stunned.

"Jeepers, sis," Pep finally said. "Remind me not to go out with you again! First the near-fatal falling pot, then a crazy car chase, now a human cannon ball—you could get a person killed!"

I was too stunned to say a word. All I could do was close my mouth, which had dropped open in surprise. Pep looked down at the red-faced farmer. He moaned. Then he belched.

"Frankie Runkle? That you?" Pep asked.

I looked back to the car, where Daphne, seated in the front seat with a frozen, horrified look, was holding her hands to her forehead. Suddenly, the newspaper teen whipped out a camera, and before I could move away, he'd run up and snapped a photo of me standing over Frankie amid all the shards of glass.

"Thanks!" he said, with a big salute. *Hee-haw. Hee-haw.* "This photo could be the big break I've been waiting for!"

Ironic, after Pep's crazy escape across the cornfield from Pat Butts and Tam See—which had been completely unnecessary because they knew where we lived and where we were headed—we'd run right into this kid with a camera, who'd caught me in yet another "newsworthy" moment.

I give up.

"Sure thing," I said to the kid with a wave. "Happy to help."

I looked at Pep and rolled my eyes.

"C'mon, Frankie, get up," said Pep, grabbing Frankie's arm. He reeked of alcohol.

The door to Carter's Country Corner Store jerked open, and the gal who worked behind the counter, Junie Mae, a husky young woman who was normally all smiles, stepped outside and wagged her finger.

"Frankie! I've gone and called your mama to come take you home. You're lucky I ain't callin' the sheriff. You go and sober up. After that, don't you ever come back to where I work, or come to my house again. You hear me? Like I said the other night, we're finished!"

She turned and went inside. The door slammed shut.

"Frankie, let's go sit over there." Pep pointed him toward a rocking chair on the big covered porch.

"I'm going to find out what happened," I said to Pep.

"I got this," she said, looking at Frankie, who, despite his drunkenness and flight through the glass window, appeared to be just fine. She handed me Daphne's twenty-dollar bill.

A bell jangled as I pulled open the shop door and stepped onto the dirty wide-pine floor. Junie Mae was talking to two thickset farmhands studying the window. The bell jangled again as the newspaper kid came in behind me. He whistled at the shattered window.

"Hey, lady," he said to me, "can I have your name? For the photo caption? This could be my big break, gettin' me outta the delivery van and into the newsroom."

"You want to be a reporter?"

He nodded.

"Then figure it out for yourself," I said.

The kid frowned before he shook his head and began reloading the box dispensing newspapers near the door.

"Thanks, guys," Junie Mae was saying to the farmhands as I hurried to a cooler in the back of the store and grabbed a bottle of water for Daphne. "Like I said, I really appreciate y'all tryin' to help out. Since Frankie and me split up, he's been a real pain in my butt. He's even been stalking me."

"We're real sorry about the window," said the first farmer.

"Ol' Cletus Carter's gonna have a hissy fit 'bout this when he sees his store window blown apart," said the second man, scratching his head.

"When Frankie rushed us, I just stepped aside," said the first guy.

"Me, too," said the second.

"I never imagined he'd just keep going!" The first guy shook his head.

"It's not all y'all's fault, really," said Junie Mae. "Maybe now Frankie will be scared enough to stop coming back to my house in the middle of the night. Y'all know it? He showed up after midnight Saturday night! Excuse me, I gotta call Old Man Carter now. He's gonna crap in his pants when he sees the front of his store."

I stepped up to the counter.

The bell jangled as the newspaper teen left the store.

"Junie Mae, what time Saturday night did Frankie come to your place?"

"I dunno, maybe about midnight. Or maybe later. He sat outside in his truck and spied on me all night. Why?"

I handed her the twenty.

"I thought that he might have passed me on the road. Guess not. The timing is wrong. Thanks."

"Um, okay. Sorry about the mess here. Careful not to step on the glass—if y'all can help it. The grill is closed but I'd sure be glad to ring something else up for y'all."

"No, thanks. Just the water. You've got your hands full. We'll come back another time."

"Sure thing, hon. Thanks for stoppin' by. Here's your change."

I grabbed Daphne's change and headed out. As I started to pull open the door, the newspapers in the box next to the door caught my eye. I stopped and peered into the newspaper dispenser, reading the headline of the next day's paper: "Chow Network Chef Knoxed Dead!"

Of course.

The front-page article went on to tell the story of Master Chef Slick Simmer's untimely death—the third death and second murder at Knox Plantation this summer.

"So much for my PR. Daphne's gonna have a cow."

I slammed the door and walked outside past Frankie,

who was sitting in a rocking chair on the store porch rubbing his head. I went over to Pep, who was waiting by the car.

"Frankie was busy stalking Junie Mae Saturday night," I said, jerking open the door to the backseat.

"So . . . ?" began Pep.

"So, we can cross suspect number four off our list."

I tossed Daphne her change.

CHAPTER 34

Later that night I was dreaming about copper pots and pans. Dolly was sitting in a copper saucepot, flying across my cottage room. Round and round she went, yipping happily as her ears flapped behind her. I was in my own copper pot, racing behind Dolly and trying to catch up.

A doorbell rang and the postmaster from the village arrived in his own copper pot. He delivered a box. The box sprang open and another copper pot flew out. Then another box arrived and another pot flew out. Then another. And another. Soon, boxes and copper pots and pans filled my little cottage. There was barely enough room as Dolly and I raced around, zigging and zagging to avoid all the pots and pans.

Below us, people seated in bleachers cheered. I saw Daphne, Pep, and Precious, all clapping and hollering for me to hurry. Dolly zoomed by as she lapped me in her saucepot.

Copper pots and pans carrying people flew toward me from the opposite direction. I careened left, missing Glen Pattershaw screaming by in a big roasting pan. I zigged to the right to avoid Ambrosia Curry on a crepe pan. She blew me a kiss as she whizzed past my ear. Miriam Tidwell zipped to my left, straddling a small lid, wagging her finger at me and laughing as the crowd below cheered. Then Frankie Runkle called out, "Don't talk about Ambrosia that way!" and he raced up in front of me. I pulled up sharply and spun to the right, narrowly avoiding a collision.

People in copper cookware careened toward me faster and faster. Dolly raced past again, barking. I swerved, barely missing a giant stockpot jammed with Sissy and Peaches Clatterbuck, who shouted, "We're gonna kill you!" as they swooshed by. The Clatterbucks, shaking their fists, were to my right as Dolly passed me on my left. Robin Harden, with a pretty green ribbon in her hair, headed right for me in a big copper saucier. There was no room, no time to get out of anyone's way.

Suddenly, the scene changed.

Blinding headlights aimed right at me as a dark vehicle hurtled down a dark, shoulderless road. I was running as fast as I could to get out of the way . . . but I wasn't fast enough. Just as the vehicle caught up with me, there was an earsplitting bang as we crashed through a big glass window and I flew—

Someone was screaming. My eyes jerked open. My heart pounded fast inside my chest as, in a sweat and panting, I shot up from the bed.

CHAPTER 35

"Eva?" It was Ian's voice. "Are ye alright?"

"Wha . . . What's happening? Where am I?"

I tried to slow my breathing. I thought that I was in my cottage, but it was dark, and the dream still swirled in my head. And Ian was there. Was I still dreaming? I was confused.

"It's just a dream, hen."

That's when I felt his long fingers slowly and deliberately brushing my damp hair from my face.

"Yer hot, Eva."

Ian bent close to me. I could smell his earthy, woodsy cologne. As the moon peeked from behind a cloud outside, moonlight filtered through the lacy curtain and fell onto Ian's handsome face. His eyes were the deepest, darkest green, and they twinkled in the moonlight. He was so close . . .

Dolly whimpered. That's when I saw her, cradled in Ian's arm.

I leaned back into my pillows. Yes. They were my pillows,

I thought. I was in was my own bed. I was at home, in my cottage.

"I don't understand. Ian, what are you doing here? It . . . it's late, isn't it?"

There was a dull ache in the back of my head, leftover from my crash at the motor home.

Time for another ibuprofen.

"Aye, it is. I was out riding in the woods when I ran into your little beastie here." He nodded to Dolly. "When I couldn't find ye out in the woods, I came to check if ye were home safe." He put Dolly on the floor. "I'm sorry if I frightened ye. I was out on the stoop when I heard ye screaming. I ran in—"

"Screaming? Omigosh. I'm so sorry . . . It . . . it must've been a nightmare." Sitting in my bed, in the dark, late at night, I was suddenly terribly self-conscious with Ian there.

"Yer alright now. Can I get ye something? A glass of water?"

"No, really, I'm fine. Thank you for bringing Dolly home. I'm sorry she was out loose. She does that sometimes."

I was sure that I looked like a fright. What was I wearing?

"Ye don't have to tell me. I know."

I looked down. I was wearing my I HAVE THE HOTS . . . FOR COLD PRESSED OIL tee shirt. If I'd felt better, I might've laughed out of mortification.

"Are ye sure yer alright?"

"Yes, yes. I'm fine. I'm just . . . a bit chagrined . . . here in my sweaty tee . . ."

"Aye, as Precious would say, yer a bit of a hot mess, hen." Ian chuckled as he tucked a strand of my hair behind my ear. "Never mind it, then. Yer fine. And yer shirt's just lovely."

"Right." I shook my head.

Ian chuckled again. "Bursting into yer place unannounced like I did, it could've gone way worse, ye know. Ye could've been sleeping in the skuddy." He winked.

"In the what?" Ian started to answer. I gave him a sideways look and held my hand up. "No. No. Don't answer that!"

Ian laughed. It was a big laugh. I'd never seen Ian laugh like that before.

"There ye go. I see yer getting yer old saucy self back now," he said with a grin.

There was a noise outside. Ian turned his head to listen a moment. Then he leaned closer.

His masculine scent—musk, leather, earthy oakmoss, and woodsy green vetiver—was like a drug whirling around me. I took a breath and inhaled as much Ian as I could . . .

"I gotta go now, Eva," he whispered. "Kyrie's waiting on me."

"Kyrie? She's . . . outside?"

Kyrie, short for Valkyrie, was Ian's majestic chestnut mare.

Wait! Ian rode his horse to my cottage in the middle of the night?

That's right, I thought. Weird as it was, I knew Ian rode his horse at night, often chasing down poachers in the woods. And who knows, maybe, just for kicks . . .

"Can I see her?" I started to get out of bed.

"Naw. Eva, ye need to get some rest, darling. And I need to get back to Greatwoods. Miss Precious'll discover I'm missing and she'll call out the cavalry."

Placing his hands on my shoulders, Ian gently positioned me back onto my pillow. Then he leaned in closer with a hug, pressing his unshaven face against mine for a moment.

And then another.

The scratchy feel of his young beard, the sweet, seductive scent of his skin, his hair, and something leather . . . It was all intoxicating. Slowly, Ian turned his face toward mine and pressed his warm lips to my cheek. Then he pulled away.

"I'll be off now. Get to sleep, Eva," he whispered.

Standing, he strode to the non-screen door, quietly pulling it open. The moonlight disappeared, leaving my room in darkness. From outside, I heard Kyrie blow her master a greeting.

"And, Eva . . ."

"Yes?" I answered hoarsely, hand to my cheek.

"Please don't tell anyone that I was here tonight."

I nodded in the darkness.

"That includes Precious."

CHAPTER 36

Of course, the moment Ian stepped out of my cottage door, I threw off my tousled sheet and hustled to watch him leave. Except when I stood, my head throbbed terribly and I had to stop for a moment as I became dizzy and lost my balance. In the moments it took me to pull myself together and get to the door, already Ian and his mighty chestnut mare had disappeared. I hurried outside; still, there wasn't a trace of Ian Collier or his horse anywhere. The moon popped in and out from behind the clouds as peepers sang their raucous songs in the trees.

I sat down on the stoop for a few minutes, daydreaming about my mysterious and oh-so-seductive neighbor.

He had my attention.

Dolly stepped through the non-screen door and sat next to me. Behind us, inside the cottage, the black Victorian clock on the mantel struck twelve times.

"Crap."

I stood up and went inside with Dolly.

The cottage ceiling fan whooshed quietly overhead as

Dolly yawned. I opened my nightstand drawer, grabbed a doggie biscuit, and tossed it to her.

"There ya go."

I figured she'd head to her bed. Instead, with the biscuit in her mouth, Dolly waddled to the screen door and stepped through the torn screen I'd still not fixed, wagging her tail on her way to the yard.

"I give up. Don't go far, Dolly," I warned.

Turning on the antique cranberry glass lantern hanging over the dining table, I shuffled to the bathroom. I rinsed my face, neck, and arms before swapping my sweaty top for a fresh black racer-back tee—my hot, sleepless nights caused me to change more times at night than I did during the day. After that, I fussed absently around the cottage, trying to memorize each moment of Ian's strange, intoxicating visit. The way he'd felt. Smelled. The look in his green eyes . . .

My aching head interfered with my reverie, so I turned the overhead light off. Then I sat and tried to remember Ian. Only this time, all I could think about was my weird dream. *What was I supposed to glean?* The vehicle chasing me was an obvious reference to Sunday night's incident on the road home, I thought. But what about the copper? Where was it all going?

Filtering through the lace window curtain, moonlight made lacy shadows on the floor.

I got up and poured myself a glass of water, grabbed a bowl from the cupboard, and filled it with Precious's freshly made olive oil and rosemary potato chips. *And why had Robin Harden been in my dream?* There was some connection to the copper, no doubt. *What was it?* The window over the sink was open. Dolly barked in the yard.

"No, Dolly," I called quietly. "Hush." At least she was staying in the yard this time, I thought.

Obviously paying no attention to me, Dolly barked again as she went running off. I put the chips on the dining table next to my little notepad and went outside to the yard, calling softly after Dolly. It was no use. She'd disappeared.

"She'll come back," I said to myself aloud. "She always does."

Or Ian will just have to bring her back home again, I thought, smiling.

I went back inside and grabbed an ibuprofen, downing it with some water before sitting down at the table. Chomping on the chips, I thought about getting up and turning the light back on to study my notes, but just thinking about any sort of light made my head ache even more. So I closed my eyes and thought about my list of murder suspects: Savannah Deats. Glen Pattershaw. Ambrosia Curry. Frankie Runkle. I crossed Frankie's name off my imaginary list. Emmylou Twitty. Sissy and Peaches Clatterbuck. Miriam Tidwell. I still couldn't shake my dream. Why had Robin Harden been in my dream?

Was my subconscious trying to tell me something?

I thought for a moment.

Robin had told me that she'd brought the restaurant copper to the cook-off for Slick. Farm manager Burl said that after the cook-off, he'd helped Robin pack the borrowed copper to take back to the restaurant at about five thirty. That had been before he'd packed up Slick's copper, ostensibly to go back to the motor home. According to Palatable Pecan waitress Wendee, all the restaurant copper had been returned to the restaurant after the cook-off. Had Robin seen Slick when she picked up the pots and pans? Was that at five thirty? Maybe . . . she'd come back? No, why would she? Still, according to Daphne, something was going down with Slick and the copper, after she'd been with him . . . around eleven or so. Did he go to the Clatterbucks' truck then? Still, that would've been hours after Robin might've seen him at five thirty.

Then I remembered that when she'd invited us to dinner, Robin had said how she was looking forward to seeing us all at the restaurant the next night. Only she hadn't been at the restaurant at all that night. Later, Wendee'd said Robin had been out sick. Then Monday night, Robin wasn't at her regular jujitsu class, and Lark told everyone that Robin was on a planned vacation. So which was it? Vacation or sick?

Or neither?

Where was Robin?

Twenty minutes later, sitting in the dark with my empty snack bowl, I was no closer to understanding my dream than I was to solving Slick's murder. If Robin had been involved, what motive could she have possibly had? And when, if ever, had she seen Slick?

I couldn't come up with a motive or a time. Still, something didn't feel right.

Finally, I got up and turned on the light. I went back to the table, grabbed a pen, flipped open my little notepad, and crossed off Frankie's name. Then, reluctantly, I scribbled *Robin Harden* at the bottom of my list. I snapped the notepad shut. I was too tired to think about it any more.

I switched off the overhead light again before crossing to the back of the room, where I plopped into my comfy armchair and put my feet up on the ottoman. I closed my eyes and tried to forget my aches and pains.

And I started daydreaming about Ian.

CHAPTER 37

Someone was creeping around outside with a flashlight. It was almost one in the morning. I'd been waiting for Dolly to come back home when I spotted the light and made out a figure dressed in black standing near the big house porch. Without turning on a light, I jumped into my black skort, slipped on a pair of flip-flops, quietly opened my non-screen door, and stepped outside, gently releasing the screen door against the doorframe so it wouldn't bang.

I snuck undetected about halfway across the lawn, when suddenly a light hit me square in the face.

"Who's there?" I cried out, putting up my hands, shielding my eyes from the glare.

"Shhh! It's me."

"Omigosh." I shook my head—big mistake; it still ached like crazy—and hurried across the yard, heading straight for the light coming from Daphne's garden, below the big house porch. "What are you doing here in the middle of the night?"

"Funny, I seem to recall asking you the same question last night, Babydoll." Buck flicked off his flashlight. That's when I saw Dolly sitting at his feet, wagging her tail. "And I never got a satisfactory answer."

"Dolly!" I cried. "What is it with you two?"

Dolly never moved. She just whimpered me a greeting.

"Shhh!"

"So," I whispered. "Again, what are you doing here, Buck? It's not exactly calling hours."

"I do my best work at night."

"Funny, that's what I said to Debi Dicer yesterday. Although I was talking about her, not you."

Buck raised an eyebrow. "I see you two are still ruffling each other's feathers."

"Something like that."

Buck chuckled.

"Honestly, I don't see what you see in her." Flashes of Buck kissing me popped into my head. I liked it. It made me all gooey inside. Then I thought of him with Debi and it made me mad. I tried to push the kiss memory aside. I decided to think about Ian instead.

My man moratorium was not looking too promising.

"My relationship with Debi is not at all what you might think," Buck said.

Whatever that means.

"No doubt."

He reached for my arm.

I pulled away. "No."

"No?"

"No. Don't touch me."

"Why not? Don't you like it when I touch you? I do."

"I don't like complications. And you—and Debi—are a mountain of complications."

"And you're not . . . complicated?"

"I just might be. That's even more reason to keep you at arm's length."

"I see. So last night in the backseat was . . ."

"Last night. That's all. A moment of weakness. Nostalgia. Guilt. Confusion. It's over now."

"Ahh. Thanks for letting me know, Babydoll."

Even in the dark I could see Buck's soft smile. I was pretty sure he didn't buy any of what I'd said. I wasn't sure I did, either. Still, I was trying. I didn't know what Buck was up to, but he was definitely up to something when it came to Debi. And I knew my psyche couldn't handle another duplicitous relationship. Buck confused me. I needed to stay away from him.

"So," I said, "I figure you're either here stalking me or working on Slick's murder. And since you really don't seem like the stalker type to me, I'm gonna guess you're working the case, even at this ridiculous hour."

"Good deduction."

"So, what've you got? You owe me that much. You scared me half to death out here."

Buck thought for a moment. "I'll share if you will."

"What if I don't have anything to share?"

"Babydoll, you never come clean. You've always got something hidden up your sleeve. Deal?"

"Fine."

"Okay. I'm here because it's quiet, no one is around to get in my way, and really because I want to see what it was like when everything happened here late at night—the Saturday night homicide in the Clatterbucks' truck, the missing copper, and even your Sunday night mishap."

"Mishap?"

"For now, for lack of a better term, mishap at the motor home. Maybe it was an assault. Maybe a burglary in progress. Maybe just an accident. Maybe something else."

"Mishap at the Motor Home. Sounds like a cozy mystery," I said sarcastically. "And none of it happened anywhere near where we're standing now. It all happened at the warehouse. So, you're here outside the big house now because . . . ?" I raised my arms and shrugged.

"Because of this." Buck snapped on his flashlight and pointed it at some tracks in the ground.

"What's that?"

"Bicycle tracks. They come and go, but I've pretty much been able to follow them all the way from the woods near the motor home to right over there." He pointed to a patch of dirt near the porch.

"So? Guests use our bicycles all the time. That's what they're for."

"Yes. Except I've found several sets of tracks that lead directly from this spot near the porch to the woods near the motor home. Then there's a set of footprints from the woods to the motor home and back to the woods. That's how the second set of bicycle tracks was discovered."

"Second set?"

Buck nodded. "The first set leads from the bicycle rack directly to the motor home and back. It took a while longer to find the second set. Actually, I found it and followed it just tonight." He pointed the flashlight around the dirt spot next to the porch, studying the area.

"In other words, your crackerjack detective, Eli Gibbit, and his team of goons missed it."

Buck wagged a finger at me teasingly. "In other words, the take-off spot in the woods was outside the perimeter of our initial investigation."

"Right." I rolled my eyes. "Wait! I saw Savannah Deats riding the three-wheeler after breakfast—"

"Yes. I know. She already explained away another set of tracks I found earlier from here to her van."

"And I remember something else! Somewhere out here, I remember seeing boxes." I spun around, looking. "There!"

Buck flashed his light on a packed area of dirt near the bushes at the corner of the big house.

"You mean over here?"

"That looks about right. And there was another box outside of the motor home. I saw it there before I fell."

"Are you sure?"

"Absolutely."

"Babydoll, there was no box at the motor home that night. I'd have seen it when I got there."

"It was there. I remember!"

Buck waited.

"Someone must've taken it before you got there," I said.

"Maybe Savannah? I saw it just before I started to open the motor home door. Wait! There's more. I saw a bunch of the same kind of boxes in the post office addressed to Glen Pattershaw in Pennsylvania."

Buck shook his head. "Always something up your sleeve. And you saw these boxes . . ."

"When I brought Daddy's olive trees to the post office to be mailed earlier today . . . I mean yesterday. Monday! Burl Lee took me. The postmaster was wrapping up a big pile of boxes behind the counter. I couldn't help but notice . . . Do you think they could've been the boxes that were here?"

"Could be. I'll get someone on it."

"So you're helping with our Slick investigation? That's good."

"*Our* Slick investigation? You mean there are more of you?"

"Daphne, Pep, and Precious, of course. You don't expect us to leave it to Eli Gibbit, do you?"

"Of course." Buck shook his head. "Abundance's own Mod Squad." He clicked off his flashlight. "Listen, Babydoll. Far be it from me to tell you how to go about your business, but have you ever thought about leaving the murder business to the professionals? You lucked out last time. But in the process, your meddling almost got you killed."

"Lucked out? That was great investigating! I wasn't 'meddling.' Don't insult my intelligence."

Buck raised his hand in protest. "I may sound like I'm kidding here, but I'm very serious, Eva. This is not some make-believe mystery story with a built-in happy ending."

"Look, I just helped you tonight, didn't I?"

"Maybe."

"Come on. Give me some credit here. Eli is not headed anywhere in the right direction."

"And you know that because . . . ?"

"You and I both know that all your detective cares about is getting a quick conviction. He doesn't care who actually commits a crime or why. And he hates Daphne. As much as or more than he despises you! Even if he can't get a conviction, he's happy to mortify her with an arrest."

"So, then, Miss Detective, who do you think killed the chef?"

"Up until now, I thought it was Savannah Deats. But after seeing this"—I motioned to the tire tracks—"and thinking about the boxes, I'm not so sure. Glen Pattershaw? The point is, there are plenty of people who could have killed the guy, and for good reason. Daphne isn't one of them."

"For example?"

I ran down my suspect list.

"Well, you are quite the investigator. I should've taken notes."

"No worries. I've got notes."

"Care to share?"

"Sure. If it'll help get Daphne off the hook. Wait here."

I hurried over to the cottage, flung the door open, and grabbed my notepad. When I got back to Buck, he was speaking softly on his phone. Traitor Dolly was curled up at his feet, snoring.

"Hey, here you go," I said, holding out my notepad.

"Alright. I'll see you later," he said on the phone before ending the call. He ran his big hand through his short-cropped hair and shook his head. He looked tense.

"Debi?" I asked sarcastically. "I told you once before, she's got a tracking device on your SUV. She'll make a dandy wife. You'll see. Talk about a ball and chain." I rolled my eyes.

Buck burst out laughing. "Babydoll, I told you not to worry about Debi," he said. "Trust me."

"I'm not worried. And I don't trust you. Still, it's all fine. She—you—are none of my business," I said curtly.

"I see."

"Here," I said, shoving the notepad into his hand. "Will I ever get this back?"

"I'll read through it, make copies of anything I need, and you'll have it back by end of day tomorrow."

"Okay. Great."

"Provided," he warned, "that you promise to stop nosing

around. You could actually do more damage to a legitimate investigation than good."

"Right. But there is no legitimate investigation as long as Eli Gibbit is running it."

"Please, Eva. Stay out of this. We'll get it right. I promise."

I sighed.

Hands on my shoulders, Buck bent down, putting his face up to mine. His dark eyes flickered. "Eva, I hate to say it, but you're a magnet for disaster. Always. And you're putting yourself in danger . . . again. Please stop."

CHAPTER 38

Tuesday evening, I was scheduled to lead the Abundance Ladies Club in an olive oil tasting party at the big house—and I'd been dreading it for weeks. Normally, it would be fine. Even fun. But not this time. Not this group.

The ladies club president was none other than Buck's mother, Tammy Fae Tanner. She was sure to be there, along with the treasurer, the lovely Debi Dicer. And of course, secretary Emmylou Twitty would be in attendance as well, in all her sweetness, no doubt. Could it get any better? Yes. Of course it could. Why, it just wouldn't be a party without membership chairwoman Pooty Chitty. Not to mention the thirty or so other members who'd spent the last few months gossiping about me and my "scandalous" return home from the Great White North. Secretly, I knew that they all loved me . . . after all, how boring would their lives be without me?

Bless their hearts.

Plus, Miriam Tidwell, Ambrosia Curry, Clementine, and Glen Pattershaw were still staying upstairs at the big house, while Savannah Deats remained holed up in her decrepit van over by the warehouse. With his investigation slowly under way, Detective Gibbit had not "released" any of our guests to leave the county. And Daphne couldn't leave town, either.

I'd spent Tuesday morning planning my tasting presentation. It was midafternoon when my non-screen door flew open.

"Fiddle-dee-dee, Eva. I thought you'd be long gone by now!" Daphne bustled in, wearing a pretty powdery pink chiffon dress.

"Gone? Me? Where to?"

"Why, to the Pickenpackers' herbary, of course. Remember? I asked y'all yesterday to pick up some lavender."

"No, you didn't."

"Of course I did. I need more for tonight's gift bags."

"Daph, I'd remember something like that," I said, closing my laptop.

"Yes, I distinctly remember the conversation!"

"No, Daphne. I'm quite sure. We did not have that conversation."

"Yes! Ohhhh . . ." And with that, Daphne flew across the room, threw herself down on the settee, and burst into tears. "I'm sorry, I must've gotten confused! So much has been goin' wrong these past few days that I can't seem to keep it all straight. Oh, why? Why-yeeeee?" She buried her head in her hands, sobbing.

I crossed over to the sofa and sat down next to her. "Daph, has something else happened? What can I do to help?"

"I'll be alright." She sniffed. "It's just that right now, everything . . . everything seems to be falling apart!" She sobbed again. "We had three more calls this morning—people canceling their reservations."

"I'm sorry. I know that's not good." I handed the drama queen a tissue.

"I can't blame them, really," she said, wiping her nose. "No one wants to come stay at a place where people are gettin' bumped off, as Pepper-Leigh says. We've just got to figure out what happened to poor Slick. Who could've done such a thing to him? Oh . . . poor, poor Slick!" She broke down into sobs again. "I'll never see him again!"

I patted her arm before reaching back to a shelf and grabbing a box of tissues. "Here," I said.

Daphne snatched the box, pulled out a tissue, and honked her nose. Dolly looked up and woofed.

"Dolly, shhh!"

Dolly woofed again and trotted out the non-screen door.

"I'm sure this will all be solved soon," I said.

"Not with Eli on the case!" Daphne wailed. "He's not fit for the job, thinking I lured Slick here to kill him. Why, it's positively insane."

"I'm so sorry. Eli will get it right. He just needs time."

"No." Daphne sobbed. "My friend Janie called from Atlanta to tell me Eli'd sent some deputy up to her place—all the way up there! She said the man was askin' all sorts of questions about me and Slick."

"Seriously?"

Daphne nodded before grabbing another tissue and honking her nose.

"If Big Boomer gets wind of this, he'll take the children from me. Everything I've done, leavin' Atlanta, comin' back here, startin' this business from home so that I could be with the children . . . it's all been for them. The children. If I lose my children because my hospitality business brought crazy killers to our home, then I'll just die!" She was heaving and sobbing again.

"Daph," I said, giving her a hug, "I gave Buck my notes about our murder suspects last night. Everything I know. He promised that he'd go over them. Maybe he can make some headway in the case. At least, he might find something to get Eli to lay off the idea that you had anything to do with this."

"Buck? Last night? Oh, please, Eva, please don't tell me y'all are back together! What next?" she wailed, throwing her hands into the air. Then she mumbled into her tissue, "I thought he and Debi Dicer were about to be married. That's what everyone says."

I ignored her question. I had enough on my mind and was just trying to get through the ladies club day. And I was so confused about my feelings for Buck—not to mention

Ian—that I'd really tried hard to keep both of them out of my mind until after the tasting. And I'd done a pretty good job of ignoring it all that day, until Daphne started.

"Ohhhh!" she wailed. "How can I go on this way?"

Really, I needed to talk Daphne down. She needed to be in control during the ladies club event.

"Daph, I have an idea. Since the chefs, Miriam Tidwell, and Savannah are all still here, maybe I can poke around a bit more this evening after they come back from the swamp tour. I'll ask them some questions. I've got a few theories. And I want to ask Lark some questions, too. About Robin."

"Lark? Robin? What on earth for?" Daphne looked up and blew her nose. She looked terrible . . . all red and blotchy. Her fair skin did not respond well to blubbering.

"Robin hasn't been around since Slick died. And I think she might know something."

"What on earth could Robin possibly know?"

"I'm not sure. But apparently, she's left town suddenly."

"Lark said Robin was traveling. Remember?"

"Yes, I remember. But Wendee the waitress said Robin hadn't been to work because she was sick."

"That is odd," said Daphne slowly. "Y'all don't honestly believe that Robin, dear, darling Robin, could have anything to do with this? Lark has raised her daughter to be a fine, upstanding young woman. A woman of culture. Why, Robin has breeding!"

"I don't know what to think. Still, I'd like to talk to Robin, and she hasn't been around when she should have been."

CHAPTER 39

When I was very young, my mother hosted parties. From upstairs in my room, I'd listen to the murmur of women's voices as they chatted in the big house parlor and porch beneath me—like a wave, the chatter would roll in, loud and excited, then ebb and die back, quiet for a while before the next animated wave of voices and high-pitched laughter. There'd be clinking glassware, clattering plates and silverware, and footsteps shuffling across the wooden floor. And as the night wore on and the liquor flowed, the waves of giddy laughter would grow louder and louder.

As I sat in my cottage that evening, again I heard that series of festive voices and noises drifting across the yard. I looked at the clock. Seven fifty-five. The business portion of the Abundance Ladies Club meeting would be over soon.

And there it was. The knock on my screen door.

"Miss Eva, your big sis sent me to get you," Precious called from the stoop. "Time for the tasting. Good luck, Sunshine. I gotta head back to Greatwoods. Oh, here's a paper for ya that I picked up in the market today. Looks like you're still a bona fide celebrity." She opened the screen door and tossed a *Southern Celebrity Probe* supermarket tabloid on my dresser. "Don't take it personal, Sunshine. Nothin' more than junk-food news."

"Uh-oh." I closed my laptop and got up to see the rag paper.

"You always say that any publicity is good publicity, right? Oooh, looks like it might rain soon! Gotta run!"

I was at the door as Precious waved and started across the lawn, picking her way over the grass in her spiky shoes. It was dusk. Storm clouds looked inky black as a gusty wind upturned the leaves in the trees.

"Bye!"

I picked up the newspaper. The front page headline read "Knox-ing 'Em Dead Again!" There wasn't much of a story, just the facts about the Clatterbuck and Simmer deaths and how I'd been involved with each and how there was an ongoing investigation regarding the famous chef's murder. Other than the headline, the main focus on the front page was a stock photo of Slick Simmer, another of Big Bubba Clatterbuck, and the photo of me, bloodied, scratched, oiled, and grass stained, sitting on the ground after I'd fallen during the cook-off. The caption read "Another Knox Down!"

"Crap on that."

At the bottom of the page, there was another story, continued on the inside of the paper, about the successful charity weekend and a "mysterious benefactor" who had donated fifty thousand dollars to the Abundance Farm Family Fare charity.

Ian.

I tossed the paper down on the bed. I didn't have time to read any more. And it definitely wasn't time to start daydreaming about Ian. The good news was that whoever wrote the article focused on me, not Daphne. So my sister wasn't in any danger of losing her kids . . . not yet, anyway.

I checked myself in the mirror. Daphne'd insisted that I borrow one of her dresses: a creamy-colored Prada cotton poplin sundress in an oversized cobalt blue and olive green tropical floral print. There was a gathered skirt with slash pockets and a fitted sleeveless top featuring a metal zipper up the front. I spun around in front of the mirror. Daphne's dress was a little tight in the bust, but otherwise, the fit was pretty good. I chose a pair of big lapis and sterling silver dangly earrings to go with the dress, along with some silver bangles. I slipped into my black Cole Haan thongs. Daphne'd brought me a pair of creamy Ferragamo sling-backs to wear. *Too fancy.* I left them on the bed.

I tossed Dolly a biscuit and gave her a pat and kiss on the head.

"Stay inside, Dolly. It's too hot in here to close the front door."

I don't even know why I'd said it; she'd blow through the non-screen door the moment I stepped into the big house— I was sure of it.

As the darkness crawled across the sky and peepers began their nightly serenade, a stormy breeze kicked up, swishing the leaves in the trees and flattening the flowers. I hustled across the yard.

When I hurried up the big house porch stairs, two by two, the ladies club members were gathered in the parlor, still babbling noisily. I stopped short when I saw Pep on the front wraparound porch.

"Pep! What are you doing here?"

Wearing a black apron patterned with little silver skull-and-crossbones motifs all over it, Pep stood at attention behind a long table covered with a white cloth displaying pitchers of sweet tea, iced water with lemons, and dozens of liquor bottles and mixers.

"I'm bartending, hon. Whatchya think I'm doin'?"

"I thought that Daphne hired someone from Dixie Shindigs to tend bar tonight. What about the Roadhouse? Don't you have to work?"

"I took the night off," she said with a little smile. "Wouldn't miss this party for anything."

"Right." I looked at her sideways. "Is Pooty Chitty here?"

"I imagine so," Pep said all too vaguely. "No worries. I'm prepared. She's a red-wine gal. I was sure to bring along her favorite." Pep held up a bottle of Chianti. "It's actually not bad. Darlin', you just do your thing with the tasting and

I'll do mine. I'm only here to serve." She winked. "You look nice tonight in your sundress. Something of Daphne's?"

"Thanks. Yes. She insisted I wear it. All I had was black." I sighed. "I refused to wear the sling-backs and pearls, though."

"Good call," Pep said, laughing. "Seriously, hon, the big silver danglies and the bangle look hot. Don't know about the sandals, though." We both looked down at my Cole Haan thongs. "Given the crowd inside, I think we need to get you a pair of boots like mine."

I burst out laughing. "Combat boots! How perfect!" I slapped Pep on the shoulder as she snorted in little giggles.

I stepped through the front door and inside the parlor, where forty or more women—ostensibly the social elite of Abundance County—were seated at round tables covered in white linen with pretty wildflower centerpieces in blue mason jars. We'd piled most of the parlor furniture in the kitchen and out on the big wraparound porch for the night.

Near the center of the room sat a group of six women, known collectively as "the B6." The clique included Marilyn Monroe look-alike Bubbles Bolender from jujitsu class; lawyer's wife Cat Blankenblatt, a tall, slender woman of Cherokee descent with exotic features, short dark hair, and a manly voice; white-haired beanpole Asta Bodean—rich and cold, from peanut money, she always wore white pants and caftans and had served on the board of every charity, foundation, and key business in the county; blonde, bug-eyed cosmetic surgery junkie Bunny Bixby—divorced from a Georgia Lottery executive, she was obscenely wealthy and owned a winery; timber heiress Bernice Burnside, who reminded me of Raymond Burr—tough, single, and cutthroat in business, she'd served in the Georgia House of Representatives for more than twenty years, and her nephew Tommy ran the tee shirt place in town; and buxom redhead Beula Beauregard—married to a railroad man, she was always seen and heard serving several philanthropic organizations across the state and had amassed a fortune marrying and divorcing rich and powerful men.

Of course, like every other woman in the county, Daphne aspired to be a part of the mighty B6 group, and given that her surname, Bouvier, began with the requisite first letter "B," she'd campaigned tirelessly for an expanded group to be called "the B7."

So far, no luck. Still, I knew this event meant the world to Daphne. It needed to go off without a hitch.

No one seemed to notice as I stepped into the room and made my way over to the mantel, where a narrow table was set up with bottles of olive oil, tasting cups, and score sheets. I heard ladies club president Tammy Fae Tanner's distinctive, low drawl and treasurer Debi Dicer's catty laugh. I looked up to find them seated right before me, front and center, along with the rest of the club's executive committee members: Daphne's friend and vice president Pickles Kibler—elegant and wealthy, the toffee-skinned descendent of Andrew Jackson and one of his slaves owned the art gallery in town with her husband, Kip; secretary Emmylou Twitty, looking just as miserable as always; membership chairwoman Pooty Chitty, wearing a very low-cut, satiny white blouse; and event and projects chairwoman Violetta Merganthal, a round, giggly woman who always wore purple.

At a far table near the kitchen, Daphne sat with her best friend and the twins' mother, tall, brown-haired Earlene Azalea Greene. Also at her table was Palatable Pecan owner Lark Harden; good-natured family friend and poultry farmer Alice Spencer; Daphne's book club friend who worked in adult protective services, Sadie Truewater; and Louisiana Heenehan, a lifelong farmer who'd recently written and self-published scandalous erotica under the pen name Kitty Kipple.

There were other women, a few of whom I knew, including school principal Belle Reede, and Angel Pride, creator of the bestselling Heavenly Bun hair accessory. There were fifteen or twenty more women whom I didn't know. As Daphne had said, every woman who was anyone in Abundance was there.

Someone rang a bell—honestly, I think it was a Swiss cowbell—and kept ringing it until eventually the yakking women quieted down. Tammy Fae stood up and cleared her throat.

"Ladies, please welcome Miss Eva Knox. She's here today"—her voice brightened to extreme fake cheerfulness as she continued—"all the way from New England, to teach us something about tasting olive oils." She spoke as if she were addressing a room full of kindergartners. And as if I hadn't grown up in Abundance.

The ladies clapped politely with their fingers.

"Miss Eva, why don't *y'all* begin. We're just *dyin'* to hear what you have to say, aren't we, ladies?"

There were some giggles and titters, and the ladies nodded and smiled as Tammy Fae took her seat.

"Good evening," I began. "Thank you all for coming. My sisters, Daphne and Pep, and I are delighted to share some of the family olive oils with you."

Smile, Eva.

Dead silence. I heard crickets from outside. Daphne, sitting between Lark Harden and Alice Spencer with her hands folded in her lap, smiled politely. From the doorway, Pep gave me a grin and a thumbs-up.

"This evening, we're going to be tasting three different extra virgin olive oil varieties, Arbequina and Arbosana, originally from Spain, and the Koroneiki variety, which is originally from Greece. We grow each of these varieties right here on the plantation."

More dead silence. A few polite smiles. A few titters.

"You'll find that at each of your place settings there are three small cups filled with a small amount of olive oil."

The women looked down at the little plastic salsa cups filled with oil. They said nothing.

Yup, there go the crickets.

"Also, you've each been provided with a goblet of water—it's purposely just room temperature with no ice. In addition, you'll find slices of green apple, to help clear your palate between tasting the different oil varieties."

Debi reached out and bit into an apple slice, right then

and there. The room was so quiet, everyone heard the *cru-unch*. She winked at me and smirked as she chewed.

"And next to your napkins," I continued, trying to ignore Debi as she reached for another slice, "there's a tasting scorecard and pen."

Finally, people murmured as they picked up the cards and took stock of what was in front of them.

"Now, before we begin, I'd like to explain the moniker 'extra virgin.'" I held my fingers up, making quote signs with them when I said "extra virgin."

"When it comes to this topic, Miss Eva is a lost ball in high weeds," joked Debi Dicer. The women all giggled.

I pressed on.

"When discussing olive oil," I said, "anything labeled 'extra virgin' should have no sensory defects. And just to be clear, all unflavored Knox Plantation oils are 'extra virgin.'"

"Good thing the oil doesn't take after the women," drawled Debi Dicer with a catty laugh.

Everyone laughed. I saw Daphne blush. Pep, standing in the doorway, made a face and shook her head before she caught my eye and gave me a wink and another thumbs-up.

Tammy Fae Tanner raised her hand.

"Regarding 'undesirable,' since you're such an expert in these things, can you give a specific example of what we should be looking for?" she asked with a smug look.

Titters.

"It's a great question. An indication that oil has gone bad might be that it smells like cucumber, meaning the oil is old and has been stored too long. Or if it has a ripe banana smell, it would indicate that it is spoiled, perhaps due to too much heat or sun exposure." I looked directly at Debi. "Too much exposure is always bad."

"Oh, I love banana smell!" said Pooty Chitty suddenly.

"Not in olive oil," I said.

"Once something's old and gone bad," cried Tammy Fae, "it just ain't worth havin' anymore." She looked at me and smirked. "Right, hon?"

Debi snarked, "When things go bad, I get rid of 'em, right quick."

She spun around in her chair, addressing the group. "Why, just last month, I stumbled upon something really old. Goodness knows, it'd probably been hidden away for eighteen years or more! Of course, I didn't even have to bother with it to know that it was . . . What is it that you said, Miss Eva?"

"Undesirable," said Tammy Fae with a smirk.

"Yes! That's exactly it. Undesirable. And y'all know how old goods spoil with age," said Debi. The ladies all laughed.

"It's true, Debi," I said, still smiling, ignoring her sassy double entendres. "Bitterness increases with age. And I'm afraid no marketing in the world can ever sell a spoiled product like that." I raised my eyebrows and smiled.

I heard Pep snort from the porch doorway. The ladies giggled and chatted.

"Okay, so, flavor in oil is determined by the olive variety and by the fruit's ripeness at harvest," I said. "An unripe olive flavor might be described as 'grassy,' whereas a ripe olive might be described as 'buttery.' Also, like wine, growing conditions—weather, climate, soil—play a role in flavor, as well as overall crop maintenance, how the fruit is harvested and handled, as well as the milling process.

"We'll first determine whether or not our oils have any sensory defects. After that, we'll describe the specific smell and taste characteristics of each."

Debi gave Tammy Fae a smug look. Tammy Fae smirked back. It was like a silent fist pump between two fourth-grade bullies. I pressed on.

"Let's take the Arbequina oil on the left. Ladies, please, if you would hold the cup with one hand and cover most of it with your other hand while swirling to release the aroma."

They all picked up their individual cups and began swirling and whispering to one another.

"That's right. Keep swirling for a bit, as you would during a wine tasting. Now, uncover your hand and inhale the aroma. Sniff for no more than a few seconds, wait for another few seconds, before sniffing again. Do this three to four times. Be careful not to sniff too much for too long at a time or you'll overload your senses."

There was a general flurry of activity as the ladies raised their plastic cups and started swirling and sniffing.

"Try to determine whether there are undesirable aromas. Does it smell of old peanut butter? Wax crayons? If so, your oil is rancid. On the other hand, if it is what we call fusty— the result of olives being stored too long before milling—it might smell like old gym clothes, sweaty socks, or decomposing fruit."

The ladies laughed and babbled about that one.

"If your oil is musty from olives being stored in humid conditions, it'll remind you of mold or mushrooms. And muddy sediment will make your oil smell like baby diapers, manure, or even sewage. A winey or vinegary oil will remind you of nail polish or solvent."

"Baby diapers!" cried Violetta Merganthal. "Lord, no!"

Everyone laughed. They were all chatting now.

"Ladies, if you look at your scorecards, you'll find a full list of defect aromas."

For several minutes, the ladies continued swirling and sniffing, chatting and checking out their scorecard descriptions. They seemed to be having a good time.

"Circle the description that best matches what you smell. If you find nothing to circle, and I certainly hope this is what you've determined with our Knox family oils, then the oil is good. If you find any of the defect characteristics listed on your scorecards, then the oil is not 'extra virgin.'"

"And we need to tell my daddy!" exclaimed Daphne.

The ladies had a good laugh and then busied themselves as they looked at their scorecards. I was happy that no one seemed to have any more snarky comments for me. Perhaps the worst was finally over.

"Now we'll move on to describe aroma."

I instructed them to swirl and sniff again, rating the intensity of the oil between zero and ten.

"Olive oil aromas are often described as basically 'green' or 'ripe,'" I said. And within each category I named specific aromas: grassy, tomato leaf, banana, pear, and butter, among others.

I waited while the ladies sniffed and noted aromas. It seemed Debi didn't write anything down on her scorecard before checking first with Tammy Fae. I was surprised. I thought Debi had more balls than that.

After a few minutes, I announced, "Once you've marked your aroma characteristics, we'll move on to taste. Is everyone ready?"

"Ready!" they called out.

"Here comes the fun part. I want you to slurp the oil, much like you would during a wine tasting, by sipping a small amount of oil in your mouth while sucking in some air. You want to cover your tongue, teeth, and palate with the oil, and you will make noise! After slurping, just swallow. And notice how it feels and tastes from beginning to end.

"And before you begin, you might want to consult your scorecard to help you determine what you're looking for. You'll want to first decide whether or not your oil is basically sweet or bitter. These are the two basic tastes in olive oil."

Imagine a roomful of women sucking and slurping oil all at once. Seeing Tammy Fae and Debi with their heads together, slurping and rolling their eyes as they conferred . . . they looked positively sinister. And Emmylou Twitty, with her already pinched-up face, looked like a miserable rodent of some kind with its head caught in a vise, trying to get a drink. Of course, Pooty Chitty was the noisiest and most proficient of all. There were all sorts of giggles and guffaws as the ladies slurped and chatted. I even caught Daphne smiling.

The women went on smelling, tasting, and rating all three oils as they listened to my instructions and tried to determine the pungency, mouthfeel, balance, freshness, and style of each of the olive oils. Finally, more than an hour later, I concluded the tasting by confirming the general characteristics of each of the three oils the women had rated.

"Ladies, when you're finished, we've paired some wine and snacks for you out on the porch. Or if you'd prefer, there are cocktails and iced tea. And before you leave tonight, there is a gift bag with a bottle of Knox Liquid Gold Extra Virgin Olive Oil for each of you on the table near the door. Please don't forget to take one with you before you leave!"

There was a clap of thunder outside. At the same moment, the women applauded—it actually sounded genuine and enthusiastic this time. About the time I reached the front door, Tammy Fae was announcing that Beula Beauregard would be heading a new fund-raiser to help the Clatterbuck family and she needed volunteers to manage the event.

Every woman raised her hand to help.

CHAPTER 40

The big house porch was jam-packed with chattering women eager to get snacks and drinks at the bar. No one noticed me as I hustled across the lawn toward my cottage. They also didn't notice when someone grabbed my arm and spun me around.

"You skank!" hissed Debi Dicer.

She gripped my arm so tight, I was sure there'd be bruises. *Hey, why not? It'd just match the rest of me,* I thought.

"Let go of my arm, Debi, or I'll call the sheriff and have you arrested for assault," I said calmly.

In hindsight, it probably wasn't the most appropriate threat, but it'd just popped out.

"Oh, *y'all* would like that, wouldn't you!" Debi seethed, still holding my arm. With her other hand she flicked a strand of her bleached-blonde bob. "You're the one who should be arrested!" she snarled. "Why, you assaulted the sheriff and got away with it! Everybody in town knows it."

Clouds covered the sky and a hot, mean wind kicked up. I loved the way it made Debi's hair stand up on end. With her free hand, she snatched at the windblown strands and managed to pull only half back down. I smiled.

"Of course, most folks think your brain is about as solid as a pogo stick in quicksand," she said. "So aside from being amused, no one really cares about you." Debi smirked. "Still, you think you've got Buck wrapped around your nasty little finger, don't you? Better think again."

"What on earth are you talking about now, Debi? Oh, wait. I don't care. Now, let go."

I pushed her hand off me, turned, and started race-walking across the lawn toward my cottage. Still, Debi chased after me, flapping her arms, spitting out insults. Around us, leaves from the trees rolled and hissed in the wind.

"I know that y'all were together again last night! Know how I know? Huh?" she demanded, running along beside me.

"No, Debi. How do you know?"

I stopped and folded my hands over my chest. Obviously, Debi wasn't going away until she said what she'd come to say. So I figured that I might as well hear her out, or she'd chase me all the way into my cottage. I didn't want Debi inside—or anywhere near—my cottage.

"I heard you on the phone!" she harped. "When I was talkin' to Bucky myself."

"I'm sure you're mistaken. It wouldn't be the first time."

"Oh, don't play Doris Day with me," Debi snapped, hands on her hips. "That ol' dog won't hunt. I'm not stupid. I know exactly what y'all were up to last night. You *do* have a reputation."

"Yes, I suppose that I do. And no doubt I have you to thank for it. So, thank you. Of course, Debi, you have your own reputation as well. Down at the Roadhouse. Do you ever consider that?"

Debi stared at me, her perfectly waxed brows furrowed. Just for a moment, I saw Debi flinch. I knew I'd hit home. Then she narrowed her eyes and looked really, really angry. Her usually neat inverted bob was mussed up, and a chunk of hair fell back down over her eyes. She raked it away with the palm of her hand before the wind blew it straight up in the air again. She snatched at her hair.

"That's below the belt!" she said between clenched teeth.

"Yes. Apparently that's what you're all about, isn't it? At least that's what they say . . ."

I had turned to leave when Debi drew in close to me and grabbed my arm again. She flung me around and with her lips barely moving she said very quietly, "I'm onto you and your silly tricks. You're not finagling your way back. Bucky's mine now. Got it?"

"I got it, Debi. But did you?"

"What on earth are you talkin' about?"

"That big engagement ring you've been pining for . . . did you get it yet?" I wrenched myself free. "I've been looking for your wedding announcement in the paper. Funny. I haven't seen it . . ."

That did it. Debi spun on her heel and headed back to the big house. I'd hit a nerve. Good to know.

"Oh, Debi!" I waved. "A word of advice . . ."

Halfway across the yard, she whirled back around and glared at me.

"When you keep calling Buck, over and over again, on the phone? It only makes you look more desperate. Especially when it's after midnight. Of course, I do admire your stick-to-itiveness."

"Bless your heart," she said smoothly before turning and marching back to the party on the porch.

Well, that was fun.

Score one for me.

A gust of wind turned the leaves on the trees upside down, whipping the overhead branches in weird circles as I headed to the cottage. The weather was looking decidedly creepy. I'd check the weather app on my phone when I got inside. Then, when I was almost to the cottage, I heard something. A small voice? I stopped to listen. Nothing. Must've been the wind. I pulled open the screen door and stepped inside. Yanking the top drawer on my dresser open, I reached in and grabbed my phone.

"At least the battery's not dead."

Then I heard the noise again, coming from somewhere outside.

"Hello?" I called out. A wave of laughter echoed across the lawn from the big house as a big wind rustled the leaves in the trees.

I heard a tiny voice. I was sure of it. And I heard Dolly squeak. It was definitely coming from outside. Absently dropping my phone into my pocket, I stepped outside. The door slammed behind me. Slowly, I walked around to the back of the cottage.

"Hello?"

There was a giggle.

And then, there they were.

"Dolly! Clementine! What on earth are you doing out here? It's almost dark outside and it must be way past your bedtime, Clementine! Does your mother know where you are?"

There were several acres of lawn between my cottage and the big house. The little girl had traveled an alarmingly long way from her upstairs guest suite. She was in her little pink pajamas, sitting behind my cottage with Dolly at her side. Both of them were covered in dirt, digging holes around the perennial flowers in the cutting garden. Clementine held a green John Deere toy tractor.

"Wanna play with me?" she said, smiling. "Mommy's sleeping."

"No, sweetie, I can't play with you. We need to get you back to your mother. Right away! What's this?" I asked, picking up the tractor. "A new toy?"

"Uh-huh! The nice man gave it to me."

"Nice man? What nice man?"

"The man Mommy took me to see. He lives in a silver house on wheels!"

CHAPTER 41

Calling Ambrosia Curry a sound sleeper would be an understatement. After hustling Clementine across the lawn, into the big house, through the laundry off the kitchen, and up the back stair as the ladies partied hard downstairs, I banged on the locked door to Ambrosia's second-floor suite for a minute or more. I got no answer. Putting my ear to the door, I couldn't hear a thing. Then I got a bit paranoid, worrying that something might have happened to the celebrity chef. And I didn't want to put her little daughter in danger or have her upset.

So I brought Clementine up to the third floor, where Daphne's oldest daughter, twelve-year-old Meg, was thrilled to give Clementine a bath and read her a story. We even found some clean pajamas that belonged to Little Boomer to fit Clementine. Afterward, I rushed downstairs to the pantry—the party in the parlor and on the porch was in full swing—and I grabbed a master key, rushing back up to Ambrosia Curry's suite.

When I finally unlocked and opened the door to the suite, I was relieved to see Ambrosia Curry unharmed, sprawled out on her bed, still in her fluffy white bathrobe, with an eye mask covering her lids. Orgasmic chef? Ha! She looked anything but orgasmic.

I shook Ambrosia and called out her name several times before she finally awakened. She became frantic about Clementine before I assured her that her little girl was safe upstairs, taking a bubble bath.

"Why did you go see Slick Simmer the other night with Clementine?"

"What are you talking about?" Ambrosia asked. Wrapping her bulky bathrobe tightly around her waist, she paced the room.

"Clementine told me. You took her to see 'the man' in the 'silver house on wheels.' It doesn't take a genius to figure out who that is. Or was. You went to see Slick Simmer in his motor home."

"I don't think Clem knows what she was saying. I never took her to Slick's motor home," she said, not looking me in the eye.

"Yes, you did take her. I even saw the toy tractor Slick gave to her."

"You're mistaken."

"Miss Curry, this is not the first time you've lied to me. To everyone. Now, if I have to, I'll call the sheriff . . ."

She spun around and looked me right in the eye. "Please," she whispered. "You don't know what's at stake. Don't do this."

"I certainly do know what's at stake. My sister is being investigated for murder. My family business—our livelihood, not to mention our reputation—is at stake. And a man has been murdered. You know something about what happened. Maybe you murdered Slick Simmer yourself. Is that it? Did you murder Slick?" I crossed my arms.

"No! No. You don't know what you're saying. I would never do such a thing." She waved me off with her hand. "Please. Just let this go," she pleaded.

"How about this for a theory? Slick discovered Clementine and threatened to go to the network, or the press, and tell them about her. And you killed him in order to keep your secret. You even threatened Slick in front of everyone on the lawn during the cook-off!"

"I did? No. I didn't. Not about that. I mean . . . Oh, mercy!"

"You did kill him, didn't you?"

"No!"

"Although I can't imagine why you brought little Clementine with you . . ."

I looked at Ambrosia's ears. Did she have pierced ears? Could Ambrosia Curry have knocked me down from the motor home doorway and lost an earring?

"Stop this! Of course I didn't kill Slick! You're as crazy as they say in the tabloids!"

I couldn't see whether her ears were pierced or not.
Too much hair in the way.

"You got Slick to come with you and your daughter for ice cream in the refrigerated truck—after all, you'd made the ice cream earlier, so you knew it'd be there. You used Clementine to distract Slick and then you choked him to death."

"That's terrible!"

"And very plausible. In fact, I'm surprised that the detective hasn't thought of it yet. Maybe I should clue him in . . . You're a good liar, Miss Curry. You've been lying to everyone and getting away with it for years!"

"No! Stop. Listen to me. Please! Why would I kill my own daughter's father?"

"What?"

"You heard me, Miss Busybody. Why on earth would I kill, or even harm, the father of my child?"

"You're kidding, right?"

"No. I'm not kidding." Ambrosia stopped pacing.

"Seriously? You're telling me that Slick Simmer is Clementine's father?"

"The reason you couldn't wake me up tonight is because I took a sleeping pill after Clementine went to sleep. Or after I thought she was asleep. I'll never do that again. This whole thing . . . seeing Slick with Clementine, then having him die . . . so suddenly. It's been . . . devastating."

She ran her hand through her curls. She looked terribly distraught as tears rolled down her cheeks.

"I don't understand."

"Slick and I go way back. And a few years ago, when I was working in Paris . . ."

"At the Crazy Horse?"

"Yes. At the Crazy Horse." She grabbed some tissues from a box on the nightstand and blotted her face. Then she threw herself into a chair. "I was a dancer in the burlesque show there. Anyway, after the late-night shows, a bunch of us often went out to a restaurant nearby for a late supper and drinks. Slick worked in the kitchen at the time. And, well . . . you know, one thing led to another . . . He and I ended up in his apartment above the restaurant."

Could this be true?

It was practically the same way Daphne'd met Slick.

"And you're telling me that you got pregnant?"

"Yes. It was just before he went back to the States. He was going to star in a new TV show that Miriam Tidwell was pitching to the Chow Network. Slick said Miriam had another show and he wanted to tell Miriam all about me. He said I'd be the perfect star for it."

"Even though you'd never worked as a chef?"

"That wasn't a problem. Slick said he'd help me."

"And did he?"

"Oh yes. He was marvelously generous. He taught me to cook and shared dozens of his recipes. Many are in my first cookbook. He never claimed credit."

"If Slick Simmer is Clementine's father, then why didn't he acknowledge his own daughter?"

"He didn't know about her."

"What? Why?"

"Because he and I both had contracts that forbid it. Clem had the potential to mess up both our careers. I couldn't live with myself if I were responsible for ruining his career as well as mine. I owed him too much—for my career. And, honestly, Slick and I were good as friends. But as a couple? Not so much. We were only together that one time. That was enough . . . for both of us. And, really, everything was fine, until Clem started to grow and she needed more attention. And I needed more money to care for her."

"Then why were you threatening Slick during the cook-off?"

"Because I'd finally decided to let him know that he had a daughter. I'd told him a few weeks earlier. And he hadn't seemed to believe me. He just said that I wanted money. It'd made me a bit angry with him, so I used that for the cook-off show."

"Well, you can hardly blame a guy for not believing you. The first he heard of his child was years after her birth, when you demanded money!"

"First of all, half that stuff we said out on the lawn was all for show. People love it when we all squabble. It makes for great entertainment. Miriam taught us that. Still, keeping Clem from Slick was not the right thing to do. I know that now, and it hardly seems fair, but I really do need money—for Clem's day care—and I was hoping for some child support. I thought Slick and I might be able to work out some sort of quiet visitation. Once this contract mess was over, Clem could get to know her father." Ambrosia sighed. She looked very sad. "At least the other night he got to meet her. And he told her that he loved her. We were going to work something out."

"I'm sorry."

"Yes. I made a mess of it. Poor Clem will never know her daddy now. It's my fault."

"May I ask what time you went to see him?"

"After dusk sometime. About eight, I think."

"Isn't that awfully late for Clem?"

"Yes. Usually. But she'd slept all afternoon. And I needed to be careful no one saw us. So we had an adventure. She rode in the basket on one of those three-wheeler bikes, and I got my exercise. It was fun."

The bicycle tracks, I thought. *One set, at least.*

"Didn't you take a risk that he'd be with a woman when you got to the motor home?"

"No. He knew I was coming. We'd arranged it earlier."

"And when did you leave Slick?"

"A little before nine, I think. He hustled us out, all of a sudden. That's when I saw your sister arrive. I didn't know who it was at the time, but later I figured out she owned the big Buick."

I reached into my pocket and showed Ambrosia the earring. "Is this yours?"

"What? No. I don't have pierced ears." She wiped a tear. "Why?"

"I found it. That's all. So, if you didn't kill Slick, do you have any idea who did?"

"If it wasn't your sister, then honestly, I can't imagine." She wiped another tear. "Slick was a scoundrel. But he was a lovable one." She sniffed. "I owe him everything."

I nodded. "Did you tell the detective that you'd seen my sister in the Buick that night?"

"No. I didn't figure out who was in the car until after he'd interviewed me. I told the detective that I'd seen a Buick."

Same thing, I thought. *No wonder he's after Daphne.* "And what about Miriam Tidwell?"

"What about Miriam?"

"Do you think she could have killed Slick?"

"Miriam? Harm Slick? No way!" She shook her head. "Miriam hired Slick and me when network management wanted to spice things up. She'd gone out and found Slick, then me, then Glen. Why kill the goose that lays the golden egg? She's a tough old bat, but not a killer." Ambrosia straightened herself up. "Now, if you'll excuse me, I'm anxious to get my daughter back. Will you take me to her?"

"Yes, of course. I'll take you upstairs." We headed toward the door. "One more thing."

"Yes?"

"Clementine said Slick gave her a toy tractor. Do you know why?"

Ambrosia shook her head. "Clementine found the tractor

on a bench outside Slick's motor home. She was delighted with it. When we showed it to Slick, he said she could keep it."

"Was it his? Slick's, I mean?"

"I don't know, really. I mean, it seems like the kind of thing that a little boy would have, doesn't it?"

"Yes, it does."

CHAPTER 42

After taking Ambrosia Curry upstairs and reuniting her with her daughter—who was deliriously happy in her bubble bath—I hurried back to the second floor, where I bumped into Miriam Tidwell in the hallway.

"Excuse me, Miss Tidwell, is this yours?" I held out the diamond stud.

Miriam pushed her big glasses up her beaky nose and squinted at the stud in my hand. "Nope. It's a nice one, though. Must be two carats or more."

"Okay. Thanks." I shoved the earring back in my pocket. "Any idea who murdered Slick Simmer?"

"You don't beat around the bush, do you? I thought you Southerners were more subtle than that."

"I've been corrupted by the North."

"So I've read."

She grinned and held up a copy of the *Southern Celebrity Probe* news rag. I grimaced. Still, I wasn't letting her change the subject.

"You told Detective Gibbit that my sister Daphne lured

Slick to Abundance specifically to murder him. Why would you say something like that?"

Miriam let out a big sigh. "Your sister's been a thorn in my side for years. She had the potential to ruin Slick's career and, by connection, mine as well. And, quite frankly, I don't like her hoity-toity attitude and her sickly-sweet, stupid Southern accent. If she says 'y'all' to me one more time, I'm gonna punch her pert little nose."

"So . . . you threw Daphne under the bus because you don't like her?"

"I didn't say that. I don't even know the woman. What I said was, I didn't like her accent and her la-di-da attitude. And the fact that she distracted my celebrity from his work."

"Are you kidding?"

"Look, Slick wasn't the only one. Ambrosia, Glen, they're always getting themselves in a jam. It's my job to see that the public never finds out. Your snooty sis made my job harder."

Just then, Clementine Curry stepped out from the back stairway—until her mother's arm pulled her back and out of sight.

"Oh!" exclaimed Ambrosia from the stair.

"Aw, hell, Ambrosia," said Miriam. "You might as well cut the crap. Go get your daughter to bed."

"Hi, Birdlady!" cried out Clem happily, peeking out from behind her mother's fluffy bathrobe.

"Hi, Chickadee," called Miriam with a wave.

"Miriam!" cried Ambrosia. "You know?"

"Of course I know! Who do you think keeps an eye on Miss Chickadee here when her mommy is performing? You can't just leave a child alone like that all the time . . . in an open trunk! What if the lid were to fall shut? Or slam on top of your precious baby? Ambrosia, haven't you heard? Raising a kid takes a village." Miriam made some sort of snorting noise. I think it was a laugh.

"But . . . the contract!" sputtered Ambrosia.

"Heck with the contract. I haven't told anybody at the network about the child. And I don't plan to. Why should I?

Those bastards screwed me over. Twice! The way I see it, I owe them." She winked at Clementine. Clementine giggled.

"Uh, okay. I think." Ambrosia looked at me. I shrugged. "I need to put Clem to bed now. Miriam, can we talk in a few minutes?"

"Sure. I'm not going anywhere. At least according to the police around here." She made a face. "I can finish my reading." She held up the supermarket tabloid and leered at me.

"Alright, we'll talk later, then," said Ambrosia as she hustled Clem into the suite and closed the door.

Miriam turned to me. "For what it's worth, Slick knew all about the kid. Even put her in his will."

"What?"

"He and I used to joke that with all his shenanigans, there was bound to be at least one slipup—one kid—out there somewhere. When I discovered Ambrosia hiding her kid, and I saw how old the girl was, I figured out the timeline. Knowing Slick and Ambrosia were friends—he was the one who introduced us, you know—I guessed the kid might be Slick's. She's got those bright blue eyes of his. Ever notice? It was a dead giveaway. I figured that he knew all about her. So I mentioned something about the kid to him not too long ago. That's when I realized that it was the first he'd heard about her."

"I don't get it. If you told him about his daughter, why didn't he take responsibility?"

"Because her mother obviously didn't want him to know. And he respected that. And of course, we couldn't be sure the kid was his. Still, even without DNA or any other kind of proof that Clementine was his, he put the kid in his will right after Ambrosia contacted him and finally fessed up about Clementine."

"But Ambrosia said that when she contacted Slick about child support, he didn't believe her."

Miriam shrugged. "Maybe he wanted to give Ambrosia a little taste of her own medicine . . . keeping a kid a secret like that—it's not kosher."

"I still don't get it. If he didn't know Clementine was his for sure, then why put her in his will?"

Miriam shrugged again. "I asked him the same thing last week. He said it was just a 'feeling' he had. Pretty cosmic, don't you think?"

"That's one word for it."

"For what it's worth, that little girl may have lost a daddy, but she gained a fortune. I was the witness when he drew up his will. His estate is a whopper. And I'm trustee of the kid's trust fund. Slick finalized it just last week. See what I mean? Cosmic."

"Do you think the trust fund could have had anything to do with whatever was going on with Glen over finances?"

"Could be. Those two go back a long ways. In fact, now that you mention it, this whole money thing between them really took off after Slick realized he had a kid and started setting up the fund. You know, you could be onto something."

"And just to be clear, you didn't kill Slick?"

"Kill Slick? My Slick? Are you crazy? I loved the guy like a son. Plus, to be crass about it, he was my bread and butter." Miriam started down the hallway. Then she stopped and turned suddenly. "Look, Chow Network fired me when I was a producer because ratings for my cooking shows had gone south, as they say. Big-time. They told me that audiences didn't want to watch a chef who could actually cook. Instead, the network said people wanted a compelling 'premise.' A 'story.' Pure entertainment."

"Meaning . . ."

"No one wanted to watch a show called *Mae's Southern Cooking*. However, a show called *Beauty Queen Swamp Cuisine* would be a hit. Once I figured that out, I made a deal with the network. If I could create three great shows with entertaining, surefire premises, they promised to hire me back. After that, I came up with the idea of a roguish, womanizing chef who'd roam across the states, lambasting and wreaking havoc on restaurants and women. Slick was a slam dunk for the job.

"Then I came up with the Orgasmic Chef concept and Slick said he knew the perfect woman for the show. He even gave Ambrosia a pile of his recipes to start her off. After that, I designed a show around Slick's old college roommate, Glen Pattershaw, and called it the Crusty Baker. Suited the potty-mouthed bugger to a tee. Then after I put it all together for the network, I assumed they'd keep their word and hire me back as a producer. Except the network cheated me. They hired me as a lesser-paid PR person. Publicity people never make any money, you know."

"Tell me about it."

"Still, I managed to get a clause in my contract that assures me a share in the profits from each of my shows. So you see, the last thing in the world I'd want would be for something bad to happen to Slick."

"Yes. That makes sense."

"Besides, I loved the guy. Now, I'm tired. Anything else you wanna know?"

"I wish you hadn't thrown my sister under the bus. She loved Slick. She didn't deserve it."

"Aside from hating her accent and Southern prissiness, she was merely a means to an end. I gotta protect my people. I needed a distraction. Last thing I wanted was to have some snoopy detective uncovering the truth about a love child between Ambrosia Curry and Slick Simmer. I can't risk losing another of my chefs. I'm only telling you now because you found the kid and connected her with Ambrosia. You understand."

I was annoyed about it all. Still, she was a guest. I nodded and started down the hall.

"Hey!" she called out.

"Yes?"

"You asked me whether or not that earring was mine."

"Yes."

"You didn't ask me if I knew who it belonged to."

"Do you know?"

"Of course. It's Glen Pattershaw's. He gets a pile of those stud earrings in the mail from his fans all the time. Usually junk. The earrings are his signature. People love to think he's wearing what they send him."

"Thanks. I'll ask him about it."

CHAPTER 43

The raised volume of raucous laughter and clinking glasses downstairs meant the ladies club party was swinging along merrily. I walked to the end of the upstairs hall and knocked on the door to Glen Pattershaw's suite. He didn't answer. I knocked again and called out his name. Nothing. I pulled out the master key.

Then I paused. Quick steps hurried down the hall toward me. Here came that unmistakable jangling bracelet.

"Thank goodness I found you!" Daphne said, huffing. "I've been lookin' all over. We need ice cream."

I slipped the master key in my pocket. "What?"

"The ice cream! From the other day. Ambrosia Curry's peach bourbon ice cream from the cook-off. It's still inside the Clatterbucks' truck. Surely you of all people haven't forgotten?"

I rolled my eyes. How could I? I'd found Slick Simmer lying right next to a dozen tubs of the stuff.

"We need it ASAP!" she ordered.

"Why?"

"The ladies are havin' a wonderful time and they've

stayed longer than anticipated. We need to feed them. The ice cream will be the perfect treat to end our evening. So, I need y'all to take the Kubota and get it now. It can't wait; there's a storm headed our way."

"You're kidding, right?"

"Eva, don't be ornery. I checked with the sheriff's department and they said we can go in the truck now. I need y'all to go there and be back with the ice cream before the storm! Two or three tubs should be enough. We'll need to get all of it out before we return the truck to the Clatterbucks. Remember? That was the plan the other day before . . ."

"Before Precious and I found Slick. I know. We never got the ice cream out of the truck."

"There y'all are! I've been looking for you," cried Lark Harden, bustling down the hall. "Miss Daphne, you're all out of those delicious crab and caviar canapés!"

She was all smiles as she offered to help Daphne with any last-minute food preparations. Of course, it was all polite code for: *Guests are hungry and you need to serve food!*

"Miss Lark," said Daphne, "you're our guest tonight. We've got everything under control. Don't we, Eva?" It was a statement. Not a question.

"Surely there's something I can do to help?" Lark asked.

"No, thank you, Lark. Eva is just leaving to pick up some ice cream," said Daphne calmly.

"Wonderful! Now, Miss Daphne," Lark asked, in a mock-scolding tone, "have you taken time to check on your kids tonight? You've been busier than a honeybee in a hive."

"Oh yes! The children are all fine. In fact, I just came down from the third floor," answered Daphne with a smile.

Daphne put her arm around Lark as they headed toward the stairs. I followed.

"Speaking of kids, we've missed seeing your lovely daughter, Robin, this week. Where is she?" Daphne asked.

"Oh, Robin had a vacation planned for months. She's off to Europe again."

"Europe! Sounds divine," gushed Daphne, stepping back to allow Lark to head down the stair first.

"When did she leave?" I asked suddenly.

"What?" asked Lark. She and Daphne turned to stare at me.

"Oh, um, you mean Robin?" said Lark. She stopped short on the stair. She looked away and said, "Saturday night."

"After the cook-off?" I asked.

"Why, yes, I suppose so. She had an evening flight." Lark looked at me and smiled. "Now, are y'all sure I can't help in some way?"

"Absolutely," said Daphne. "I'll walk with you down to the parlor."

CHAPTER 44

Rumbling across the lawn in the Kubota, against violent gusts of wind and rain, I raced to the Clatterbucks' refrigerated truck to get the stupid ice cream for Daphne's party. Given that the last time I'd been inside the truck I'd discovered Slick Simmer's frozen dead body, it was about the last place I wanted to see again. And trying to beat a big storm—for ice cream, of all things—didn't make the chore any more palatable.

Ears flapping in the wind, Dolly was riding shotgun.

As we rode under live oak trees on the edge of the lawn, the moss above us fluttering wildly in the blustery wind, I couldn't get the conversation with Lark out of my head. It just wasn't right. What she'd said about Robin's trip made no sense. The closest commercial airport was nearly two hours away. And it was a smaller airport, which would've had a connecting flight to a bigger hub airport—like Atlanta—that serviced international flights. Even if Robin had left right after I'd seen her on Saturday afternoon, by the time she'd gotten to the airport, no flight would've connected so late in the evening to a bigger flight bound for Europe.

So the scenario that Lark had described couldn't have happened.

And hadn't Wendee at the Palatable Pecan told me that Robin had been the one to bring back the restaurant copper that night? How could she be in the restaurant and at the airport at the same time?

She couldn't.

Then why was Lark lying?

And where was Robin?

There was a flash of lightning and the night sky lit up cobalt blue. My phone beeped. The screen read "Buck." He was calling from some "secret" number that he'd entered himself on my phone during the last murder investigation. He'd said even Debi didn't have the number. I didn't know whether to believe it or not. I ignored it.

A minute or so later, the screen flashed "Buck" again.

Fine.

"Hello?"

"You okay? I saw a report about a tornado near your place." Buck's drawl was deep and soft.

"Tornado? No, not here. We're fine."

"Where the hell are you? What's that noise?"

"Dolly and I are riding in the Kubota."

"The Kubota? In this weather? What's going on?"

"I'm getting ice cream."

"Ice cream?"

"Daphne dispatched me to the Clatterbucks' truck . . ." There was a big clap of thunder as a neon bolt of lightning streaked across the sky.

"What's that noise?"

"Nothing. Like I was saying, Daphne dispatched me to pick up the ice cream that Ambrosia Curry made during the cook-off. It's still in the Clatterbucks' truck. I was supposed to get it the first time I was there, but of course, badness happened. It's okay for me to go in there now, isn't it?"

I was kind of hoping he'd answer "no."

"Yes. The investigators are finished there."

"Nothing scary left behind?"

"Not as far as I know."

"Daphne wants to serve ice cream to the ladies club. She's determined to impress the hell out of them. You know, because she wants to be a part of that ridiculous B6 group."

Buck laughed. "A group named after a vitamin."

"Did you learn anything about Savannah or Glen Pattershaw and the boxes?"

"I'll fill you in later when I return your notes. That's why I called."

"Aw, c'mon! I can't wait!"

"I'll be headed over to your place in about an hour."

"C'mon! Tell me what you know."

"I've got work right now."

"Please?"

Buck sighed. "Only for you, Babydoll. Okay, quickly, both Glen and Slick came from old-money families outside Philadelphia. And they were roommates at Amherst College. You know, in Massachusetts."

"I know all that. And I know where Amherst is," I said, rolling my eyes.

"Right. So when Slick's college grades bottomed out, his family stopped supporting him. After that, they never gave him another dime. Meanwhile, Glen lent Slick money from his trust fund so when Slick dropped out of college he had something to live on while he got started working in restaurants. As far as anyone can tell, Slick never paid back the loan."

"Okay, so Slick owed Glen money, right?"

"Not exactly. Years later, when Glen wanted to start his bakery chain, Slick lent *him* money. And lots of it."

"Probably from his first wife's estate."

"Exactly."

"Meaning, Slick paid back Glen's loan."

"Not exactly, because Slick lent Glen way more money than Glen had given Slick earlier."

"I'm so confused."

"Well, basically, the way I'm seeing it, Glen owes Slick a heck of a lot of money. Plus, by all accounts, Glen's DaBomb Bakery chain is in the toilet and is either going to have to shut down or he's going to have to declare bankruptcy any day now. My sources say that his finances are completely upside down."

"So, he has reason to steal fancy copper."

"Yes."

"Hey! Also, I think Slick wanted his money back because he'd created a big trust fund for his daughter."

"What daughter?"

I told Buck about Clementine and the trust.

"So, Slick Simmer was a daddy. I'm sure my detective hasn't figured that angle yet. Good work, Detective Knox. We'll look into the trust fund. You've been busy."

"Wow!" I cried, as a huge crack of light sliced the sky, followed immediately by an earsplitting snap and crack of thunder.

"I heard that!" said Buck. "Look, I'm not crazy about you riding around alone out there during a storm. There's a tornado watch . . . Wait! Aw, damn. It's a warning now. Just changed. There was a tornado over in the next county. Baby-doll, skip the ice cream and get back home!"

"Not if I want to live to see tomorrow," I said with a grimace. "Daphne was deadly serious about this. And she'll lose face with Lark Harden and the B6ers if I don't come through!"

"May I remind you about what happened the last time you took a Kubota ride at night?"

"Listen, if I don't get Daphne this ice cream, she's going to kill me, so I'm kinda dead one way or another."

"Eva, this weather is no joke! Just get yourself back to the house and wait until I get there."

I didn't answer.

"Eva!"

"Yes?"

"Are you headed home?"

"No."

I might have heard him curse.

"Are all the ladies still at the house?" he asked after a moment.

"If you mean is your sweetheart, Debi, there, the answer is yes. Along with your charming mother and everyone else."

Buck mumbled something I couldn't hear.

"So, maybe by the time you get here to arrest Glen for stealing copper—and maybe murdering Slick—we'll have the ice cream out and we can have a party." I laughed.

"By the way, when you get back, if I were you, I'd stay clear of Debi. She's been madder than a hornet about you. If I didn't know better, I'd think she was jealous." He chuckled.

"We already had our smackdown tonight."

"Babydoll—"

"She started it."

"Aw, hell, I gotta take this call—"

"Wait!" I cried. "There's something else!"

"What?"

"Something isn't adding up with the Hardens. Lark said Robin left for Europe on Saturday night, right after the cook-off. Except I think Robin took the borrowed copper back to the restaurant that night and I can't figure out how she had time to do all that and still fly out that same night. And she'd said that she'd see us all the next day and never did."

"Get to the point, Babydoll."

"Can you check and see when, or even if, Robin Harden left the country? It would've been Saturday night or Sunday."

"Yes. I gotta go—"

"Okay. Bye!" Before he could answer, I hung up.

Always leave them wanting more, I thought. It's an old trick that I learned from Daphne.

CHAPTER 45

The wind had picked up considerably. And the rain was moving sideways. Even under the Kubota roof, I was getting wet in the open vehicle. Dolly sat huddled next to me, shaking when the thunder went off—which was often. Still, I thought, I had time to get the ice cream from the truck and head back home before any super-dangerous storm activity kicked up.

Or Daphne would have my hide.

The dusk-to-dawn light at the warehouse still was not working. So once again, the gravel parking area was dark. I pulled the Kubota up to the back of the Clatterbucks' truck, left the Kubota running with the headlights on, and stepped into the rain and onto the gravel. Dolly hopped out and, for once, stuck near me. A broken piece of yellow police tape flapped in the wind off the back of the truck.

Just when I stepped up to the rear of the truck, pretending that nothing was wrong and that I was fine with returning to the scene of the crime in the dark night all by myself during a raging storm, Dolly started barking. A giant floodlight snapped on over at Savannah Deats's yellow van. It was a huge spotlight, much bigger and more powerful than the one Savannah'd had the other night. She'd been shopping.

"Who's there?" she screeched through the wind. Dolly kept barking as Savannah marched across the drive.

Man, that chick isn't afraid of anything.

"Dolly, stop!" I warned. "Savannah! It's just me," I shouted back. Her light was blinding. Dolly kept barking. "Shhh! Dolly."

"What do you want? Why are you here?" demanded Savannah. She wore a bright yellow rain slicker with a hood. "Oh God." She groaned. "I figured. It's you. And you brought that nasty barking mutt again."

Dolly jumped up on Savannah's leg, greeting the woman with wags and whimpers.

"Dolly, get down. Savannah, what do *you* want? Why are *you* here?"

Savannah's coat flapped open and I saw that she wore an oversized SLICK EATS AMERICA tee shirt. She probably slept in the shirt. Dolly, showing an uncharacteristic display of obedience, came back to my side and sat down.

"I have every right to protect myself and my property," Savannah said with a huff. A big puff of wind blew her hood back, tossing her long braid in the rain. "Especially since I'm stuck at this deadly place."

I reached up and pulled open the rear bifold door on the Clatterbucks' refrigerated truck. Dolly shot under the truck, out of the rain and wind.

"Hey! What are you doing?" cried Savannah. "That's evidence. Or is it a crime scene?"

Cool, dry air wafted from the back of the insulated truck as sheets of rain poured down outside.

"Whichever it was, it isn't anymore," I shouted, reaching up and pulling myself into the dark refrigerated box. The truck insulation muffled the noisy storm outside. I was sure there was a light switch. I just didn't know where . . . Savannah pointed her big light inside. I looked down. "Uh-oh." I'd gotten grease on Daphne's Prada sundress.

"Why are you here?" shouted Savannah.

"I'm getting ice cream."

"Oh!"

Savannah placed her ginormous lamp inside the box, lighting the truck interior. She hoisted herself up into the back of the truck, out of the rain and wind, where we stood face-to-face in the refrigerated section of the box.

"Apparently, the investigators don't need anything here anymore," I said. "So, Savannah, have you figured out that I didn't kill Slick and steal his copper?"

"I guess so," she admitted.

Outside, there was a flash of lightning and a loud boom of thunder. Thinking about Dolly, underneath the truck, I turned toward the freezer section, eager to get the ice cream and return home as quickly as possible. Savannah kept talking.

"You probably wouldn't have brought your stupid dog to steal stuff. I was kind of upset," she said. "About Slick and all."

"Yeah, well, I might be thinking the same thing about you." Savannah was so devoted to Slick, somehow, I just couldn't see her as his murderer. Over and over again, I'd tried to convince myself, and everyone else, that it'd been her. I just hadn't been able to make the idea stick. As eccentric as she seemed, my number-one suspect was the only person connected with Slick who seemed . . . genuine.

I made my way to the freezer door. "If you want a giant container of ice cream, you're welcome to it," I offered.

"Really? That'd be nice. Except I don't have anywhere to put it . . ."

"Maybe you should find yourself a place to live, Savannah. And a job?"

"I suppose . . ."

Not exactly anxious to see the inside of the freezer again, I stopped with my hand on the door. "Listen, Savannah, you were here. Please, can you tell me what really happened on Saturday night?"

"What do you mean what happened? Slick was murdered!" She grabbed the end of her braid and gnawed on it.

"I know that. But you were here. What did you see?"

"I wasn't here. And besides, why should I tell you?"

"I'm trying to help figure out what happened."

"Why?"

"Because, Savannah, my family can't afford to lose our livelihood when people don't come here or buy our products anymore after people get murdered. We didn't do anything wrong and we need people to know that. And besides, I want to know."

"Well, with your reputation and all . . ."

"Savannah, I have a rep for being a klutz and running away from men. Not murdering people!"

"But people keep ending up dead and you do keep finding them!"

"You don't need to remind me. Still, I didn't kill any of them. And, really, if you were me, wouldn't you want to know what happened . . . at any cost?"

Savannah didn't say anything. She chewed on her braid.

"C'mon, Savannah. What do you mean you weren't here Saturday night? You've been parked over here since last week, right? We owe it to Slick to find his murderer."

Savannah looked away.

"If you really cared about Slick, then help me find his killer. Do it for Slick."

Savannah sighed. "Alright. That Detective Jibet, Giblet, Gibbit . . . or whatever his stupid name is . . . seems like a jerk anyway. He came to see me yesterday and I didn't like him one bit."

"Join the club."

"He said that I killed Slick so I could be famous."

"Sounds like something he'd say," I said.

"You don't like him, either?"

"Not even close."

Savannah breathed a deep sigh, then closed her eyes.

"Okay. I'll do it for Slick."

"Good. So what happened?"

"I've been parked here," she said. "But I haven't been here the whole time. Slick sent me away Saturday night. To get something for him. And I almost think it was on purpose. You know, to get rid of me. I didn't tell the sheriff, any of the deputies, or that piece-of-work detective, though. I have to protect Slick's reputation. Even in death."

"Can you explain?"

Savannah took a deep sigh. "I don't think so."

"I promise to keep your secret. Slick's secret, if that's what it is. Please? Tell me. For Slick."

She let out a long breath.

"Alright . . . For more than a year now," she began slowly, "I've been following Slick wherever he goes. I . . . I loved him. He . . . he was my life."

"I understand."

"Well, I got to know him pretty well. And most people don't know this, but Slick has a thing for certain foods."

"Certain foods?"

"Uh-huh. Junk food. And lots of different takeout. Also Thai food."

"Okay . . ."

"Often, he'd send me out to pick up food for him so people wouldn't know that he liked junk food. That wouldn't have been good for his reputation, you know."

"I get it. A famous chef who eats junk food is not cool for business. Go on."

"Well, Saturday night, a little before seven thirty, he came over and asked me to get him an order: tom yam goong, pad Thai, khao pad, and Thai tapioca pudding. I'll never forget it."

"That's not junk food. That sounds like Thai food. Right?"

Savannah nodded.

"Except, we don't have a Thai restaurant in Abundance," I said. "Junk food we have!"

"I know that. So did Slick. And there isn't a Thai place in the next county or the one after that. The nearest Thai restaurant is more than an hour away, and that's using the highway. Round trip, it was at least a three-hour trip. But that's not all."

"No?"

"He told me he wanted a Willy's Wicked Whoopie Pie from Willy's All-night Diner."

"Where's that?"

"About twenty minutes past the Thai place. And when he asked me to get him the food, Slick knew exactly where each place was and how far it was from here. He handed me directions, money for the food and for gas, patted me on the butt, and told me to go. So I did. I always did. And later when I thought about it, I realized that he'd kind of rushed me along . . . like he wanted me to be gone."

I remembered how Daphne'd said she'd arranged to meet Slick around nine. And how Ambrosia said she and Clementine had met with Slick at about eight. That's exactly what he'd done, I thought. Sent his little pain-in-the-butt groupie away so she wouldn't interfere with his two extremely important rendezvous.

"Okay, so you left at seven thirty; that means you got back at ten-thirty or eleven, right?"

"No. My gas gauge is on the fritz and I ran out of gas on the way. So I didn't get to the Thai restaurant until way after eleven o'clock, and they'd already closed. I don't have a cell phone so I couldn't call Slick and tell him. By the time I got the Willy's Wicked Whoopie Pie and came back, it was almost one in the morning. The motor home was dark. I knocked on the door, just in case Sick was up, but he didn't answer."

"Because he was probably already dead, here."

We both turned and looked at the freezer door inside the truck.

"Oh!" Savannah put her hand to her mouth and closed her eyes.

"I'm sorry. Then what happened?" I asked.

She looked down and said quietly, "I put the Willy's Wicked Whoopie Pie in my icebox—I still have it—and I went to bed. Then I knocked a couple of times on Slick's door in the morning—I still had his money for the Thai food, you know—and there was still no answer. I figured he was mad at me."

"That must've been when Precious and I saw you walking back from his motor home. Just before we came here."

I looked at the freezer door a long while before finally pulling it open.

CHAPTER 46

As I tore across the grounds, headed back to the big house in the ice-cream-loaded Kubota, the rain slowed and there was an odd, eerie stillness about the night. It was as if we were in the center of the storm. Or on the back side of the storm's spin. Or a nearby tornado had sucked up all the air . . . All bad. Remembering Buck's tornado, I pressed my foot on the metal gas pedal and wished Dolly and I were home already.

Every so often, the sky would light up and look blue as lightning struck. Bigger flashes of light would make the sky white. And I could see all the clouds. The scariest strikes were the intense neon bolts that pierced the sky in quick, jagged stabs—sometimes just a single, fat, crooked spike. Even Dolly didn't like them. She huddled next to me, whimpering after the big booms. Of course, the thunder never really stopped rumbling.

Finally, when I steered around the corner of the big house, Dolly jumped out of the Kubota, running off across the yard toward the cottage and her non-screen door. The ladies still clamored away on the big porch, laughing and drinking. I noticed that a car that'd been parked next to the bicycles when I'd left in the Kubota earlier was missing. Since I'd seen the same vehicle for several days, I was pretty sure that it was one of the rentals belonging to the guests.

Just as I parked the Kubota next to the empty space, the big house went black.

Everything went black.

Everywhere.

"Ohhhh!" exclaimed the ladies on the porch. There was laughter and more chatter.

The power was out.

Big raindrops began pelting the Kubota as I hustled out, grabbing the first big tub of ice cream.

"Slumber party!" a woman shouted from the porch.

"Yes! Yes!" shouted others. "Let's do it, ladies!"

Then the lights came back on.

There was applause, then more laughter and merriment. I hustled through heavy rain, onto the rear porch, and through the kitchen door. I dropped the first ice-cream tub on the kitchen counter along with my phone and raced back twice more for the second and third tubs. Afterward I made my way to the front porch, hoping to find Daphne. Her soiled Prada sundress was completely drenched, sticking to my legs.

The wind was coming from the other side of the house, making the big front porch a great spot for storm watching. All the ladies were there, some standing, others draped in chaises, collapsed in chairs, and swinging in the hammock as they chatted away merrily. A mega-shot of lightning, close enough to flash yellow and red, struck the front yard as a noisy clap of thunder cracked and exploded, shaking the house.

"Oooooh!" The ladies cheered and applauded, as if they were watching a fireworks display. The bolt of lightning had struck the ground no more than fifty feet from the house.

I couldn't find Daphne anywhere. I made it to the end of the bar, where I grabbed a couple of paper napkins and began patting my face and arms dry. There was a loud cry from the other end of the bar.

"Oh, Pooty, hon, I'm so sorry!" I heard Pep exclaim. "And that was *such* a pretty blouse."

Pooty Chitty stood opposite Pep at the bar, and Pooty's bright white silk blouse, as well as Daphne's formerly pristine white linen tablecloth, were absolutely soaked in crimson red Chianti. Regardless of how Pooty responded about her ruined blouse, I was darn sure that Daphne would have a fit when she saw the red stain on her fancy tablecloth. And I was equally sure that Pep's spilling wine all over Pooty had not been a mistake.

"What the hell were you thinking?" shrieked Pooty. "This is my brand-new silk blouse! It was a gift!"

"I'm so sorry to spoil your gift," said Pep, smiling superpolitely. "At least the winey color looks lovely on you. Actually, now that I think about it, hon, it suits you better than virginal white . . ."

I tossed my paper napkin and quickly moved away from the bar.

There was another blinding bolt of light followed by a loud crack of thunder in the yard. Women squealed.

"I don't understand why you have to be so greedy!" shouted someone behind me.

"I'm not greedy," answered another voice.

I turned and saw the preacher's estranged wife, Emmylou Twitty, arguing with Angel Pride, the Heavenly Bun woman. Emmylou was in her clogs, with a long denim skirt and floral-print cotton blouse. Angel wore a bright yellow imported suit, and her long hair sat atop her head like a big bird's nest. Each woman clutched one side of a Slick Simmer cookbook, and they were tugging at it, pulling it back and forth, like two preschoolers arguing over a toy.

"You said you wanted the book!" screeched Emmylou. "So I brought it tonight, just for you!"

"You didn't tell me you wanted five hundred dollars for it! Five hundred dollars for a used cookbook! I thought we were friends." Angel huffed. "Now, give it up! I'll give you ten dollars for it."

"We are friends. You said that you wished you had a Slick

Simmer cookbook, and this is the last one that I have. I brought it here tonight, just for you!"

"It's old and used. And it's all dog-eared, with spaghetti sauce stains on the pages!"

"You can buy it from me now, or you can spend even more on eBay later. The chef is dead and he isn't coming back to autograph any more books—thank goodness!"

"Shhh, ladies! Let's be civil, please," scolded prim school principal Belle Reede. Then she tripped over herself and cursed.

I looked around for Daphne, but I couldn't find her in the buzzing crowd. I turned back to the bar just in time to see Pooty Chitty as she finished shaking a Coca-Cola can. She ripped off the tab and pointed the can at Pep. The fizzy soda squirted Pep right in the face.

Completely unfazed, Pep turned to giggly Violetta Merganthal, who was waiting with an empty glass, and said, "I'll be right with ya, hon, just as soon as I finish settin' up this gin fizz . . ." Smiling, with her eyes on Pooty, Pep reached down and grabbed a big seltzer bottle.

Yikes!

I turned away as I heard a fizzy-sounding *whoosh*, followed by Pooty's squeals. I forced myself not to look back. Instead, I scanned the crowd, trying to find Daphne. Whoops! Tammy Fae Tanner caught my eye. Raising her glass, she gave me a sneer. Someone bumped into me.

"Watch it! Oh, it's you. Again." Emmylou Twitty groaned as she backed away from me. "Don't y'all ever watch where you're going? You're the clumsiest woman ever!"

"Maybe that's why she keeps falling over dead people," said tall, skinny B6er Asta Bodean with a snort as she sauntered by with a bottled lite beer. She laughed at her own joke. I decided her stupid turban and white caftan made the willowy woman look like a Q-tip.

Emmylou still clutched her old Slick Simmer cookbook. She must've won the tussle with Angel Pride, I thought. Angel and her big bun were nowhere to be seen.

"Emmylou! Lovely bumping into you again." Inside my

head, my eyes were rolling. "I see you have another one of Slick Simmer's books. Is that one autographed, too?"

"Yes. It is. And it's five hundred dollars. Do you want to buy it?"

"I might. Can you tell me something about the book? How did you get it?"

"I bought it online. Years ago. And it's in pristine condition. Angel said she wanted it, but she's pooped out. I'll let you have it instead, if you want it. Otherwise I'll sell it on eBay, like the other one."

"Emmylou, I meant to ask you last time we bumped into each other . . . when exactly did you get Slick to autograph your books?"

"Saturday, of course."

"Both of them?

"Yes."

"But you told me when I saw you at the cook-off Saturday afternoon that you'd missed the autograph signing in the morning. Were you mistaken?"

"I don't see how that's any of your business," she snapped.

"Well, I'm thinking that if I'm about to spend five hundred dollars on a Slick Simmer autographed book, I need to have some idea of the book's history and its provenance. Autographs are so difficult to authenticate these days, you know."

"Are you calling me a liar? This is a genuine Slick Simmer cookbook, signed by Slick Simmer himself." She threw open the cover and showed me the title page, where, sure enough, not only had Slick signed the book, but he'd made it out to her.

"Wow!" I said, reading the inscription. "'To Emmylou Twitty, one hot dish! Thanks for the memories, Slick Simmer.' Are you sure that you want to sell this, Emmylou? After all, it has your name inside."

"Good riddance! That man was a pest. An animal!"

"I don't understand."

"Like I told you, Kyle and I waited for hours to meet him on Saturday."

"Ohhh!" A giant gust of wind whipped rain onto the porch and the ladies all shouted as they got drenched. Then they started laughing. Emmylou didn't seem to notice and kept talking.

"I waited until everything was over and I saw the chef at his cooking station, packin' his pots and pans. I ran back to the car and grabbed this book to get it autographed along with the brand-new book that I'd stood in line for so long to purchase. Except when I got back to where I'd last seen him, Chef Simmer and all his things were gone!"

"I see . . ."

"Well, as y'all can imagine, I was beside myself that I'd missed an opportunity again! So I asked around where he might have gone. A man who looked like a cheap imitation of Jimmy Carter gave me his last bag of peanuts and told me that the chef's motor home was parked on the other side of the plantation. So, despite the fact that it was already suppertime, Kyle and I hiked over to find the chef and beg for his autograph. I even got blisters. See?"

Emmylou pulled her foot out of her clog and held it up for me to see. I didn't look too closely. I took her word for it about the blisters. She had huge feet. Then she put her foot back down. There was a big clap of thunder. People applauded. Despite the wind and rain, the ladies around us had remained on the porch, apparently having a grand old time.

Emmylou prattled on, paying no attention to the crazy weather. "It took us nearly forty-five minutes to find him. We even ran part of the way!"

"Yes, it's a bit of a hike from here to the warehouse. I'm surprised you made it that quickly."

"And it was hardly worth it." She seethed.

"Did you find him?"

"Oh yes. He was there, alright." Emmylou tightened her lips and her eyes flashed.

"What happened to get you so upset, Emmylou?"

"At first, the chef seemed like such a gentleman. And so happy to see me. After I asked for his autograph, he suggested that I leave Kyle outside to play with his toy tractor in the yard while I joined him inside his motor home. He offered tea and promised to sign both my books."

"And did he . . . ?"

"Oh yes. He signed the books, alright! But afterward, instead of tea, he started coming on to me! It was 'quid pro quo,' he said. He just wanted me for my body. I hate men! All of them!"

As Emmylou's voice got louder, several of the women moved away. Except redheaded Raymond Burr look-alike Beula Beauregard. Holding a drink in her hand, she was moving toward us from the other side of the porch.

"What did you do next, Emmylou?"

"Why, what do you think I did? I marched outside, grabbed Kyle, and we hauled ourselves back here to the car and then home for a pot roast."

"What time was that?"

"What does it matter what time it was?"

"The more details I can get about the book—"

Emmylou threw a hand up in exasperation. "I don't know. It was around suppertime."

"Can you be more specific?"

"No."

"And you didn't kill him?"

"Kill him? Kill who? Slick Simmer? Of course not! I am a good, honest, churchgoing woman. I would never kill anyone. Even a despicable, perverted chef. Except, maybe, my poor excuse of a preacher husband . . . I'd sure like to wring his neck!"

Red-faced, Emmylou was positively shaking with anger.

"Here, Emmylou, have a drink," said Beula Beauregard as she pressed a tall, icy glass of something into Emmylou's free hand.

"I don't drink!" squealed Emmylou.

"Maybe you should, dear," answered Beula, putting her arm around Emmylou's shoulder.

"Just one more thing, Emmylou," I said quickly. "When you were inside Slick's motor home, did you see any copper pots and pans?"

"Oh yes. Chef Simmer's precious copper pots and pans," she said sarcastically. "They were everywhere. He was hanging a bunch up when I got there—"

"Thanks," I said.

"Take a sip, Emmylou. Everything will be alright," ordered Beula.

"But wait!" shouted Emmylou to me. "What about the book? Don't you want the book?"

"Maybe. I'll get back to you," I said.

"Please, take it. I don't want it! And I could use the five hundred bucks!"

"You and me both," I said to myself.

"Y'all need to come inside with me, sweetie," said Beula as she ushered Emmylou through the ladies toward the parlor door. "We'll talk."

There was another flash followed by an earsplitting roar of thunder as buckets of rain pounded the roof. A bunch of ladies swinging on the porch hammock oohed and aahed at the summer storm.

So, I thought, Daddy's farm manager, Burl, had said he packed Slick's copper pots and pans for the motor home at about five thirty on Saturday night. Emmylou had said it took forty-five minutes to walk over there, so it had to be about six thirty when they were at the motor home; Savannah had said she was there between seven and seven thirty; then Ambrosia and Clementine showed up around eight; and Daphne was there from nine until between ten thirty and eleven.

So, who came—or came back—to see Slick after that?

CHAPTER 47

The master key was burning a hole in my pocket. I still had it from when I'd used it to check on Ambrosia Curry. Also, I had the diamond stud earring in my other pocket. And there was a rental car missing from the parking area. Everyone was distracted by the storm. And I hadn't seen Glen Pattershaw all evening. I slipped out of the parlor and headed up the stairs to the second floor.

At the end of the hall, I knocked on Glen Pattershaw's suite door once more. I called his name. I knocked again. I waited. Then I slipped the master key into the lock, turned the handle, and peeked inside.

"Hello?"

Silence.

Located in the back of the house, Glen's room was the smallest of the guest rooms. It'd been Pep's room growing up—she'd liked the fact that the little corner room was the darkest in the house. In fact, to keep it that way, when we were teenagers, she'd painted the walls black. With that in mind, Daphne'd chosen a dark navy blue paint when she renovated the room for guests, sure that she'd never be able to cover Pep's "hideous" black walls. Also, Daphne had added floor-to-ceiling bookshelves along one wall and filled them with books.

I stepped inside the bookish blue room and closed the door. Now that I'd had time to think about it, I was pretty sure this had been the room from where I'd seen a light late Sunday night.

Front and center was a heavy four-poster king-sized Empire-style bed surrounded by more antique dark Empire-style tables and dressers. Glen wasn't the neatest fellow; the bed was a mess, his suitcase lay open on the floor, there was a pizza box tossed in a chair, and there were dirty clothes, chef's jackets, toques, clogs, tee shirts, towels, and old junk food packages scattered everywhere. There was even an empty donut bag from Duke's.

"Looks like there's more than one chef who likes junk food." I chuckled to myself.

Something caught my eye peeking out from under the linen bed skirt. I crossed the room and lifted the skirt to find a big cardboard box—like the others I'd seen with the postmaster. Sliding the box out from under the bed, I pulled open the flap and peeked inside. There was a large object wrapped in bubble wrap. Slowly, trying not to disturb anything, I pulled out the object. It was heavy. And I could easily see through the wrap.

It was a copper pot.

"Dang! So now we know who stole Slick's copper collection," I said to myself. "Which means—"

Heavy footsteps sounded outside the door. Quickly I jabbed the pot back in the box and kicked the box under the bed.

If Glen comes in here, what will I say?

I spun around, eyeballing the room as I heard someone fiddling with the door latch.

CHAPTER 48

Fortunately, Glen Pattershaw was a big man who moved slowly. And noisily. By the time he got himself into the bedroom suite with the door closed behind him, I was ready.

"Chef Pattershaw, I'm so sorry!" I said with the biggest, most sincere smile I could muster. Stepping from the bathroom, I held a stack of fluffy white towels in my arms. "I thought that I could slip in here and deliver these fresh towels while you were out."

I hoped that he didn't notice that my hair and sundress were totally soaked.

"Umm, sure. Okay," said the burly chef. His eyes shot nervously to the bed skirt. Then around the small guest room. Then back to me. He frowned as he snatched at his blue stud earring. It looked like a sapphire. And it was every bit as big as the diamond stud in my pocket. I thought about showing it to him, then changed my mind. Already I had a sick feeling . . .

Wearing a white tee shirt and rumpled jeans and sneakers, Glen dropped a pizza box down on the bed and tossed a big paper bag next to it. A roll of packing tape fell out. I pretended not to notice.

"I'll just set these towels in the bathroom and be out of your way," I said quickly.

Of course, the fresh towels had been in the bathroom the whole time. I was sure Glen didn't know about Daphne's obsession with fresh towels and bed linens, and most likely, he'd never known that the towels in my arms had been stashed in an oversized hassock under the bathroom window.

Quickly, I arranged the towels in the bathroom as I heard Glen moving about the bedroom. When I turned to exit the bathroom, Glen stood in the doorway, blocking my way. He smelled like a bar, smoky, with alcohol breath. And the moment he got close, I knew he'd been the person who'd knocked me down at Slick's motor home. I could just feel it. A wave of dread and uneasiness swept over me.

Outside, the wind blew hard. A branch scratched against the house.

"Looks like the storm is kicking up," I said, trying to sound casual.

The lights flickered.

"Um-hum," Glen mumbled, looking around. Then he spun around and put his hand around my wrist.

"Ow!" He'd grabbed the same wrist that Deputy Riddley had bruised. I thought I'd die . . .

"What the hell are you doing in here? Really?" he demanded.

He was a big man. No wonder I'd hit the ground so hard at the motor home when he'd run into me. And he was big enough to have easily done away with Slick Simmer, I thought.

I needed to get away.

I yanked my wrist free and wriggled around the bulky chef.

"Like I said," I stammered, making my way across the little blue bedroom, "I'm just bringing you some fresh towels. I'm afraid my sister Daphne is a stickler about linens. She was beside herself when she realized we'd not kept up this weekend. You know, with all that's happened . . ."

Moving quickly between me and the hall door, the chef said, "Next time, let me know you're coming. I don't like surprises."

The wind blew harder outside as rain spattered onto the shingled house.

"I'm sorry I disturbed you," I said, trying to step around the baker. "Now, if you'll excuse me . . ."

All I wanted to do was get out. Call Buck. Let him deal with it this time. I knew Glen had knocked me down at the motor home. No question about it. Just seeing him close up had set off all sorts of bells and whistles. And, of course, Glen knew he'd knocked me down all along. And now he'd caught me snooping in his room.

"Sit down," he said roughly. He pointed to the bed.

"No, really, I've got to run," I said, smiling. "As you can hear, we've got a full house downstairs. People are waiting for me."

The lights flickered again. I turned, headed straight toward the door. Glen grabbed both my wrists this time.

"Sit the"—he swore—"down!"

"Let go!" I cried out. With hands as big as Buck's, the baker's solid grip was unyielding.

"Don't bother yelling. No one can hear you with all that chattering downstairs. Now, I gotta talk to you, dammit!" he growled, holding my wrists even tighter.

Do something, Eva!

At once, I bent my elbows outward and clasped my hands together, making a fist. Quickly stepping in toward Glen, I jabbed my two-handed fist, punching him in the gut as hard as I could. Surprised, he swore again as he staggered backward. That's when I yanked my wrists free.

Jujitsu to the rescue.

I rushed to the door and threw it open. Then I ran down the hall and down the stairs. I'd never been so grateful to be among a group of drunken, gossiping women in my life!

Then, just as I hit the bottom stair, the power went out.

CHAPTER 49

A few minutes later, candles and hurricane lamps lit up the big house interior. Outside, gusts of hot, mad tropical air roared and rattled the doors and knocked the shutters on my family's old place, while fat lightning bolts and powerful rumbles of thunder sliced into the night. As torrents of rain pelted the house, out in the yard, spear-like leaves of tall palmetto trees swished and rolled in the cutting wind. Limbs and leaves on the ancient oaks furiously twisted and turned, helpless in the tropical storm.

Still, despite Mother Nature's brouhaha, the ladies club members remained happily gathered in the parlor and on the big front porch, camped out in the hammock, big wicker chairs, settees, and rockers, socializing and watching the storm. They were, quite literally, having a blast.

Except for Emmylou Twitty, of course. She was off somewhere bending Beula Beauregard's ear.

And although I kept a lookout, I didn't see Glen Pattershaw. He must've stayed up in his room. After all, with the weather continuing to worsen, there wasn't anywhere to go. If he'd driven through it once to bring a pizza and packing tape home, he knew how bad it was out there. I doubted he'd want to risk it again—even if he could. Surely the roads were flooding. I just needed to keep away from him and not get cornered again.

A cowbell rung out from inside the parlor, its low, melodious bellow somehow drifting through the unbridled laughter and shrill cackles of four dozen inebriated women. To be clear, not everyone was drinking alcohol. But there were enough confirmed partiers in the group to put the "social hour" up and over the top.

"Ladies! Ladies! May I have all y'all's attention, please? Ladies!"

After she repeated herself another three or four times, savagely waving and ringing the bell, finally Tammy Fae Tanner held the group's attention. Candlelight from giant hurricane lamps flickered as a warm breeze puffed through the suddenly silent house.

"We've learned from the weather service that there are reports of severe flooding and dangerous wind gusts in the area. And there's a tornado warning until eleven o'clock tonight," she announced.

Half the women groaned and the other half cheered. Tammy Fae signaled for silence.

"Since there is a travel advisory with the roads bein' flooded, trees bein' down, and power bein' out almost everywhere, we're askin' that y'all please remain here at Knox Plantation tonight until it's safe on the roads again—we'll be sure to let y'all know when that is. Probably just a couple more hours. Meanwhile, we'll keep the bar open. Our gracious hostess assured me that there are plenty of delicious snacks on the way!"

Ladies erupted into polite applause, and there were mumbles of approval. Still, most people headed back toward the bar on the porch. If bartender Pep and her husband's mistress, Pooty Chitty, had finally finished tossing and shooting beverages at each other, then all would be well, I thought. Pep was the best bartender in the county; she could easily keep this crowd satiated. Still, last I saw, she was covered in cola and aiming a seltzer bottle at Pooty . . .

I scanned the porch again for Daphne. Then, through the torrents of rain outside, I saw headlights flickering down the long drive. Who on earth would be out in this weather?

My heart skipped a beat.

It was Ian Collier's dark blue Hummer. Slowly it rolled down the gravel drive, passing the front corner of the house to park near the back, close to the kitchen door. I went onto the porch, watching, eager to see Ian. The driver's side door opened slowly. A tall man wearing a long black raincoat with a hood stepped out into the rain.

Except it wasn't Ian.

It was Ian's gangly manservant, Lurch. The lanky bloke fought the driving wind and flipped open a huge umbrella before pushing through the weather and around the vehicle to open the passenger-side door, where out stepped Precious, wearing tall, spike-heeled patent leather boots and a long, leopard-print raincoat with a red-lined hood.

By the time I'd fought through the chattering ladies in the candlelit parlor and made it back through the dining room into the kitchen, Precious was already inside with her coat off. Wearing a black catsuit with giant gold hoop earrings and tall black boots, she stood at the back door taking a box from Mister Lurch, who bolted back to the Hummer for something else.

"Precious! Why are you out in this crazy weather? And what's in the box?"

I grabbed the box as she handed it to me and placed it on the counter next to the ice-cream tubs.

"Your big sis called about fifty minutes ago to say that you had a houseful of women trapped here on account of the weather. And the twins left earlier on account of them both having migraines."

Precious made a face. I rolled my eyes.

She continued. "Your sister said that I needed to get over here quick as a bunny 'cause she knew these ladies were all hungry as bears after winter. Since I had a ton of snacks and frozen canapés stored at Greatwoods—it's what I used to do in my spare time before you needy Knox girls came along and upturned my life—I said that I could bring 'em. So I grabbed Mister Lurch, and we hustled right over with my goodies."

"I see that you didn't have time to change." I stifled a giggle, taking in the skintight catsuit.

Precious gave me a warning look.

It was all I could do not to ask her what the hell she was wearing. Except I already knew. The crazy catsuit was probably inspired by Ambrosia Curry's bodysuit a few days earlier. Precious ignored me. Even in her silly suit, she was all business as she emptied the boxes.

"It was good of Lurch to bring you," I added.

"*Mister* Lurch. And ya don't think I was gonna drive though this cuckoo weather by myself, do ya? Mister Lurch is a ninja. He can get anyone through anything." Precious clomped over to the red Lacanche, turned the knob, and lit the gas oven. "Good thing you folks got a gas oven, with the power bein' out and all. Y'all need a generator."

Precious fussed around the kitchen as Lurch brought in another box.

"Precious, I need to talk with you about our investigation. So much has happened. I think Glen—"

She interrupted me, slamming a drawer closed. "Okay, Sunshine. We'll talk. But can it wait a few minutes until we get organized here? Those women are social flesh eaters out there, and we're really under the gun. Miss Daphne wants to make a killer impression. Of course, when I put it that way, y'all already have done that!"

Precious cracked up at her own joke. Then she slapped a doily on a big tray and began arranging cold canapés on top of the doily.

"Sure. It can wait, I guess," I said.

"Good."

"Besides, I need to check on Dolly." I couldn't remember whether I'd put Dolly inside the cottage after we'd gotten back from the ice-cream run.

Lurch stepped out from the laundry room. Standing straight and tall, dressed in black slacks, a pressed white shirt, and a black tie, with a matching black vest, he smiled. And he

looked almost handsome, in a peculiar, dark sort of way. He
mumbled something to Precious, who was madly clomping
about the kitchen, taking out food, arranging it on cookie
sheets and platters, and shoving things into the oven.

"Now, careful about the refrigerator," she warned.
"There's no electricity and they ain't got generators hooked
up here yet. So only open it if you're in dire need of something. There's ice at the bar with Miss Pep. Where's the bar,
Sunshine?" She turned to me.

"On the front porch," I answered. "And these tubs of ice
cream need to be served before it melts."

Precious nodded. "I reckon so." She turned to Lurch. "Go
get 'em, tiger."

She shoved a tray with cold canapés in Lurch's hands
before he pushed open the kitchen door and ambled out.

"Poor guy. When those cats get their paws all over him,
he won't know what hit him." Precious chuckled.

Moments later, we heard cheers as Ian Collier's manservant offered snacks to the ladies.

I looked over the farmhouse sink and out the rain-soaked
window. A crack of light lit up the yard. Then came the roar
of thunder.

"I've got to close the cottage windows and doors and
check on Dolly," I said.

"You kiddin' me? Y'all are going out in this crazy-ass
weather?" asked Precious. "Miss Daphne will have a fit if
you wreck her pretty party dress." She turned to look at me.
"Oh, never mind. I see you've already done that. Tsk." She
shook her head.

"Hey! How did you know this dress is Daphne's?"

Precious rolled her eyes. "Honey, I know everything.
Take Mister Lurch's umbrella. It's over by the door. If you
don't blow away, we'll be here when y'all get back," said
Precious without looking up. She tore open an aluminum-
foil package. "Unless lightnin' sets the house afire . . . and
I wouldn't be surprised about that one bit. There were trees
down everywhere. We even passed emergency crews chain-
sawin' in the road!"

I heard a roar of giddy laughter from the parlor as I grabbed the big umbrella.

"Thanks!"

I charged out the back door, then across the porch and down the stairs into the storm. Drenched flowers in Daphne's garden were pressed flat to the ground. Leaves and sticks littered the lawn everywhere. And the very second the big black umbrella went up, a huge burst of wild wet wind nearly carried me away. I hunched down, pulling hard against the umbrella as it shot up into wicked gusts of wind.

"Sheesh! Precious wasn't kidding!"

The wind howled in a constant low-pitched roar as limbs and leaves wrenched and twisted in the gale. Sheets of rain spattered sideways. Pulling the umbrella down against the top of my skull, resisting the strong, blustery yanks, I pitched myself forward and dashed across the slippery yard, all the while tugging and fighting the umbrella to keep it—keep myself—from flying away.

Completely soaked, I figured that I'd change out of Daphne's ruined dress when I got inside the cottage. And I hoped to find Dolly safe and dry there as well. Yet as I neared my place I saw that my front door and window were closed.

What?

Since I didn't have air conditioning, I always kept the wooden front door open and used just the screen door. Or, rather, the non-screen door, as Dolly would have it. Regardless, I was sure that I'd left all the windows open earlier. Someone must've done me a favor by closing up my cottage—protecting it from the weather. *That's swell,* I thought, staggering closer to the cottage. *I just hope Dolly is safe inside.*

I landed on the stoop, closed the umbrella, and threw open the screen door. The wind snatched the door and slammed it against the front of the building. Then, keeping hold of the latch, I pushed open the big wooden door.

"Dolly?"

I didn't see Dolly anywhere—normally she'd have been right at my feet when I came in. And it took me a few moments before I realized that something was terribly wrong.

Rotten eggs.

Yes. It smelled like rotten eggs. Everywhere. My entire cottage was filled with rotten-egg smell.

"Hell no!"

I turned and bolted, leaving the umbrella behind. Except about halfway across the lawn, there was a terrible clap of thunder and a flash of light, and the ground shook and I turned my ankle, slipped, and fell face-first onto the wet grass.

"Eva!"

In the wind-smacked, pouring sheets of rain, Buck came from nowhere. Wrapping big arms around me, he easily lifted me up off the slick wet ground before charging back through howling, gale-force winds. We were headed to the big house, where all the ladies watched from the porch, cheering and laughing.

"Gas!" I shouted against the wind and rain as Buck raced with me in his arms across the lawn.

"What?" Buck shouted though the torrential rain.

A red bolt of lightning exploded into the ground near the big oak tree. Buck's body jolted as he kept running.

"My cottage . . . it's filled with gas!"

CHAPTER 50

With an earsplitting crack and a flash of crimson, a huge lightning bolt struck the far corner of the plantation lawn. Surging forward, Buck held me tight in his arms as we plunged through the raging storm. A tree branch flew by. Then another. A big one. I heard the ladies cheer from the big house porch.

"Put me down!" I yelled in Buck's ear as he carried me across the lawn. "You need to find Glen Pattershaw. He stole the copper and knocked me out! Besides, you're embarrassing me. Everyone's staring at us!"

"What?" he shouted, putting his mouth closer to my ear.

"You're em-bar-rass-ing me!"

I pointed to the people watching on the porch.

"You should be used to it by now!"

I frowned and pointed to the ground.

"Your mother and Debi are there!" I shouted as Buck set me on the soaked grass.

He took out his phone and braced against the wind and rain as he called in the gas emergency. Then he grabbed my hand and we hurtled through the shrieking storm toward the big house. Finally, we flew up the back porch stair and threw open the kitchen door. Buck didn't stop until he reached the stairway in the laundry off the kitchen.

"Stay here and wait for the crew. They're just down the road. Where's Pattershaw?"

"Hopefully, still in Pep's old room."

Soaking wet, Buck headed upstairs.

"Wait!" I cried, fishing the diamond stud earring from my pocket. "Ask Glen about this. It fell into my bra when he crashed into me at the motor home."

Buck's eyebrows went up as he returned down the stair. He couldn't hide an amused look as I handed him the earring.

"And you were going to tell me about this . . . when?" I opened my mouth to say something, but he waved me off. "Never mind." Then he turned and, still sopping wet, ran three steps at a time up the staircase.

"Cute butt," said Precious, looking up the stair. "He looks mighty hot all wet, don't he?"

We heard the dining room door swing open. We stepped into the kitchen to see Lurch standing with an empty tray. He had lipstick on his cheeks and shirt collar. Without a word, Precious marched to the counter and handed him a fresh tray of canapés before he turned and sped back into the dining room. Precious looked at me and shook her head.

"Told you the ladies would like him. Now, you!" She looked me up and down. "Sunshine, I ain't figured out whether you're the luckiest or unluckiest woman I've ever known. For sure, you're a disaster waitin' to happen." She handed me a dish towel.

"Magnet. Magnet for disaster," I mumbled, drying my face and arms with the towel. "That's what Buck says."

"No kiddin'!" Precious raised her eyebrows and smiled. "I don't suppose you brought back the umbrella."

"I'm sorry. I left it over at the cottage, waiting to be blown up with all of my earthly possessions."

"Huh?"

"I smelled gas."

"What?"

"My entire cottage is filled with gas."

"Lord have mercy," said Precious.

"There y'all are," cried Daphne, stepping through the dining room door. "Eva, I've been lookin' all over for you! Where have y'all been? And, ohhhh! What have you done to my dress? It's soaked! And . . . is that . . . grease?"

"Uh-oh," said Precious.

"And your knees . . . they're green!"

There was an earsplitting siren outside.

"Gracious, what now?" cried Daphne.

Outside, fire engines roared and rumbled down the drive. Red swirling lights lit up the rain-soaked plantation grounds. Vehicle doors slammed and men in black and yellow rain gear fought the storm, swarming around my cottage across the lawn. Daphne rushed to comfort her guests, while I stood at the big house kitchen door, watching the crew prop open my cottage door and open all the windows.

I stepped onto the back porch and greeted a fireman who explained they were responding to Buck's call, and as luck would have it, they'd been just down the road, returning to the fire station after removing a tree from the road. As he retreated to my cottage, more county vehicles carrying deputies flew up the drive, their blue lights flashing. I watched as Detective Eli Gibbit skittered through the storm to the front porch.

The Abundance Ladies Club couldn't have asked for a better show.

"Dolly!" I called out from the back porch. Where could she be? "Dolly!"

Something chirped. From the kitchen, Precious called to me, "Sunshine, is this your phone? It's been peeping."

I stepped inside. Precious handed me my phone.

"Thanks."

I had a message. Except I didn't recognize the number. So sick of all the media calls about the runaway-bride and dead-men stuff, I almost erased it. But it was local, so for once, I decided to listen.

"Hi, Eva," said a cheery female voice. "This is Wendee from the Palatable Pecan. I hope you don't mind my calling. I got your number from Tommy at Hot Pressed Tees. You asked during lunch whether there were extra copper pots or pans brought to the restaurant by mistake after the charity cook-off. Remember? I asked our sous chef while you were at the restaurant? At the time he said no. But later, after you left, he remembered that there'd been one extra saucier, and it'd belonged to Master Chef Simmer. So Robin returned it to the master chef after we closed the restaurant on Saturday. I don't know why you asked about it, but I thought it might be important, so I'm just letting you know. Hope this helps. Have a nice evening, and stay dry! Bye."

CHAPTER 51

"Here's your notepad."

I jumped as Buck slapped my little notebook down on the kitchen counter next to me. Still listening to Wendee's message, I hadn't heard him come into the room.

"You okay? I gotta catch up with Eli and Pattershaw . . ."

"Yes. So you found Glen?"

He nodded before turning to leave the room. "Eli's on it."

Dolly stood wagging her tail at his feet.

"Dolly! Where have you been?" She spun in an excited circle. "Wait!" I called to Buck. "Did you find out anything about Robin Harden leaving for Europe?"

"Three o'clock Sunday departure from Atlanta. Standby to Amsterdam," Buck said hurriedly. "Gotta go now." He strode out of the kitchen. Dolly followed him. I shook my head.

"That's not what Lark said at all," I said to Precious.

Precious raised her eyebrows.

"Lark said the trip was planned and that Robin had left on Saturday night. And I just got a message from waitress Wendee at the restaurant. She said Robin brought Slick

Simmer a copper pot after the restaurant closed on Saturday night."

"That'd be eleven o'clock," said Precious. "That's when the restaurant closes."

"So, we've finally confirmed that Lark lied. And Robin was with Slick sometime late Saturday night after the restaurant closed at eleven, returning a copper pot. And then Robin left the country on Sunday, on standby, which meant it wasn't planned at all. What does this look like to you, Precious?"

Precious shook her head.

"I don't understand. Robin is a good person."

"Sometimes good people do bad things," said Precious. "Like my cousin Dewanna, remember? She shot her husband after catchin' him and the babysitter—"

"Yeah, yeah. I remember."

CHAPTER 52

As the night storm pummeled Knox Plantation, there was
a knock at the big house kitchen door.

"Hello? Folks?"

It was the fire chief. And he was asking for me. I stepped
out on the porch.

"Your place is fine now," he said. Wearing a long yellow
slicker and big fire hat, he was totally rain soaked. "Looks
like you left the knob turned open on that old gas range."

"But I don't cook," I said, pushing a wet clump of hair
out of my eyes.

I'd been so caught up in everything that had happened
that night that I'd completely overlooked the fact that I was
still soaked to the bone. Despite the warm weather, I was
getting chilled. I crossed my arms across my chest.

"These things happen," he said gently. "Sissy!" he called
to someone behind him. "Can y'all get us a blanket over
here? Miss Knox is shivering."

"I'm fine," I said. "We've got a whole house full of blan-
kets inside."

My mind raced, trying to remember that last time I'd

even been in my kitchenette, let alone used the range. It occurred to me that during the short time I'd lived in the cottage, I'd almost never used the oven. I was a terrible cook. And over the years, I'd just stopped trying. Besides, there was always food in the big house . . .

"That mini range of yours is ancient," the chief said. "Y'all might want to consider replacing it with a newer model. Most new ranges have automatic cutoffs to prevent this kind of thing from happening. A few minutes more and the whole place could've gone up."

"No, you don't understand," I said, shivering. "I don't cook! I've never even used that oven. I didn't turn on my stove. Are you sure that's what went wrong? Could there be a leak in the line somewhere?"

"We've checked it out completely. The gas company sent a guy here, too. There's nothing wrong with the lines or connections. Maybe you bumped into the knob on the range by mistake?"

"No."

"Like I said, if it were me, I'd purchase a newer-model range. Just to be safe."

Something wasn't right, I thought. But my pondering was interrupted when someone threw a blanket over my shoulders. I turned to see big Sissy Clatterbuck, dressed in a slicker and emergency gear. She was a volunteer on the emergency crew! A radio squawked loud static, then voices. From one of the emergency vehicles, a big person lumbered quickly across the lawn.

"Chief! Chief! We gotta go!" the big person called out. I recognized the voice.

The chief waved. "Coming, Peaches!"

Peaches Clatterbuck.

The rain still poured sideways, and the crew was busy loading up their equipment in the muddy yard as the ladies on the porch cheered and offered them refreshments. The chief and Sissy, who'd draped the blanket over my shoulders, jumped off the porch and hustled against the wind and rain, joining Peaches before heading to their vehicles.

"Thank you!" I called after them, waving.

Sissy turned and waved back.

Talk about a mindblower. Although anything was possible, certainly, seeing the sisters in this context made it harder to imagine they could be murderers . . .

I wracked my brain trying to figure out how I could have turned the knob to my oven. Had I hit the knob getting a bowl of chips? The bowl had been in a cupboard near the oven . . . Still, who'd closed the windows and doors?

"Just one minute, missy," hissed a voice from behind me.

Tammy Fae Tanner stepped out from the kitchen, joining me on the back porch. The door slapped shut behind her. She held her hands on her hips. "I have somethin' to say."

A flash of lightning cracked over the house. Thunder exploded.

"What is it, Missus Tanner?" I pulled the blanket tight around me.

I wondered where Buck was. I wanted to find out what Glen had told him. Was it Glen or Robin who'd murdered Slick? After all, it was pretty clear that Glen had stolen the copper. But then, why had Robin disappeared?

Tammy Fae cleared her throat and started slowly through clenched teeth, "I watched—with everyone else on the porch—as y'all made a spectacle of yourself in the yard tryin' to seduce my son."

She had a way of speaking that made it look to anyone passing by like she was smiling; however, close up it only looked like a menacing sneer. It was an art that most of the women in Abundance had perfected.

She continued in her low, deep drawl, "As I live and breathe, makin' a scene seems to be somethin' y'all are very good at here. And when it comes to men, you, my dear, have elevated it to a high art."

"Thank you."

"Aren't you cute as pie!" Tammy Fae cried with a big grin. She patted me on the arm. "You think that your little damsel-in-distress routine, faking a fall in a thunderstorm and such similar nonsense, will lure Buck back to you."

"Exactly where are you going with this?"

"Sweetie, I'm here so we can come to an understanding. Even though Buck is a grown man, he is still my son. *My only son*. And as his mother, I'm fixin' to move heaven and earth to protect my only child from any harm or pain—two words for which you, bless your heart, are the very definition, especially when it comes to my son. So, I'm telling you now, stay away from Buck. Or else."

"*Missus* Tanner, you wouldn't be threatening me, would you?"

"Threatenin' you! Why, bless your pea-pickin' heart, of course not, sweetness! What a silly notion." She flapped her hand dismissively. "I'm just clarifyin' a point. If you can't run with the big dogs, then you may want to stay here, on all y'all's little ol' porch—just to be safe." She raised her eyebrows and tightened her mouth. "My son has a girlfriend."

"Yes. It's funny how you both need to keep telling me that . . ."

With roaring engines, sirens and lights ablaze, the fire trucks and emergency vehicles churned down the drive. I shivered under my blanket. From the kitchen, Precious pushed open the screen door a bit and reached around Tammy Fae, who didn't budge, to hand me my phone.

"Sunshine, your cell phone's cryin' for ya again."

"Thanks," I said.

Tammy Fae kept talking. "And really, darlin' Eva, I'm tickled pink you've come back home. I look forward to seein' y'all at our next jujitsu class. Maybe you and I can partner up sometime." Tammy Fae smiled wickedly before pulling open the porch door and slipping back inside the house. "I'd love to show you some of my moves."

She closed the screen door softly behind her and I heard her strut across the kitchen floor.

"Hell hath no fury like a mother scorned," said Precious from the other side of the screen door.

CHAPTER 53

I sighed, looking down at my phone. There was another message from Wendee. A text. It read, "Chef said Boss returned another Simmer stockpot taken by mistake late Saturday. Cheers! Wendee."

"Are y'all sure there isn't something I can do to help in here?" restaurant owner Lark Harden asked, stepping into the kitchen with a smile.

"Actually, Lark," I said, "may I talk with you, privately, for a minute?"

"Of course, Eva, sweetie," she said. "How can I help?"

I grabbed two kitchen chairs and dragged them into the laundry room near the back stair to speak with Lark in private. All week long, I'd been listening to mothers prattle on about how they'd do anything to protect their children. Daphne. Emmylou. Ambrosia. And now Tammy Fae. And then there was Lark. A mother with a beautiful daughter. She followed me into the laundry room, where I set an oil lamp on the washer and we sat down.

"Lark, I don't know any other way to say this. Please

understand, you've always been a close family friend and I'm sick at heart about this . . ."

"What is it, Eva, darling?"

"You're the one who killed Slick Simmer, aren't you?"

"What?" Lark's hands flew up, her eyes got big, and her face flushed. "Eva, what do you mean?"

"I've been thinking it was Robin. But it wasn't Robin at all. It was you, wasn't it?"

Lark was like family. Accusing her of killing Slick Simmer was light-years out of my comfort zone or experience. Still, she was a dear family friend, not to mention a pillar in the community, and I needed to hear her out before I ran off to Buck with my theory. Maybe—hopefully—I'd missed something and was wrong about everything. Maybe Glen Pattershaw had done it after all.

"Eva, sweetie, I don't know what you're talking about."

"Yes, I'm afraid that you do. Something happened between Robin and Slick. I know they were together because he told Daphne when he was with her earlier that night that he had to meet someone, and it had something to do with copper. And Wendee at the restaurant told me that Robin left the restaurant after work to take Slick one of his copper pots that was mistakenly mixed up with the restaurant copper—a saucier, she called it. I don't know why Robin and Slick were in the Clatterbucks' truck, but with the scoop that I saw there next to Slick, I'd guess that they were eating ice cream."

Lark looked down at the floor and said nothing. So I kept talking.

"Since she was there, and since she left town so suddenly, I'd been thinking—as incredibly difficult as it is to fathom— that it was Robin who killed Slick. Maybe it was in self-defense. After all, by everyone's accounts, Slick was kind of an animal."

Looking horrified, Lark still said nothing.

"But then, I just got this text from Wendee saying the 'Boss'—that's you, Lark—returned a stockpot to Slick late on Saturday. Robin had already returned a saucier. So that means there were two mixed-up pots, and you each returned one. First Robin, then you. Only now I'm thinking that when you brought yours back, you found Robin and Slick together . . . in the Clatterbucks' truck? Lark?"

She was sobbing.

"Oh, Lark! Please tell me I'm wrong! I'm so sorry. I know this sounds crazy!"

I got down on my knees in front of Lark and took her hands in mine. I looked up into her face. She was whimpering.

"He was her father," she whispered, tears streaming down her cheeks.

"What?"

"And I found them together."

"What . . . what are you saying?"

"Neither of them knew. I had to stop them. I . . . I just panicked. Reacted."

"Please. Lark. What do you mean . . . ?"

"I was pregnant when I married the man Robin has always believed was her father. He's the only one who knew the truth . . . all these years. He took the secret to his grave, God bless him."

"I don't understand . . ."

"Slick and I met at culinary school when we were both in our twenties in Europe. He'd lost a wife. And been divorced. He was bitter. And I was just . . . young. There'd been a wine-tasting party. And we'd ended up together. It was one night. When I found out I was pregnant, I knew my parents would kill me."

Could it be? The same story . . . again?

I waited.

"I'd just started seeing an older confirmed bachelor whom I'd met at a museum fund-raiser. We enjoyed each other's company. When he recognized my distress, he prodded. For weeks he bugged me to tell him what was wrong. Finally, I told him what happened with Slick and about my pregnancy. He offered to marry me on the spot. And much to my surprise, I accepted. It was the perfect arrangement.

I needed a father for my child and he needed someone on his arm to attend and hostess all sorts of charitable and royal events. He was such a lovely man, really . . . We were never really in love, but we grew to love each other very deeply. And he always loved Robin as if she were his own child. Well, she was, really, in every way. Oh, it doesn't really matter now, does it?"

Tears streamed down Lark's cheeks.

"Lark, I'm so sorry. Please, can you tell me what happened Saturday night?"

She sighed. "It was almost midnight. Wendee was right. I came back here late to return Slick's stockpot. I was afraid he'd leave early the next day and we'd not get it back to him in time. Chef found it after Robin had left with the saucier that our sous chef had found. It's always so busy and confusing in the kitchen during weekend nights . . ."

"Yes."

Lark wiped her eyes and took a deep breath.

"When I got to Slick's motor home, I was surprised to find Robin's car. I saw a light in the refrigerated truck, so I went there. That's where I caught them . . . Robin and Slick . . . together. They were giggling and feeding each other ice cream. He was flirting. He had his hands on her. Robin had always idolized Slick as a master chef—she had no idea he was her father, of course, so I didn't doubt that she was totally taken by him. Just like I'd been once."

She stopped and blotted her face again.

"I freaked out. His back was to me. I ran up behind him . . . and I . . . I . . . I . . ."

I knew instantly what she'd done. The jujitsu move. The one Ringo had demonstrated with me. The one he said could be so dangerous if you weren't careful.

"The neck nerve press," I said. I remembered how helpless I'd felt when Ringo had demonstrated the choke hold on me.

Lark nodded.

"All I could think about was protecting Robin. After Slick fell, I grabbed Robin and dragged her out of the truck.

I don't even remember closing the freezer door. I didn't realize Slick was dead until I heard about it later . . . on the news." Lark broke down in hysterical sobs. "Oh my God, what have I done?"

"Eva," murmured a deep, low voice, "I'll handle this now."

It was Buck. We hadn't even heard him descend the back stair, where he'd been listening to Lark's confession.

CHAPTER 54

Three-quarters of a day later, the big storm had blown out of town. Late Wednesday afternoon at Knox Plantation was all blue skies, puffy white clouds, and sunshine.

We'd worked most of the day tidying up after the ladies club event the night before. Finally, with the massive cleanup complete, the twins had gone home—they'd actually shown up for work—Daphne was out with the kids somewhere, Pep was at the Roadhouse, and Precious was finishing up in the kitchen before returning to Greatwoods. Dolly and I were lounging in the hammock on the big house porch, enjoying the peace and quiet.

Precious stepped out from the parlor and crossed to the hammock, handing me an icy-cold, fresh-squeezed strawberry lemonade before plopping down into the cushioned wicker chaise next to me and raising her feet. She placed her own drink on the wicker side table. Her butterfly-print blouse coordinated with a pair of lace-up platform Louboutin espadrille wedges, each with a beaded butterfly embroidered on the black canvas toe. The lace-up ribbons were wrapped several times and tied around her big ankles. Giant bejeweled butterfly earrings capped off her summery outfit. Reaching into a pocket, she pulled out a big doggie bone and tossed it on the floor.

Dolly scrambled unceremoniously across my stomach. Lemonade sloshed on my leg.

"Hey, Dolly, watch it!" I cried, trying to steady my tall glass of lemonade.

Jumping out of the hammock, Dolly landed with a thud on the painted porch floor. Wagging her tail, she pounced on the doggie treat and carried if off somewhere.

"Thanks, Precious." I plunked the fresh strawberry garnish into the drink and took a long sip from the straw. "Mmmm, this hits the spot."

"Sure thing, Sunshine. I figured you could use a little refresher. You've been workin' hard. And you've been kinda scattered lately. Forgettin' to turn off the oven in the cottage—that was bad, Sunshine."

"But . . ."

Precious put her hand up. "No buts. When you get too much goin' on up here"—she tapped a finger on her temple—"you get paranoid and distracted, and then accidents happen." She sipped her drink. "You need to chill."

"You think I'm paranoid?"

"I think stuff happens and you jump to conclusions sometimes. Like that car the other night . . . the one you said was chasin' you. It was probably just a drunk person. Or an old person who couldn't see at night. And that pot that fell . . . it was probably just the wind. Y'all said yourselves that it was windy that evening."

I sighed. "Maybe you're right. Still . . ."

Ignoring me, Precious glanced at the little Cartier watch on her wrist.

Not only did Precious have the run of the Greatwoods estate next door, but it was clear that Ian Collier paid her handsomely.

"What is it you said that Ian Collier does for a living?" I asked.

"I didn't say."

"Oh, come on, Precious. What gives? The man owns one of the biggest, most opulent estates in the country, he's the most handsome guy on the planet, and he sneaks into town to hand Lark an 'anonymous' fifty-thousand-dollar donation for charity, and I still can't find anything about him online. It's like he doesn't exist!"

Precious just shrugged.

"You're not going to tell me anything?"

"Nope. It's nothing personal, Sunshine. You know that I love you. It's just a big part of my job not to say anything. That's Mister Collier's prerogative, not mine."

"Fine," I said with a shrug. "I'll figure it all out. I just need a little time." I jabbed the straw into my mouth and sipped more lemonade. "In fact, I'm taking it on as a personal challenge."

"Suit yourself, Sunshine. Although I wouldn't be counting on findin' out anything. Like I said, if Mister Collier wants ya to know, he'll let ya know himself. Besides, some mysteries are better left unsolved."

"So there is something to know, then!"

Precious laughed. Across the lawn, a black Cadillac Escalade came tearing up the drive.

"Uh-oh. It's way too early in the day for Miss Biggity," said Precious with a frown.

"Precious, it's nearly four o'clock!"

A swirl of dirt churned from behind the roaring Escalade. I cocked my ear. Something about the engine sounded familiar . . .

"You got that right, sister." Precious chuckled. "The way I see it, any time of day is too early to deal with the likes of Her High and Mightiness."

The Escalade slammed to a stop near the porch. With the engine still running, the vehicle door flew open and Debi Dicer sprang out onto the gravel before charging though the garden.

"He's not here," I said from the hammock. I took another sip from my drink. I didn't get up.

"What?" Debi stomped up the porch stair.

"I said, he's not here. Buck. Surely that's why you're here? Looking for your 'Bucky' again? I can't imagine any other reason why you'd be here without an invitation, Debi." I was rude. Still, I said it with a smile, so it didn't count.

"Well, aren't y'all the hostess with the mostest this afternoon!"

Precious coughed.

"I called first," Debi said with a huff. "I'm here to pick up my official notebook. From the ladies club meeting? I left it by mistake last night. Miss Daphne told me she found it."

"Oh yeah, I remember seeing it. Musta slipped my mind. So much other important stuff to think about," said Precious, standing up. She set her drink down. "It's in the kitchen. I'll be right back." The screen door slammed hard behind her as Precious clomped into the parlor.

"Like a bull in a china shop," muttered Debi as she put a manicured hand on my hammock. "I'm sorry, Miss Eva, did I catch you napping? You look all tuckered out today. Chasing after my Bucky all these nights must be messing up your beauty sleep. Goodness knows, you need it. Why, your wrist is positively green! Although I think it suits you." She pushed hard on the hammock, swinging it so that my drink sloshed all over me.

"Careful, Debi," I said, brushing myself off. "You don't want to break your pretty nails. It'll be harder to claw yourself around town." I set my drink on the side table.

"Oh, I get around just fine, sweet thang. You, on the other hand, are another story. Why, y'all just can't go anywhere without somethin' bad happenin'!" She smirked. "A little birdie told me that you nearly lost your pretty little head after jujitsu class. And running alone down a dark country road at night—a little bitty thing like you could get run clear off the road!" Debi cackled hard. "But then, y'all aren't any safer in your own home, now, are you? Forgetting to turn off the gas on your stove last night . . . Tsk, tsk, Miss Eva. Why, you're lucky y'all weren't *killed*!"

I sat up and looked hard at Debi. She stared right back and blew me a little kiss.

"Find another boyfriend," she said coldly.

"Here ya go," said Precious, stepping back onto the porch. "Have a nice day, now, ya hear?"

"I'm sure I will. Thank you," said Debi. She tucked her notebook under her arm and descended the stair. Shocked at what she'd said, I didn't dare let her know she'd gotten to me.

"Bye, now!" I waved. "Careful not to trip on the stairs."

Debi waved back before marching past Daphne's flowers and onto the drive. She slid into her Escalade and slammed the door. A moment later, she was flying down the drive, honking her horn as the dirt swirled behind her.

"Ain't she the Wicked Witch of the South," said Precious.

"I'm afraid she's way more evil than that, Precious."

CHAPTER 55

Even knowing that Debi was self-absorbed, mean, and sneaky, I'd never imagined the extent to which the woman would go to get what she wanted. Had she actually chased me down the road with her Escalade? The big engine sounded eerily familiar. Had she pushed a pot over the balcony to hit me? She certainly had access to the upstairs apartment. And was it possible that she'd turned on the gas in my cottage? When? Had she gone back to the cottage after we'd argued on the lawn . . . while I'd been in the big house with Clementine? Certainly, she had time. And if she *hadn't* done all this, how else would she have known about it all? And she'd seemed so pleased . . .

"You okay? You're lookin' a little peaky," said Precious.

"I'm fine."

"Too bad about everything that's happened. Poor Lark Harden." Precious plopped back into the wicker chaise. "And Robin. And little Clementine."

"And Slick."

"Yeah. Him, too." Precious sipped her lemonade.

"Plus there's Daphne—she really did love the guy. Although I can't figure out whether he was a total cad or a total romantic."

"Probably a little of both," said Precious. "Folks ain't just black and white, ya know?"

"Tell me about it." I took a swig of my lemonade as I considered Debi Dicer.

"I figured Miss Daphne could use some kiddie time and the kiddos could use some mommy time, so I sent Mister Lurch over with some fixin's in that monster picnic basket. He drove the Kubota with Miss Daphne while all the kids were piled into the back with the basket. I imagine right about now they're all settin' on a blanket under that big oak tree just this side of your daddy's olive grove—the one with the little birdie houses hangin' from it."

"That was a great idea. I'm sure Daph will feel better after some quality time with the kids." I took another sip. "And I'm sure she's thrilled to have a man around. Not that I'd ever imagined her with Lurch!" I chuckled.

Ian, more likely, I thought. But then, he'd shown up at my place in the middle of the night, hadn't he? I shook my head and smiled.

"*Mister* Lurch. Say, did Ambrosia Curry end up leavin' this morning?" asked Precious. "I forgot to get her autograph after breakfast."

"She left you an autographed cookbook before she and Clementine headed out with Miriam Tidwell. And she left the big Louis Vuitton trunk for Daphne. Said she didn't need it anymore. Daphne nearly wet her pants, even with the holes drilled into the back of it."

"Ya don't say!"

"Miriam, Ambrosia, and Clementine are going to vacation in the Florida Keys before Miriam takes on her new duties—"

"As trustee of Slick Simmer's multimillion-dollar trust fund!" Precious interrupted with a big grin.

I nodded. "They looked like a little family together. I'm happy for Clementine. And I think Miriam is planning a new television series for Ambrosia, one that will feature Clementine."

"Aw, that's sweet." Precious popped a cherry into her mouth. "Are you goin' to the service for Big Bubba tomorrow? No doubt the entire county is gonna be there."

"I was planning on it."

"Wanna ride with me?"

"Sure. Thanks."

"Hey," she said, "did you know that the fire department started an Internet funding page for Sissy and Peaches Clatterbuck this mornin'? Already they've raised six thousand dollars in scholarship money! Coretta Crumm called a few minutes ago to tell me all about it."

"And the ladies club is sponsoring a 'no-tie' fund-raiser dance for the Clatterbuck family. We should go."

"I dunno, Sunshine. I'm not really into that froufrou kind of stuff."

I burst out laughing. "Right! Says the woman wearing a Cartier watch and Louboutin shoes! You kill me, Precious."

"Hey, I'm game for the memorial bash for Slick Simmer that the Roadhouse is holdin' this Saturday night. Now, that should be a *par-tay*!"

Precious took a final, long sip of her lemonade, then plucked the strawberry off the rim and dropped it into her mouth, leaving nothing but ice in the tall glass. I noticed that her "strawberry-drop" style was distinctly similar to Ambrosia Curry's sensuous handling of the berries. I smiled.

"Daphne told me she's invited Savannah to stay the rest of the week in the big house so she can go to the Roadhouse memorial on Saturday. I don't know what the woman will do without Slick after that."

"Me, neither," said Precious. "I actually feel sorry for her. She must be feelin' low as a toad in a dry well."

I nodded.

"Listen, Sunshine," continued Precious, "I'm gonna head to town tonight. Mister Collier said life's too short to just work all the time, so he gave me the evening off. I'm gonna get a facial."

"Okay, thanks for the lemonade. And I'm not going to ask where you're going for the facial—since there's only one place in town." I rolled my eyes as I thought of Tammy Fae Tanner and Shear Southern Beauty.

"Don't worry, Sunshine," Precious said with a smile as she hoisted herself up from the chaise. "I'll get all the dirt and come back and tell ya all about it!"

"Don't bother!" I shook my head. "Ow!" Shouldn't have done that. My head was still sore.

Precious clomped down the porch stair and crossed through the garden to the parking area. Then she stopped.

"Say," she said, "I forgot to ask. Who won Saturday's cooking challenge?"

"Slick Simmer. He won hands down," I said. "There'll be a big commemorative plaque in his name downtown. And Daphne arranged to have a key to the city presented to Clementine."

Precious nodded her approval. Then she gave me a little wave good-bye.

"Bye." I waved back.

A moment or two later, I watched as Precious revved up her little Corvette and flew down the drive. I set my lemonade on the table next to me, closed my eyes, and settled back into the hammock, enjoying the fresh breeze. A mockingbird chirped from high in a tree as the wind moved the leaves on the branches. Suddenly sleepy, I breathed a deep sigh. After a few minutes, I was almost asleep . . . dreaming of riding Kyrie through an ancient Scottish forest . . .

Someone brushed a lock of my hair from my forehead. Startled, I jerked upright and nearly tumbled out of the hammock.

"Hey!"

Dressed in jeans and a fitted gray tee shirt, Buck stood next to me on the porch with a dimpled smile, chuckling behind his dark aviator sunglasses. I tussled with the hammock, struggling to keep myself from falling on the wooden floor.

"Buck . . . Ack! Why are you here?"

He reached out and steadied the hammock. The sleeves of his tee fitted tightly around his bulging biceps.

"I thought you'd want to know that Robin Harden is flying home from Amsterdam," he said, sitting on a wicker ottoman. "She admitted to rendezvousing with the chef in the Clatterbucks' truck when she returned one of his pots late Saturday night. Daphne arranged for a pair of top-shelf criminal defense teams from Atlanta to represent Robin and Lark. They're in good hands."

Buck helped himself to my watered-down strawberry lemonade.

"Is Lark going to jail?" I asked.

"Probably." He took a giant sip from my straw. "Gosh, that's good."

"Help yourself." I shook my head, slowly this time.

"I don't know for sure about jail. Certainly, being such a beloved community leader and the fact that it appears Lark didn't mean to kill the chef should work in her favor. It'll be up to the prosecutor and her attorneys."

"And Glen Pattershaw?"

"He's still being detained. I think he's planning to sell the diamond earring you gave me to return to him last night. It's worth quite a bit." Buck set the empty lemonade glass down on the table and popped a strawberry in his mouth.

"So he can use it to pay off his business debts?"

I waited while he swallowed my strawberry.

"Either that or pay for a lawyer. He'll need big money for both. You were right. He's the one who stole the copper from the chef's motor home. He lifted boxes from the warehouse, then brought them over to the motor home to carry away pots and pans Sunday night. He figured with the chef dead, no one would notice the missing copper until it was too late. Only, he didn't count on eagle-eyed Savannah. And then you showed up right when he was stealing everything. Although by the time you got there, he'd already hidden boxes of the copper stuff in the woods near the motor home, keeping it under cover as he shuttled it back to the trunk of his rental car with the three-wheeler bike. If you hadn't bumped into him at the motor home, remembered the boxes outside, and then seen the boxes in the post office, I doubt we'd have connected the dots so quickly."

"Not with Detective Gibbit on the case."

"Pattershaw's arguing that the copper pots and pans he stole from Slick Simmer's motor home pay a debt owed to him, and that the copper collection is actually his. I don't see how he can win that one."

"Me, either."

"Are you sure you don't want to press charges for his threatening you last night?"

"No. Like I said last night, I'm sure."

"You feelin' better?" Buck gave me a once-over that made me blush. "You're lookin' good, Babydoll." He raised his eyebrows and smiled. "I like that little racer-back tee."

"Stop it." I reached over with my left hand and smacked him on the shoulder, almost falling from the hammock again. Buck chuckled, but this time he made no effort to steady the hammock. "Does Debi know you're here?"

"Why do you keep asking about Debi?"

"You're practically living together, aren't you?"

"Now, darlin', you of all people know that you can't believe everything you hear."

"Look, I don't know what's going on with you two, but I want no part of it."

"I'm not asking you to be a part of it." He grinned. "Although, if that sort of thing appeals to you . . ."

"Stop it! I hope you're kidding. And you know what I mean. You're with Debi now. So stay away from me. Besides, I've self-imposed a man moratorium."

"A man moratorium, huh?"

"Yes. And not only are you a man, but you're a man who is supposed to be marrying my archnemesis. So this book is closed." I folded my arms.

"Are you sure?"

"I'd say, I'm sure."

"Then I'd say there are a couple of chapters you still haven't read, Babydoll."

Buck lifted his sunglasses, leaned over, and cupped my face in his big hands. He pulled me in the hammock toward him, with his deep chocolaty eyes flashing, the corners of his mouth turned up, and then he moved in and planted the biggest, wettest, mushiest kiss ever on my lips.

"Mark my words, Eva Knox—this story is just beginning."

Buck stood up, lowered his aviators, and ambled down the porch stair.

Dolly barked twice.

RECIPES

Slick Simmer's Killer Sweet and Slightly Spicy Barbecue Sauce

Rich and satisfyingly complex, this lightly fruity, slightly spicy, and delightfully sweet condiment is scrumptious as a marinade and grilling sauce for meat and poultry. Try marinating chicken pieces—either with or without skin—for 45 minutes before placing chicken on the grill over medium heat, turning and basting chicken with sauce until done. Serve warmed sauce tableside to slather on the chicken after plating!

- 1 tablespoon olive oil
- 1¼ cups chopped rhubarb (about two stalks)
- 1 peach, pitted, skinned, and chopped
- 1 medium sweet onion, chopped
- 4 garlic cloves, chopped
- 1 cup molasses

- 1 tablespoon Worcestershire sauce
- 2 tablespoons balsamic vinegar
- 2 tablespoons brown sugar
- ⅓ cup apple cider vinegar
- ½ cup tomato paste
- 1 teaspoon paprika
- 1 dash cayenne pepper
- 1 teaspoon salt
- ¼–½ teaspoon black pepper
- ¼ teaspoon cinnamon

1. Warm olive oil in saucepan. Add and stir-fry rhubarb, peach, onion, and garlic over medium-low heat until softened.
2. Add molasses, Worcestershire sauce, balsamic vinegar, brown sugar, apple cider vinegar, pepper, tomato paste, and spices.
3. Stir and warm mixture over low heat.
4. Spoon warm mixture into blender and puree until smooth.
5. Return mixture to saucepan and heat over medium heat, bringing to a boil.
6. Reduce heat to low and simmer until sauce thickens, up to an hour.

Precious Darling's Balsamic Berry and Peach Olive Oil Scones

Olive oil scones are super-moist on the inside and deliciously chewy. This recipe reads long, but is easy to make and yields double the amount of most recipes—you'll have plenty for a large tea party! Of course, you can freeze a good number for yourself—that's what I do, pulling out a scone from the freezer each morning and popping it in the oven for 15–20 minutes before enjoying it with a fresh cup of coffee.

If using just one baking sheet, keep remaining dough chilled between baking rounds. Smaller berries are best; big berries get in the way of the dough layers and may end up making a wet mess of the dough. Don't be afraid to use flavored balsamic vinegar . . . I like cranberry.

Also, make sure your extra virgin olive oil is fresh. Look for a mild buttery variety suitable for baking, like Arbequina, which is available online if you can't find it locally.

And if you prefer smaller, tea-sized scones, slice dough triangles in half again before baking. Remember, the dough triangles *will* expand in the oven!

- 4–6 ounces blackberries
- 2 ounces raspberries
- 1 peach, pitted, skinned, and diced, separating ¼ of the diced peach from the rest
- 4 tablespoons balsamic vinegar
- ½ cup demerara sugar
- 4 teaspoons demerara or granulated sugar
- 4 cups all-purpose flour, plus additional flour to dust work surface and ¼ of the diced peaches
- 2 tablespoons baking powder
- ¼ teaspoon salt
- ⅔ cup Arbequina extra virgin olive oil or similar
- 2 cups buttermilk
- 2 large eggs

FOR WASH
- 1 large egg
- ⅓ cup milk
- Enough demerara sugar to sprinkle over scones

1. Preheat oven to 400°F.
2. Line baking sheet(s) with parchment paper. You'll have enough scones for more than one baking sheet, so plan to reuse one or have more than one ready.
3. In small bowl, combine blackberries, raspberries, ¾ of the diced peach, balsamic vinegar, and 4 teaspoons sugar.
4. In medium bowl, whisk together flour, ½ cup demerara sugar, baking powder, and salt.
5. Add olive oil to flour mixture, stirring with fork until coarse crumbs appear.
6. In separate bowl, whisk buttermilk and eggs.
7. Pour buttermilk mixture into flour mixture. Combine until just mixed. Do not overmix.
8. Dust remaining ¼ of diced peach with flour (for ease of mixing into dough), then add and stir into dough, just enough to mix.
9. Refrigerate dough for 10 minutes or until chilled.
10. Turn chilled dough onto lightly floured surface. Shape into ½-inch-thick rectangle. Do not overwork.
11. Pour half of berry mix lengthwise down center of dough and press berries into dough.
12. Fold one half of the dough over berries in center, pressing dough layers together.
13. Add more berries to the top of the folded section and press berries into dough.
14. Fold remaining dough layer over berries, pressing layers together.
15. Refrigerate 10–15 minutes or until chilled.
16. Whisk one egg with milk for wash.
17. Cut chilled long rectangle of dough into enough triangles to fill baking sheet. Chill any remaining dough.
18. Place triangles on baking sheet, about one inch apart.

19. Brush egg-and-milk wash over triangles on baking sheet.
20. Sprinkle triangles with demerara sugar.
21. Bake triangles until golden, about 12–17 minutes. Thinner scones will take less time; thicker scones will require more.
22. Remove scones from oven and immediately sprinkle more demerara sugar over just-baked scones.
23. Cool scones on rack.
24. Repeat steps 17 though 23 until all the dough is cut, washed, sprinkled, baked, sprinkled again, and cooled.

Ambrosia Curry's Boozy Peach-Bourbon Ice Cream

What better summer treat could there be than peaches with ice cream and a kiss of bourbon? Yummy served with ginger cookies and a mint sprig garnish.

- 5 ripe peaches, pitted and halved
- 4 ounces (¼ cup) bourbon, or more, to taste
- ⅓ cup olive oil for grilling peaches
- 1½ cups heavy cream
- 2 cups half-and-half
- 6 large egg yolks
- 1 tablespoon sugar for peaches on grill
- 1 tablespoon sugar for peaches in blender
- 1⅛ cup (9 oz) turbinado sugar for ice-cream custard base
- 2 tablespoons–¼ cup olive oil
- 2 chopped ripe peaches (skinned or unskinned)

1. Lay peaches on cookie sheet. Drizzle with half the bourbon and sprinkle with 2 tablespoons sugar. Marinate for half an hour.
2. Start medium fire on grill—about 400°F.
3. Brush olive oil on peaches.
4. Place peaches cut side down on grill for 5 minutes or until grill marks show on peaches.
5. Flip peaches and grill another few minutes, again until grill marks show.
6. Remove peaches and cool.
7. In blender or food processor, puree cooled peaches. Refrigerate.
8. Heat cream and half-and-half to point of steaming, but not yet bubbling.
9. In large bowl, whisk or whip egg yolks until light yellow.
10. Gradually add sugar to egg yolks.
11. Slowly add cream mixture to egg yolk mixture, one tablespoon at a time, stirring with heatproof silicone or wooden spoon, tempering egg yolks for first one-third of cream mixture addition before adding the rest.
12. Heat mixture over low to medium heat, stirring frequently for about 4 minutes, or to a simmer (170°F–175°F), until the mixture coats the back of a wooden spoon.
13. Remove mixture and add grilled peach puree and remaining bourbon, stirring well.
14. Pour through fine-mesh strainer into container in an ice bath. Stir until cooled.
15. Refrigerate, at first uncovered if still not completely chilled, so as not to form condensation on the cover. Cover when cool enough that it won't form condensation. Chill another 4 hours or overnight, until custard base is as very cold (40°F or lower).
16. Whisk in 2 tablespoons of olive oil.

17. Process through ice-cream maker.
18. After ice cream stiffens in ice-cream maker, with just two to five minutes left, add chopped ripe peaches. Do not add fruit too early or liquid from peaches will mix into ice cream and render it icier and less creamy.
19. For soft-serve ice cream, serve immediately. For firmer ice cream, freeze for at least one hour.

Precious Darling's Olive Oil and Yogurt Waffles

Makes 6–7 square waffles

The olive oil coating renders a soft crust to these deliciously sweet, fluffy, and moist waffles. Try adding your favorite fruit to the batter, or topping waffles with real maple syrup, a dollop of yogurt, and fresh fruit—such as strawberries, blueberries, and raspberries—mixed first with a touch of sugar.

Recipe is easily doubled for more waffles, and cooled waffles are easy to freeze. Pop frozen waffles into the toaster or oven for a quick, no-mess meal!

- 1½ cups all-purpose flour
- 1 tablespoon baking powder
- 1 teaspoon baking soda
- 3 eggs
- 1½ tablespoons brown sugar
- ½ teaspoon salt
- 1½ teaspoons vanilla

- 1½ cups whole-fat vanilla yogurt
- 1 tablespoon olive oil

1. Preheat waffle iron.
2. In large bowl, whisk together flour, baking powder, and baking soda.
3. Whisk together eggs, sugar, salt, vanilla, and yogurt.
4. Add egg mixture to dry mixture until batter is just moist. Do not overmix.
5. Lightly coat heated waffle iron with olive oil, using a brush, paper towel, or wax paper.
6. Pour batter onto waffle iron. Close and cook until waffles are browned to your liking.
7. Remove waffles. Serve immediately or keep warm while re-oiling waffle iron and repeating for next batch.

Precious Darling's Famous Cold-Pressed Olive Oil Peach Cake

Dense, moist, and delish, this treat is yummy when topped with fresh fruit and whipped cream or crème fraîche. My family is addicted to this one—especially my husband, who, after eating too many peaches once as a kid, normally doesn't care for peaches at all!

- 3 cups peeled and chopped peaches
- 2 tablespoons peach-flavored brandy (optional)
- 1 tablespoon demerara sugar (for peaches)
- 3 large eggs

- 1¼ cups all-purpose flour, plus extra for pan
- ½ teaspoon salt
- 1 teaspoon baking powder
- ½ teaspoon baking soda
- 1 cup sugar
- ¾ cup extra virgin olive oil, plus extra for pan
- 1 teaspoon vanilla extract
- 1 teaspoon almond extract

1. Preheat oven to 350°F.
2. Sprinkle demerara sugar on peaches.
3. Marinate sugared peaches in brandy (optional).
4. Oil and flour 9-inch springform pan.
5. Separate egg whites from egg yolks and set aside. (You'll be using both.)
6. In a small bowl, whisk flour, salt, baking powder, and baking soda and set aside.
7. Set aside 2 tablespoons of sugar before putting the rest of the sugar into a large mixing bowl.
8. Using electric mixer, slowly beat olive oil into sugar until the oil is absorbed. Beat on high for several minutes, until fluffy. This might take awhile. You might want to read a few pages of your favorite cozy mystery while you wait.
9. Add egg yolks to olive oil and sugar mixture. Beat until well blended, about 5 minutes.
10. While still beating olive oil, sugar, and egg mixture, adjust mixer to low and add flour mixture, about ¼ cup at a time, incorporating each addition before adding the next. Do not overbeat batter.
11. Mix vanilla and almond extracts into batter.
12. In a separate bowl, add a pinch of salt to egg whites before beating whites into soft peaks.

13. Sprinkle 2 ounces of sugar over peaks and continue beating until the peaks become stiff.
14. Fold stiff egg whites into batter until the two are thoroughly combined. Do not overmix.
15. Place half the batter into the springform pan.
16. Spread three-quarters of the peaches over the batter.
17. Cover peaches with remaining batter.
18. Add remaining peaches over the top of the batter.
19. Place into preheated oven and bake, rotating pan after 20 minutes, for 45 minutes or until sides pull away from pan and toothpick comes out clean from center.
20. Cool on rack before removing from pan.

The Olive Grove Mysteries

By Kelly Lane

Eva Knox and her family are experts at crafting fine oils at their upscale olive plantation—and even more skilled at solving slippery crimes.

Find more books by Kelly Lane
by visiting prh.com/nextread

Praise for Kelly Lane's novels

"An intriguing mystery and plenty of Southern atmosphere."—Peg Cochran, national bestselling author of the Gourmet De-Lite Mysteries

"Quirky characters and broad humor enliven this Southern belle mystery, and suspense keeps the reader guessing."—*Gumshoe Reviews*

kellylanewrites.com
🐦 KellyLaneWrites